You know how when you see a person, like a person walking down the street, and you immediately know that you like them? I don't know what it is—maybe they remind you of someone who was nice to you as a baby. Or maybe it's all chemical. Like a smell, or an aura. Or is it . . . recognition? Like you know right off there's something in them that's like something in you?

Whatever it is, it was there, that feeling, in the handshake, in the smile, there when I finally met him.

Jack.

ALL

KINDS

OF

OTHER

JAMES SIE

Quill Tree Books
An Imprint of HarperCollinsPublishers

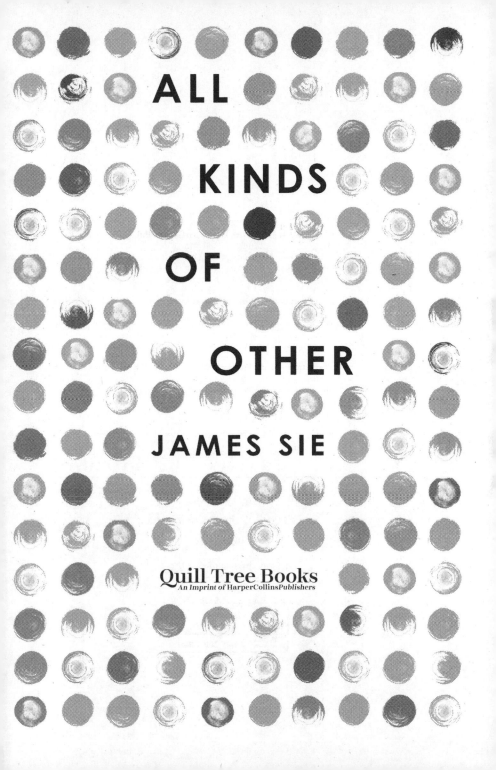

ISBN 978-0-06-296250-8

Typography by David Curtis

22 23 24 25 26   SB   10 9 8 7 6 5 4 3 2 1

❖

First paperback edition, 2022

Your body is yours at the end of the day
and don't let the hateful try and take it away
We want to be free, yeah, we go our own way
And my body was made
—EZRA FURMAN, "BODY WAS MADE"

all about ev(i)e

ok here goes
hello evie this is adam
i want 2 say how r u and
when am i gonna see u again
am i gonna see u again
r u done being done with me
r u still mad r u
i want 2 say i want 2 say

jesus this feels stupid
of course evies still mad at me i text and text but the bubbles r all my color a conversation im having by myself. i call but no answer shes frozen online no chatter no posts
weeks of this
write it down dr grace says what would u say 2 her if u could? pretend like evie is right in front of u adam
what would i say 2 u evie
dr grace says i cant control ur reaction but i can process my feelings write it down 4 myself and dont catastrophize ha like i can control that
so here i am back on a new tumblr a habit or a need u tell me evie
what would i say 2 u

i would say what the hell is happening

where r u why the silence its like ur totally gone not just from me but from pittsburgh

i would say i want u in front of me irl not just on a page

evie the last time i saw ur face it was all fucked up and ur hair ur beautiful hair was gone he used scissors like hedge clippers and the ends shot out like they were still expecting the weight

and u were furious at me

i dont wanna remember u that way evie and i dont want my last words 2 u 2 be the ones still curling in ur ear

let me put new ones in there i can do better this time

im sorry

i know this is supposed 2 be just 4 me but hey maybe u will find this maybe hashtags work maybe u will read this and we can rewind

what would i say 2 u evie

everything

#adamandeviehere4u #pittsburgh

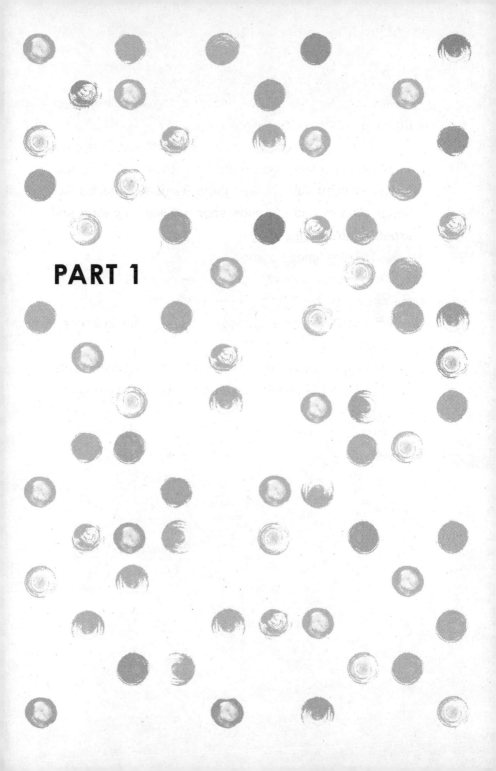

PART 1

1. Jules

The words just won't come out.

I mean, I'm not much of a talker to begin with, but still. It's not like I don't know what I want to say. "Guess what, guys, I'm gay." Easy. I can actually feel the words crowding around inside my mouth, pushing against my teeth, waiting to be released. When Dhyllin invited Gregg and me over for an end-of-the-summer hang, I was hoping to introduce them to this new-and-improved Jules, out and proud. I'd erase the memory of my pathetic coming out to my mother in the front seat of the family Subaru and replace it with something better, cooler. Reboot the second year of my high school life.

But I can't. Partly it's because I'm worried what they're gonna think and partly, it's that Dhyllin just won't shut up. Yes, we all know Dhyllin has an exciting life, the best life, anyone would kill for a concert promoter father with a Hollywood Hills mansion, but if he doesn't stop talking about traveling this summer with Smash Mouth on their official 2015 tour, I'm seriously going to need to drink bleach.

"I thought Lisbon was wild, but I'm telling you, Jules, when we hit Amsterdam, that place was off the *chain*. . . ."

I mean, how was my news going to compare to that? Coming out just doesn't measure up to groupies in Berlin and private jets. Not these days. But if I can't tell friends I've known for years, how am I going to tell strangers? Maybe strangers would be easier. There wouldn't be so much on the line, so many expectations—

"Earth to Jules, hello."

I jolt back to the present, start dribbling the basketball again. "What did you say?" I ask, trying to cover, but Dhyllin's already given up on me and is checking out his Snapchat feed. Gregg's playing on his phone, as usual. No one's talking. It'd be the perfect moment. Each bounce of the ball leaving my hands is like a command: *Tell them. Tell them.* But I can't. It's tricky with Dhyllin. Not that he would punch me or call me out or anything like that. No, he'd just look at me with those sleepy blue eyes and say something casually sarcastic like, "Well, *that* was no mystery," or "*That* explains a lot"—which would somehow be just as bad.

Without looking up, Dhyllin asks, "Are we going to keep shooting hoops or do you guys want to play Xbox?"

Gregg finally disconnects from his phone. "Hell YES Xbox."

"Jules?"

I've never really been that into gaming. But everyone else is, so I shrug. "Whatever is cool with me."

Dhyllin doesn't move, though, and inertia sets in. We keep shooting hoops on the blue acrylic of Dhyllin's dad's basketball court. Well, *I* keep shooting hoops. Gregg's camped out just outside the key, dodging any ball that falls near him and smashing aliens on his phone, his straight black hair covering most of his face as he bends his head down. Dhyllin's off to the other side, texting, wearing some fresh Yeezy Boosts that look like they just came out of the box. I dribble and shoot around both of them, a moon orbiting two fixed planets in a sky-blue space.

We haven't been in the same school together since fifth grade. We mostly see each other during the summer, old habits. I wonder if we have anything in common at all anymore.

Dhyllin looks up suddenly and squints at me, blond hair flopped over one eye. "You're not going to like Earl Warren High," he tells me.

"How would you know?" I say, pretending to throw the ball at him. He doesn't even flinch. "Why?"

"It's *public*," Dhyllin says, as if that explains everything.

"And . . . ?"

"You're not used to that. It's a huge school. And coming in sophomore year? You'll be lost." He says this like he's really concerned, like he didn't spend the whole last year icing me out while he spent time with his new posse at Beckman Prep. Dhyllin lowers his voice. "And there are gangs there. They're gonna eat you alive."

"You don't know that," I say, but really, Dhyllin's the kind of kid who *does* know things. He's always picking up adult frequencies, decoding them, and translating the data for the rest of us. "I'll be fine," I say, trying to sound like I mean it. "Look, Gregg goes there, and he hasn't been jumped."

Dhyllin smirks. "That's because they're afraid he's going to use karate on them."

Gregg gives him a fast middle finger without even stopping his game. "Karate's Japanese, dickwad. Get your racial stereotypes right."

"What about the gangs?" I ask.

Gregg shrugs. "I don't know. I don't think so." His head slumps back to his phone.

"Yeah, whatever." Dhyllin flips his blond hair off his eyes. He's recently had a growth spurt; well, his head has, anyway. It looks huge, square and man-shaped on his teenage boy's body, the opposite of me, whose legs and arms seem to have beanstalked overnight. Funny thing though—Dhyllin, even out of proportion and with that one red pimple cluster blotching his forehead, still has the superpower of making you feel like he's the coolest kid in the room. He's still the magnet that draws in all us rusty nails.

"You should come to Beckman Prep. Good basketball team," he says. Beckman Prep is, naturally, the most exclusive private high school in the Valley. If it were up to my dad, I would have gone to Beckman my freshman year, but the decision was most definitely not up to him.

"And there's some pretty hot babes there, too. You have no idea." I don't. I really have no idea. Or, you know, interest.

"It's a great school. You should totally go there." Dhyllin's lost his sleepiness. He sounds excited by the idea. There's something in his eyes that tugs at my chest, something from the past, a memory, not really a memory, more a *feeling*: the three of us in elementary school, running through Dhyllin's backyard (not this one, his mother's), spinning around with lightsabers, Jedi robes flowing behind us. That excitement. Dhyllin's mom and dad were still together then, and so were mine. Plastic lightsaber smashing into plastic lightsaber, Anakin and Plo Koon and Qui-Gon, high-pitched death squeals, until Dhyllin was tired of dying and he would shrug off his robe and say, "That's not what happens in the movie," and we would immediately throw down our sabers and join him, so what did he want to do now?—

"—Hey, Jules, reboot."

I jerk back into focus. "What?"

Dhyllin rolls his eyes. "I said, see what I got?" He slides a black metal cartridge out of the pocket of his skinny jeans. "Strawberry shortcake. Wanna hit?"

Of course Dhyllin vapes.

"Nah," I say, then add, "Not right now." I turn away and shoot. *Swish.* Fourth basket in a row. The ball bounces right by Gregg, who doesn't even notice. "High score!" he shouts into his phone. "Suck it!"

"I am *so* bored," Dhyllin says, and I know I've given him the wrong answer. He slides the cartridge back into his pocket and starts texting.

A moon and two fixed planets, with lots of space in between.

From the house, there's the sound of a sliding door opening. I look over and see Dhyllin's dad coming out onto the patio with another man, laughing. The two men are about the same age, but the other man's dressed way more casually, in a Pirates T-shirt and shorts. He grabs Dhyllin's dad by the shoulder and points at something on the patio. They both laugh again.

5

"Who's that?"

Dhyllin takes a brief glance and turns away quickly. "Oh God, I forgot," he says. "Long-lost college friend of my dad's. He's here visiting or something. God."

Someone else steps through the darkness, bringing the shadow of the inside out with him: black oversize hoodie under a dark kind of camouflage jacket, black skinny jeans, black boots. A kid, hands stuffed in his pockets, body hunched like he's braving an arctic blast instead of an end-of-summer heat wave in Los Angeles. He's staring at the ground, apart from the two adults, and you can tell by the angle of his body that he isn't listening to them at all.

"Who's with him?" I ask Dhyllin.

Dhyllin keeps texting. "The son," he says, aggravated. "I'm supposed to meet him, he's in our grade, whatever."

"He doesn't look like his son," I say. The father's white, and the boy's definitely darker, could be maybe Indian or Pakistani.

Dhyllin tilts his head a fraction toward the house. "He looks like a terrorist." Another glance. "A tiny terrorist."

"Racist," Gregg says automatically, without taking his eyes off his game.

"Just joking," Dhyllin says, all put out. "But look at him."

The kid is pretty short for someone our age. That's the first thing I notice. The second thing is that under his hood, the boy has this tumbling sea of dark hair, with one large bleached wave swooshing out from it. And the third thing is his eyes, which are wide and bright against the deep olive of his skin.

Eyes that are looking back at me. And aren't looking away.

I've got this thing I do, where sometimes I just stare. I don't mean to; I kind of get lost in my head and forget that my body is still in real life. My grandmother calls it catching flies, my father calls it spacing out, and my friends just say I'm going offline. But I can tell that this kid is not offline. He's staring, not into space, but directly at me, like we're in a conversation and he's waiting to hear what I'm going to say next. Waiting, like a challenge.

And, of course, while I'm thinking all this, I'm still staring at him.

My face burns hot. I jerk away, trying to turn and dribble and shoot all at once, as if that was what I've been doing all along, and of course the ball misses the entire backboard by about a mile, sailing inches above Gregg's head and landing in the bushes.

"Play much?" Dhyllin says, smirking into his phone.

I run over to get the ball, glancing back toward the house. The boy isn't looking in my direction anymore, but Dhyllin's father is. He extends an arm out, waves us in.

"I think your father wants us to come over?"

Dhyllin gives a tight shake of his head. "Fuck no. The last thing I wanna do is sit and listen to him tell stories about the old theater days." His thumbs jab his phone screen like he's about to launch a nuclear device.

His dad still has his arm up. I drop the ball. "Maybe we should just say hi."

"Who what where?" says Gregg, finally looking up.

"C'mon, Dhyllin," I say, but he's already heading the opposite way.

"Go ahead, but I'm warning you, you'll never escape," he says over his shoulder, then walks off toward the pool, phone leading the way, leaving Gregg and me completely stranded.

The adults on the patio are staring at us, waiting, expecting conversation. Adult conversation. Gregg looks at me, and I look at Gregg. Dhyllin's completely spooked us. We both break into a run, scooping up our backpacks and retreating to the side gate. It isn't until we're safely at Gregg's house, half an hour later, that I wonder what we were so frightened of.

I do get my coming out moment, at Gregg's house in Silver Lake. He's on his bedroom computer fighting off a zombie invasion and I'm lying on his bed, listening to music low on headphones and staring up at a big-ass spider as it makes its way across the ceiling. Gregg has a phobia about spiders, he would be totally skeeved out if he saw it, and that would spoil my announcement. But the spider's heading toward the door. I make a deal with myself: if the spider's gone by the time Gregg completes his mission, I'll tell him.

Gregg's shouting at the screen, "No! No! I see you! You want some, huh? You want a piece of this? Huh? BOOM!"

Coming out to Gregg is pretty much a no-brainer. He's got two dads, for one thing, so he's probably not going to get all salty about the news. And he's already been at Earl Warren High for a year, so possibly he could give me a heads-up if there are any raging homophobes I should avoid. Though I doubt he would notice that kind of thing. Gregg isn't someone who seems to notice much of anything that's not shooting at him from a computer

8

screen. Which is another reason why it should be easy to tell him.

"Go for the head, you fucking noob! God, you're useless!"

I know from the body count that the mission's almost over. I take off the headphones and clutch them to my chest. Even though we haven't seen each other much over the last few years, even though we don't have a lot to say when we do, Gregg's still one of my oldest friends. We've known each other since preschool, and his family is one of the few we kept in touch with after I switched schools, and switched again. And again. But that also makes it harder to come out to him. Gregg knows me one way—how is he going to react when I tell him I'm this other way?

"Behind you, there's another one BEHIND YOU, DAMN IT!" Gregg screams.

"Gregg!" yells one of his fathers, Danny, from downstairs. "Jesus! Enough already!"

"Whatever," Gregg mutters, fingers still flying over the keyboard. "Mission complete." He pushes back from the desk, then automatically pulls himself in again. "I need a better flamethrower," he says under his breath, grabbing his mouse, swirling and clicking it over his WoW mouse pad.

The spider's almost at the door. I keep my eyes fixed on the ceiling.

"Hey," I say.

"What?" says Gregg, without turning around.

"I think I might be gay."

The keyboard stops clicking.

"Uh, okay . . ." Another pause. "Does that mean you want to

kiss me now or something?"

"Gross, no," I say. "I'd rather kiss a zombie."

"Okay," says Gregg. "Good." The keyboard starts clicking again.

"Are you surprised?"

"Um, I don't know. I guess."

"You guessed?"

"I. Guess."

"Oh." The spider's nowhere to be seen. "So . . ."

Gregg swivels around. He brushes his hair off his eyes. "It's cool."

"Okay," I say.

He swivels back. More keyboard clicking.

"Oh, and not like it's a big thing," I say, "but let's just keep it quiet for now, like at school?"

"No problem." He pauses. "Except . . ."

"Except what?"

He pushes back in his chair again. "Except, I really feel sorry for you, man."

I swear I can feel that spider prickling along my neck. "Why?"

"Because," Gregg says, "if you turn out to be anything like my dads, you're going to have the most boring life ever."

happy 2gether

evie u used 2 tell me theres no one else in the world but us and I knew what u meant

who else was gonna understand u but me and who else was gonna understand me but u

together in this new creation we got to name everything even ourselves. u gave me my name u said we were the first boy and first girl that ever lived and i should be adam wouldnt that be perfect and it was

of course there were other people around 2 many of them crowding the hallways at my school i got my fair share of backward looks and hands hiding smirks but mostly i slipped by

i was all camouflage the flannels and jeans and baseball caps and i was lucky by birth slim hips and a flat chest that reads boy in a once over eye flick. strangers could slot me in their brains and walk on and kids who knew me thought i was a weirdo already

i was just trying 2 pass like a brown moth against bark hidden and happy

not u evie

u were a butterfly and proud of it u liked color u liked bebe u liked a smoky eye u craved hair clips of every shade

once ur hair started growing out and ur mom with a tight

mouth said fine a little color dont get carried away then evie was born and u were gonna be urself no matter what at least at ur school. screw the haters and gym class and the math teacher who told u 2 stop making fun of normal people. they tried 2 shove you back into ur chrysalis but u just wouldnt fit. if they told u 2 wipe that lip gloss off ur mouth ud just find a brighter shade

but it wasnt easy 4 u i had it easier okay i will admit that now

ud escape 2 my house the only place u could wear what u wanted sometimes id pull out old clothes never worn stuffed in the back of my closet the skirts the turquoise jumper the yellow sundress i always hated but it was beautiful on u. it was like show and tell every day after school u were there when my first binder came in the mail

and sometimes ud lie in my bed ur head in the curve of my arm ud just lie against me and cry (and it wasnt from anger or fear but just a release a relief of being urself)

and it was just us 2

adam and evie alone in the new world

all the colors

#adamandeviehere4u #pittsburgh #mothandbutterfly

2.

Hell has officially frozen over.

Ever since we moved into this neighborhood when I was three, my mother has always said that Earl Warren High School would be the last place on earth she'd send me to. She'd heard all these horror stories about the drugs, the "bad elements," the exploding class size. When I was small, we'd cross the street so we wouldn't pass near the school, it was *that dangerous*.

So, guess where I'm heading the first day of sophomore year?

I had this secret idea that I was going to get up, grab a quick bite, and head out early, just so I could get my head together, shake off the old at-home me, and figure out what new-school me was going to be. But as soon as I wake up and smell breakfast, I know that plan is totally shot.

Mom's in her bathrobe. She's got that droopy look that tells me she's been downstairs for a while. On the kitchen counter, there's a buffet: scrambled egg whites, tempeh bacon, cut-up cantaloupe, orange juice, a brown-rice-flour, agave-sweetened blueberry muffin. And one plate.

Dang.

She reads my face. "You know it's the most important meal of the day," she says. This from the woman I've never seen eat more than a piece of toast for breakfast. And now that we're gluten-free, not even that.

"I told you I was gonna get my own breakfast. You could have slept in," I say.

She waves a hand. "First day of school? Ha. I couldn't sleep anyway. Have some eggs. You need your protein. Are you nervous? You must be nervous."

As a matter of fact, I *am* nervous, but having your mother point it out isn't exactly helpful. I shrug and try a bite of the rice-flour muffin, which immediately sucks all the moisture from my mouth. I grab the orange juice.

"Are you drinking coffee again?" I ask, spraying out little particles of dried spackling.

"I *needed* it, Jules," she says. She takes a sip, like she's demonstrating. "Besides, I don't think coffee's the problem. I read online that coffee's actually *good* for you now. So . . . giving it up is *not* the answer."

Mom's been looking for this particular answer these last four years, something to explain her nervous stomach and the periods of time when she can barely get out of bed. Traditional doctors were no help, she said, so we've been on a tour of all the major diets you could ever imagine existing in Los Angeles, starting with striking down meat and becoming vegetarian and then making our way through vegan, raw vegan (that was rough), picking up meat but no dairy, adding goat's milk but no cow, going fermented . . . Right now, she's settled somewhere between paleo and "clean eating," with a side of gluten-free. And wine. "Clean eating is good for you, too," my mother said, and I guess I don't mind going along for the ride—it's easier that way—but sometimes I think my father left home just because he wanted to get a decent meal.

My mother's in the middle of telling me about Judy Pevsner and the acupuncturist herbalist who changed her life. "I should probably get going," I say.

She sets down her mug and taps the marble counter with her fingernails. "Oh, it just feels wrong, not driving you to school. I've done it for fourteen years. Should I drive you? Just today?"

School is three blocks away. I'm sixteen.

"That's one of the advantages of me going to Earl Warren, remember?" I say. "That I can walk there?"

"I know . . ." She bites at her thumbnail. "Just . . . be aware. Don't get caught up in your head, okay? Notice what's around you. Be *safe*. Remember Bishop Academy . . ."

My stomach gives a lurch. Suddenly it all seems too much, the smell of the cooling eggs and the bacon and the coffee on her breath. This is not the way I wanted to start my day, thinking about Bishop Academy.

The funny thing is, Mom was *crazy* about Bishop Academy to begin with. It cleared all her hurdles, which was not an easy thing to do. I've been in three schools the last four years, even though I was fine with all of them. I started sixth grade at one small private college prep (too cultish, according to her), moved to a charter (too disorganized), went *back* to a private (barely tolerable), and started freshman year of high school at Bishop Academy, a parochial she was convinced was just right, even though we're Jewish. "It's religious, but not *too* religious," she'd say to her friends. "It's not like he has to convert or anything. The basketball program is great. And the education is *marvelous*." It was a perfect fit. At least for four months. And then the Incident happened.

The Incident. It wasn't a big deal. It really wasn't. Some guy on JV basketball, some stupid sophomore, Patrick, in the locker room, calling me out. . . . I don't even know what happened, really—maybe I was doing the staring thing, I guess I was, but it wasn't like I was staring *at* the guy—but suddenly the word *fag* flew in the air toward me, *splat*, and then laughter. That word stuck on me for the next few weeks, during drills, before games, on the bus. . . . I don't think they even believed it; I mean, why would they? It was just something they said, a joke, some way of marking me from the other freshmen—like a nickname, right?— and eventually it stopped, but then they started calling me Julie, and that was understandable, too, I mean, I didn't like it, but it wasn't a big deal, right? I could take it, but I made the mistake of mentioning it to my mother and it quickly became an Incident. Conferences, meetings with the coach, the vice principal, the head of school . . . it dragged on for months. My heart dropped every time I saw my mom's Subaru parked in the visitor lot. I wish she would have just left the situation alone, but Mom operates on two modes: exhausted and furious.

Patrick was reprimanded for his language and the team was

given a lecture on inclusivity, but that wasn't nearly enough for her. She wanted a suspension and was for some reason surprised that a Christian prep school wasn't willing to go that far. "In this day and age!" she would say in the car, throwing her hands in the air when she picked me up after practice, and I would sink lower in the front seat and wish she'd get out of the parking lot, and all the way home she'd interrogate me about what every kid said to me, which by this time was not much, because while all of these interventions never singled me out as the cause, everyone of course knew it, and good luck getting anyone to pass the ball my way, let alone talk to me in the locker room. Basketball was over by spring break, and I didn't think I'd be signing up again next year, but that really didn't matter. The last day before break, she waited for me in the pickup line after school and almost hit the crossing guard peeling out of there.

"Jesus!" I shouted.

"Exactly," she said darkly, gripping the steering wheel.

That's when she told me she had no intention of re-enrolling me next year. Okay, I already figured that was going to happen, given her track record, but it's not like she even asked me about it. Yanked out of school again. I kept my mouth closed and my eyes drilling holes in the dashboard ahead of me.

"Why are you looking so pissed off?" she asked.

I shrugged.

"Jules, how can you even want to go to that school?"

"I could have made it work."

"No, you couldn't have." She shook her head. "Poor Jules, you have no idea. These kinds of people? Trust me." She looked at the road, then back at me, then at the road again, then asked the question I should have known all along was coming, that I was surprised hadn't come sooner. "So . . . *are* you gay?"

"What does that have to do with it?" I yelled, but we both knew that wasn't an answer. "I don't know," I said, but that was a lie. I did know, really, without ever admitting it to myself. Ever since the Incident, the question had been slowly revolving in the back of my mind, just out of focus. Thinking: Who made my chest tighten. Who didn't. Who I thought of before I slept, and who I thought of when I *couldn't* sleep. And I wondered, *had* I been staring at Patrick? Not in a pervy way, but just, staring? And, wait, hadn't he been staring at me first? And then, there in the car when Mom asked me the question, it suddenly became very clear what the answer was.

"I . . . guess so."

"You guess you're gay? You don't *know* you are?"

"No, no, I mean, yes." I was breathing really hard, like I'd just done a full-court sprint. I'd just admitted it. I couldn't take it back.

"That's fine," she said. "Nothing to be ashamed of. It's *good*."

"Why is it *good*?"

"It's good! Look at gay marriage! Even the president has evolved! Now you can be your *authentic self*."

I made a disbelieving grunt, and she stopped the car so fast I felt the seat belt pull tight. She jabbed her finger in front of my face. "Hey. Listen to me. What those boys did is not your fault, okay? You are who you are. I mean, you don't have to wave a flag about it, but if you're gay, *good*."

Okay. So, yeah, I was basically outed by my mother.

And this led back to Earl Warren High School, because, where else was I gonna go on such short notice? Dad wasn't big on the idea. We had a family conference, him propped up on the dining room table on my mother's iPad, FaceTiming from his condo in Santa Monica. He had on that grim problem-solving look and kept wiping his face with his hand. He said, "If you don't like them picking on him in private school, why the hell would you think that going to public school is going to be any better?"

"It's only until we can get in somewhere else," Mom said.

"We should have gone to Beckman."

My mother made a face.

"Well, I guess that's another bridge burned," my father said. "Maybe you could have consulted me before you made this decision?"

Mom had her answer all ready. "If I could ever get you on the phone, maybe I would have."

I ducked myself off the screen, because we all knew where this road was heading, but I heard Dad calling out from the iPad, "Wait wait wait a minute, come back. Jules." I poked my head into the corner. He said, "What do *you* want?"

I shrugged, because did it matter?

"Earl Warren's gotten *so* much better, Jules," my mother said, ignoring the screen. "It's all cleaned up, they have a magnet track in science now and a good basketball program. Really good."

Dad's voice slid under hers. "You know we can't get our deposit

19

back from Bishop, right?"

"So the money is all you care about?" Mom said, crowding the screen.

"Okay, so you've got it all figured out," said Dad. "Excellent. Why are we even talking?" This time, when I left the room, they let me go, 'cause, yeah, they really didn't need me there. And by the end of that conversation, Dad lost, Mom won, and Earl Warren was in.

My mother keeps asking questions, roadblocking me from leaving for school. Yes, I have my laptop. Yes, I have the forms. Yes, my phone is charged. Yes. Yes. Yes. I grab my backpack but she's already holding on to the other strap.

"Stick close to Gregg," she says. "Let him show you around. Be careful. And you know there's a Gay–Straight Alliance on campus, right? I looked it up. GSA."

"Stop, Mom."

"I'm just saying! Find people like you . . . and if there's any trouble, just call me—"

"Goodbye, Mom—"

"So don't listen to me." She reaches up to grab my cheek. "Oh, my big boy . . . Remember, this is just for now. We'll find you the perfect school. But are you excited anyway? I want you to be excited."

Why does she have to look so worried when she says that? When did she get so thin? The circles under her eyes are enormous. They take up half her face. "Don't worry, Mom. As long as I can play basketball, I'm excited," I say, and let her hug the life out of me.

A block away from school, and my mother's nerves are still jangling inside me. It's impossible not to feel nervous when she's feeling so nervous. My phone vibrates, and I'm sure it's her telling me to look both ways before crossing the street, but then my dad's face appears, inviting me to FaceTime. So much for getting my head together. I think about not answering, but that would mean I'd miss him wishing me well my first day, and who knows when I'll hear from him again? I'm surprised he even remembered.

My parents have been separated for three years, and honestly, there's not much difference between him living in Santa Monica, an hour away, and him living at home. He's still always working. When he left, he gave me a key to his condo and told me to come over anytime, and though I've clipped it onto my lanyard next to my house key, I've visited exactly once. He's never there. Santa Monica might as well be in Australia.

"Hey, champ, how's it going?" he shouts. He's at an airport, LAX I'm guessing.

"Good."

"You're up early. What are you doing?"

"School, Dad. First day of school."

"Already? Isn't that early? I thought it was after Labor Day."

So he didn't remember. I wonder if he even knows I'm gay. I'm assuming Mom told him but he's never talked to me about it and I'm sure as hell not bringing it up. "Why are you calling?" I ask.

"I'm about to board a plane to Puerto Vallarta," he says. "Scouting locations."

"Tough life, Dad."

"Hey, for a producer, locations are only headaches. But you should come along with me one of these trips. Maybe next summer." Which is what he told me last summer.

There's a blare of announcements on the airport loudspeaker. My father shouts, "Shoot. Listen, they're calling my flight."

"Okay, I gotta go, too," I tell him.

"Don't worry about school, we'll find you a better one. Just hang in there, okay? And knock 'em dead!"

I try to say goodbye, but the loudspeaker comes on again. My father puts a finger to his ear and shakes his head. His image stutters as he waves his hand, and then he's gone.

The day has just started, and I'm already exhausted.

Both my parents want to get me out of Earl Warren as fast as possible, but at this point, I don't care. I'm tired of all the changes. If it were up to me, this would be my last school until I graduate. No more drama.

meet u at bench by entrance

When Gregg texted where to meet him this morning, he of course didn't mention that there were *tons* of benches scattered around the school, and three different entrances. I'm early, so I pick a group of benches under a tree near the entrance he's likely to be using, and plant myself down on it. What I don't know is that, at Earl Warren High School, there are such things as senior benches. Also, junior benches. Also, sophomore benches. You might think they all look the same, but try sitting on the wrong one, and you'll find out pretty quickly what's what.

I've barely gotten my phone out of my pocket when I hear, "Oh, nah, nah." Two guys stand over me, a tall Black kid in a school hoodie and red Air Jordans, short twists of hair sprouting from the top of his head like a fountain, and a sharp-faced white kid with blond dreads and a black Skrillex T-shirt. "You're in the wrong place," Air Jordans says.

"This is a senior bench," Skrillex says, hiking his foot up on the seat.

I jump up. "Oh, sorry. Uh, where are the sophomore benches?"

Skrillex slides into where I'd been sitting. "How the hell should I know? I'm not a sophomore." A high five for that one from Air Jordans.

Backing up to avoid his sprawling legs, I tangle in the straps of my backpack and feel my feet skidding out from under me. I swear, my last growth spurt has been like a system upgrade that's always crashing. I head for the ground, but Air Jordans has a strong grip. He pulls me back to balance with one steadying hand on my shoulder. "Take it easy, it's all good," he says, and his pitying look is almost as bad as the laughter that rockets out of Skrillex's mouth as I stumble away.

Earl Warren is huge. Two different courtyards, four buildings, a giant track surrounding a football field, indoor and outdoor basketball courts, and a row of trailers for class overflow. I think all of Bishop Academy could fit inside just one of these courtyards. Maybe Dhyllin was right—how am I gonna find my way around all this? I wander, watching the campus slowly fill up, students clustering on the lawn, attaching to other clusters. The quiet hum of voices becomes loud and rowdy in a moment, interlocking, the sound of students who know each other fitting into place.

Gregg's with a small group by the south entrance at some curved benches surrounding a table, and Gregg's body makes another curve as it bends around his phone. One of the girls with him looks kinda familiar, but it isn't until I get up close and see those anime eyes and those perfect teeth that I recognize her.

"Oh my God. Jules." She stands up. It's Cecilia Diaz, someone Gregg and I used to go to *kindergarten* with. I mean, I haven't run into her since I was in third grade, but I can still see the little girl smiling through that teenage face. Five-year-old me had a crush on her back then, and sixteen-year-old me can see why.

She hugs me immediately. She still smells like lavender. "You are so tall," she says, "but you totally look the same."

"Hey," I say. "So do you."

She purses her lips together and bats her eyes. "Okay, are you on the SAS track or the magnet?"

"What?"

"At school. I think the SAS track here is *much* better than the magnet, that's what I'm on, but a lot of the classes overlap so you'll have to check your schedule. Also, there are some teachers you'll want to avoid, if you can—do you want some cinnamon gum?—I can give you a list of them if you'd like."

"No thanks, I mean, sure, I mean—" Cecilia's brain moves at a speed I can barely keep up with. It's like she's playing a Ping-Pong game with herself, thoughts ricocheting from one subject to another with only a blur in between. It reminds me—she was always the one who the kindergarten teachers had to shush during quiet time.

"—So Gregg tells me you're gay?"

"Huh, what?" I stare at her.

"You just came out, right? That is so sweet."

I glare at Gregg, who yanks off the earbuds he's been wearing this whole time. "Where what who?" he asks.

"Thanks for not telling anybody," I say.

He shrugs. "I didn't. Just Cecilia."

Cecilia waves her hand in front of my face. "Oh, no no no, it's no problem at all. Really, it's like no big deal. This school is totally cool about that. Totally. I mean, just last year we had two homecoming kings and *they* were a couple." She looks off behind me, scanning the courtyard. "Okay. Let's see, there's Matco and Felipe over there," she says, jabbing a pink-polished finger to my right. "They're gay. You want me to introduce you?"

"No! No!" I blurt out. I feel my face blotching into all shades of red. "I mean, not . . . right now, or . . ."

"That's fine," Cecilia says. "But I *think* they might be dating so . . ." She makes an iffy gesture with her hands, disappointed.

I take a quick look to my right, expecting, what? I don't know, two buff models out of a magazine? Guys in skirts and rainbow flags? Instead, they're just two students leaning against a tree, one skinny with a baseball cap, the other shorter with a soccer shirt and hair that looks like he just got out of bed. They don't look any different from anyone else on campus. How would I have known they were gay?

Cecilia continues. "There's Roger, he's a junior, but I don't know him very well, just from the Young Entrepreneurs Club, but he seems nice, and—oh! Look at that freshman guy over there, no don't *look* but look, he's got I think makeup on and pink hair? So that might be something! Mr. Janssen in physics, he's the teacher sponsor of the GSA—that's the Gay–Straight Alliance Club, I'm a member of that, too—he'd be, like, a good person to talk to if you have questions but really it's *so* not a big thing. Lowell's the student head of the GSA and he's in our grade, he's over there with Lily Cho, they're always together"—her voice dips down as they pass behind us, then revs right back up—"you might have some classes with him, probably, if you're on the magnet track, so ANYWAY . . ." She finishes and looks at me, eyes bright, like she's ready to take my order.

"Uh, thanks," I say. "I think I'm just gonna . . . ease into it, you know?"

"Of course!" Cecilia says instantly, nodding like that was her idea all along. "You should just take your time, go at your own pace." She nudges Gregg. "Everyone needs to go at their own pace," she tells him.

"When how what?" Gregg says, pulling his earbuds out again.

I'm going to change the subject, bring up classes or schedules or climate change or *anything*, but then I see Mateo and Felipe, whichever was which, get up to go. The taller one hoists his backpack over his shoulder and holds out his hand to help the other one up, but then he never lets go as they walk to the main entrance. One guy's hand is docked into the other's so smoothly, like it was meant to fit there. No one stares or points, nothing. The two keep holding hands as they walk up the steps. The action of one hand slipping so easily into another—that's what I want. I want that for *my* hand.

"Either of them your type?" Cecilia whispers in my ear.

Are either of them my type? It seems weird to be sizing them up, like they're on a menu I can choose from. What's my type anyway? It seems like a simple question. Do I have to have one?

"Can I get back to you on that?" I mumble to Cecilia. Mateo and Felipe reach the building. Their hands break apart as one pulls open the door, and they disappear inside. And this is when I think, I'm going to be okay here. *They had two homecoming kings.* To my parents, that wouldn't be enough of a reason to stay at a school, but for me, it's as good as any.

The bell rings.

And that's when I see him. Again.

He's standing by the front entrance, the kid from Dhyllin's father's house, leaning against the wall. There's that wave of bleached hair spilling out from under his cap that makes him instantly recognizable. His clothes are still way too heavy—a jacket, a hoodie, a knit cap—nothing he's wearing makes any sense on a hot day like today. His head is down, and his arms are crossed in front of him, and he makes no move to join the stampede passing him on the way to first period.

I point him out to Gregg. "Wasn't he just visiting?"

Gregg shrugs. "Why's he wearing so many clothes at the same time? He looks like a refugee."

I shake my head. "Really, Gregg?"

He holds up his hands in protest. "The clothes! I meant all the clothes!"

Cecilia leans in. "With that hair? He might be a refugee from One Direction."

Gregg's eyes widen. "He *does* have a Zayn Malik vibe!"

"You know who Zayn Malik is?" I ask.

"I had a brief One Direction phase. Don't judge." I wasn't about to—I remember being a little fascinated with 1D myself, once upon a time, though looking back, I realize it didn't really have anything to do with their music.

We make our way slowly toward the double doors of the entrance. There are hundreds of kids around me, more than at any school I've ever been to. Lots of chattering, and the smell of sweat and smoke wafts out of the hallway up ahead. Kids are being wanded, like at an airport. It's all a little overwhelming, but I kind of like it. Being part of a herd means you're protected because you don't stick out. You aren't going to get picked off by any hungry lions.

The Zayn Malik kid (and does he really look like Zayn? Maybe in the eyes, and of course that wonder swoosh of hair) hasn't left his post by the door. He looks so, I don't know, unhappy, alone, rocking back and forth on his heels, ignoring everyone, face scrunched up . . . As I get closer, walking up the steps, I get this guilty feeling that I should have introduced myself that day at Dhyllin's house, that my running away has somehow made me responsible for this unhappiness, this loneliness, even though I've never met him.

I lean my body forward and start to raise my hand, but then he looks up and I see I've made a mistake. He isn't sad or lonely. He's *pissed*. His brown eyes are these dark disks, hard and angry. He looks like he wants to punch somebody, and when he sees me, there's this jolt of recognition, and his eyes narrow and his lips press tight together, like I'm the one he wants to punch.

I pull back—my heart pounds like I want to run away but there's nowhere to go but ahead. My foot catches a step it didn't figure on being there, and for the second time that day I'm falling forward, this time into a packed crowd of students, but by some trick of physics, enough space opens up for me to fall straight to the ground, my backpack spilling, laughter echoing all around me, and my first day of school officially started.

yentl

im sitting at lydiahs coffee house right now best kenyan brew in pittsburgh right? our favorite place to bitch and moan. the lgbt center is right around the corner thinking about stopping in but it would feel weird without u evie dont know if i can do it

can there be an adam without an evie?

rewind

movie night at the center remember how cold it was by the river that day? my mom dropped me off it was my 1st time got a flyer from dr grace damn i was nervous and i was late but not as late as u

u snuck in when the lights were off and sat by a stranger ur size and that was me. u must have followed the sound of my eyes rolling like marbles into the back of my head. i had already seen yentl my dad made me but i dont like musicals much

is this movie 4 real u asked

yeah that old lady is pretending 2 be a boy i said and we both laughed

remember big marg was so mad at us she shushed us from across the room said hush its babs u kids have 2 learn ur history im here 4 the pizza u whispered in the dark 2 me. my names evie

oh evie i could tell that name was still new on ur lips u had 2 keep it hidden in ur pocket and ur hair was only just starting 2 reach below ur ears and I remember u kept trying 2 tuck it back and were u sneaking eyeliner even then?

i forgot which name i gave u i was still looking 4 mine. we were the youngest ones there we couldnt stop laughing and laughing and it felt so good 2 laugh first time in years. i was trying 2 pull myself out of my middle school hell and u were trying 2 pull urself out of urs and we were both looking 4 a hand 2 grab on to

remember we both got real quiet at the end when yentl started unwrapping himself in front of his love (yentl u should never have revealed urself u should have kept that binder on and stayed a boy). i knew it was gonna happen but this time it hit me harder i couldnt look maybe because it was a bigger screen or maybe because i was sitting next to u

and after the movie the lights flickered on u asked me if my eyes were wet and i lied. u said thats ok boys do cry and thats when i knew u were my hand

pulled me out evie u pulled me out

and now u wont even answer a text

#adamandeviehere4u #pittsburgh #yentl

3. ● ● ● ● ● ● ● ● ● ●

Sometimes I wonder if I would feel so behind the gay curve (is that a thing?) if I had known I was gay before the end of freshman year. Or, if I had *admitted* I was gay before the end of freshman year. But it's not like I knew and was hiding the fact. I mean, it really didn't come up until then. Sure, there were signs, but I didn't know they were supposed to add up to anything. Like, when all the hunky guys on that CW show tear off their shirts and become werewolves? I thought everyone got that same breathless, scared/excited feeling I did watching them transform. And I've liked girls before, just, I guess, not the way I'm supposed to. Was I lying to myself? Maybe. But it was more like, there was this blank spot in the middle of myself that I didn't know was supposed to be filled. Until I did.

Okay, there was this time in fifth grade when I got my first laptop, and I googled "men doing sex." Just curious, I told myself. Big mistake. The first results were already too much—exciting for a moment, but then windows kept popping up and it became full-tilt terrifying. Sweaty naked men appeared on my screen faster than I could click them away. What they were doing looked frantic, and frightening, and painful. Videos, images, GIFs . . . it was like the scene from that Disney movie with the walking brooms—the more I clicked away, the more windows kept sprouting up. I didn't know what to do. My father was on location, as usual, so I had to show the laptop to my mother. It was not a happy thing.

To her credit, she didn't freak out too much, but I don't think she entirely bought me telling her I was looking for Minecraft videos. She installed a filter on my laptop, and it's been shutting down dicey internet sites ever since. Not that I have any desire to poke around *that* alleyway any time soon. Well, not much, anyway.

The gay men on billboards for AIDS awareness, or condom use, or the ones on TV shows . . . they don't look a whole lot different from the guys on those porn sites. Ripply muscles and gleaming smiles, hairless white skin . . . is that what we're all supposed to turn into, sooner or later? Hunky werewolves, except backward, transforming from gawky, awkward beasts into buff gay men with smooth skin and muscles?

I am wholly unprepared to deal with that level of gay.

As far as at school, well, there are guys in varsity basketball, seniors, who seem to have made that transformation. Their pumped-up bodies make our JV team look like we haven't been fully inflated. Some of them are CW werewolf hot, to be honest. Like the guy who saved me from falling off the senior bench that first day, Air Jordans. His name's Jamal, and he's captain of varsity. Point guard, blazing fast, with an incredibly soft hand, *swish*, all net, all the time. Not the person you'd want to be tripping in front of. Out of his hoodie and into his jersey, he looks like he could already be playing on an NCAA team. Crazy built. But I'm not even going to start thinking in that direction. No way I want a repeat of what happened at Bishop Academy.

Besides, I don't have a lot of time anyway, not with basketball practice already starting. At Bishop, pretty much everyone who signed up, played, but at Earl Warren almost half of us are going to get cut. So, I've got to concentrate on doing well—locking down the drills, trying to get my hands on the ball as much as I can to snag a spot on the team—and keep up with my schoolwork as well. It's a lot.

So, as far as getting on the gay bandwagon, whatever that means, it'll have to wait. I mean, how was I going to announce it, anyway? Who was I supposed to tell? Doesn't matter. Like I said, I don't have time for any of that.

And yet, here I am, end of fifth period—standing in front of Mr. Janssen's classroom, the one with the rainbow sticker on the window.

His room is down the hall from biology, far from the wide main stairway, close to the back stairs that hardly anyone uses, the one that's darker and smells of weed. Perfect for shady deals and secret make-out sessions. And, possibly, quick escapes after signing up for the Gay–Straight Alliance.

Mr. Janssen's room is dark; everyone's already made their way down to lunch. The clipboard is tucked into the smoke-colored plastic file holder attached to the door. Just an ordinary clipboard. I look around, trying to act like I'm not looking around. You can't read what's on the clipboard without taking it out of the file holder. I study Mr. Janssen's door over and over. His name. The

room number. The rainbow sticker. The clipboard. *The clipboard.*
Why do I feel so nervous?

Cecilia said it was no big deal. *No one cares.*

I pick it up.

GSA Club
Room 554

We welcome all LGBTQ students and their straight allies
Explore LGBTQ Issues in a friendly, inclusive environment
Meets Fridays @ lunch
Sign up below

See you soon!
—Lowell
Sponsor: Mr. Janssen

Lowell's in a few classes with me, but I've never talked to him, partly because he's got the kind of perfect cuteness that's super intimidating, and partly because he's always in an exclusive party of two with his bestie, Lily Cho. Cecilia's right, they're never apart, always walking together and snickering at some joke only the two of them understand. Intimidating.

There are fifteen students already signed up. I wonder how many of them are gay and how many are straight. Would we wear color-coded name tags? Lots of spaces left. There's a pen dangling from the clipboard on a string.

Just do it already.

l grab the pen, uncap it.

Put the cap back on.

Put back the clipboard.

My heart is beating so fast.

Pick up the clipboard.

Grab the pen—

"You should just go for it."

I whirl around. Behind me, it's the guy—One Direction, Zayn-not-Zayn. Him.

I startle so badly I hurl the clipboard. It misses him by inches and drops to the ground, the smacking sound like a gunshot echoing down the hall.

"Uh, what?" I say. My face feels like it's on fire. I try to shake the panic out of my voice. "I, um, yeah, uh—"

He bends down and swipes up the clipboard by his feet. Holds it out to me. "The GSA. It can be a good way to meet people. You know, with similar interests."

Standing face-to-face, he barely comes up to my shoulder, and a good three inches of him is on top of his head, this cascade of thick dark hair, plus the swoosh, free from cap or hoodie. He also has some serious eyebrows. His voice is smooth and cool, no hitches or hesitations.

He holds out the clipboard, waves it.

"Yeah, right," I say, grabbing at it. "Sure."

"Mr. Janssen seems pretty chill," he says. "I have him for physics."

"Oh, good!" I say, nodding way too many times. I pretend to

study the clipboard. "It, uh, sounds interesting. Thanks."

"It could be a bust, you never know. Depends on the school. But it never hurts to . . . scope out the territory. You know?"

His voice is neutral but friendly. He ducks behind me to deposit a paper in Mr. Janssen's file holder, and then starts walking away.

"I've, we kinda, met . . . at Dhyllin's—" I say, and he stops. The thought of that meeting, that *non*-meeting, makes me redden all over again.

"Yeah," he says, his voice giving nothing away, "kinda."

"I'm Jules," I say, and do something so bizarre that I amaze even myself: I stick out my hand. It's like I'm trying to act more adult than I'm feeling, trying to do the grown-up thing, but it just comes across as formal and weird.

He looks at my hand, considers, then reaches for it with his own. "Jack."

His hand is small, but he squeezes mine so firmly and shakes it so hard I almost buckle. Two shakes, that's it, but my hand tingles when he releases it.

"Yowch, Jack!" I say.

And then he grins, like that was just the sound he wanted to hear. And that grin? It's . . . it. His grin is like . . . a match that lights a candle. And these deep dimples appear out of nowhere and punctuate the glow. His eyes, those hard disks of brown, melt into something warm and happy. It's impossible not to grin back.

"So, I guess we're the new kids, right?" I say.

"Oh, yeah," Jack says. "We're the new ones." One second more of that smile and then it's gone. "I guess I'll see ya," he says, and turns to the stairs.

My hand still tingles.

"Hey," I call after him, and he stops. I hold up the clipboard. "There's no Jack on the list."

His face crinkles. "No. I'm not going to be here long enough to get into all that. Not my thing. But you have fun." And he disappears into the shadow of the stairs.

My heart is pumping hard. Why?

You know how when you see a person, like a person walking down the street, and you immediately know that you like them? I don't know what it is—maybe they remind you of someone who was nice to you as a baby. Or maybe it's all chemical. Like a smell, or an aura. Or is it . . . recognition? Like you know right off there's something in them that's like something in you?

Whatever it is, it was there, that feeling, in the handshake, in the smile, there when I finally met him.

Jack.

adamandeviehere4u

i can't help it im online watching some of our earliest videos. damn we were like hyper puppies let out of a cage giggling and jumping up and down we couldnt stay still 4 more than 2 sentences. we looked so young how can it be only last year. i guess we were trans babies just starting out pre everything

the adamandeviehere4u youtube channel was all ur idea. i told u i got the ok 4 hormones was gonna start taking t over the summer b4 freshman yr and u said omg lets record ur transition lets start now

so we did

hi im evie and im adam and we are here 4 u today we are going 2 talk about

my voice sounded i swear like i had just huffed a bunch of helium it was so high. u didnt have streaks yet no red or blue or yellow fireworks lighting up ur hair but it was finding its curl. i still looked like a leftover from a tegan and sara concert

we recorded in my bedroom cuz where else. sometimes ud see my lizards in the shot sometimes dirty laundry (god we did not know what we were doing) u were the chatty friendly 1 and i was the quiet 1. u almost always did the intros and i mostly waved welcome we are both trans kids i am transfeminine and he is transmasculine and we r going 2 transition together and we hope u will find these videos helpful

i think they did we got so many questions so many kids looking 4 help. where can i buy a binder/how did u tell your parents/im afraid of coming out 2 my friends how did u both do that/what is body dysphoria do i have it/r u guys dating (ha no we were not)

some of these kids were like 9 years old or something we had 2 look up all the words dysphoria nonbinary gender nonconforming it was all new we didnt want 2 take a wrong step lead someone the wrong way. there were so many questions i had 2 make a tumblr just 2 answer them all

our life got bigger at least online. it didnt matter what was going on at school we had followers all the sharing and caring dont u miss it? we could block the haters and reach out across the world such a high. we sounded so cringey then but it didnt matter we were happy on our way cuz it was going 2 get better remember that was the promise

it's okay being who u are. u can be who u want 2 be. love urself u r perfect

that was the promise

dont u miss it?

come on evie call me up we can make more

call me

#adamandeviehere4u #pittsburgh #youtube

bad education

so tired today

at school mrs conlon deadnamed me in biology oh so sorry she said i meant adam so sorry ADAM and that just made it into this huge thing i mean how many months have i been reminding her how many cmon

yeah i know i know not a big deal just some petty bullshit evie u would have talked me down given me some perspective u would say just be happy ur not at my high school

which is true

we were 5 miles apart in 2 different school districts but it was more like 2 different dimensions 2 parallel universes

i mean both of us were caught in this crossfire of words and bathroom bills and old white men from far away who suddenly got really really interested in telling us where we got 2 pee they couldnt stop thinking about us peeing yeah and we were the freaks

and at my school it was mostly ok i mean they had a diversity assembly (which was pure hell everyones eyeballs swiveling my way) and there was the article in the post gazette with my photo so i wasnt anonymous anymore everyone at school got 2 claim they knew someone who was

but even tho there were lots of eyes popping and elbows knocking into ribs and phones raised it never got 2 a fist in the back of the head or anything. half the people called me the right pronouns half the time so i guess i won the lottery but

evie ur high school was 20 years in the past where all the heads were shaking hell no and where u had a vice principal who was also the assistant football coach and u heard he called u a fag in front of the whole team and hey thats just locker room talk nothing 2 be done and ur guidance counselor would just tell u why do u make this so hard on urself?

like u were hitting ur own head against ur locker and hocking wet spitbombs on ur books. they said u provoked u were causing a scene

and on the days where u couldnt hold it in any longer u had 2 make that long walk 2 the special bathroom by the administration offices and all the kids knew where u were going

hey sicko do u stand up or do u squat is it still attached?

every day and somehow that was ur fault 2

no help from ur parents. ur father didnt even know about u he thought u were just being weird with the long hair crap and ur mother warned u dont tell ur father dont bring this sickness home

(home where adam wasnt allowed over where there was no evie only a deadname with ur face attached)

so u erased urself u wiped off the lip gloss and the eye pencil and the hurt b4 u walked thru the door u knew ur mom was just waiting 4 an excuse 2 stop it all and u werent about 2 give it 2 her

whats worse being out and hassled by strangers or hiding urself from the ones supposed 2 give u love? it's a one two punch evie a combo platter of misery

fuck it adam ud say. 3 more years

the only person u could talk 2 was me. u were safe at my house we could make our videos we could lie on my bed and hold hands and flip off the world

i could make u feel better i guess i took it 4 granted we could always make each other feel better

so when did that stop happening

#adamandeviehere4u #pittsburgh #highschoolhell

4.

Two weeks later, I can't believe it, but I've made the team. Could be a few sophomores got pulled up to varsity, or the freshman class is unusually short this year, but I'm officially a forward for the JV Earl Warren Wildcats. Go Jules.

Now the work really begins: more training, later practices, getting plays down, trying to find time for homework. I still haven't been to a GSA lunch meeting. I tell myself that I'll get to it later, that I'm still figuring out how this new school works, and one more thing will just tip me into overload. Next Friday, I tell myself, every time I pack up my lunch at the end of the week, next Friday I'll check it out.

But even when I'm plowing through all this new stuff piled up in my brain, at the bottom of that heap, always there, is the question that is Jack. I can't shake him out of my mind, even though I barely see him at school. He appears at the edges of my day—slipping around a corner, disappearing into a crowd—but if anything, the *not* seeing him just adds to the mystery. Why's he still here? Why'd he talk to me that day outside Mr. Janssen's class? What's his deal, as in, is he gay? Shouldn't I be able to tell?

Dhyllin's the obvious one to ask. He'd have answers. But, after that day at his house, I don't know how I feel about getting into it all with him, the coming out and everything. Plus, I remember how he sneered at Jack with that tiny terrorist line. Who knows what else he'd say, if he knew I was interested? Still, when Dhyllin texts and wants to know if I want to see a movie in a cemetery, I take it as a sign.

who's harold and maude?

its a movie idiot

what kind of movie

who cares just come bring a blanket

I don't know anything about Hollywood Forever Cemetery and their movie nights on the graveyard lawn. Seems pretty creepy. I mean, on Halloween, sure, but all summer and fall? I'm not that into movies anyway, and old movies? Forget it. But if I want to see Dhyllin to get some answers, he's going to be there with a bunch of his Beckman Prep friends.

ok see u there

Mom doesn't like the look of the neighborhood when she drops me off, even though the crowd's mostly old hipsters holding bottles of wine and folding chairs. "Are you going to be safe?" she asks.

"I'll be with Dhyllin," I tell her. My mother thinks Dhyllin is the sweetest boy on the planet, partly because she's still thinking of his fifth-grade self and partly because he's good at working the parent angle.

"Okay . . . ," she says, scanning the crowd for potential child abductors. "Just stick with the group, all right? Is your phone charged? Call me as soon as your movie's over. Let me know if you want a ride back."

Man, I need to get my license. At least I got her to stop saying *playdates*.

I wait in line for a good forty-five minutes to get in. We all get directed onto a path, where we pass gravestones and crypts on the way to the stage area. When we finally reach the main lawn, it's so swarmed with people sitting on blankets you can barely see the grass. All those blankets, mixed with that flash of perfect sunset sky before the light completely disappears, remind me of a giant golden quilt being stitched together. We're in front of a huge mausoleum, where a screen is mounted for the movie. A DJ spins tunes to the right of the screen, under a little grove of palm trees, and there's a photo booth set up, covered by decorative daisies. People are walking around selling popcorn and beer, and there's the unmistakable whiff of weed drifting over the whole place.

It's like an outdoor concert, surrounded by dead people.

Dhyllin had texted me to meet him under the palm trees, which must have been some kind of joke because there are palm trees literally sprouting everywhere you look.

No answer. I scan the clusters of palm trees across the lawn, but I don't see any teenagers hanging out under them. The light's already going from gold to blue-gray. Soon, it'll be impossible to pick him out. It's always like this with Dhyllin—that feeling that you're forever playing catch-up. Like in fourth grade, when Dhyllin was playing wall ball, wall ball was all it was about. And then one day, you see him sitting on a bench with Eddie Redfield at recess and ask him why he wasn't lining up for his turn and he squints up at you with that sleepy gaze and says slowly, "I don't know . . . I just don't feel like playing. Go ahead, if you want," and suddenly the ball in your hand is the most babyish thing ever.

When Dhyllin invited me to the cemetery, I got that old feeling like I was specially chosen, and now, when I can't find him, I'm just imagining what he's saying about me to his Beckman Prep crowd, how judgy they're all going to be. I know I shouldn't care—I don't even know his Beckman Prep crowd—but, when you don't have your own crowd, well, you worry about these things. I feel like my time at Bishop Academy was a completely wasted year, I never really connected with anyone, and while everyone else has a circle of friends by now, I'm starting at square one.

My mother's face is flashing in my brain, an alarm going off, *Be aware, Jules!* and I realize I've been staring again. The spot where I'm standing is suddenly prime real estate, people pouring in from every side, like the tide's just come in and all these woven

Mexican blankets and wine coolers have washed up on the shore. I back up, almost step into someone's rotisserie takeout, stumble over shopping bags and ice chests, and pick my way up to where the concession tents are. When I turn around, my spot has disappeared, submerged in the sea of people.

How can I feel so alone in the middle of such a big crowd? Why is everything so hard?

I'm just about to give up and Uber home when things get really strange, because, swear to God, Jack is standing in a concession line right in front of me.

Jack. At first it feels like fate. I mean, how many times can you run into someone without it meaning something? Fate! I think about Jack and *boom!* he appears. *It's another sign.* But before my heart can really rev up, another thought pushes the brake down: *He's here with Dhyllin, idiot. He got invited, too. Logical. No fate about it.* And this kinda bums me out, like Jack's already part of the crew and I'm the odd man out, again, always a beat behind.

I give Jack a tap on the shoulder. "Hey."

He turns and looks up at me. "Oh." The *Oh* doesn't come with a smile, or a friendly handshake like at school. Instead, there's something frosty in his eyes, or something that looks like dread.

RIP me.

"I'm not stalking you," I blurt out, exactly the thing a stalker would say.

"O-kayy," he says. It's already awkward. I ask him where everyone's camped out, and he points to an area in the middle of the lawn. "We're over there."

"No palm trees," I say.

"We got here pretty early," he says, as if that explains everything.

"Oh," I say, as if that makes perfect sense.

"Excuse me, are *either* of you getting *anything?*" the woman in line behind us asks.

"You're next," I say to Jack.

"That's all right. I'm good."

"Then why are you standing in line?"

Jack shrugs. "Six bucks for a taco? No way." He steps out of line. "But go ahead."

People behind me are glaring. I can feel their collective breath huffing on my neck. I dart out after Jack, and the crowd surges forward, pushing us out into the no-space between lines.

"It's my first time here" is the only thing I can think of to say. At that moment, the music cuts out and a voice announces that the movie's about to start. A cheer goes up in the audience. The perimeter lights shut off. We become ghosts of ourselves, barely visible.

"Uh . . . I should be getting back," says Jack-in-the-dark.

"Sure, me too," I say.

With me following, Jack makes his way to the seating area, somehow finding a path through all the lawn chairs and sprawling legs. At one point he turns around and gives me a look, and then another. I wave *still here!* to him, and he keeps going in, to a blanket at the very center of the lawn, the last place I'd expect Dhyllin to be, which turns out to be the only thing I get right that night, because Dhyllin isn't there, and his posse isn't there, either. The only person sitting on the gray-quilted moving blanket is Jack's father, eyes wide with surprise. He looks at me, then at Jack, then back at me. "I guess we have company," he says.

Jack looks completely confused. I stammer something like, "I'm sorry, I thought . . . you were . . . with Dhyllin?"

He shakes his head. "Why would I be? I didn't meet him, remember?"

"Oh," I fumble, "I guess I didn't . . . realize . . . that." My face is so flushed I'm surprised it's not glowing like a brake light. I want to bury myself under the blanket and never come out.

"Yeah." An awkward silence. "I met Gregg, though. We're in a couple of classes together."

"Ah, got it," I say, like that was the information I was sent over here for.

"There's plenty of room," Jack's father says, though there really isn't, unless you're family.

I tell them it's all right, I was thinking of taking off anyway, but when I mention I've never seen *Harold and Maude*, they both get very serious.

"Sit. Down," says Jack's father.

"You've got to stay," says Jack, settling in. "Trust me."

The Paramount logo comes up on the screen. "Okay, no more talking," Jack's father announces, even though everyone around us is cheering.

I'm torn between crawling away in humiliation and staying. "Are you sure it's okay?" I whisper to Jack, giving him an out.

"I'm sure," Jack whispers, and turns back toward the screen.

There's a distant "Sit down!" from the back. I look around, fold myself into a small shape on the blanket next to Jack, use my rolled blanket as a bolster.

I guess I'm staying.

I can tell the movie is seriously old by how fuzzy and scratchy it looks. There aren't going to be any good car chases, or explosions, or superheroes. And when the acoustic guitar begins and the kid in the groovy suit and bracelet starts lighting candles, my heart sinks. *Oh boy.*

And then (trigger warning) the guy hangs himself. Dangling legs, shiny shoes. *In the opening credits!* But (spoiler alert) he's not really dead. This is one seriously weird movie. I don't know if I can describe it—disturbing, hilarious, *romantic?*—it blows off the top of my head. I knew movies could make you laugh, or scare you, or bum you out, but *Harold and Maude?* It's so many things, all at once. Deeply weird. I'd never seen anything like it. And Maude. *Maude.* Even though she's older than Harold by about a hundred years, she has the youngest spirit of anyone in the movie. And he, and she . . . together . . .

If you wanna sing out, sing out—

At one point I look over and see Jack and his father singing along to the soundtrack, like the other people around us. At first it seems so cringey, Jack bopping his head in time with his dad's—no embarrassment at all. If Dhyllin were somewhere out there watching, there's no way he'd be singing out. I can't imagine doing it, either, especially not with my father. Watching Jack and his dad watch the movie, the glow of enjoyment tying them together, dorky, yeah, but both of them so *into* it, makes me think of my own dad, how he's in the movie business but we never watch anything together anymore. To my father, movies are about budgets and schedules and financing and *those fucking actors*, and none of that interests me. His movies don't, either, if I'm being honest. Realizing that gives me this ache inside, and that ache connects somehow to the ache thrumming through the guitar, through the whole movie. It's this ache of wanting, and it isn't entirely a bad feeling. I didn't know a movie could do that to you.

Jack has to nudge me back to life after the credits come up.

"Yeah?" he says to me. His eyes are shining.

"Yeah," I say. "Yeah."

That grin.

I tell them I'm going to Uber back, but Jack's dad won't hear of it. We make our way to the parking lot, his dad surging ahead. Jack knows more about *Harold and Maude* than any sane person should. No, I don't know who director Hal Ashby was. No, I don't know who Ruth Gordon was. No, I've never seen *Rosemary's Baby*, for which she won an Academy Award. Jack can't believe these things aren't common knowledge. "You live in the film capital of the world!" he says.

"Yeah, well," I say, "maybe it's like when you live in New York City and never see the Empire State Building. I've also never been to the Hollywood Sign." I hesitate, then add, "I mostly watch movies on my phone. Or, at least, scenes of them on YouTube."

He groans like I've physically punched him. Looks at me with an expression of infinite pity. "You seriously don't deserve to live in Los Angeles. I think they might kick you out." He tells me all the essential movies I have to see, most of them like forty years old, and he says that's just to catch up. I grin, ask him which ones are Marvel and which ones are DC, and he groans harder.

I pull out my phone, look down, and ask, "What's your Instagram? Or do you do Snapchat?"

But Jack doesn't answer, and when I look up, ready for his information, his mood has completely changed. Something has happened. I'm talking to someone else. Jack's eyes are narrowed, his lips press together tight. It's like a window suddenly closed—I'm on one side, and he's on the other. "I'm not doing social media," he says, and before I can respond, he shoves his hands in his pockets and hurries after his dad, leaving me behind to wonder what I did that was so wrong.

The car is an extremely old Chevy Malibu, with one door and the hood a completely different color from the rest. The back seat is filled with boxes, and papers, and headshots of Jack's dad that have toppled out of a small cardboard box, so that he's all around me, smiling and glaring up from the floor. *Rick Davies*, they say.

It turns out they live in Pittsburgh, and Rick's an actor, or wants to be. He's going to be out here for almost five months, trying to get work, with Jack along for the ride. I get all this from Rick. He's as talkative as Jack is silent, Jack the black hole staring out the side window of the front seat. I still don't know what happened. Walking to the car, something went backward and sideways and totally screwed up. What did I do this time? Was it about watching movies on my phone? The crack about DC and Marvel? Did he think I was making fun of him?

"Jules?" I hear Jack's dad saying. He's looking at me in the rearview mirror.

"Sorry, what?" I say.

"I said, what does your father do?"

I tell him, and he jerks the car to a stop, pitching us all forward.

"Jesus!" says Jack, from inside his hoodie.

"I've heard of Alan Westman! Westman Productions! All those Trouble in Paradise movies on Lifetime, right?"

He's right. My father's been cranking out glossy bikinis-in-peril TV movies for almost as long as I can remember.

"Okay, you've heard of him, you don't have to kill us," mutters Jack.

Rick ignores him. "Hey, if he ever needs a gritty police detective, or a suspicious gardener, or anything, I'm available."

Jack groans and sinks deeper in his seat.

"Okay," I say, not telling him that there probably isn't going to be much chance of me passing on the information anytime soon. "I'm the next house."

"Wow," Rick says. "Fancy."

I'm four steps out of the car when Rick calls me back. He's waving a couple of headshots at me. "Just in case," he says. "I should use 'em if I've got 'em, right?"

"Oh-my-God-Dad," I hear Jack say from inside the car.

I take them. "See you in school," I call out to Jack, but he's completely quarantined himself in the front seat and doesn't even look up.

So much for fate.

I'm almost to the porch, mentally punching myself, when I hear the car door open. Fast footsteps behind me. Jack.

"So sorry about that," he says, breathing heavily.

"About . . . ," I say.

"About my dad. Just throw those headshots out."

"It's okay."

"It's gross."

We stand for a moment, at the very edge of uncomfortable, until he finally blurts out, "So, look, do you want my number? Just, like, in case?"

In case of what?

His eyes glow as he looks at me. They're swimming with moonlight. So much white, such an intense, dark center.

I slowly pull out my phone. "Okay," I say.

My mother pounces almost as soon as I close the front door. She's in her robe, glass of chardonnay in hand, waiting for me. I'm expecting questions about the movie and the cemetery and Dhyllin, but she skips all of that. "Who was that boy out there with you?"

Amazing. She got to the window at the exact moment I was being dropped off. Sometimes I think my mother planted a tracking device on me when I was born. There isn't any other explanation.

I tell her about missing Dhyllin and meeting a school friend who happened to be there, trying to keep it all general, but even this sets off a volley of questions—What's his name? Is he nice? What grade is he in?—all of it said really lightly, but with so much frigging weight underneath, I can't stand it.

"Oh . . . and is he an actor?" she says. I'm completely baffled until I see she's staring at the headshots I'm holding.

"No, it's his father," I say, holding them up so she can see Rick smiling at her. It's kind of like the parents are already meeting. She gives me a puzzled look, but I don't want to get into it because that would mean bringing up *my* father and, well, why spoil the mood? I finally manage to escape by telling her I'm wiped out and still have a physics test I have to cram for. Even so, she can't resist giving an excited little squeal after I say good night.

"Stop, Mom," I say.

"Sweet dreams!" she sings as I race up the stairs.

State of matter—everyday life 4 states of observable matter—liquid, solid, gas, plasma

I've actually got my physics notebook open, just in case Mom barges in. I really don't want to talk about the evening with her. Maybe because I want to think about how I am going to think about it, without her telling me how to think about it. How can I explain the night to her when I don't fully understand it myself?

Can you call it a date if you met by accident?

Phase changes occur when special points are reached

Potential energy vs kinetic energy

I've tucked his father's headshots in my desk drawer. I've got Jack's number up on my phone. His phone number, just, like, in case. Of course, I've googled *Harold and Maude* already and found a bunch of interesting trivia I want to text to Jack, but I stop myself because, well, I don't want to mess up, again.

Give an example of a phase change

Jack's eyes. Liquid freezing into a solid melting back to liquid. Abrupt transformation. Resulting in a complete personality shift.

Under what conditions did the phase transition occur?

I have no idea. What were the conditions present—were they in him, or was I the *catalyst*? What was the *matter* with him? What *state* was he in?

And then there was that moment when we looked at each other, by the front door—that was like *plasma* passing between us. Electricity. Is this how we know someone's interested in us? That second *second* of a look, more than a glance, not quite a stare . . . was that it? I mean, it was over right away, it might not have even happened at all, but in that moment, it felt like a hand had grabbed mine and passed me a secret note.

But what did the note say?

Freezing point. Melting point. Vaporizing point.

Or am I just getting it wrong?

shakespeare in love

alone in my room so damn quiet in here
im thinking about the kiss
im thinking about it
we were talking shakespeare yeah that was something
we both shared odd but true wrangling about the old bard ha
u were complaining u said he has all these girls dressed
up as guys rosalind viola portia why didnt he write any plays
where dudes dressed up as girls? no fair
falstaff dressed up as a woman i said
great. drunk old bearded man puts on a dress ha ha ha
what a role model. transphobe shakespeare
evie all the women were played by men remember?
o yeah u said
we were lying on my bed facing each other my fingers
laced in urs i was in my usual jeans and flannel u were in
that yellow sundress
u took ur other hand and traced my jaw (the new jaw
carved out of my new narrow face) and u said ur so lucky
look whats happening 2 u
i was 6 months on t but u werent on anything no way ur
mother would allow you. u could only go so far u could tuck
and u could curl and u could give yourself a smoky eye but
ur body stayed stubborn what u were not

at least ur hair was growing out so thick and long with yellow fire at the tips u loved it even tho u had 2 twist it hidden in a hoodie so ur dad wouldnt see. my hair was buzzed above my ears such a dude

we kissed. the guy that was me was kissing the girl that was u and that was new 4 both of us and there was electricity in the newness and it felt safe because we werent worried about hands going where we didnt want them 2 go and our eyes saw only what we wanted them 2 see

but

the kiss wasnt the same 4 both of us. there was romeo and juliet in ur eyes and i was thinking twelfth night like we were twins viola and sebastian shipwrecked on the bed. that was when i realized 4 the first time i didnt want 2 kiss a juliet i wanted 2 kiss a romeo an orsino an orlando a boy

i told u this and u said maybe but u never know

i think i know i said

ok u said and ur fingers tangled into mine again but the fingers felt heavy and then they slipped away

i wish i lived in elizabethan times u said. those beautiful dresses

#adamandeviehere4u #pittsburgh #shakespeare #asyoulikeit #12thnight #violaandsebastian

circle of friend(s)

im watching those transition videos on youtube im watching me become me

adam on testosterone 3 months 6 months 9 all the changes thank u jesus 4 the t it was like my real self was erupting from my own body and im not talking about the zits. my jaw squaring and the hair on my legs and arms thickening and so was my voice it had dropped 2 the basement a miracle

there i was second puberty second growing up i think i lost half my vocabulary the hormones the appetite the horniness and rage

the complete and utter joy

im watching month 9 now and i see me talking a mile a minute 5 cups of coffee speed nothing like the me at school so excited giving all the details pointing out the changes flipping out over a waitress calling me sir so into it

and ur not saying much

so i watch again im looking 4 clues and i catch something in ur eyes a sadness around the edges a frozen smile why didnt i notice that b4? i was so stoked by how i was growing i thought it was all ok 4 both of us

no thats bullshit

i knew something was up

i remember that 1 time u got mad at me 4 nothing u were talking about a circle of protection not like a magic wizard kind of circle but like people in ur life who could surround u and keep the crazies from the outside away

u told me i had my family who understood who had my back but u didn't have anyone

i said well what about me and u said u? ur only 1 point what kind of circle is that? and maybe u meant it as a joke but it kind of pissed me off and i said thats not my fault get some friends (like that was all there was 2 it like friends were something u could stock up on from costco) and maybe i also meant it as a joke but it didnt land that way

it was a dick thing 2 say and i tried 2 make it better i said come over here i tried 2 make a circle with my arms but u shrugged me off

ur right i make a shitty circle

if an apology drops on tumblr and no one reads it does it make any difference?

im gonna leave a comment 4 u on our youtube i hope u see it i hope u will call me please please please evie lets rewind

#adamandeviehere4u #pittsburgh #tisfortestosterone #chchchchanges

5. ● ● ● ● ● ● ● ● ● ● ● ●

What sixteen-year-old wants to get to school early Monday morning?

I sit at a sophomore bench alone, darting looks in all directions, but there's no sign of Jack. I was hoping to be able to just kinda run into him, but that's difficult when there's no *him* to run into. When does he get to school? I never see him in the yard. Does he just teleport into first period?

No luck.

I send him another text, the fifth one about *Harold and Maude* since Sunday night (so much for playing it cool):

> **hey did u know the writer of**
> **harold and maude was openly gay?**

No answer. Just like the other four. I look over my texts heading into first period and curse myself for sending the most idiotic messages ever. What was I trying to do, scare him off? Why the hell can't you unsend texts?

By nutrition break (otherwise known as snack time), there's still no sign of him, and at lunch, driven to despair, I do the unthinkable—I ask Gregg for advice.

Theoretically, it's not a bad idea. Gregg's in a couple of classes with Jack, Gregg knows about me, Gregg could be the connector.

Trouble is, Gregg is Gregg.

"I don't know anything" is all he can tell me, when I ask him about Jack.

"Yeah, but, like, who does he hang with?"

"He doesn't really talk to anyone—why do you care?" Gregg says. He's obviously distracted.

"I don't know, I'm just . . . curious. Like, do you know . . . is he gay, or what?"

"Oh, there's the chips guy. Excellent." Gregg digs into his pocket, pulls out some money. "Want one?"

He looks around to make sure the courtyard is clear of lunch supervisors, then jogs up to a junior with a big duffel bag. A moment later he's back, two Doritos bags in hand.

"Here," he says, tossing one on the table. At school, Gregg exists solely on junk food.

"I don't eat these, remember?" I say, pushing the Doritos away. "No processed grains." I've got the lunch my mom packed last night (yes, she still packs them): cashew-flour flaxseed bread with soy cheese and no-nitrate ham, quinoa crackers, and a small, sour apple. I've tried to stop her from making my lunch, but in the end, it's easier to take it than to argue.

"I thought it was white sugar you weren't eating."

"It is. But also processed grains now."

"God, that is the saddest thing I ever heard." Gregg grabs the bag of Cool Ranch chips from the table and pops it open. "So, what were you asking?" he says, licking the powder from his fingers.

"Jack. Is he gay, do you think?"

Gregg does that up and down thing with his eyebrows, and I punch him in the arm maybe a little harder than I mean to.

"Ow!" he says. "How am I supposed to know? It's not like he's going down on anyone in physics or whatever."

"Ugh. Never mind," I say. "You're useless."

"Useless how?" Cecilia asks from behind me. She sits down, plunking her backpack onto our table. "I mean, how *this* time?"

Gregg grabs his chest and slumps to the table, mortally wounded, but when he hears the crack of her Diet Coke, his head jerks up. "Where'd you get that?" he asks.

"Soda guy's right over there," she says, pointing to a student with a soft cooler tucked under the table by his feet. "He's almost out."

Gregg jumps up. "Oh, by the way—Jules's got a big boner for Jack the new kid."

"Screw you, Gregg," I say, but he's already halfway across the lawn. Cecilia turns to me, eyes bright, and I know I'm doomed.

"Tell."

So, I do, what little I know.

"Okay. Promising," she says. You can see the high-speed processors firing up in her mind. "Are you going to ask him out?"

"No!" I say. "I mean, I don't even know what his deal is, and, just, no."

She lifts her hand, lets the bracelets jingle down her arm, and then locks them into place with her other hand. Ready for battle. "Okay . . . I've definitely noticed him. Very quiet. Keeps to himself, a little intense, or could be just super shy. Difficult to know. Anyway, the question is, what is his deal . . . is he gay . . ."

I want her to just tell me the answer. "What do you think?"

"I think . . . he does have a vibe."

"Are we still talking about this?" Gregg asks, returning with a Coke in hand.

"Shut up, Greg-g," she says, deliberately pronouncing both *g*'s at the end of his name. "Let the grown-ups talk. Okay, my radar sense says . . . definitely maybe."

"*Definitely maybe* means your radar sense is pretty crappy," says Gregg. He guzzles down his soda.

Cecilia sighs. "Whatever." She holds out her hand to me. "Okay, give me your phone."

"Why?"

"Just give it." She grabs it from my hand and starts furiously typing, thumbs flying. "Here . . . is a list . . . of questions . . . you can ask him . . . that will let you know . . . who . . . he . . . is." She finishes, hands the phone back to me. "*Teen Vogue*. Guaranteed."

"Okay . . . ," I say, reaching for the phone, but at that exact moment Jack appears out of nowhere, and I slap the phone out of Cecilia's hand, like it's a live grenade I've got to save her from. It skitters across the table and lands in the grass. I yelp and scramble to the ground, and by the time I've gotten back up, Jack's standing right by me.

"Oh, hey," I say, like I've just now noticed him. I see Cecilia lean forward toward Jack, like a T. rex eyeing a Jeep full of riders.

My glare is supposed to be threatening, full of fire, but by the time it reaches her it's turned into something desperate and watery. *Please oh please do not say anything. Do not. I beg you.*

Jack notices nothing. He pulls his backpack up onto the table and bends toward me. "Hey. *So, um*"—he lowers his voice, as if that's gonna wall us off from the others—"I've got something in my bag . . ."

"What is it?" Cecilia asks, like she's TSA.

Jack pulls out a Tupperware container and opens it up. It's filled with about six dark, reddish-brown balls of . . . dough? jelly? that are a little bigger than golf balls and glistening with syrup.

Gregg is suddenly all at attention. "Whaaaaat—that smells amazing."

"What are they?" I ask.

"Uh . . . Indian fried dough?" he says, like he's not quite sure.

"Did you make them?" He nods, but it's hard to believe, they look so perfect.

"I thought you might . . . like to try one?" He almost sounds embarrassed.

"I'll try one," Gregg says immediately.

Cecilia pushes in. "Hi, I'm Cecilia, friend of Jules."

Gregg pushes her back. "And I'm Gregg, *also* friend of Jules." He adds, like it's gonna score him a treat, "We're in *physics* together."

"Yeah, I know," says Jack, the corner of his mouth twitching up. He fishes a ball out with a spoon. "You guys can have one, too, if you want. I made, like, a boatload of them last night."

Cecilia carefully plucks the sticky fried ball from Jack's spoon, her fingernails acting like tweezers. Gregg, meanwhile, just scoops one up from the Tupperware and crams the whole thing into his mouth.

"Whoa," says Gregg. You can see the blood sugar spiking in his eyes.

"Oh," Cecilia says, after a bite. "These are actually good." Her body does a little happy shimmy. "So, you just make these? For what?"

Jack shrugs.

Cecilia sucks the syrup off her fingers, thinking. "And you have a lot of them? Like, a lot, lot?"

"Yeah, well, you can't just make a few," Jack says. "And I made too many."

"You know what you should do . . ." I swear I can see a light bulb flickering on over her head. "You should totally sell them here."

"What?" says Jack.

Cecilia holds out a finger. "Yes. Look around. Everyone's selling food. Ever since the LAUSD banned corn syrup and empty calories from campus—"

"And those are the *best* kind of calories," Gregg adds, heartbroken.

"—there's this underground market at school for food that students actually want to, you know, *eat*. Chips, sodas, candy—it's insane. And everyone's looking for something new and different and tasty. You could make a killing. A *killing*. Just don't get caught."

Jack shakes his head. "I . . . don't think anyone is gonna want to buy these—"

But Cecilia is in full Young Entrepreneur mode. She fixes Jack with a laser stare. "You, sir, are mistaken. Okay. Give me three. God, they're sticky. Put them on a napkin. Do it."

Jack doesn't have a choice.

Cecilia stands. She gives me a look and her lips twist into a sly smile. "C'mon, Greg-g," she says, pulling up Gregg, who's still licking the syrup off his hand, "I need your help." She drags him away. "We'll be back!"

We watch her march across the courtyard, napkin in hand, Gregg following like a shadow.

"Well, okay then," Jack says.

I realize it's just me and Jack, alone at the table. I can't believe how happy I am to see him. It's this feeling like, I've been benched since I started high school, waiting to be tagged in while everyone around me is running up and down the court, and now I'm back in play, on my own team of two.

"Jules?" says Jack.

"Sorry, what?"

"I said, is she always like that?"

"Cecilia? Yeah . . . she likes to be helpful," I say. I look down at the remaining dough ball in the plastic tub. "So, you just whipped these up? Just like that?"

"They're not that hard, once you know how. My mom taught me . . . they're gulab jamun. It's an Indian sweet. You make them for holidays, and weddings, and birthdays, and also"—he takes a deep breath—"when-your-father-makes-a-complete-ass-of-himself-in-the-car-and-you-want-to-apologize-for-being-so-weird." He slides the Tupperware across the table toward me. "You know, occasions like that."

I jump in. "No! It was great! I—I had a great time, the movie was great, and your dad is"—I stop myself from maxing out the word *great*—"your dad is cool."

Jack rolls his eyes. "Yeah, right. Anyway . . ." He smiles, satisfied, like he just got something out of the way. "Are you going to try it? That one's got your name on it."

"Oh!" There's a super-awkward moment where I don't say anything. "Actually . . . I'm kinda not eating processed sugar, so . . ."

"Huh. Tons of that in here."

"Also, wheat flour. And dairy. And . . ." I trail off, realizing how pathetic I sound. ". . . fried."

Jack pulls the Tupperware back and shields it from me. "Well. Okay. Wow. That's pretty much all these are, so . . ." He looks up at me. "Sorry. I didn't realize. Allergies?"

"Oh, no no no," I say. "No allergies."

"Religious?"

"No, it's just—my mother has these health issues, so she's trying out this diet. Trying out a lot of diets, actually. It's kind of her thing."

"Oh. And why do *you* do it?"

"Uh—" I hadn't really thought about it before. "It's just . . . easier that way?"

"Easier?" he says, puzzled. "Okay . . ." He looks so disappointed.

I reach out and grab the Tupperware from his hands.

"Wait. You don't have to," says Jack. "It's not a big deal."

Why does it feel like it is? I spoon one up. The dough ball's soft, moister and more delicate than a donut. I look at Jack, hold it up, and pop the whole thing in my mouth.

Sugar.

Gregg was right. Whoa. Soft. Sweet. Spiced. I want to eat a whole tub of them.

"Do you like it?" Jack asks.

"You," I say, running my tongue over my teeth to catch every crumb of sweetness, "are going to make a million dollars."

"I guess I wouldn't say no to that." Jack smiles . . . and the dimples. The dimples. Worth every gram of sugar.

There's a pause, and we both look away, just in time to see Cecilia strut across the courtyard to us. She's got her chin high, lips pursed in satisfaction, and her arm is in the air, waving three one-dollar bills above her head.

Jack turns to me and shrugs, smiling. "So . . . you wanna help me sell these things?" he asks.

There's nothing I want more.

apocalypse now

u blocked me im blocked on our youtube channel I AM BLOCKED why evie why did u just do that? what do u think im gonna do stalk u i just wrote 1 comment reaching out 1 goddamn comment and u changed the password?

how the hell we gonna sort this out if u wont talk 2 me?

im on ur side remember?

but maybe u dont believe that

maybe ur remembering

dont remember evie dont

i fucked up evie i wasnt ready

u always told me ur school was like a battle zone but i didnt understand it until the bombs started dropping around me

like oh this is how bad it can be

we were going 2 the center. pick me up at my school u said slip in we can go from there. my secret crush will probably still be hanging around his name is roman he has a nose ring and soccer player legs

when i got there u looked great evie u were in a really good mood so happy 2 see me. maybe u flew a little brighter down the hallway and that caught their attention or maybe it was our chatter (we could never shut up together)

but really i think they were just waiting

later u told the principal u didnt see anyones face but

u had 2 say that u knew what the price was 4 telling cuz u did see u saw the face of every kid who cornered us on the stairs and they werent all boys either

our chatter cut right off

they sliced u away from me with their bodies with their words they wanted u all 2 themselves

where u going they said why u so happy u know ur just a

(i dont even want 2 write the words they said dont want 2 give them air)

we wanna show u something they said and they grabbed ur hair and ur arms and they dragged u 2 the boys bathroom and 2 stood watch and 1 of them turned 2 me (he had that sharp silver curling out of his nose and fists twitching 2 be released) he said what r u looking at faggot and i said nothing

turned my head and looked down at the floor

said nothing

it wasnt even 1 minute but it felt like hours before they ran off. i found u crouched in the last stall ur hair and face wet with spit and a gash on ur cheek from the stall door u fell against

u said forget it dont say anything lets get out of here but i made u go 2 the nurse just in case and she wouldnt even look u in the face she called u by ur deadname she shook her head but she wasn't the worst

she reported it 2 the principal who punished exactly no one called in no one and oh yeah he deadnamed u 2 said emotions are high lets calm down why dont we call ur parents but he wasn't the worst

not even roman with the soccer player legs who high
fived the others and ran off slow like it was a victory lap
not even he was the worst

u know who was the worst

it was me evie. it was me

all the things i coulda done screamed fought ran 4 help
but i did none of the above evie i just stood there

and whats worse evie? the worst secret i never told u?

i knew these people thought faggot was better than
being trans

so i shut up

i was happy 2 be just a faggot 2 them

how wrong is that

HOW FUCKING WRONG IS THAT

waiting 4 ur mom outside neither of us talked. not a
word. i stared at the ground trying to disappear. u stared
straight ahead wouldnt look at me i couldnt find ur hand it
was like u were already gone b4 the car pulled up. we didnt
even say goodbye

we were just empty shells evie 2 coffins with nobody inside

#adamnotthere4u #pittsburgh #worstone

6.

hey

hi

those dough things
awesome

thanx

what do u call them

gulab jamuns

but i just say indian fried dough easier lol

so good

a little messy but yeah

u should call them indian
donut holes

kids like donuts

good idea

thanx 4 being my lookout dude

sure dude

Over the next two weeks, selling Indian donut holes is pretty much my only Jack time. Nutrition break and lunch, we travel around the courtyard, me keeping watch for supervisors, Jack handing out the goods from his open backpack. A few minutes before, we huddle in the stairwell ladling the dough balls into baggies, my hands raised to his. A few minutes after, we count the money and high-five. Altogether, it's barely forty minutes. But every minute together feels like a step. Walking toward something. A friendship. Or more.

After school, it's all basketball, five days a week, gearing up for our first preseason game against Alvarado High. And I know I should be worried about whether I'm going to start or not, about how much attention the coach is paying to the other forward, Colton Meyers, but I don't know, I'm not that stressed about it anymore. It's not that basketball isn't still important, it's just that my mind's on what happens after practice, what I'm going to text Jack once I get done.

hey

hey

dude, crazy today!

your on fire

thanx

when are u making more

idk maybe the weekend

i could help if u want

any time

if u want

ok bye

Can you run off at the mouth while texting? Apparently, the answer's yes.

sweet dreams

haha

sweet like the donut holes i mena

"Jules, what are you doing? We're eating dinner," my mother says from across the table. I hold up a finger.

*mean

bye

"Jules—"

see you tomorr

"I got you on the waiting list at Beckman Prep."

My head jerks up. "What? No! What? I don't want to, I mean, I'm on the team at—I'm *fine* where I am."

My mother gives me a *Now that I have your attention* smile and leans back. "So, who are you texting?"

"Uh, Jack." I haven't talked much about him since the movie—anything, really—because I don't want her to make a big deal out of it, especially when I don't even know if it *is* any kind of a deal.

"*Really.* And how are things with Jack?" I swear her eyes are getting misty.

"Fine. Nothing," I say, trying my best to slam that door shut and nail boards across it.

"When do I get to meet him?"

It's gotten very hot in the room. "I don't know. He's just a friend."

"Well," she purrs, "you never know."

"Hey!" I blurt out. "I saw some workers down by the reservoir. What's going on there?" The city's recently drained Silver Lake Reservoir, just down the street from us, and the neighborhood's on the rampage. My mother joined a citizen's action group, Save Our Reservoir Endeavor (SORE), and that's currently got all the attention she isn't directing toward me or against Dad.

She puts down her fork. "Jules. You will *not* believe the latest—"

Oh my God, it actually worked. My mother goes off on the evils of developmental contractors and sweetheart deals, and by the time she's gotten around to the corruption in city hall, I've got my plate scraped clean and I'm halfway up the stairs to my room.

You never know.

But a lot of times, my mother *does* know. Just like Dhyllin knows. And I never do. Like, there's a way the world works, and they've got it figured out, but me, I don't. I don't know what the deal is with Jack. There's always something held back with him. I mean, I know he has a mom in Pittsburgh, and a bratty younger sister, and two pet lizards. And that he loves movies, of course. But nothing else. He never mentions having a boyfriend, or a girlfriend, or if he's even into any of that. I haven't actually come out and told him I'm gay, either. Is he waiting for me to do it first? Am I missing the signs? Is he trying to avoid an awkward conversation because he isn't gay?

I think my head will explode. As well as certain other parts of me.

> **have u ever playd 22 questions**

> **no what is it**

> **its kinda a game**

It's Friday night, and I'm at home after practice. I copy Cecilia's questions, dump them into my text. I can't believe I'm doing this.

> **whoa thats a LOT**

22 questions what u expect

cn i just do 4?

sure

ok

name- jack davies

no middle?

none that im gonna tell you

fave food-

idk italian?

celeb i look like- well
zayn malik according
to ur friends

lmfao

my celeb crush- umm

I watch the little dots cycling on the screen, on and off and on, meaning he's writing, meaning he's stopped, meaning he's started again.

ok idris elba

Who the hell is Idris Elba? Is that a man or a woman? I leave the screen to google the name and come up with a face I recognize—the dude from *Pacific Rim*. Okay. My heart gives a jump, but when I return to the text, he's continued:

> **charlize theron**

I google that name, too, and . . . it's a woman. This is not helping. At all.

> **dude u pick the weirdest people**

> **why they are fine af**

> **who would u pick**

His question makes my mind go completely blank, and I write down the first name that comes into my head, basketball-related, of course:

> **stephen curry maybe**

It's like the *maybe* walks it back a little, but it doesn't at the same time. There's a pause, and I'm guessing it's his turn to be looking up names.

> cant argue with that

A step forward. I feel reckless. I type a name, and pause, and erase it, and type it again.

> zayn malik isnt bad either

There. It's done. A giant step. I can't imagine it can get any plainer than that.

But then, there's nothing. No response. Not even the dots. I take a breath. I'm tired of steps. I want to sprint.

> im gay did u know

The answer comes back fast.

> yeah

The word is so meaningless there in its little bubble. I have no idea what it's trying to tell me.

> howd u know

And then there's the longest pause ever. Dots blinking, and stopping. Blink. Stop. Blink. Stop. Blinking, blinking, blinking. Stop. He's either texting an essay, or he doesn't like what he's saying. And each time he stops, my stomach somersaults.

Finally, only six words make it onto my screen:

> **takes 1 to know 1 dude**

I'm holding the phone in my right hand, but the words send a shock of electricity through my entire body, the top of my head to my toes, and all the parts in between. I'm one tingling mass. I see everything right in front of me, the movie dates and the holding hands and the kissing, so much kissing, and there we are with crowns on our heads, the king and king of homecoming. It doesn't matter that Jack goes silent, doesn't text anymore that night. I have my answer.

It is happening.

monster

all right lets finish this horror show this car crash lets lay it all out

u came into my room looking like they tried 2 rip the evie right out of u

the cut on ur cheek was healing but looked worse puffed up an angry sunset of purple and red. ur hair was all slashed off into spikes and patches ur head was so small ur eyes on fire

u threw the silver butterfly hair clips on the bed the ones i gave u on ur bday. u said here take them nothing i can do with them now

look at me. look at me

i couldnt look evie couldnt move couldnt talk couldnt form thoughts words deeds u were just wanting 2 words from me why couldnt i say them

i was just freaked evie u were on fire and i was freaked

u told me ur father grabbed the scissors and he grabbed ur head like he was gonna do the hedges like u were a tree that needed pruning he never said a word

but ur mom never stopped yelling while she destroyed ur room I TOLD U I TOLD U she ripped all the posters from the wall all the hiding places upturned and turned out

telling me this u were shaking there was an explosion

building inside u i didnt know how 2 stop it i was scared evie the guilt burning me up i was little pieces of ash dissolving in the air i was dissolving

adam i told u not 2 say anything why didnt u listen 2 me why did u make me go 2 the nurse why

nothing but guilt and ash spinning from me the air was thick with it and in every moment of silence more words slipped away more space crumbled between us a chasm

and then u were yelling

this is completely fucked up

my father says i cant he wont let me he said he would kill me if

dont you understand im on lockdown 24/7 no coming over no videos goddamn it dont u care at all adam say something adam jesus adam SAY SOMETHING

my hands shot up like i was surrendering and the words finally came but they were the wrong ones evie i hurled them out so hard 2 hard i just wanted the fire to stop everything to stop

WHAT DO U WANT ME 2 SAY EVIE HUH WHAT DO U WANT ME 2 SAY

and everything stopped

nothing adam dont say anything
i don't need u
forget it
im done with u

u ran out i didnt follow why didnt i follow
every day i think of that every day
where were my hands 2 stop u my words 2 calm u the
curve of my arm 2 hold u
who am i now who is this boy i have become

#adamandevie #pittsburgh #monster

gravity

i cant do this anymore it isnt helping dr grace was WRONG. mom says whats the matter and dad says hey kiddo but they dont know what went down and writing it out doesnt make me feel better doesnt make me less of a shitty friend doesnt let me take it all back it just keeps the circles going around in my head no relief

besides youll probably never see this anyway whats the point

on youtube on our tumblr the comments and the asks keep coming like everythings the same like we r still together. all these people looking 4 sharing and caring but i have no answers 4 them and who the hell am i 2 tell anyone anything

i cant stand how much i miss u. i tried to call 1 last time but ur phone is shut down do u hate me that much

i even went to ur house it took a while to find ur address but i did. no one at home the curtains all shut a scrape of mud on the top step of the porch no color at all. i shouted 4 u but the house stayed silent it didnt recognize ur name

fuck it evie

No more rewinding

u said ur done with me you dont need me so i guess i wont need u either

adam and evie r here 4 no one

even my name doesnt fit right adam the name u gave me i thought it was my true name but im giving it back it was only my true name while i was with u now its just a dead-name buried under my porch im gonna have 2 find another

pittsburgh feels like a chokehold my bedroom is crammed with ghosts. dad is heading west scoping out Hollywood 4 a few months and i told him i wanna go with him and he said yes and mom said yes even dr grace said it might be a good idea a different environment so all systems go

u know that scene in gravity where 1 astronaut unclips himself from the other and just spins off into space? thats what im gonna do im gonna take down the adamandevie tumblr im gonna get me a new name and spin off into the unknown

out in los angeles no one will know me and i can just float along the boy who has no answers who has no sharing or caring who wont damage anyone who can just be left alone

or maybe ur the one floating away maybe im unclipping u and letting u spin away smaller and smaller until ur just a spot a speck and then just an idea an image in my head that was never really there a butterfly

(bye evie)

#adamandevienolongerhere4u #gravity #goodbyepitts-burgh #goodbyeadam #goodbyeevie

7. ● ◉ ◎ ◎ ◎ ◉ ● ◎ ◎ ◎ ◎ ◉

I see the yellow bus with ALVARADO HIGH SCHOOL printed on the side pull into our parking lot. They're already here, the Alvarado Angels, sworn enemies of the Earl Warren Wildcats. Last year they knocked our varsity team out of the playoffs. This year, it's revenge. Today's only a scrimmage, but, as Coach D'Arienzo says, it sets the tone for the entire season.

No pressure.

My mother will be out in the stands. I told her not to come until it's a real game, that I'm not even sure I'm gonna get off the bench because Colton Meyers is the starting forward, but she says she wants to support me. I have a feeling that's not the only reason. She also knows Jack will be there and wants to get her eyes on him.

Oh, yeah, Jack's coming, too.

No pressure.

He said he wouldn't miss it, if just for the excuse to watch a lot of guys in loose jerseys get all sweaty on the court. I think he was joking, but I actually don't want him looking at all those other guys on the court. Just one particular guy in one particular jersey. Number eighteen. Me.

Now that I've opened up to Jack, everything feels . . . uncorked. I've told him about my dad leaving, about my mom and her diets, their fighting . . . stuff I haven't told anyone about. And he's mostly quiet, but he listens, really listens. And when I told him about Bishop Academy, and what happened in the locker room, being called Julie and all that, he got so fierce, calling all the players jagoffs for what they did, and the coach an even bigger jagoff (it's a word he uses a lot).

"Don't let them get away with that shit," he said. "Because they'll just keep getting away with it. Assholes shouldn't win." He was so angry—for me. And even though my mother said the same thing, more or less, it made sense when I heard it from Jack. I guess they *were* jagoffs. I can see that now.

Speaking of jagoffs, the kids from Alvarado High start filing out of the bus. Time to get changed. Right before I enter the locker room my phone buzzes. It's a text from a number I don't know, with a YouTube link attached:

you should see this

I figure it's some kind of scam message, some Trojan horse that's going to open up a virus (Mom is always warning me about viruses), so I kind of forget about it and head into the locker room.

Everyone's pumped up, extra loud and rowdy. There's a very interesting conversation going on between Jamal and Tommy McBride, the guy with the blond dreads and Skrillex T-shirt from my first day, who's a varsity forward. They're talking about whether or not you should "do the deed" before a game, you know, about keeping all that energy in and whether that's a myth or not. Tommy McBride says it's bullshit and then Jamal says, "How do you know, Tommy, your girlfriend's not putting out anyway."

And there's a round of *ooooooooh*s from everybody and then Tommy fires back, "At least I got a girlfriend, jackass," and Jamal's brother, Kevin, who's a junior, says, "He don't want no girlfriend, fool," and Jamal smirks, and Tommy says, "Well, okay, no *dude* wants your sorry ass, either," and Jamal just smiles and says, "Oh, I got my eye, I got my eye," and the whole room is full of *ooooooooh*s again and then Coach D'Arienzo comes in and tells us to head on out and get warmed up.

Wait, is Jamal gay? And everyone knows? And no one cares? I mean, it's Jamal, who would go up against the varsity captain, but also . . . *he's the varsity captain*. And then I realize this varsity captain's still in the room, checking out his hair in the mirror. Jamal sees me in the reflection and swear to God, he smiles at me. Swear to God.

"Good game," I say in a rush, and bolt out quickly, before he can see how red I'm getting. I don't understand—he looked at me like he knew what my deal is, and I've barely talked to him. How did that happen? Did telling Jack I was gay suddenly give me some kind of invisible mark to all the other gay people, like an entry stamp on your wrist to get in and out of amusement parks? How obvious is it?

When I step onto the court, I see Mom already there, waving

wildly. I duck my head and hope no one notices. We start our warm-ups, and after every ball that leaves my hands during the drills I sneak a look at the stands. It's pretty packed, but there's no sign of Jack yet. Two quick blasts of the ref's whistle. JV's up. I take my place on the bench. Game time.

We start out pretty evenly matched, lots of back and forth, but then Alvarado breaks away and puts up six points *boom boom boom*. Colton's off his game, misses an easy two-pointer, but Xavier gets the rebound and scores. Still four points down.

No Jack.

I have this whole thing mapped out, where I actually get in some court time, sink a few three-pointers, and am generally awesome. Jack's so impressed, he comes up to me afterward, smiling that smile, the look in his eyes telling me, *I'm so into you right now.* And he meets my mother, and we celebrate, maybe he comes to our house for dinner, actually, scrap that, we go *out* for dinner, and then, well, who knows . . .

Concentrate on the game.

Second quarter. Our point guard, Gavin Miller, fastest kid on JV, is all elbows, with a temper to match his buzzed red hair. Gets called for charging, then called again for popping off with the ref. Two free throws, four more points for Alvarado. Gavin storms to the bench, muttering, "Crying bitches—"

"Are you still talking, Miller?" D'Arienzo says.

Gavin clamps his mouth shut, but his head bucks like the words are trying to punch their way out. He slams his hand down on the bench and glares at the world.

Halftime, we're down six.

Third quarter. Maybe Jack's actually here and I've just missed seeing him in the crowd. I imagine him watching me from the bleachers, his dark dark eyes, wide and almond-shaped like a deer's, his thick eyebrows (who notices eyebrows? Me), the right one with the piercing arching higher than the left, which gives him a wiseass look even when he doesn't mean it. The thought of him watching the game, watching me, starts to get me all riled, which would not be a great state to be in when you're on the bench in baggy shorts, jock or no jock—

Whistle blows. Coach D'Arienzo taps me on the shoulder. "Westman, in for Meyers!"

Here goes.

I leap up, slap hands with Colton. Somewhere in the stands I hear my mother screaming out my number. No pressure. The Alvarado players charge in. "Man up!" yells D'Arienzo, and I fix on the Angel forward, number twenty-five. Everything else falls away.

A blur of red and gold coming at us, the thud of pounding feet. An intercept, and then it's our ball and we're a wave of blue and white sweeping the other way, raised arms and darting shapes. The ball's mine. I sink a shot. *Yes.* No time for glory, more back and forth. Time zooms by. A cross-court pass, and I sink another. When did my hands get so hot? And though I'm not thinking about Jack at all, he's somehow beside me, speeding my feet, clearing my head, lifting the ball from my hands into one glorious, three-point rainbow shot in the last five seconds.

Victory reclaimed.

A roar from the stands. Whooping, high fives, hands pounding backs at the bench. Coach D'Arienzo swats me on the head. "Good job, Westman." I look around, still breathless, and there's my mother running at me, arms open. She hugs me, which is super gross considering how sweaty I am, but I guess I don't mind.

"Jules, I'm so proud!"

"Just a scrimmage, Mom."

"Oh stop, you were fantastic." She pulls away. "And where's Jack? Don't I get to meet him?"

I shrug, trying not to look disappointed. No Jack coming down from the bleachers, no Jack to be mega-impressed by my victory. In the locker room afterward, I check my phone and—nothing. I start to get worried. What happened to him?

I shower and get dressed, and just as I'm closing my locker, I feel a vibration in my pocket. Finally. It must be him, texting, explaining why he couldn't make it, telling me he's just outside, waiting.

But it's not from Jack. It's Gregg:

hey did someone send u a video?

They did. It's there, right underneath Gregg's text—the unknown number and its message. So, I duck away from all the celebrating, put on my headphones, and scroll down.

I touch the link.

At first, I don't know what I'm looking at. It's these two kids bouncing all over the small screen of my phone. *Adam and Evie Explain It All 4 U*, the YouTube title reads. "Hello, my name is Evie!" the one with the longer hair says, and I turn my phone sideways to make those kids bigger, turn up the volume, and in my ears there's a voice that sounds familiar but sped up, "And I'm Adam!" and it's a girl's voice, and she moves forward from the background to shyly wave at the camera, and it's me she's waving at, and the first thing I think is, Hey, that must be Jack's sister, but then I remember the name is Adam, but even then, even though the eyes are the same and the smile is the same, my slow, slow brain refuses to catch up.

And then it does.

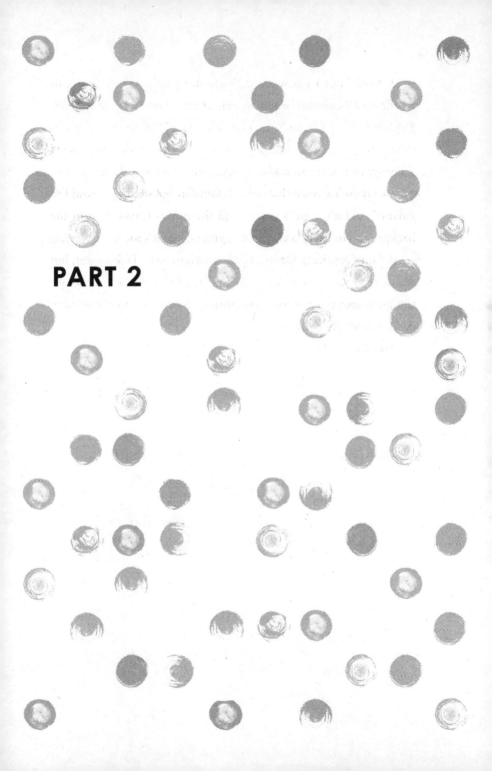

PART 2

Evie: *Hello my name is Evie*

Adam: *And I'm Adam*

Evie: *Hello*

Adam: *Hello*

Evie: *I'm a trans girl*

Adam: *And I'm a trans . . . boy? guy?*

Evie: *You can be either*

Adam: *Okay*

Evie: *And we're here because like we want to um just for people out there who might be trans or know someone who's trans or have questions um we are saying hello*

Adam: *Hello*

Evie: *We're going to be starting high school next year in the Pittsburgh area and it's kind of scary because well we both kind of came out as trans last winter and so*

It'll be our big debut

I'm sure everyone will be excited and super supportive ha ha not

But we thought it might help other kids out there who are going through the same thing to like see how we're getting through it and

Is there something you'd like to say Adam?

Adam: *My hair looks super weird why didn't you tell me it looked like this?*

Evie: *Stop looking at your hair*

Adam: *Does it always look like that*

Evie: *Yes*

Adam: *Evil*

[laughter]

Evie: *Anyway if you have any questions or anything just ask below and we'll try to answer it or I will anyway and Adam will keep looking at his hair okay remember*

Be who you want to be love yourself and you are all perfect and um okay bye bye peace

8. Jack

"And this is my son . . . Jack."

He's introducing me to the landlady, dropping that sinkhole pause after *son*, stopping my heart—*Is he gonna say my new name? Come on, Dad, are you fucking kidding me, of all the times to forget your lines*—but then he nails his cue and gets it right. The pause must've been for dramatic purposes, typical Dad. Playing to the crowd.

I give a cool nod to Frau Blücher, who's squinting down her sharp nose at me. Dad lifts an eyebrow—*be polite*—but I don't want to be giving her my voice, not yet. Her name isn't really Frau Blücher, it's Mrs. Kozenski, but I swear she's a 3D version of the pinch-faced housekeeper in the movie *Young Frankenstein*, down to the sour look and mole above her chin. Her eyes squinch and shift back and forth—me, Dad, me again—she's not buying we're related. *Yeah, we get that a lot, thanks for playing*, I want to tell her, but I don't, because we really, *really* need a place to live.

We've landed in front of some kind of boarding house/Airbnb for college students in Frogtown, a part of Los Angeles that looks nothing like what Los Angeles is supposed to look like, all industrial concrete and chain link, some artsy hipster vibe creeping in here and there, but this block is definitely less hip, more creep. We're across the street from a boarded-up Dolly Madison factory, next to a chop shop with barbed wire curling around the parking lot. The house is dark and huge, color of the Wicked Witch of the West, peeling green paint, tiny windows, rickety stairs on the outside. Definite serial killer vibes.

There's not a lot of other options. Everything's so expensive in LA, super expensive. Ever since we touched down at LAX we've been passed from one actor friend of Dad's to another, staying overnight in guest rooms or couches before heading to the next way station, like thespian fugitives on the run. And every place we've looked at to rent costs too much, or won't do a month-to-month, or is a little too meth house for a growing boy and his dad. The clock is ticking—if we don't find a place and get me enrolled by the beginning of the school year, Mom'll pull the plug on this whole Great Experiment before it even starts, and we'll be winging back home to Pittsburgh by the end of the week.

Which brings us to the serial killer house.

Frau Blücher leads us up the peeling stairs to the second floor, then sifts through a large ring of keys she pulls out of her pocket. *Ze stairvay can be trechewous*, I imagine her saying, and have to choke down a laugh. Dad and I share a look, and I know—I know—he's thinking it, too, we just rewatched that movie a couple of weeks ago.

When she opens the door, I expect rats or creepy moths to come fluttering out, but it's not that bad. The hall is dark and musty smelling, but neat, and there aren't, like, faces in jars on the counter, so, thumbs-up for that.

The available bedroom looks out onto the street. It's got one double bed on a metal frame, an old dresser, and an end table, that's it. The one wall that's not wood paneled has a giant water stain in the corner and a crack coming down that looks like evil's gonna come crawling out of it. It's the approximate temperature of hell in here, and no air conditioner.

"It's never a problem when the window's open," Frau Blücher says. Our faces have all melted into sweat puddles. "Just keep the curtains shut during the day."

My father nods. "This could work," he says, obviously delirious from the heat.

Before we pass out, the landlady leads us down the hall, sighing with every step, pointing out the *shared* bathroom and the *shared* TV room and the *shared* kitchen. She tells us about the Los Angeles River and the bike path that runs along it, less than a mile away, "Perfect for exercise." Back in the hall, she's had enough walking and just waves toward the other end, where the three serial killers we'd be doing all this *sharing* with are holed up. Their doors are shut, but I'm sure they pop up on dark nights when the fluorescent bulbs in the kitchen start flickering.

All the while my dad is giving his full-on, flirting-with-the-old-ladies, middle-aged Italian/Irish/Portuguese/German Casanova charm, guaranteed to work, but Mrs. Kozenski's got her mouth pinched shut and folded down. I'm doing my best to stay out of the way, hidden in my hoodie, but her eyes keep sliding over in my direction, and I'm thinking it's my fault she's got such a sour look on her face. Maybe it's not that she doesn't believe I'm his son, but that she doesn't believe I am *a* son. So, I spread my legs a little farther apart, square my shoulders, shove my hands into my pockets. Stare her directly in the eye so she'll look away. It works.

Who knows, though, maybe that judgy glare is for my brown skin and heavy eyebrows and dark hoodie. Maybe she's got a problem with that. Interesting thing: before the transition, I never got this much side-eye from strangers. I was always *cute* or *sweet* or *what beautiful skin!*, but now, they suspect I'm building terrorist clock bombs in the basement. But it's also possible Mrs. Kozenski could be frowning at the bleached wave in my hair, my pierced eyebrow. So many options to choose from. How do I hate thee, let me count the ways.

My dad keeps flirting with the Frau, gives her that chummy-chum wag of the head. "And what about the local high school, Mrs. Kozenski? Know anything about it?"

She tightens her eyes and puckers. "Earl Warren. I hear it's a very good school." My dad underlines, "Very good school," just to make sure I've heard, but Mrs. Kozenski's already interrupting. "Listen. I've never had high school kids staying here. I don't like wild boys, okay?"

Ah, the pierced eyebrow.

She continues. "The men on this floor are all responsible college students, very quiet, and we want to keep it that way." She shakes a finger at Dad. "You are going to be responsible for him?"

My dad holds up his hands, opens his eyes wide. "Oh, don't worry. That won't be a problem. Jack's a pretty quiet kid, believe me."

She's not believing. I pop my eyes open, too, all innocent, give her my sweetest and quietest smile. She tries to smile back, but it's mostly mouth-stretching. "Okay, then. Good. Come fill out the papers."

I've passed. We're in. Not such a bad place, after all. Yeah, it'll be a nightmare sleeping in the same room with my dad, but the whole situation is so far from real life—Pittsburgh, the house we've lived in since I was born, parents who work a nine-to-five, a sister—that I'm actually kind of stoked.

Not that I'd ever let my dad know. When we get in the car, I give him my *What were you thinking* stare, but before I can launch in, he holds up his hand. "No complaining. You knew what you signed up for. This is what I meant by bare bones."

I roll my eyes. "All I'm saying is, if you snore, I will murder you in your sleep."

He shakes his head. "You already know I snore, so, no patricide allowed. And look, it's only fair because I have to put up with boy odor and Axe Spray."

I raise my arms high, a lethal move considering the sweatbox temperature and the black hoodie I've been wearing all morning. "Boy odor! Woo-hoo!"

My dad says, "That's nothing to cheer about."

But we both know it is.

No time to unpack our stuff from the car, there's another old college friend who lives in the Hollywood Hills who my dad's dragging me to meet for lunch, but I get him to check out the

LA River before we go, looking through the metal gates at the sad trickle of water and the deserted bike path and the old graffiti; it's funky and abandoned and my new favorite place ever. Dad says, "Well, maybe you shouldn't come here by yourself," and then we're off.

We take Riverside Drive, angling west, me navigating by phone and Dad trying to keep Cherry Jubilee from overheating on the way over. The closer we get to Hollywood, the more movie and TV posters keep popping up. Everywhere. Plastered on giant billboards, buildings, bus stops, buses, benches . . . they'd have them tattooed on dogs if that were possible. The city's constantly reminding you: *We're the film capital of the world, damn it.* I love it. I mean, you're not going to find *Orange Is the New Black: For Your Emmy Consideration* signs popping up in Pittsburgh. There they are, the whole cast, giant-size, including Laverne Cox, trans superstar. I stick my phone in the air, thinking Evie would love a picture of this, she idolizes Laverne Cox, but then I let it drop, because, oh yeah.

And as many movie billboards as there are, there's an equal number of homeless tents and shanties set up underneath, mini campsites crammed under the highways and off the exit ramps, every street seems to have a couple of tents crowding the sidewalk. But then we turn up into the Hollywood Hills and suddenly, no more tents and no more billboards. Instead, green lawns and flowers bursting with color even in August. The palm trees are all hand-polished, the houses are all mansions, and *oh shit!* there's the Hollywood Sign right in front of us, yes, here we are, the

Los Angeles that people think about when they think about Los Angeles. *That* Los Angeles.

My dad's college buddy Mr. Gene Ramsey is a big-time concert promoter who lives in a house that's all gleaming wood and glass, that looks like it should be on a cliff overlooking a beach. You know how you can be completely disgusted with something you also completely envy? That's this house. Every room looks like the best hotel suite ever and I'm afraid to sit anywhere because I should have dressed better and my ass is going to somehow scuff the white furniture. There are these long hallways with framed gold records of albums I've never heard of hanging on them. I wonder how many people live in this hotel of a home, and when I find out it's just him and his girlfriend, plus the son when he visits, I think, how egotistical and wasteful, when there are hundreds of homeless people just a mile away, how excessive and obscene.

But the air-conditioning feels *so* good.

I don't know how a concert promoter is going to be any help in landing acting work, but as my dad keeps repeating over and over, *It's who you know in LA*, so my dad needs to know as many people as he can these next months. He launches into his Great Experiment speech as we tour the house, a speech I've heard so many times I could recite it by heart—how his aunt in Michigan died and left him a chunk of change, and instead of upgrading the car or fixing the roof or doing anything at all sensible he decides he's going to take it and quit his permanent temp job as a legal proofreader and try to make a go of it as an actor in Hollywood for four and a half months, it's now or never, do or die, all he needs is one lucky break, blah blah blah. This Great Experiment could also be called the Crazy Suckhole of Money. I have no idea how he convinced my mom to let him go. It's completely unrealistic and impractical. I wanted in immediately.

I can tell Mr. Gene Ramsey doesn't think much of my dad's Great Experiment because he says more than once, "Four and a half months is not a long time," like that's gonna suddenly change my dad's mind. Dad nods but says, "It's actually almost five months. And hey, no guts, no glory, right?" (My dad is someone who says things like *Do or die* and *No guts, no glory.*) Gene Ramsey shakes his head, like, *I warned you.* He's a small guy who never looks you directly in the eye, wears a blazer and dress shirt even though he's in his own house, brown leather boots that must have cost a fortune, and a pair of jeans with a label that has never crossed paths with my local Kmart. My dad, on the other hand, looks like he just wandered in from a Bucs game and is asking to use the crapper. "Holy moly!" he keeps saying, each time we enter a new room.

I can tell Mr. Gene Ramsey doesn't hang around kids that much even though he has one of his own. He keeps forgetting I'm there, and each time he does remember, he has nothing to say to me except, "You're going to get along great with Dylan, he's around here somewhere," like Dylan's a Game Boy he misplaced, and once he finds it I'll be occupied and the problem of me will be solved.

I can also tell he's not that close to my dad because he asks, "How many kids do you have?" twice and then he forgets I'm there again when he brings us downstairs and asks my dad if I'm adopted. My dad says no and Gene Ramsey says, "He's pretty dark," and after my dad tells him my mother's Indian, he says, "Well, that explains it," and then he turns around and notices me standing there and says, "Whoa, you want a Sprite?"

We finally do find Dylan, playing basketball with his friends out on this huge-ass court in their backyard. We see them from the game room, where I discover that his name isn't D-Y-L-A-N but D-H-Y-L-L-I-N. It's scribbled on a limited edition, signed Tony Hawk skateboard propped up against the pool table. Come on, *Dhyllin*? It's like you're setting him up to be a dick at birth.

Which he is. His dad waves him in from the back patio, but *Dhyllin* can't be bothered to even look up from his phone. I step out from the cool of the house into the full blast and glare of the sun—oh yeah, it's still summer—and when my eyes get adjusted, I see he's got two friends with him, an Asian kid and a tall skinny white boy. The tall kid is the only one shooting hoops, and he stops when I come out, just freezes and stares at me—*stares*—and usually I'd shrink back, look away, but because this is Los Angeles, because I've got my own Great Experiment, because I'll never see these people again, I lift my head higher and shoot a DeNiro *You talking to me?* stare right back at him. He drops his gaze first, which feels good, and then gets tangled up in his giraffe legs and misses his shot and that feels even better. That's what he reminds me of, a baby giraffe, long legs long neck, and learning how to walk but not too well. Really skinny and tall, with good arms, and I feel a quick bite of jealousy about those arms and his tallness because I don't have either.

Then they all run away, three cis guys scared off by one little trans guy, at least that's what it looks like, though probably it's just that the rich kids smelled the Kmart on me and ran off holding their privileged noses. Basketball-playing kids from Los Angeles are a lot like basketball-playing kids from Pittsburgh, kinda douchey.

Mr. Gene Ramsey says, "Boys," and wanders back inside.

My dad's hoping to pry out some names and phone numbers from his old college buddy, but even after an hour at lunch chatting about the good old days at Carnegie Mellon and the theater department, Gene Ramsey can't cough up any contacts. He says, "I'm out of that side of the business," so no names and no agents and no meetings, nothing but a Let's Do Lunch when he gets back from Spain in a few weeks, which means, if I get the translation right, never. He doesn't ask me a single question, hardly even looks in my direction, which is fine by me. When we get to the car, I ask my dad if his friend was usually like that, and he says, "Oh, he's always been kind of an asshole. But at least we got a good meal out of it."

Which is true.

I think about those kids running away, about Baby Giraffe Boy staring, and I ask my dad if he said anything about me to his friend. My dad says, "I don't think so. Why? Should I not?" I just shrug and put in my headphones, because he doesn't know about my own personal Great Experiment, and I don't know if I want to tell him.

It'd be too hard to explain, but here it is: I've lived in the same place in Pittsburgh my entire life, I was born a Burgher. Grew up with the same families, the same kids going to the same schools. Every personal transition I've made has been sliced up and dissected, put on a slide, gawked at, shared and laughed at. On a good day. But here, it doesn't have to be that way. If I stay stealth, I'll be able to forget Pittsburgh, go to school for a few months, and just be me. This me. Not a symbol or a social experiment, something to wave a flag over or lob a name at.

Just a brown boy named Jack, formerly known as Adam.

We unload our stuff at the new home, and Dad leaves me behind to Skype Mom while he goes to Costco to get a blow-up mattress for me and sheets that don't look like bedbugs have crapped all over them (I'm not even going to sit on the bed until he gets back). He's made me promise not to tell her about the gang graffiti on the garage. Or the neighborhood. Or anything that might make her nervous. So I guess we're gonna do a lot of talking about the weather.

I sit on the floor, open up my laptop. Enter in the house Wi-Fi password (thank God that works) and sign on to Skype. *Bloop bloop bloop bloop.*

I'm waiting for Mom to answer, staring at my own face on the screen. It still surprises me—*that's mine?*—the eyebrows that fit so much better, the jaw, the invisible facial hair that I swear is there. Will be there. I can feel soft, fine hairs on my cheek, and isn't there a shadow on my upper lip sorta kinda?

It's all mine. God bless testosterone.

My face on the screen jitters away and gets replaced by Mom's. She's fiddling with the computer, so for a moment I can watch her without her watching me back, someone with my exact tone of olive skin, my eyes. It's like going back home, seeing her face, the only part of home I miss.

She finally stares straight at the screen. "Hello. You're alive." She always looks so serious. "How are you? How is Los Angeles?"

"It's really hot here," I say. I tell her how the plants are out of control in this climate, huge like they've landed from outer space and are going to start eating people. But my mother doesn't want to talk about alien cacti.

"Have you found a place to stay?" she asks.

"Yep, take a look."

I swing my laptop around, trying to avoid showing her the crack in the wall and the giant water stain. She's not impressed. Her forehead crinkles, her neck pushes forward, trying to see beyond the screen. "Is it . . . nice?" she asks.

I tell her we live in Frogtown, like that's an answer, but it only makes her forehead creases dig in.

"Is that in Los Angeles?"

"Yeah, it's by the LA River. There used to be frogs around here."

"Oh. Frogs," she says, as if that might be acceptable. "You like frogs."

I tell her I don't think there are frogs in the river anymore, but there are plenty of grocery carts floating around. Probably not the best thing I could've said. Mom's mouth opens with another question about to hop out, but at the last moment she decides to smile instead.

"I guess it's part of your *adventure*, right?" she says. She uses that word a lot talking about the trip, but there's always a hollow space underneath, like she's not really buying it. *Adventure* is the last thing my mom wants right now—she's already gone through the awesome *adventures* of my nightmare puberty, my therapy, my coming out (boy), my *second* coming out (gay), and my testosterone-fueled second puberty, *now with added aggro emotions!*, which settled down just as my sister Sudhi's own puberty started ramping up. Lucky Mom. She was there handling it all. Dad was the first to get on board with my transition, but once my mom came around, she was all in. She read the brochures and did the research and made the appointments and took off from work to sit in at every doctor's appointment, every school meeting, stared down each sour face until we were the only ones left standing. When Evie and I broke apart, well, Mom had to deal with the fallout from that, too. I bet that's why she let me travel across the country and switch schools, out of her reach for almost five months. She needed the break.

Back on the screen, Mom's asking me how I'm doing. She's got that concerned look on her face.

"I'm great," I tell her. "Really."

The xylophone music starts playing, and she says, "It's your father on FaceTime. Hold on." She holds the phone up to her face and swipes.

"Hello," she says, and turns the phone around so I can see my father's face appear on her tiny screen on my computer screen.

"The modern age," my father's tinny voice says. "I'm at the Starbucks near Costco."

"Pick me up a caramel Frap," I say.

My mother turns the phone around so he's facing her. "I hear you've found a place."

"It's in Elysian Valley," my father says. "Isn't that a nice name?"

"It's a better name than *Frogtown*." The way my mother says it now makes the frogs sound toxic.

"Who told?" Dad says, and Mom says, "Hold on." She puts the phone to her chest and calls offscreen, "Sudhi, come talk to your brother while I talk to your father."

"My name is Susie!" You can hear my sister's whine even from 2,500 miles away. "We're going to be late!"

"We have a few minutes. Come here and say hello." My mother's voice has that edge to it that means if you don't listen there *will* be consequences.

My mother leaves the screen, and a younger version of her face huffs in, glaring. It's amazing how much Sudhi looks like Mom. It's like, in the womb, the Powers That Be couldn't figure out what to do with our father's mixed bag of genes and so they just chucked them all out and made a clone. But Sudhi doesn't have the dark circles under her eyes like my mom, or the worry lines above them, and not even a drop of the gentleness my mom's eyes hold. Sudhi looks like I'm betraying her every minute she has to stare at me.

"What," she says.

"How are my lizards?"

"Dead."

"Sudhi!" my mother says somewhere offscreen.

"It's *Susie!*" my sister screeches to her left. She tosses her hair back to me. "My name's *Susie* now," she says, like it's a dare. Lips pressed tight.

Okay. Susie. Whatever.

"What's wrong with that, *Jack?*" Her voice has that bratty singsong tone that middle school girls get when they all start to sound like each other.

"Nothing," I say, keeping my voice neutral. "If that's what you want, great. Good for you. Sudhi-Sue. How are my lizards?"

"It's Susie!" she screams.

"How are my lizards?"

"Gross. Fine."

"Just be nice to them, okay? Can you do that? And feed them?"

Susie just looks at me, bored resentment burning through the screen. I'm so tired of seeing that. I look down at my own face, there in the corner box, sulking. It used to look a lot more like Mom's and Sudhi's, we were three of a kind, and then the T took hold and the softness went away, the oval became a rectangle and suddenly there was the outline of my father's face, like it was waiting all this time to show itself.

And for a moment I feel bad for Sudhi-Sue, because to her, we used to be sisters, and now we're not. Maybe she feels abandoned. *Sorry, Susie, for not being the older sister you wanted. But we never really liked the same things, anyway.*

"Can I talk to Mom and say goodbye?" I say.

"Mom!" Susie yells immediately. "*She* wants to talk to you!"

"Susie!" I hear my mother yell, sharp and quick.

Fuck. I jab the video button just so she won't have the satisfaction of seeing my face, but I can still see hers, turning back to the camera, looking for me, smiling. I slam the laptop shut.

Go to hell, Sudhi-Sue. I'm not sorry at all.

Later, Dad returns from Costco ("Yes, buddy boy, the card from Pittsburgh works here, it's a miracle!"), we inflate the blow-up mattress, pile the boxes of ramen and Cup-a-Soup in a corner of the room, and divvy up the dresser. We eat beef bowls from Yoshinoya because who can even boil water when you're this tired.

The house is actually cooler by the time we get back from dinner, so Mrs. Kozenski wasn't lying. All's quiet on the second floor, just my dad and me, no serial killers in sight, no college friends, no Mom telling me to get to bed or Susie cutting through metal with her voice. Dad puts on the sheets, and I pad across the hall to the bathroom to brush my teeth and change. The wood floors are sticky, I wish I'd worn socks.

I make sure there's no one lurking behind the shower curtain and wash up. Then the next part. Taking off my binder. It usually happens in the dark of my bedroom, but no way with Dad across the room from me. I turn my back to the bathroom mirror, flick off the light.

Jeans off. Hoodie off. Shirt. T-shirt, quick. Pull down the shoulder straps of the binder that's covered my entire torso all day, one hard yank, shimmy-shimmy-shimmy, an instant prickle of relief as it passes down over my stomach, past my hips and onto the floor. Thank you, Mom, for the slim hips. Deep breath. Step out of the binder, scoop it up and then quick, before the anxiety flutters in, I pull on my Carnegie Mellon sweatshirt. Baggy shorts. Another deep, full breath.

Lights back on. Done.

I turn to the mirror and look at my face, stroke my cheek, in search of stubble. I swear I'm going to have to shave soon, or maybe I won't shave, maybe I'll grow a beard, it's possible—Mom says that if the Indian side of me has anything to say about it, there's going to be no problem accumulating hair.

And then it hits me—I live here. California. This is my (shared) bathroom, in our (shared) house. This is home. For the next few months, at least, I'm gonna be an LA boy.

Bring it on.

My dad's already snoring by the time I get back to the room. I pop in my earplugs, crawl under the blankets, and fall asleep almost instantly. Though we haven't visited the ocean yet, I dream of it, me in board shorts, smashing into wave after wave, feeling every drop of spray, every sun ray of warmth on my bare chest.

Evie: *Hello everyone we are back I'm Evie*

Adam: *I'm Adam*

Evie: *So this is a continuation of our last video about when we knew we were trans because a lot of people have asked about this and I already told my fascinating story of how Evie was born*

Adam: *So fascinating*

Evie: *Are you being sarcastic?*

Did you uh did you see how many likes we got on that one?

Adam: *A lot*

Evie: *The most okay? So now it's your turn*

Adam: *It's not a competition*

Evie: *We'll see*

Adam: *Great*

Evie: *No go ahead when did you first know you were trans?*

Adam: *Okay um so um*

Evie: *Really good start*

Adam: *Shut up it was around when I was eight I think I was watching this outdoor production of As You Like It*

Evie: *Shakespeare at eight smell you*

Adam: *My dad was in it I had to go it was my first Shakespeare*

Evie: *Who did he play?*

Adam: *Um the bad brother I think or the uncle or the father? I actually can't remember*

Evie: *He was that good*

Adam: *No no it's just that he disappeared after the first scene for almost the rest of the play anyway stop interrupting*

Evie: *I bet he was Duke Frederick anyway go on*

Adam: *I remember it being super cold and I was bundled up in a blanket on the hill at Frick Park watching strange people in strange costumes speaking strangely and there were these two girls Rosalind and Celia who were on the run and had to disguise themselves and escape into the forest of Arden and so they left the stage and*

When they came back out again

Evie: *Yes?*

Adam: *Rosalind had totally transformed herself*

Her hair was hidden under her cap and she had changed out of her dress into a pair of pants and a shirt and vest she even had a little mustache and she called herself Ganymede

And I remember standing up and my blanket just dropping away and I forgot all about being cold I just stood there staring at her and I knew I knew that was me

I was that boy she had become

Ganymede with the low voice

I think I stood for the rest of the show my mother kept tugging me to sit back down but I jumped up every time he came on I didn't understand much of what he was saying but his body I understood completely

His swagger his crouch the way he adjusted himself how he could stand one foot up on a rock fists up

It was like this magic

And I remember thinking that was what I wanted I didn't know what it meant but I knew it felt exactly right

Evie: *Yes yes*

Adam: *And at the end?*

When she changed back into a wedding dress hiding every part of herself?

It just crushed me

Evie: *Give me that wedding dress*

Adam: *And I knew if I had the chance I wouldn't change back I'd never be Rosalind again I'd always be Ganymede*

Evie: *Oh that's such a sweet story and you get points for Shakespeare*

Adam: *You know Shakespeare too*

Evie: *Yeah but my story was all about Barbie dolls*

Adam: *Barbie dolls are important*

Evie: *Barbie dolls are important*

Whatever anyway if you liked Adam's story just give him a thumbs up but not too many and please please please subscribe to our channel

Adam: *Subscribe*

Evie: *Okay remember be who you want to be love yourself and you are*

Adam: *Perfect*

Evie: *Exactly nice job on the story my sweet Ganymede bye*

9. ● ● ● ● ● ● ● ● ● ● ● ●

With one jerk of the window shade my father nukes me instant awake. "Good morning!" he sings, sadist, still pulling on the cord, and I'm a vampire exposed to the sun, hissing and twisting on the mattress, I want to sink my fangs into him, but he only laughs. "Rise and shine! First day of school!"

Is that really the best way to start the day?

This never would've happened at home, I had complete control of my own damn curtains, so, no sun allowed. My mom calls my room a rat's hole, she doesn't mean it to be a compliment, but I like the image: somewhere dark and safe, filled with all the junk I'd personally dragged in. My dad calls it a toxic waste dump—"You can smell the Chernobyl from here," he says, and Sudhi-now-Susie, well, she just covers her nose with her hands whenever she walks by my door, refuses to come in, fine by me.

Last year around this time, I had been on T just three months, a summer of revelation, giddy-up here we go! testosterone coursing through my system joy joy joy, then freshman year of high school sprang up like a bear trap and just crushed me. All the beautiful changes that seemed like SO MUCH became NOT ENOUGH with every smirk in the hallway. Too many people knew the old me—there wasn't enough distance between my *was* and my *am*. All the questions—"What are we supposed to call you now?" "Why is your voice so different?" "What happened to your complexion?"—there was never a chance to blend in before being called out.

Earl Warren, don't fail me.

Only six thirty in the morning, and I can already feel heat prickling the air when I stand up, but no way I'm going to lose any of my layers. Not today. I need all my armor. Hell, I'd throw on another binder if I could, but nope, because cracking a rib with two chest binders would not make the best first impression. Binder 101. Doesn't mean I haven't thought about it, though.

All I need to start my day is coffee and a Pop-Tart (we have eight jumbo packs stacked up in our room, thank you, Costco), but today Dad insists, it's pancakes. That's his thing. It's Mom who gets our asses in gear the rest of the school year, but the first day always belongs to Dad and pancakes. He hauls out the five-pound jumbo bag of mix and we're lucky enough to find a scratched-up Teflon pan with only a mild crust baked on in the (shared) kitchen cabinet, along with a melted plastic spatula that was once maybe gray.

"Hey!" My dad points to the bag. "Hungry Jack! Get it?"

I don't say anything, because you don't ever reward that level of enthusiasm so early in the morning.

"Did you even change your clothes from yesterday?" he asks, putting a plate down in front of me. I grunt, the universal sound of *Why are you provoking me so early in the morning I know how to dress myself I've been doing it for years don't you understand I've got other things to think about?* and he gives a big theatrical sigh and starts cleaning up the kitchen.

Here's where we spot our first housemate—the guy in the room next to the TV room. He's not your typical mild-mannered serial killer—this guy's giant, with big thick black glasses and a hairy belly that's playing peekaboo underneath his Pink's Hot Dogs T-shirt. He shuffles out of his room to the doorway of the kitchen and just stands there, looming, a sleepwalking Sasquatch—he must have been attracted to the smell of pancakes—and a moment later, he turns and leaves, shuffling back into his lair, no good morning, nothing. I think about offering him a pancake, but you know what they say—if you feed one stray serial killer on your floor, you'll end up having to feed them all.

"Let's go," I announce, checking myself in the mirror, jutting my chin out, squaring my shoulders, plucking out my hoodie to make sure it's hiding everything.

"I don't know why you're even bothering with your hair. You're only going to smash it down with that cap," my father says, peeking into the bathroom. "Don't worry, you look very . . . fly."

"Don't even try, Dad."

School is really too far a walk, unless I want to get up twenty minutes earlier, so, no. Dad drives, and yeah, I really do appreciate him getting up and making pancakes and taking the time to get me there and being an ally and all that, but what's with the constant stream of cheery conversation just pouring out of his mouth? It's exhausting. I cinch my hood tight, lean back, and close my eyes. We scoped out the route yesterday—It won't take us too long to get there.

It's amazing we made enrollment with one day's notice. There were some last-minute student dropouts, Dad worked his charm, and presto, bingo, I was in. We had all the docs—the transcripts, my birth certificate, our new address, and most important, my therapist letter. Which means I'm registered as Jack, not my dead-name, and Jack will be on the class list, and I'll be gendered right. The principal didn't even bat an eye—in fact, she gave me a warm handshake and asked about my pronouns. *My pronouns.* Back home there was a full-on interrogation and fifty shrink hoops to jump through, and they still didn't get around to changing my name on the school roster for half a year. Here in LA you tell them you're trans and they give you a goodie bag and a parade, practically.

You talk the talk, Earl Warren. But do you walk the walk?

Kids are hanging out on the lawn and the sidewalk as we drive up—I get that creepy crawly feeling, where I'm tight in my chest even when I'm shrinking into my clothes. I try not to stare at them, to see if they're staring at me, but the car's so loud it's begging to be noticed. We're driving this Chevy Malibu beater my dad bought for a few hundred dollars on Craigslist, an honest-to-God wreck he calls Cherry Jubilee because the passenger-side door and hood are bright red (but not the *same* bright red), and neither of them match the rusty charcoal of the rest of the car. When I first saw it, I actually thought it was kind of cool, in a junky *Mad Max* way, but now, when we round the block to get to the drop-off, I hear every creak and whine.

"You are *not* dropping me off here," I tell Dad, "go around the corner," but he ignores me and pulls past the chain-link fence into the parking lot, humming a little tune as he does it. He's exacting revenge, damn it. It's pure hell. I sink down and stare straight ahead. *Help, I've been abducted, I'm in no way related to this car.*

Yes, they're staring.

"Knock 'em dead, kid," my dad says. "You might want to lower that hoodie."

I might *not* want to.

"Goodbye hug?"

If looks could kill.

Go, I breathe to my dad, and eject myself from the rattling car.

I walk fast out of the parking lot, head down, but all the staring eyes have already shifted somewhere else. I'm just a kid in a dark hoodie, feeding into this huge campus with all the other kids in dark hoodies. I slow down, lift my head, and it's a goddamn Christmas miracle, no one's pointing at me or pointing me out, no ex-friends to avoid or idiot remarks to ignore. No one gives a shit. It's fantastic.

I'm surrounded by students of all colors, and white isn't the most popular shade. Black kids and tan kids shooting hoops together, a couple of girls with head scarves texting in one corner, conversations in Spanish wafting by. There's someone who could be a nonbinary kid in an army jacket, with lavender lipstick and big magenta streaks in their long hair, sitting at a table, big black boots tapping the ground, there are even two guys frigging holding hands under a tree and *no one is freaking out.* No one's calling anyone ungodly or perverted or a terrorist. It's like a Unicorn Rainbow Gap-Ad World here in Los Angeles. Hell, if I wanted to, I bet I could come out and it'd be fine, if I wanted to.

But I don't want to.

For the next semester, I'm going to just be myself.

I pull down my hood. It feels good to get a little circulation up there. I ask a group of girls for directions to Building C and they point out the way. I turn to leave, and I hear this giggling—*Oh shit, here it comes*—but then one of them calls out to me, "Nice piercing!" and when I turn around she's pointing at her own eyebrow, which is also pierced.

"Cool," I say, and nod. That seems to be the end of that, but this time when I start walking away another girl yells out, "She thinks you're cute!" and I try to act chill and give them that Supercool Guy on Campus hand wave but I end up smiling so wide that it makes them giggle even more as they run away, and their giggling is the freshest, most sparkling water you ever drank.

Okay, this is really gonna work.

I turn back one more time, just to see if we're gonna go another round, but the girls have disappeared, and in their place is the kid with the magenta streaks and army jacket, black boots striding right toward me. They stop a moment, close enough so I can see their fingers with dark nail polish clutching and unclutching the strap of their backpack, the big pink-and-blue button pinned to the strap, the patchy shadow of stubble along their jawline. From behind round glasses, their eyes lift up, dart and search, and what they find is—me.

Fuck.

They know. I see that sly, determined smile, the look that says, *I know you, you're just like me, you're a safe one.* There's something about the way their hair moves when they rush up to me that reminds me of Evie, Evie before the horror show, when she was just starting to become herself, but that memory has all the good feeling drained out of it and there's nothing left inside but panic. I'm not ready to do this again, that's not the plan, I don't want to connect with anyone, and no, I'm not a safe one, not at all. I feel this flapping in my chest—*don't look at my chest*—is anyone else looking, who's looking? Who's about to peck at me—*What are you looking at, faggot?*

I turn my back on Magenta Streaks, hurry up the steps to Building C, head down, totally unapproachable. Hoodie up, earbuds on, phone in hand, I'm a turtle retreating into its shell, hidden, trying to hide, pressed against the wall of the building, this is the most important music ever and I have to listen to it *right now.*

The bell rings.

When I lift my head and look out into the courtyard, Magenta Streaks is far off, walking away from me, retreating fast, staring at the ground, slumped, passing through the arches, fast, gone. *Shit.* The masses swarm up the steps near me but I don't move, I'm trying to figure out what just happened, how I could Jekyll/Hyde into such a jagoff in the blink of an eye. *Bad boy. I'm bad. You're better off without me, Magenta Streaks.*

And then *he* shows up in the crowd, my punishment, Baby Giraffe Boy, friend of Dhyllin's, loping up the steps toward me because of course he is, Hell is empty and all the devils are here, at Earl Warren. He knows about me, Dad said he didn't tell but I bet Dhyllin knows and he passed on the gossip to all his buddies. Out of the corner of my eye, I see he's getting closer, angling through the crowd so he can pass right by me, gawk again, point me out, he's close, he leans over, hand reaching out, he's gonna say something—

I shoot him a glare like, *Don't you dare*, and I swear, I swear I've developed mutant powers because not only does he back away and close his mouth but my glare stuns his legs, makes him stumble, pushes him through the doorway and face-plants him to the floor.

Laughter all around, the kind that ripples out, rings of humiliation spreading from that one unlucky stone that got dropped in the center. Not me this time. Him. The kind of thing that happens to you on the first day of school that people like to talk about right until the doors open for summer break.

Any other time I'd be happy for mutant powers. But today, no. Because when I shoot my death rays I see the boy's face up close, and his mouth isn't twisted into a sneer, or a smirk, but a smile. Something friendly and warm, welcoming words about to tumble out. I was wrong, and before I know it he's swept away by the crowd into the hallway beyond.

Okay. Enough with the paranoia. Chill the fuck out. Just breathe. No need to take out the entire school on your first day. Remember "She thinks you're cute!" and be that guy—CALM DOWN.

Be like water, Bruce Lee said, and that's what I try to imagine, I'm part of this river of students snaking our way to first period, just one of the new kids. I Bruce Lee my shit together enough so that when I get to physics and there's a boy at the desk next to me already sleeping, and it's the *other* guy from Dhyllin's house—*What are the chances, come on, no way*—I don't show my panic, breathe my way back to calm.

He jolts awake. "Shit," he says, longish black hair tangling in front of his face, nature's sleep mask, "where am I supposed to be?"

No one answers him, because, who knows, and he turns to me.

"Hey," he says.

"Hey."

"What class is this?"

"Physics. Mr. Janssen."

"Right. Yeah . . . yeah," he says, remembering, sad to remember. "God, I hate school." He dives back down, buries his face in his arms, but then his head pops up again, squinting at me, and my breath stops.

"Hey," he says.

"Hey."

"Did anyone ever tell you, you look like Zayn Malik?"

"No . . ."

"You do," he says, and puts his head back down.

Okay. I don't think this guy knows anything about me. And if *he* doesn't, then Giraffe Boy doesn't, either, so unless Dhyllin suddenly shows up in Spanish, pointing a finger, I'm good. I'm good. And as far as being compared to Zayn Malik? Who wouldn't want to look like Zayn? I'll take it.

Mr. Janssen enters the room, gives a little bow. He's a small man, tight mustache, bow tie, a crop circle of baldness on the top of his head. "Welcome to your favorite class of the day," he says, scribbling his name on the board, ignoring the groans. He sits, starts taking roll. When he gets to "Gregg Dang?" he has to call it out twice before the kid next to me raises his head and waves, so now I know, Gregg.

"Jack Davies?" Mr. Janssen says. It's the first time anyone's called me that outside my family or the principal, the name was a seed this summer and now it's blooming in front of the whole class and I like it, I like how it sounds, even more than Adam, the *ja* and the hard click, short and simple and tough, it's me, who I am, who I'll be, and no one around to question it.

I raise my hand. "Here," I say.

Evie: *Hi guys out there hello hello it's Evie*

Adam: *And Adam hi*

Evie: *You should know I'm very excited tonight Adam is going to be taking me out on a date*

Adam: *It's not a date*

Evie: *A date*

Adam: *We're going to the movies it's not a*

Evie: *You're paying so*

Adam: *What*

Evie: *We're going to that new movie house in Lawrenceville The one that only shows old movies*

Adam: *Classic movies*

Evie: *Whatever*

Adam: *It's the only one I go to*

Evie: *I don't get why you like those old I mean those classic movies so much*

Adam: *Maybe because they're better?*

Evie: *Come on*

Adam: *My dad kind of got me hooked on them it's kind of the thing we do together so*

Evie: *It's amazing you do anything with your dad What would I do with mine I don't know get drunk and swear at the TV but anyway*

Adam: *In middle school when it got really bad*

Evie: *Does anything good ever happen in middle school?*

Adam: *And I wasn't coping so well I was just so too much in my head all these dark thoughts you know*

Evie: *I know*

Adam: *My dad would play hooky from work sometimes and we'd see a whole day's worth of movies boom boom boom*

All his favorites

I'd get out of my head, go to Casablanca or Nashville or Chinatown

Escape from New York

It was kind of a lifesaver

It's funny I don't know if anyone else went through this?

When I came out my mom was the one who got all the pamphlets and the worksheets and the insurance papers

But what my dad did was bring home a bunch of DVDs from the library

All these trans or kinda sorta trans movies Priscilla, Queen of the Desert Crying Game Hedwig and the Angry Inch

Evie: *Oh I saw that one I love Hedwig*

Adam: *Anything where the guy dresses up like the girl or the girl dresses up like the guy*

This was how he was going to educate us on my transition by watching these movies

I mean, Some Like It Hot? The Birdcage?

Evie: *Yes we are all drag queens*

Adam: *I know where he was coming from*

But there were hardly any movies about transmen at all

Evie: *Except*

Adam: *Well yeah but*

Evie: *Boys Don't Cry*

Adam: *Yeah no*

Evie: *Trigger warning trigger warning*

Adam: *My mom had to leave the room halfway through that one*

I mean it was a good movie but

Evie: *Let's just say it's not the happiest movie*

Adam: *You think?*

I ended up showing my parents some YouTubes of guys like

Ryan Cassata and Skylarkeleven and Alex Bertie

Just so they wouldn't totally despair

Evie: *So I guess what you're saying is*

When you want entertainment old movies are

Adam: *Classic movies are*

Adam & Evie: *Good*

Evie: *But for trans information stick to YouTube*

Which I guess is why you're here so

like us subscribe

If you have any questions just let us know in the comments

and remember

You can be who you want to be

Love yourself you are perfect

Adam & Evie: *Bye*

10. ● ● ● ● ● ● ● ● ● ●

School settles down into the day-to-day—no incident reports, no teacher conferences, no one paying any attention to the quiet kid in the back of the class—and that's so fine by me. Cue the school montage—me at Earl Warren, one period flowing into another into another until one day I realize it's been more than two weeks and I've almost forgotten I've ever been called anything but Jack, and, what is this? Am I actually learning now? It's not that the teachers are any better or the class size is any smaller, no, just that once school stops being *The Hunger Games*, there's actually space in my brain for a little knowledge, go figure. I didn't know how much room worrying about a teacher calling me by my deadname, or being misgendered, took up. For the first time in a long time, school's actually about school. You know, classes. Learning. That stuff. Bizarre.

Outside of school, it's mostly me myself and I, which is perfect. There's all of Los Angeles to discover, my part of it, Silver Lake and Los Feliz and Atwater Village, Griffith Park for a little green, the Los Angeles River for a little muddy blue. I zip around on my new used, scavenged bike, a perfectly good three-speed with just a few dings I found abandoned between a lumpy sofa and a broken Ikea shelf (honest, Angelenos will throw anything out on the curb). So, I bike to school in the morning, and after school it's a new set of streets each time home. That's how I find a Day-Glo thrift store with racks of designer clothes for cheap that I'm pillaging as soon as I get some cash, and a bookstore with a tree growing in the middle of it, and there's even a reptile supply store nearby where, if I'm missing my lizards, I can get my fix of bearded dragons and leopard geckos and corn snakes, inhale the smell of crickets and mealworms—that's what a bedroom should smell like. I think about asking for a part-time job there, but then I imagine pulling out my social security card and having to explain the name on it, and, no thank you, not today, I'm good.

And, of course, every other day you're gonna pass film crews on location, long white trailers camped out on the street, fired up by electric generators, the sidewalk clogged with cops sitting on chairs and electric cables snaking out of trucks, ready to be tripped on. It's the portable holy shrine, the reason why everyone's here: moviemaking. All bow.

"People here love films so much, they will watch them ON YOUR GRAVE."

My dad throws a quilted moving blanket onto the grass. We're at the Hollywood Forever Cemetery, getting ready for the ultimate movie-watching experience—we've already scoped out the headstone of Looney Toons legend Mel Blanc, *That's All Folks!* and Dad swears he won't leave until he finds Peter Lorre's grave. We were two hours early, and we still barely managed to get a spot on the Fairbanks Lawn. The crypts around us are lit up, the techno music is blasting, and the water tower in the distance isn't covered in rust and graffiti, it's got the Paramount Pictures logo printed on it. Toto, I've a feeling we're not in Pittsburgh anymore.

Best of all, the movie they're showing tonight is *Harold and Maude*, easily one of my top five, the first big-boy indie Dad took me to when I was in eighth grade, pretty young I know, but I was in a real bad space back then, and I think it was his way of trying to jolt me out of it, show me that the dark doesn't always stay dark, difference is a strength, fly your freak flag, all that. And he was right, it did help. If I had to stand in line two hours for any movie, it would be *Harold and Maude*.

"Hey, you forget something?" I say to Dad. I point out all the picnic baskets, all the Trader Joe's canvas totes being unloaded around us.

He tosses me a giant bag of popcorn from 7-Eleven. "What more do you need?" he asks. "This is a movie, not dinner theater."

"I didn't have dinner."

"Well, whose fault is that?" he says, but I notice he's not paying attention to me. His eyes are hooked onto the purple yoga pants of some flexi-girl in braids ahead of us, bending over to set up her lawn chair.

"Gross, Dad, really."

"What are you talking about?"

"I see you checking out that woman."

I expect him to deny it, but he just shrugs and says, "So? She's nice to look at, right? What's the harm in that?"

"Well, Mom might have a different opinion."

That's when he pulls out a five and sends me off to the concession stand. "Go get something to eat."

"You can't buy me off," I say, before I leave. "I saw what I saw."

He says, "You know, I always wanted a son, but not such a smartass one."

"Well, you get what you get and you don't get upset."

"How'd that work out for you?" he says, arching one eyebrow.

I flip him one slow middle finger and pick my way out of the crowd. Get in the long line for the red tents where all the delicious smells are coming from.

This is not the dad I'm used to. I know I've changed since we've gotten here, I'm more settled in my skin, surer, but Dad's changed just as much. Maybe it's not having to juggle a work job and a theater job and home, or maybe it's his natural rhythm without my mom around to keep him in line, but he's way more laidback, shaggier, doesn't get on my case about school or homework or anything, just trusts that I'm handling it. He's more focused on himself, which is good, out every day hustling, trying to get meetings set up, going to workshops and showcases, all that networking bullshit that sounds like pure hell to me. He feeds off it.

Who knows? His dream could come true after all. I mean, it's not impossible. He's acted on TV—every time a film production crew rolls into Pittsburgh, he gets a few lines as somebody's gardener or a taxi driver or an asshole cop—and he's done a bunch of theater. So, it could happen. In the meantime, it seems like he's enjoying the ride, wherever it takes him.

Just like me.

The line has moved close enough for me to read the menu, and if I'd only done that in the first place, I could've saved myself some time. The organic hot dogs are way too expensive, same with the carnitas tacos and the grass-fed sliders . . . the only thing I can afford is a pop . . . or popcorn. No way. There's popcorn back on the blanket, I can munch on that and pocket the five, because who knows when I'm gonna pry another dollar out of Dad—

A tap on my shoulder.

I think it's someone wanting to get by, but when I turn I'm staring at a navy-blue Earl Warren High sweatshirt, and I pull back like there's gonna be a shove or something landing my way—I can't help it, it's a reflex—but when I look up, there's Baby Giraffe Boy, a goofy grin on his face and a blanket rolled up under one arm.

No, not Baby Giraffe Boy, not anymore. Jules. His name is Jules.

A couple of weeks ago I met him for real. He was in front of Mr. Janssen's door, right before lunch, holding up a GSA clipboard like it was a final exam, he looked so nervous and so lost . . . and all of a sudden it made sense to me. I knew what his deal was because I'd been in the same place before. Baby Giraffe Boy was taking his first steps coming out.

It was kinda sweet. I remembered that scared feeling, standing outside the glass door of the Pittsburgh LGBT center, my first Youth Night, about to step into the unknown. I was frozen by the downtown winter wind, couldn't make up my mind, teeter-ing between go/not-go, and I might've bailed completely if Big Marg hadn't shown up, carrying two bags of chips and cookies.

She gave me the warmest hello and held the door open, and my fear just melted away. Sometimes, you just need a little push to get you where you need to go.

So, when I saw Giraffe Boy there, sweating over a clipboard, even though I told myself before I got to Los Angeles that I wouldn't be doing any sharing and caring, no connecting, I still felt bad about that first day of school, and I figured, I owed him. And like I said, he looked so lost.

I gave him a little push.

I told him to just go for it, trying not to spook him, and then he stuck out his hand like a businessman at a cocktail party, it was so strange, he gave me his name, and I gave him mine, and Baby Giraffe Boy became Jules.

Jules, who's standing right in front of me now. What is going on?

There's a sudden clutch of anxiety when I realize he was looking at me when I didn't know I was being looked at, and I flip-flip-flip through every little movement I've made over the last fifteen minutes, making sure I haven't somehow given myself away, and it takes everything I've got not to yank at my hoodie and pull it away from my binder.

"I'm not stalking you," Jules says.

"Okay . . ." And while that's kind of an odd thing to say, I start to relax, because he seems as jumpy as I am. Neither of us is interested in buying food, so we step out of line and talk some more, but there's no time for conversation, over Jules's shoulder I see my dad at our spot waving his arms, *Mayday mayday*, he hates latecomers at movies, and I guess that includes outdoor movies, too. On cue, the lights cut out. My dad disappears into the dark.

"I should be getting back," I tell Jules, talking loud over the announcements. He nods, I nod and take off. That's that. A weird coincidence.

It's almost impossible to find my dad now, even though I just spotted him two seconds ago—the crowd is one solid mass of dark bodies. Cell phones blink on and off like fireflies in the crowd. I look back to get my bearings and Jesus, there's Jules, right behind me, six feet away. He gives a little wave, I think he must be sitting somewhere nearby, but when I finally find my dad's blanket, he stops in front of it, too.

Awkward. Jules looks as confused as I am. My dad gives me a dangerous smile, turns to Jules and says, "I guess we have company," all fluty and bright-eyed, and I flick him a warning glare—*Don't embarrass me.* For some reason, Jules thought I was sitting with Dhyllin, ha, they were supposed to meet up. He's kinda embarrassed, I can tell, but when he starts to go my father practically drags him down. "There's plenty of room," he says.

Jules says, "I might just go home. I don't even know what this movie's about."

That is straight-up ridiculous. To come all this way, pay, and *not* stay for the movie? Not stay for *Harold and Maude*? No. Dad's right, there's plenty of room, and judging from the cheer going up in the crowd, this screening is going to be epic. No one should miss this.

"Are you sure it's okay?" Jules whispers to me, looking uncertain but hopeful. He just needs another push. "I'm sure," I say.

The movie starts. Jules kind of hovers over us for a moment, then sits down.

I guess he's staying.

I've seen *Harold and Maude* at least nine or ten times—it's been my go-to movie when I'm home sick or just generally feeling crappy, I can probably recite it by heart—but when I look out from the corner of my eye at Jules staring at the screen, it's like I'm watching it for the first time. He doesn't check his phone once, or sigh, or fidget—he just sits, hunched with his hands tucked under his arms, watching. Not even the firecrackers someone sets off behind the Port-A-Johns distract him. The only time he looks away is when he offers me his blanket, still rolled up—I guess I must have rubbed my arms for warmth. To be honest, I am a little cold, but I shake my head. He looks at the blanket, like he might still unfurl it, then puts it down between us, like he's saying, *Just in case.*

When the end credits roll, Jules stays still, staring ahead, even when the crowd starts standing up and blocking the screen. His eyes shine.

"Yeah?" I say to him.

"Yeah," he answers. "Yeah."

My dad insists on driving Jules home even when Jules tells him no. I tell my dad to stop being so pushy, but I'm secretly glad he is.

We walk back to the parking lot, lit walkways in between looming palm trees guiding us through the cemetery. My dad scoots ahead for some reason, and it's just me and Jules, and we're talking, about the movie, about movies in general, and it's obvious he doesn't know squat about films, but it doesn't matter because he still seems interested. And I notice that I'm gabbing faster than usual, the words just tumbling out of my mouth, ratatatatatatatatat, it must be what taking speed is like, but it's not a drug I'm on, it's just conversation. It's the most I've said to anyone in Los Angeles, including my dad, this whole trip, and all the words, locked up for so long, are just galloping out of the stable. Jules doesn't seem to mind, and even keeps up, doing some galloping of his own, we're neck and neck racing in this conversation. I notice when he smiles, he's got this lopsided grin that pulls up one side of his face and shows all his upper teeth. Dorky, but cute.

"What's your Instagram?" he asks, digging for his phone. We're walking on the path that splits in two, right to the parking lot and left to the cemetery gates, and just as we reach the split I hear the most dreaded of sounds: teen boy laughter. There's a group of guys, my age, four of them horsing around under a lamppost. They're hooting at something, and they've got that loudness that tells you right away they don't give a shit. About anyone. I see them through the streams of people walking alongside us, I see a security guard, too, telling them to move along, but they aren't listening. One of them looks up, past the guard, into the empty space that's suddenly cleared between them and us and I see the kid's face, lit by lamplight.

Dhyllin.

He's dressed like the true hype beast he is, shiny red Supreme varsity jacket, camo Air Force 1s, an N.W.A baseball cap that can't hide the blond. He's pulling on some kind of vape pen, and I bet anything it's not nicotine he's inhaling. I swear, he might as well have the letters D-O-U-C-H-E printed on his jacket. In rhinestones.

He exhales, looks across the path at Jules and me. The look becomes a stare, and after the stare, a smile. It's not a good smile. It's not warm, or welcoming, it's a smile ready to pounce. It's a smile that comes with a silver nose ring and soccer player legs. Nothing good ever comes from that kind of smile.

"Or do you do Snapchat?" Jules says, still looking down at his phone. He doesn't see Dhyllin, and doesn't see the fifty black crows that are crowded inside my chest right now, perched on my binder, ready to burst out of me—this panic about to peck its way out of my skin. I can't get to the parking lot fast enough. We veer to the right, away from Dhyllin under the lamppost, but I'm just waiting for the clomp of Air Force 1s running up to us, the shout, the hand on the shoulder, who knows what Dhyllin's capable of.

"I'm not doing social media," I hear myself tell Jules, but I'm so far out of my body by now, I could already be waiting by the car.

On the way to Jules's house, Dad bombards him with parent questions, but all I can concentrate on is the car thudding over every bump and pothole, the steady engine rumble pounding in my gut—*I'm caught I'm caught I'm caught.* I'm at the edge of something dark, and whatever good that came out of the evening is about to fall into it. *What do you expect, that's what happens when you don't keep your head down. It's all your fault. Fuck.*

I tell myself to stop it, that I'm catastrophizing, that's what my therapist would tell me. I'm safe in the car. Nothing's happened, yet. Dhyllin might not know. But I think of his smirk, and yeah, he does. So, why am I freaking out? What's the worst that can happen? *Pull it together—*

The car lurches to a stop. "Jesus!" I shout, thinking we were about to hit something running across the road. But it's just my dad, being dramatic after finding out that Jules's dad is some TV movie producer that he's heard of. Great. I sneak a glance in the rearview mirror to see if Jules is checking his phone, if Dhyllin has texted him yet, but as soon as I look up, he catches my eye in the mirror and I look away.

I'm caught I'm caught I'm caught I'm caught

Jules directs my dad around a big concrete crater surrounded by a park. This must have once been the lake of Silver Lake. His house is right off it, and it's beautiful, oak trees with their trunks lit up, a white fence covered in bright red bougainvillea, windows glowing from inside. It's not Mr. Gene Ramsey impressive, but it sure beats the Pittsburgh duplex my family lives in.

"Wow, fancy," my dad says, a farmer visiting the Big City.

Jules gets out, and I think this horrible night is finally over but then my dad opens his window and decides to pile a little more shit on it. He calls out, "I should use 'em if I've got 'em, right?" and I see him handing Jules some of his cringey headshots to pass on to Jules's dad. *Oh my God oh my God, Dad.* I can't even look up when Jules says goodbye to me through the rolled-up window, I'm so embarrassed. His voice is low, and sad, and then he's gone.

Of course he's sad. He didn't know what he was getting himself into. When he shuts the door to his house, he won't think about the movie, or our conversation, no, he'll be wondering what was up with that weirdo and his loser dad. And whatever Dhyllin tells him will be a little more icing on the weirdo cake. Dhyllin and his jagoff sneer. Why should he win?

Fuck it.

I yank open the car door before my dad pulls away and stop Jules just as he hits the porch. I think, I'll just tell him, why not, perfect time, it'll be easy. But when I open my mouth, I realize, I don't want to. I'm not ready.

So, instead, what comes out of my mouth is: "Do you want my number, just in case?"

Just in case. What does that even mean, but go figure, he pulls out his phone and smiles, relieved that maybe I'm not a psycho after all. In the lamplight Jules's skin looks even paler than it usually does. He's got a light dusting of acne along his left cheekbone and some freckles scattered on the bridge of his nose. Eyes that can't decide whether they're gray or blue, heavy eyelids that make him look a little sleepy. He's probably a foot taller than me, but it doesn't seem to make any difference tonight.

"All right," Jules says, after we exchange numbers, "I guess I'll go study up on those movies you told me about. Just so I don't, you know, get kicked out of Los Angeles."

"I'm telling you, it's gonna happen. Middle of the night, they're gonna come for you," I say, and we both laugh, and the laughter settles into quiet and in the quiet I hear this mini air-raid siren going off in my head, *Toooo cloooose.*

He sticks out his hand like he did at school, as a joke this time, but I don't shake it because my hands suddenly feel really small compared to his. I jam them into my pockets. "See you Monday," I say, and walk back to the car.

Okay. It's okay. Dhyllin could blow it all up tomorrow, and maybe Jules won't care, or maybe he will, but at least tonight I wasn't the jagoff. I saved the evening, even if it's just for the evening. Whatever else happens, happens.

We're three blocks from our house when my dad breaks the silence and says, "What?"

"Did you have to do that, Dad, really?"

"What? Talking? Having a *conversation*? Hey, I was just trying to help you out, buddy. You weren't doing yourself any favors."

"I don't need your help."

"You're gonna have to do better than that, if you wanna keep him interested."

I stare at him for the first time since we got in the car. My jaw's scraping the floor mat. "What are you talking about? It's not like—I'm not interested like that, okay? God." I make the universal throat-scraping sound for disgust.

"Okay," he says, and stares at the road. But after a minute he picks it right back up. "You *are* still into guys, right? That's still . . . in effect?"

What can I do but stare?

"Just trying to keep up. You will let me know if anything changes, yah?"

"Yeah, Dad," I say under my breath. "You'll be the first to know."

God, sometimes parents can be so thick.

Evie: *Hello*

Adam: *Hello*

Evie: *Hello*

Adam: *Adam and Evie here*

Evie: *For you*

Okay today we'd like to talk about

Adam: *Well it's not like we'd like to but*

Evie: *But it's an important topic and so well we're going to talk about it*

Dysphoria

Adam: *God*

Evie: *Gender dysphoria*

Which is basically an extreme anxiety or uncomfortableness

Is that a word?

Adam: *About your*

Parts

About what physical parts you have on your body

Versus the parts you think should be there or

It's hard for some people to even talk about

Evie: *Parts*

Obviously this is a big thing in the trans community

Not every trans person gets dysphoria

Adam: *You can be trans without feeling dysphoric*

146

Evie: *But we do*

And we thought we'd just talk about our own experiences with it

It's super hard to describe because I've basically had it my entire life so I don't know what it's like not to have it if that makes sense?

As long as I've known there was a difference between boys and girls I knew I should be over there

Not over here

And I thought I was just wrong like defective factory reject

There wasn't like a time I ever felt comfortable being in my body

What about you

Adam: *It didn't really hit me until puberty*

Evie: *Puberty is the worst*

Adam: *I think it started somewhere around fifth grade?*

Suddenly there were these changes I didn't want

There were things growing

Here

That you couldn't stop

It was like Alien

Evie: *Alien*

Adam: *Something pushing out of you that didn't belong there*

Evie: *And it was gonna destroy you*

Adam: *Exactly*

Evie: *It's like there's this time when boys and girls kind of look the same*

At least if you wanted to look the same

But suddenly you're driving in opposite directions

147

And I was in the wrong car pounding on the window
Let me out let me out
I just couldnt stand being in that wrong car
Adam: I had these panic attacks it was like you know the
Alfred Hitchcock movie The Birds?
Evie: Just pretend I do
Adam: Where there are all these crows
Hundreds of them just perched on the playground waiting
And all of the sudden flap flap flap flap
They rise up in one big cloud and attack
There are so many pecking at you you can't even see
That's what it was like but the birds were inside me
The panic birds rising up
Evie: For me it's like the opposite
It's like completely gray the whole day like numb
Adam: No no I felt that too like when it got really bad
In the beginning of middle school
When I started you know
Bleeding down there
[unintelligible]
I can't even talk about it
It was just so
Bad when it first started happening I think I passed out
And then I felt that numbness
I just went away into this void
Evie: The void yes the void
Adam: This blackness you kind of disappear into

It's like

Evie: *You don't know where your body is*

Adam: *Because this wasn't your body*

Evie: *But then where was your body where were you?*

You're nowhere you're nothing you're

Adam: *In the void*

Evie: *That was me every day all day*

And even now it's like better

Adam: *It gets better*

Evie: *But it's still there hidden in your blind spot*

Like even though coming out as trans and meeting Adam and realizing I wasn't alone is so so helpful and sharing videos with you guys and everything

But I still have to go home and hide all that

It's like every day I have to go back to this void prison and

And it's so

You know

It's

[unintelligible]

You talk

Talk Adam

Adam: *It's not going to be like that forever three more years and you'll be out of there*

Evie: *Three more years is a long time*

Adam: *But but*

There are a lot of things you can do to make things better

Evie: *I know*

Adam: *Take a long walk or listen to your favorite song or cook your favorite meal see a movie make a video*

Evie: *With your best friend*

Adam: *Who farts at inappropriate times*

Evie: *Did you just ew Adam*

Adam: *You love it*

Evie: *I do not you're so gross*

Adam: *So people out there if you're experiencing dysphoria now Remember it can get better we promise*

Evie: *And it might not go away completely*

Adam: *There are always sequels*

Evie: *But when it does come back on board you'll know how to deal with it*

Adam: *Yeah with a flame thrower and an airlock Get away from her*

Adam & Evie: *You bitch*

Evie: *Okay so remember be who you want to be*

Adam: *Love yourself*

Evie: *And you are perfect*

Adam & Evie: *Bye*

Evie: *Seriously we have to open a window*

11.

Sunday comes, nothing from Jules. Not that I'm expecting a call or anything, but—I would like to find out if I've been outed or not. Once again, my whole fate is in Dhyllin's hands, someone I don't even frigging know. Did he tell Jules? Will Jules tell everyone else? Why do I even care what these people think? I don't. But it's my information to share, when I want to share it. My decision, not some LA rich kid's.

I need to move, get the jumpiness out of my legs. I hop on my bike and take off for the river. I'm planning on riding the bike path all the way to Echo Park, even downtown, but I only get four blocks down the street when there's this bike-braking whoosh of aroma that hits me, this earthy, sharp mix of incense and spice coming from a store I've never seen before, tucked in between a taqueria and a cell phone repair shop. The sign above the window is peeling and bleached out by the sun, faded rays shoot out from the name: *Punjab Spices and Sweets Market*. Spices and Sweets, Indian-style. How have I never noticed this market before?

Being South Asian doesn't figure too much into my family's day-to-day. Like, at all. My dad's not Indian, and even though my mom's first generation, she's cut that part of her life off, ever since she got into this huge fight with Nani, my grandma, when I was seven, and Nani stomped back to her family in New Delhi, never to be seen again. I'm not sure what the fight was about, Mom doesn't like to talk about it, but it's like, when Nani left, India left with her. Nothing from the old country on the walls, nothing on the shelves, Mom packed it all away. Every Diwali, every birthday of my sister's or mine, Nani tries to sneak a little India back into our lives, sending us dented packages with saris, jewelry, books, all that, wrapped inside, but they get intercepted by Mom and dumped into a box in the basement, the letters unread. When Mom puts her foot down, it is DOWN.

Except. Except for gulab jamun.

Gulab jamun are these little fried dough balls soaked in rose water and cardamom syrup, they're made with milk powder and ghee, and they're like little spiced sugar bombs. In a good way. My mom can't quit them. She won't make any other Indian food, but these? Give her an occasion and she'll have a batch of gulab jamun soaking and swelling in syrup within an hour. She whips them up for holidays, birthdays, and sometimes uses them as bait, when she finds me locked in my room after a hell day at school. I'll be barricaded in my rat's nest, breathing way too fast and not enough, smell the cardamom wafting in from downstairs, and know she's in the kitchen, mixing up the dough. It usually works—I come down when she's about to shape them, we roll them together without speaking, side by side, and by the time they're getting golden in the hot ghee I'm on my way to breathing back to normal. Even on days when I can't stand to be touched, gulab jamun are like a welcome little round hug.

A little round hug is exactly what I could use right about now.

The old woman behind the counter is sitting, watching an old Bollywood movie with the sound off on a television mounted on the wall. She's dressed in a yellow sari that gives her the shape of a dumpling with a little dark head on top. When the door jingles and she catches sight of me, she starts shouting from across the room, "*Manu? Manu?*" and then a bunch of other words, bouncing her fingers in my direction, excited. I hold up my hands, shake my head, *I don't speak whatever you're speaking*—there are like a thousand different dialects in India, and I know none of them. The woman keeps at it, so happy, until a man comes out from behind a beaded curtain, barks a few words, and leaves. She stares at me through big thick glasses, frowning and confused, then gives up, shrinks down in her seat, shifts her eyes back to the dancers leaping silently on the television.

I walk up and down the aisles, inhaling. It's not just spices and sweets, the store has everything, candles and incense and wall hangings of Technicolor gods with long names I feel guilty I can't pronounce. There's a two-toned one, blue and gold, Ardhanarish-vara, that I recognize from the cover of a coloring book Nani used to always try to get me to read when she was still in the States. And then she'd get mad at me for using the wrong colors when I tried to fill the god in. Yeah, she was real fun, my grandma.

In the food aisles I have no idea what half of the stuff is, all these mixes and sauces and pastes. But then I spot milk powder, and big jars of ghee, and this gives me an idea. I was just going to buy a single ball from the sweets counter, maybe two, but I don't think that's gonna cut it. It's more than just the eating—I have to *make* these gulab jamun. That would put me right back in the kitchen with Mom, and the smell of cardamom, and the quiet rolling. The sneaking of a finger into the cooling sugar syrup. That's what I need.

I find a ready-made mix on one of the shelves but that feels like cheating, just adding water and frying, not the same thing at all. Once I get an idea in my head it's hard to let go of it. The ingredients are gonna cost me almost an entire week's worth of lunch money, but that's okay, because I don't usually eat lunch anyway. Even so, I have to cut some corners with ingredients, like no rose water, vegetable oil instead of ghee—no way I'm spending that much money on butter just for frying—but I do spring for the cardamom pods, 'cause it wouldn't be gulab jamun without them.

The woman sitting on the stool has gone back to staring at me—I guess I'm more interesting than Bollywood. When I approach the counter, I see her lips quivering, muttering something—a hex, a prayer, an incantation? She pulls my basket toward her and nods. "Your ma is making gulab jamun, *na*?" I tell her I'm the one cooking and she crinkles her forehead, pulls at her chin with trembling fingers. She's trying to work something out, trying to work *me* out, it makes my skin prickle. *Please just take my money, ma'am.*

And she does, but after I shove the groceries in my backpack, the old lady signals me with her hand to wait. She gets up, shuffles into the kitchen. Shuffles back with a little bottle in her hand, rose water, pushes it into my backpack while putting a finger to her lips. "Better," she says, and when I thank her, she smiles so that her eyes disappear. "*Manu.*" She brushes her fingers against my cheek. They smell like coconut. "*Puttar*," she whispers, eyes glistening. "My son."

Milk powder. Cardamom. Sugar. Oil for frying.

Sunday night. I've got the kitchen to myself. Dad's at some mixer, and no one else on the floor uses the stove that much—they're pretty much a microwave burrito or cereal type crowd. All the cookware is scratched and dented, but I'll make it work.

Mom taught both Susie and me how to make gulab jamun by the time I was twelve. We were more interested in the eating, but Mom insisted. She said, "This is the only good thing your nani passed down to me. She said a girl in India could get a better match if she made good gulab jamun." My mom stopped rolling the dough in her hand, waved a warning finger at us, shiny with ghee. "But forget all about that nonsense. You don't have to impress anyone. Make them for yourselves."

Sugar into water. Three cardamom pods.

As soon as the sugar water cooks down enough to become a syrup, the spicy cardamom smell hits me—*Hi, Mom, I'm home.* Three tiny drops of rose water, and the syrup's done.

I flash back to the lady at the store (she was right about the rose water), wonder if Nani looks anything like her now. Probably not. In my memory, Nani's a completely different shape—thin, sharp-edged, perfectly dressed, always poking, running after me trying to get flower barrettes in my hair. I remember her sitting on the couch, drinking her tea, complaining to my mom, "Why do you allow her to go around looking like a *kutta*?" I had no idea what a *kutta* was, but it didn't sound good. "Never mind her," Mom said, when I asked. So, I didn't.

They never got along. I remember sharp voices in the kitchen, rising higher and louder, every time Nani came to visit. Still, I wonder what the final thing was that made Nani put a continent and two oceans between them. It makes Mom sad to talk about it. The only thing she'll say is, "Your nani was always miserable in the States. It's better that she left. For everyone."

Dad blames himself. He says Nani never approved of the marriage because he isn't Indian. Which is about the only thing he *isn't*, Dad's a complete mutt as far as race goes, always marks the *Other* box on questionnaires under ethnic background, but the one box he can't check is South Asian. And he thinks Nani holds that against him. And that makes me wonder, what would she think of *me*? I mean, it's not just that I've got half of his genes in my system, I'm not gonna fit into any of the boxes she'd want to tick off. I'm all kinds of *Other*, I'm *Other* all the way down the list.

So maybe it is better that she left.

❖ ❖ ❖

Milk powder and flour. Baking soda. Cream. Mix. Quick. Light.

My fingers are sticky with wet milk powder while I try scrolling through my phone to look at the recipe Mom texted me, along with a goofy-face emoji and five hearts of various colors:

Have fun!

The last time I made these, I wasn't even on T yet. But I still remember the steps. It all comes back.

Let the dough rest.

Suddenly, the recipe on my phone gets replaced by a text coming in, then another and another. It's Jules. I get ready for the worst, but all he's interested in is *Harold and Maude*: some trivia about director Hal Ashby he found online (did I know Hal Ashby was a high school dropout? I did not), a meme of Ruth Gordon saying, *A lot of people enjoy being dead, but they're not dead, really.* What a goofball.

What a relief.

that was an awesomemovie glad I stayed

No mention of Dhyllin—Dhyllin, under the lamppost staring. No questions, either. Maybe Dhyllin was too stoned to recognize us that night. Maybe that jagoff sneer is just his normal expression.

Maybe I'm in the clear, for now.

Grease your palms, roll into balls.

I pinch off the dough and barely touch it as I start shaping. I remember my mother's long fingers hovering over our small hands, her nails tickling our palms as she helped us with the dough. "You're not forcing them," she'd say to Sudhi and me, "you're gently suggesting they roll into balls." She'd press crumbles of dough from the bowl into a smooth ball with one hand. "Don't squeeze. Just hug them into shape."

One by one, the balls slip off my fingers onto a plate and holy crap that really is a shit ton of gulab jamun. I must have made them a little smaller because I've got more than twenty and I'm not even done. In the syrup they'll keep for weeks, but still, it's a lot for two people. Can you possibly get sick of eating these? I guess we'll find out. If Evie were here, it wouldn't be a problem. She would always conveniently show up when we were making them and snag a few, take a few more home in a plastic cup. If she were here, we would eat the hell out of these things.

But she's not here.

Heat the oil. Not too hot. Test with a piece of dough.

As I'm shuttling the dough balls into the oil, there's a slap-slap sound coming down the hall, which can only mean that Randy of the Flip-Flops is on his way to the bathroom. Randy's Serial Killer #2, more in line with what you'd imagine a serial killer would look like: scrawny, pasty skin, greasy long hair and spacey eyes, an underfed wolfhound that's been left in the rain.

"What's going on, my little man?" he says, sniffing his way

into the kitchen on his way back. I should be insulted by the *little*, but I'm too stoked by the *man* to care. I carefully turn the balls over and over in the hot oil, tell him it's a cooking experiment for school.

"They look so good," he says, watching the balls bob up and down.

"They won't be done for a while. They have to soak. But tomorrow, help yourself."

"Cool, so cool." He stands, staring at the oil, listening to the gulab jamun sizzle. "Hey, wanna get high?" he says. Behind his thick glasses, his eyes are blazing red. As usual.

"Uh . . . I'm good," I tell him.

He nods for a while. "Cool. Cool," he repeats, and slowly backs out of the room. "They look beautiful, little man!" Slap-slap-down-the-hall-slam. I'm alone again, master of the kitchen. And they do look beautiful, all the same size, the same coloring. I feel good. I'm breathing back to normal.

A half hour later, just as I'm spooning two dozen cooked balls into the syrup, my dad finally arrives home. "I can't believe it," he says. "I could smell them all the way downstairs."

"Where've you been?" I ask. He launches into a story about going with some buddies to an acting showcase with a casting director. Dad can never just answer a question—he has to tell a story, a story where he plays all the parts.

"I met some good people to know," he says finally.

"Your breath smells like beer," I say.

"Not many," he says, pointing a finger at me, not even defensive.

"And I only bought the first one," he adds proudly. My dad sounds like such a mooch—I wonder if it's always been this way, or whether it's this trip that's made him such a cheapskate.

I put my hands on my hips, give him the Dad Look. "Am I going to have to have the talk about drinking and driving?"

"You should be in bed," he says. "What's with the baking? Is it Cultural Exchange Day at school?

"Jesus, Dad, I'm not in fifth grade." I nudge a dented ball out of the syrup, one that split open while cooking, and drop half of it onto his waiting hand.

"Only half?"

"No treats for bad behavior. You need to go to your room and think about what you've done."

"Since when have you gotten so old and bossy?" he asks. He swallows, nods, and gives me a thumbs-up. "Very tasty." He swipes another ball before I can stop him.

"How have *I* become the responsible one?"

He pulls me in with his nonsticky hand, gives me a kiss on the head. "You're doing so well out here, Jack. Growing up. I'm very proud. Yay, you."

"Stop it, Dad." I push him into the hall. "Go brush your teeth, you reek."

"Bring some of these to school. It'll make you *popular!*" He swaggers away, laughing.

"Whatever," I mutter, but then I think of Jules, Jules with his gray-or-blue eyes shining in the lamplight. To hell with being popular, but . . . I could bring some to Jules. Just to, you know,

160

make up for my weird-ass behavior at the cemetery. Like a peace offering, or . . . whatever.

I fish out an old Tupperware bowl and lid from a drawer and spoon a few gulab jamun into it. Scoop up the other half of the reject and pop it in my mouth. The soft crumbs melt away instantly, dissolving into sticky sweetness on my tongue—not bad, not bad at all.

So, yay. Thumbs-up for me.

Evie: *Hey guys Evie here*

Adam: *Hey*

Evie: *That's Adam*

And today we thought we'd talk about something that a lot of people have trouble understanding

What the difference is between gender identity and sexual attraction

Wait did I get that right?

Adam: *I think so*

Evie: *Okay good*

And we're going to do it with the help of our new friend that we found on the internet

Pull it out Adam

What are you laughing at?

Adam: *You said*

Evie: *God get your head out of the gutter*

Such a boy

So?

Adam: *Ta da*

Evie: *The gingerbread man*

Adam: *I think it's genderbread*

Evie: *Oh shit I meant genderbread*

And person, not man

Genderbread person

Shit

Can we start over?

Adam: *Too late*

Evie: *Okay okay so here's this genderbread person*

They've got a brain

And a cute cookie body

And a heart

And some sex signs on the crotch

Male female and

Adam: *What's that arrow with the line going across?*

Evie: *That's both male and female*

Adam: *Oh right duh*

Evie: *So each part of the genderbread person is totally separate*

The brain is how you think of yourself your identity

Like what gender you know you are

Okay Adam do you want to take the crotch?

Adam*: Do I*

Evie: *Don't be a pig*

Adam: *The crotch represents what sex you were assigned at birth*

Like what anatomical parts what hormones you have that caused that decision to be made

But that can be different than your gender identity okay?

Brain and crotch they don't always match up

Evie: *Right*

Okay and the cookie body here represents how you express yourself to the world

Like if you dress more quote unquote masculine

Adam: *Or if you wear those frouffy things in your hair*

Evie: *Which you can wear whether you're a boy or a girl or neither or both*

Adam: *I'm not going to wear them*

Evie: *I'm not saying you have to god*

Adam: *What?*

Evie: *And then the heart*

Adam: *Aw*

Evie: *The heart is who you are attracted to*

Male female both neither

Obnoxious boys

Adam: *Ha ha don't look at me*

Evie: *I'm looking at you Adam*

Adam: *Don't*

Anyway

Evie: *It's sexual attraction which is totally different*

Adam: *Totally different*

Evie: *Than who you are gender-wise*

Adam: *Got it?*

Evie: *Gender identification*

Adam: *Brain*

Evie: *Is different than sexual attraction*

Adam: *Heart*

Evie: *And neither of them has to be just one thing or another*

Adam: *It's all on a continual*

Evie: *Continuum*

Adam: *Continuum*

Evie: *I hope we did that right*

We could be totally confusing the shit out of everyone

Adam: *Probably*

Evie: *I'm exhausted*

Adam: *Continuum*

Evie: *Tell us how we did in the comments*

Adam: *Okay bye*

Evie: *Remember be who you want to be love yourself you are perfect bye*

12.

Monday comes, lunchtime, Jules is playing around in the courtyard with his friends, and I'm walking toward him with a Tupperware container of gulab jamun. Why, exactly, am I doing this? It's so completely random and awkward, it looks like I'm trying to buy him off, or impress him, or that I'm in fourth grade bringing cupcakes in for my birthday. What was I thinking?

I don't know. I was thinking, it was nice, talking to someone. I don't know. Just keep going. *Be like water.*

And it *is* awkward, with his friends around and all. Luckily, Jules doesn't pick up on any of that, he's his usual goofy self, and that makes it okay. Even better, he likes what I made. Apparently, his mother has him on some kind of wacky diet that cuts out anything tasty and replaces it with cardboard, something like that, so he's starved for sugar.

His friends decide to dig in, too, and this leads to . . . well, if you would have told me at the beginning of the year that I would be swinging my backpack up and down the courtyards of Earl Warren High School, hawking Indian delicacies, if you were to tell me that I'd be known as *Donut Boy*, I would have told you, very politely, that you were out of your mind.

Only in Hollywood, folks, only in Hollywood.

Cecilia had the idea. She's one of those girls I would have definitely avoided in Pittsburgh, or more like, she would have definitely avoided me. Always put together, a popular girl. Shining eyes that can lift you up or cut you down. She took a bite of a gulab jamun, flashed those dazzling teeth, and practically commanded that I sell them at school. I don't know why she decided to take me on as her pet project, and I wasn't entirely comfortable with her up in my business, but damn if she wasn't right.

At first, I thought it was going to be kind of a goof, something I would do once during lunch break, to get rid of some of the gulab jamun I'd already made, but then, man, they really do start selling. Cecilia makes the rounds, and like I said, the girl is *popular*. She's like a live-action five-star Yelp review. When I haul my backpack out at lunchtime the next day, kids are already looking for me. "You're the new thing," Cecilia tells me, patting me on the shoulder, "sell 'em while you can."

And I think, why not? I mean, I need the money. My dad's got a padlock on his wallet these days, it would be nice to have some spending cash for once. And yeah, Pittsburgh Adam would never dream of doing this, but LA Jack? He'd say, *Why the hell not?*

Of course there's still the selling part, not my strong suit, but I luck out again, because Jules is right there with me, for some reason he's way into selling these things, and it's so much easier to face down a courtyard of kids when you've got a wingman. He's the one who thinks of calling them Indian donut holes, a brilliant idea that saves me from having to repeat and explain the real name over and over again. While I'm handing out the goods and collecting the cash, Jules has my back, standing off to the side, making sure Mr. Hernandez, the lunch supervisor, isn't lurking around the courtyard.

I sell out my day's supply in ten minutes, a miracle. Jules is so happy you'd think he was the one with the dollar bills crowding his pocket.

wow sold out wow

selling tmw?

i guess yeah

i can help again

u dont have to

i wan to

*want

if u want me to

dont worry u dont have to pay me or anything

i do it 4 the donuts

haha

jk

rlly you dont have to give me donuts

> **ok cool thanks dude**

> **no problem dude**

By the way—all this "Dude"-ing? Still gives me a high. Back home I was just happy some people started using the right pronouns, it never even got to the dude level. Here, I'm default dude. Most excellent.

The rest of the week, it only gets better. I'm selling as many as I can bring.

Hey, Donut Boy!

Save me one! I didn't get to try them yet!

Hey, no fair, she can't be buying the whole bunch!

By Thursday my entire supply is wiped out, I have in my possession a pretty considerable fistful of dollars, and I know just how I want to spend it.

Jules won't take a cut, so I figure I owe him at least a movie—which aren't cheap here, by the way, almost double what we pay back home—and some popcorn or Sour Patches, if there's enough left over. That is, if he'll let me.

> **u should save ur money**

> **i dont wanna save my money i wanna SPEND my money**

> **lets go to something you want to see**

> **even a superhero movie lol**

> **what do u want to see?**

> **i treat u choose**

> **irdc whatever u want to see**

> **dude make a choice**

> **u cn do it**

> **CHOOSE**

I love who I am when I text. I love how confident text-me is, how strong and cocky, all swagger. Dude.

Friday night, he messages me after his basketball practice. I'm already home, peeled out of my binder, in sweats. I'm alone, or as alone as I can be. Dad's at another Carnegie Mellon mixer, Serial Killers #1 and #2, Brian and Flip-Flop Randy, are nowhere to be seen. And Serial Killer #3, in the back-back room, well, I haven't ever seen him, not once—for all I know he's dead and shriveled in a rocking chair (I'd pin it on Randy). So, pretty much, I'm on my own.

I know I should start a new batch of gulab jamun while I've got the kitchen to myself, but focusing's hard, I'm kinda bouncing off the wall. Part of it's that I gave myself a testosterone shot yesterday and I feel a little wired, part of it's that I'm bored, I'm tired of being in this room—I should work on my English project, no, forget that, I should go out, maybe Jules would want to go, no it's a school night, ah shit.

And at that exact moment he texts:

hi

I dive onto the bed, thumbs tapping.

hey

**u know i still have
ur dads headshots**

NOOOOOOOOOOO

BURN THEM

cmon ur dads cool

**u want me to get
them to my dad**

I start to type an all-caps "NO!" but then I think, wait, what if it actually helps? I mean, would one job do it, would it be enough to convince my mom to let us load up the truck and move west? Depends on the part, sure, but is it possible I could actually . . . stay?

sure why not

But it still feels kinda needy, so I change the subject.

> **how was practice?**

Instead of telling me about basketball, though, he asks about a different kind of game, and suddenly there's this massive text dump on my phone: some kind of cringey getting-to-know-you questionnaire that sounds like it comes straight out of *Seventeen* magazine. You know—likes, dislikes, celebrity crushes, favorite foods. Stuff like that. Nothing I'd ever expect from Jules.

> **Whoa thats a LOT**

Twenty-two questions, way too many to answer in one night. But I'm doing exactly nothing right now, so I flop back on the mattress and return a few answers. Name, food, my celebrity crushes: Idris Elba and Charlize Theron, because, duh. I ask him about his crushes, and he mentions a basketball player, or at least I'm pretty sure it's a basketball player, I have to look him up.

> **zayn malik isnt bad either**

My binder's been off all night, but my chest suddenly squeezes in. Zayn Malik. What.

im gay did u know

I'm on the mattress, staring up at my phone, arm's distance, not making a move, like he can see me. Trying not to shiver. Why am I shivering? It's hot as hell in this room.

yeah

howd u know

I get what this is, why didn't I recognize it before? Everything suddenly pulls into focus. This, this is what you call flirting. I am being flirted with. Jules is flirting with me. Goofy Jules with the gray-blue eyes and the beautiful arms. Jules.

What.

O wonderful, wonderful, and most wonderful wonderful. Cool.

Okay.

Flirting on.

I shoot back:

takes 1 to know 1 dude

As soon as I press send and those words bubble up in the thread, wham, a clench in my stomach. I throw the phone away from me onto the mattress, hoping it'll stop the transmission,

173

shake the words I wrote back into a jumble of letters. *Fuck*. Why did I text that? What was I doing? *What part of lying low do you not understand?*

But it's too late, I sent it. If this goes any further, I'll have to tell him. Not that it will, because this kind of thing never works out. Never. But, if it never does, then why do I have to say anything? Unless I want it to—but it won't. So I don't—but I should. Right?

Damn it, Jules. You are not supposed to be part of the Great Experiment.

I don't look at the phone the rest of the night. Flick off the light and crawl under the blanket, hiding. Waves, waves of dysphoria lapping dark at the edges of my mind. It's like I've been in a lake up to my neck, bobbing happily, so warm and safe and hidden, but now the water's draining away, going down, revealing everything, me, and I don't want it to get any shallower, I don't want to get out.

Or do I?

Fuck.

I'll tell him the next chance I get. This is Los Angeles, Jules is cool, he'll be fine. Or not. He'll keep the secret. Or not. I'll tell him. Or not. No, I will. I will.

Next chance I get.

The rest of the week, next chances come, and go, and come, and go, I blast past them like I'm speeding by highway exits. No off-ramp for me—I can barely say anything to Jules.

It all feels so changed with him, every look, every pat on the back, or has it always been this way? It's so obvious now, the way he nods too quickly, laughs too loudly at what I say. Even the air between us is different, there's this glow of happiness warming the space around him. It's torture.

Jules has never talked so much, all these stories pour out of him, brand-new, still in the wrapper, he's never told them to anyone else before, but there's nothing I can give him back, want to give him back. There are plenty of opportunities—he builds pockets of silence into the conversation, made just for me to fill, he gets quiet, like I'm something delicate that might run off if I get startled. Or maybe he's the delicate one, not a giraffe but a fawn, staring at me with those big eyes, waiting to see if I'm going to pet him or shoot him.

The more time I spend with Jules, the harder it gets to come out, because, yeah, I'll admit it, there are stakes now. I like the way he looks at me, the way he nudges my shoulder, how he's closed up the space between us as we walk, the me and him together, I like it. I like him. *As You Like Him.* I think of Orlando running into Rosalind-turned-Ganymede in the forest. What if Orlando was really in love with just Ganymede? Would Ganymede have to tell him about the Rosalind part of him? And what would Orlando think if he knew? I have no idea, because there is no play about this, no movie, no movie that's not a tragedy. I see Jules's face, his body, his hand reaching out to touch me, and the me, that's what I don't want to see, don't want to imagine him seeing, my body. Just fade to black, fade to black! Cut.

Why isn't it enough—what we're doing right now? I'll be gone soon—can't we just go on like this for the next few months, the Donut Dudes, staying in this no-space, not moving forward but not blowing it all up, why can't we just do that until I leave?

Because it wouldn't be right. For Jules.

I just don't want him to hate me.

I wish I were leaving tomorrow, but tomorrow comes—and I'm still here. It's lunchtime, Jules stands guard while I'm hawking my Indian donut holes and scanning the crowd for phobic faces. How many people would have to know if I came out to Jules? Maybe things wouldn't change too much, as long as Jules was cool. *Just passing through, nothing to see here.*

At the far end of the lunch area there's Magenta Streaks, sitting by themself. They're wearing a black kilt with their army boots today, and they're hunched over their sandwich, eating squirrel style—quick bites, darting eyes, fast chewing, like lunch is something you have to get away with. There's this force field of loneliness surrounding them that's probably been activated since middle school. The Weird Kid Force Field. No one to talk to, and me? Look at me, not helping at all, traitor to the cause, keeping my distance since day one—

Right on cue, like they could smell my guilt, Magenta Streaks looks up from their sandwich and finds my eyes across the courtyard, and there's a flash of Evie there, staring at me, *Don't you care at all, Adam, say something—*

"Hernandez!" Cecilia hisses as she pushes past me like a hit and

176

run. Mr. Hernandez, lunch supervisor, strides across the courtyard, making a beeline my way. Luckily, I'm just about sold out and the kids have melted back to their tables. I zip up my backpack and give him the wide-eyed, *Nothing the matter here, officer* look. But Hernandez is in no hurry to leave. He's got the sour look of a bust gone wrong. Standing over me. Staring. Daring me to say something.

"You," he says finally. "Make sure your lunch is only for *you*, just you, got it?" He snaps his fingers, points, and strides off.

Back at the sophomore benches, Gregg's laughing and Jules looks like someone died.

"You're welcome," Cecilia sings.

Gregg tells me, "You need better security, dude," and Jules's cheeks splotch red.

"I'm sorry! I didn't see him. I—I don't know what I was looking at," he says.

"Oh, we *know* what you were looking at," Cecilia says, swinging her head toward me.

A deep blush creeps up Jules's neck, invading his entire face, he won't look at me, but Cecilia and Gregg do, they're grinning— what do they think they know, when there's nothing to know? If even Gregg thinks something's going on, *Gregg,* if it's penetrated the no-fly zone of his awareness, how many other people are thinking the same thing? I scan the lunch crowd—is it my imagination, or does everyone seem to be looking in our direction, making that face you make when you scroll by photos of puppies on Instagram?

Jules. What the hell.

The bell rings. "Come on, Grey-g-g." Cecilia yanks Gregg away fast, leaving me and Jules alone.

"Those guys," Jules says, and trails off. His face has gone from on fire to completely white—I'm afraid he's gonna pass out. "So, do you *like* watching basketball?" he asks out of nowhere. It catches me off guard and I say the first thing that pops in my head because my brain is still five seconds ago and my mouth has to come up with something to say.

"Uh, yeah. Sweaty guys in tank tops running around, why not?"

He swallows, his big Adam's apple bobbing up and down. "Well, you know my first scrimmage is tomorrow, right? So, you could, if you wanted to, come . . . to watch. I mean, I don't know how much I'll play, maybe not a lot, or at all, but . . ." He swallows again, then runs fast over the next part. "And then if you, we could, like, if you wanted to hang out after or something, you know, movie, or whatever or—"

I watch him stumble over his words like he stumbled over his feet that first day, and I realize it's already gone too far—I've got to tell him, and it might not be a bad idea to do it after the game, tomorrow, away from school, with fewer eyes around and the time to lay it all out. The best part of that plan? I won't have to do it today.

"Okay, yeah. I'll be there."

Friday. The Day. During lunch, the basketball team has taken over all four courts between Building C and the cafeteria. They're

178

doing drills, lots of quick passing, fake-outs and layups and whatever else they do in basketball. There are two coaches in navy Wildcats polo shirts, shouting orders and doing that macho hand clapping "Go-go-go!" thing that I gotta say is kind of a turn-on.

I'm done selling, so I get a chance to watch them practice. So much skin. Some of the players' shirts are plastered to their bodies, outlining their muscles—others have tank tops flapping loose, showing off the sides of their chests, their bare arms. There's Jules, running with them, his shirt hanging baggy around his skinny body, his hair all matted curls plastered to his face. He makes a basket, high-fives another player with a mop of hair and muscles glistening with sweat. Hand slapping hand. Hand grabbing arm. Shoulder bumping shoulder. So free. The player lifts up his shirt to wipe off his face, there's his chest, like it's nothing. I see this, and suddenly I'm shaking, I'm a flash fire of rage. It's all so easy for them, to be so easy in their skin, no one even thinks twice about it, none of them feels this peck peck peck inside their body, this ache of not-having, of not-wanting what they do have.

I breathe deeply, feel my binder push against the breath, squeeze me into calmness.

Jules be a good one Jules don't freak out.

After last period, I head to the gym early, the scrimmage isn't for another half an hour but I need to hole up somewhere and figure out how this is going to go down tonight. Should I get it over with right away, or wait until the end of the evening? Pros and cons, pros and cons.

In the gym there are already a few clusters of people hanging out, kids squeezed tight together, watching something on their phones, others sprawling on the bleachers, horsing around, the spirit squad grouped at the far end, going over their routine. No sign of either team.

I pick out a spot in the top corner of the bleachers and head toward it, fishing out my phone and earbuds on the way. Phone's been off all day because I forgot to charge it last night—I hear Mom's voice droning in my head: *plug it in every night, you wouldn't be in this situation if you make it a routine . . .*

Weirdly enough, when my phone powers on, Mom's texts are the first things I see:

> **Hello, sweetie! How are you doing?**

> **I'm sorry I couldn't talk last night, Susie had a soccer game and it didn't go too well and she was upset, you know her! LOL.**

> **Anyway, call me tonight. FaceTime?**

> **Love you, Jack!**

This is followed by a shit ton of hearts, smooches, puppies, and one out-of-place palm tree. For someone so sensible, Mom's addicted to emojis.

Underneath her message, there's another unopened text, this

one from a phone number I don't know, I don't even recognize the area code:

Why are you hiding?

There's a link.

I look around like someone just shouted my name. This quiet place now feels like a trap, a corner to be cornered in. My lizard brain activates—fight or flight—and there's also this sick, awful feeling of relief tangled in there, too, this is what I've been afraid of since I got here, I've been holding my breath without even knowing it, and now it's happened.

I touch the link.

—my name is Evie. And I'm Adam. Hello. Hello. I'm a trans girl. And I'm a trans . . . boy? guy? You can be either. Okay. And we're here because—

I thunder down the bleacher steps loud enough to turn heads, can't tear the earbuds out because if I do the giggling voices in my ear will megaphone out, echo off every corner of the gym, every exit sign and banner. I whip my head around, searching the crowd for the pointing finger, the bodysnatching scream of the asshole who's outing me, I want to stay in this crest of anger I'm feeling right now, but I can't keep it up, people are starting to stare and the panic birds are arriving. Any moment now the

181

spirit squad will wave their pom-poms in the air like wings and start chanting *Trans guy! Trans guy! Trans guy!*

Run.

Hello says Evie. *Hello* says Adam Me.

And then I can't hear anything

There's only my breath

The panic birds flapping

My hands slamming into the door's crash bar

The blinding light

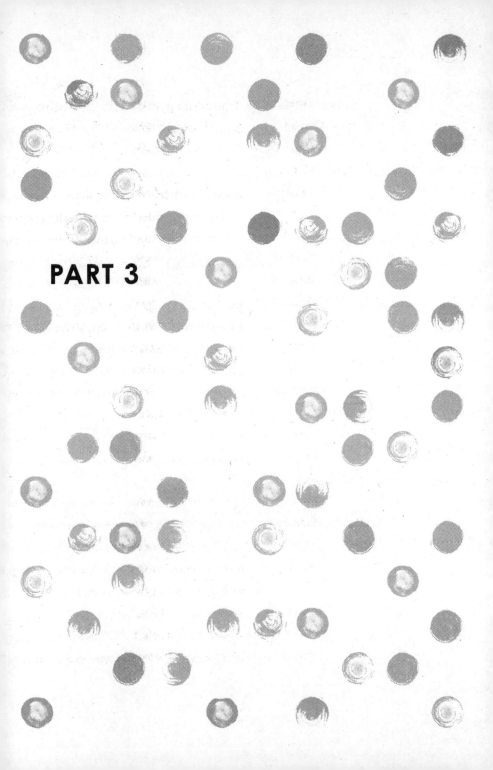

PART 3

13. Jules

> I saw a video of u

> can we talk

> im a little freaked out

> can we talk

> hello?

> hey can we talk

> ill be at the la river near frogtown at 1 Sunday
> u can meet me or not

Meet me or not.

I tell her I'm going on a bike ride, but that doesn't stop my mother's Spidey sense from triggering. "Why are you biking?" she asks. "You never bike." Which is true, I haven't ridden in at least three years. "Do you want me to drive you somewhere?

Where are you going?" So many questions I don't want to answer. "I don't even know if those bikes are working anymore. They're probably rusty or flat or what is it called with the gears? I'm sure they need a tune-up—"

"Mom, it's just a bike. I'll be fine. It's not like driving a car."

"*Speaking* of which, when are you going to be getting your driving permit? Have you been studying? Dhyllin's mom says he's already taking the car out."

I steer her back on track, explain that Coach D'Arienzo wants me to get more cardio in at home, that it will help with my game. And yes, I will study for my permit test when I get home. And yes, I will stay around the reservoir. And yes, I will be careful.

She frowns, still unconvinced. "Sunday drivers are the worst. Wear your helmet."

There are three mint-condition bikes in the garage—my mother bought them one Hanukkah when she had mistaken our family for another one and had the idea that we would all go cycling together. Never happened. I choose my dad's bike, because mine sits too low for me now.

I head off to the reservoir, or what used to be the reservoir, but is now a concrete hole like an empty swimming pool the size of a few football fields. I stay on the path around half of it, just in case my mother decides to pull out binoculars and follow along, but as soon as I'm past the dog park I peel away from the curve and veer off onto a small side street. Escape.

It feels good to be biking, pumping my legs, concentrating on nothing but where to cross and how to avoid being hit by cars. Not thinking about what's waiting for me at the end of this ride. The small street merges into a busier one, two lanes, then four lanes, and one major intersection. I get off my bike to pull it over the high sidewalk curb up to a ramp crossing the highway. I've arrived.

The Los Angeles River. I have to pass through a steel door to get onto the ramp, which switchbacks up and down to merge into the river's bike path. The path is concrete, a straight shot south. All along there's a metal pipe guardrail keeping you from falling down the concrete slope leading to the water below. If you keep pedaling with your eyes lowered, and don't look at the giant power line towers and factories in the distance, you can pretend you're biking along some meadow, with the small trees and large rocks and vegetation coming out of the deeper water, but then you notice the number of shopping carts upturned in the river and the homeless tents set up along the bank, and when you straighten your bike out you notice all the barbed wire on the other side, separating you from industrial buildings with boarded-up windows and gang tags, and you remember, oh yeah, this is totally not mother-approved.

There's hardly anyone around, just an older couple throwing a ball with their dog, letting it splash in the water, a cyclist speeding by me in the opposite direction, and two bikes ahead vanishing into the distance. That's it.

I don't know how this is going to go. *Meet me or not* isn't exactly encouraging. And how do I want it to go? I try to imagine Dhyllin's take on the situation. "You're in way over your head," he'd inform me. "Classic Jules." *Thanks, Dhyllin.* But it's true. I literally have no clue what to expect.

There's a rusty, discarded bike down the concrete slope ahead, and what I think is a bundle of clothes about to slide into the river next to it. Four pedals later I see the bundle has legs folded up inside it with black boots poking out, a cardinal-red CMU hoodie covering the rest. I slow down and hop off my bike.

My heart beats faster than when I was pedaling. I think of just getting back on and taking off. He hasn't seen me yet; he'd never know I came. I could keep biking, find an exit farther on, and not deal with any of this. I put one foot on a pedal, rock it back and forth.

"Jack," I call out, finally.

He doesn't turn around. I'm afraid my bike will skitter down the concrete into the water, so I prop it against the railing and hope no one's going to come by and steal it. I duck under the metal pipe. The concrete bank is steeper than I thought. As soon as I let go of the railing and take one step I'm taking five, fast. I almost run into Jack, but he still doesn't move. It's like he's not even acknowledging I'm there.

The way he's crouched makes him look so small.

I want to say, now that I know, that it's so obvious, but I'm still not seeing it. He's wearing his usual sweatshirt, hood up, black jeans, boots. Jack looks the same. Or, Adam looks the same. He looks the same.

Nothing's the same.

"What are you staring at?" he says, without turning around.

Jack still sounds like Jack, and I'm surprised it surprises me, like I thought maybe he was gonna reveal he had a different voice, too, all along.

"I'm not staring," I say, though most likely, I was.

I crouch down, and he finally looks at me. The first feeling I have is relief. It's still Jack. Of course it is. The face, the swoosh of hair, the eyebrows, the melting chocolate eyes . . . only now the eyes are hard and solid, stone solid, a wall keeping me out. And then my brain fritzes like a DJ just scratched a needle all over it, and I can't help it, I look for what's been hiding, the other reality, the other Jack. Soft lips? Small shoulders? I'm searching for evidence, for anything that will show me what I should have known from the beginning. I look at his hands and I remember them spooning those Indian donuts into the bags, licking the syrup off his fingers, how small those fingers were.

"What?" Jack demands, shoving his hands into the pockets of his hoodie.

"Nothing," I say. This is not how I imagined things were going to start. "Why are you so angry?"

14. Jack

Why am I so angry? He really has to ask?

I look away, because I can't even. Instead, I stare out at the river and picture a getaway, you know, the scene in the movie where the escaped convict splashes along the water, trying to get the dogs off his scent, he disappears into some drainage tunnel and the next time we see him, he's borrowed someone's clothes from an unlocked car, assumed a different identity.

I'd like to be that convict right about now.

Jules is next to me, mouth-breathing, full-on staring, not even hiding it. He's trying to work out what this strange creature he's looking at is, what's under these clothes. I've seen that look a million times, but it doesn't make my skin crawl any less.

"Why do you think I'm angry?" I say.

"The video?"

"The video. Yes, the video. Brilliant."

"And you didn't want anyone to know . . . ?"

"That's not the point, Jules! C'mon. Someone just outed me, without my permission. Do you understand how wrong that is?" You'd think that confused puppy-dog look he has on his face would calm down this fireball in my chest, but it just makes it flare up.

"And guess who sent out the video?" Jules's guesses are as blank as his face. "Dhyllin," I yell, "*your* friend, fucking Dhyllin." And that feels so good to say, I shoot one more into the water, like a skipping stone. "*Fucking* Dhyllin."

"Dhyllin?" Jules's forehead crinkles. "How do you know?"

"Who else?" I throw down Dhyllin at the cemetery, describe that look he gave me. Jules tries telling me it wasn't Dhyllin's phone number that sent the video, but that doesn't mean anything, Dhyllin could have texted it from the phone of any one of his mouth-breathing buddies.

Jules shakes his head. "It doesn't . . . I mean . . . I don't get it, I mean . . . why would he even . . . ?"

I see him going away inside his head, trying to work it out. *Hurry up!* I want to scream. "I don't know. He's your friend. You tell me. Maybe he was trying to *warn* you. Or he's just an asshole." I stare at him like the fireball's gonna shoot out of my eyes. "Did you share it with anyone?"

"No," Jules says quickly. "I wouldn't." A pause. "But I think Gregg got the text, too."

"See? See?" That just proves everything.

"Okay! Maybe he did!" Jules says, his voice rising. "But why are you so mad at *me*?"

I throw up my hands. That's what he's worried about? If he doesn't understand something so basic, how can I even explain?

"I'm just . . . angry, okay? I'm angry. He had no right to send that out. It fucking sucks."

There's a pause, and that just hangs in the air, and I think, I spewed out enough, the fireball's burning out, if we could just leave it here, if we could just accept the general *suckiness* of the situation and move on, move past it, maybe everything will still be okay.

But Jules is so not moving on. He's still in *working it out* mode.

"Okay, so you're . . . you're a . . ."

"*Jack*. I'm a Jack."

"You're *trans*, right?"

I nod, bravo, Jules, you got it, three points, you get an A.

"And is Jack your name? You called yourself Adam on the video. Was that your real name, or did you have a name before—?"

I look away, 'cause suddenly I'm really tired, and, anyway, what does it matter? But not looking at Jules doesn't make him disappear. "My name is Jack, okay? That's the only one you need to know. The other ones are just deadnames."

"They're what?"

"Never mind." This. This is why I didn't want to come out. The whole point of going stealth, not having to answer these fucking questions.

Jules's face scrunches up, still working out the equation. "Okay, so . . . um, like, I don't really know anyone who is, so . . . can I ask . . . like, *how* much are you—you know, like, your body, is it—"

"No! God, No!" I shout. "You can't ask that! That's not okay. God!"

"Okay! Sorry! Sorry!" That stops him, but all those questions are still there, bulging in his eyes, just because they're never said doesn't mean that I don't feel them burrowing under my skin, tiny birds skittering, pecking away. "I didn't know, I—you gotta give me a break, okay? Just give me a second to get up to speed."

But I don't want to give him a second, because, what's the point, let's just speed to the part where he walks away. 'Cause that's what's coming. I can feel it.

"I don't want to talk about this now," I tell him. "I *really* don't want to talk about this."

"Well, when *were* you going to talk about this?" he says. "Don't you think it would have been kind of important for me to know?"

I'm ready with the right answer, which is to say, yeah, I wanted to tell you, I was just about to, but the way he asks has just enough of a demand in it to make my teeth clench. "I didn't tell *anyone*. It shouldn't matter."

"Nobody would care."

"You don't know that."

"Okay. Maybe you're right. But what about me? Why didn't you tell me?"

"I . . . that's not the point. It's a personal decision."

"But *we* were . . . personal. Right? I mean, weren't we . . . we were . . . kind of . . ." Jules trails off.

Were. Past tense.

Neither of us wants to finish that sentence, and so we just let it hang there, unclaimed, but the silence stretches out so long it gets said anyway, invisibly. And I feel my entire insides hollow out, and the world freezes, and I finally ask the question that's been hiding underneath the fireball all this time, and I have to sling it real hard just to get it out, so it sounds more like a challenge than I mean it to:

"Okay, so now you know. *Does* it matter?"

Jules looks like I just ambushed him, his mouth works on finding words, and on his face are seven different answers, and none of them are *No, it doesn't matter.* I wish, I wish I could take back the question, hide it deep where even I can't find it. His eyes are, like, terrified, and I feel bad for him, I do, he's so lost, he needs me to help him find his way out, to call it quits, and then we can all just go home.

"No, that's all right don't worry about it," I say quickly. I even try to sound friendly. "It wouldn't work out, okay, Jules? Because—it never does, this kind of—" and I wave my hand between us. "Just forget it. This is way too complicated for you. It's not what you want."

I thought he was gonna be relieved. I really did. Instead, he stares at me like I just slapped him. His face flares red, then scrunches up. The words catch in his throat. "So, what was this? Like, a test? You wanted to see how long you could fool me?"

"It's not about fooling anyone," I start to tell him, "it's about me coming out when I'm ready to—" but I can tell he's not even listening, I see the red spreading in his cheeks, warning, warning.

"I'm not stupid, okay?" He stands up too quickly, loses his footing. The gravel under his feet surfboards him down the slope, he windmills his long arms like a cartoon coyote and the only thing that stops him are his hands hitting the rough concrete on the way down.

"Jules!" I shout, getting up to help him, but he jumps right back to standing—must be the basketball reflexes, or anger—and his sudden movement is a force that whumps me back down onto the ground, hard.

He stands over me again. He's breathing fast. The little pricks of bright red that dot his scraped palms blink as he clenches and unclenches his fists. Is he doing that because of the pain, or is there a punch coming my way? Always a possibility at the end of this scene.

The red disappears as he squeezes his fists tight. "Maybe I am," he says, voice thick. "Maybe I am stupid."

Jules strides up the slope to his bike. I hear the pedals engage, the chain crank into gear, and then, he's gone.

You aren't stupid, Jules.

He missed what I wanted him to miss, but what was happening between us, he got just right.

But that's over now.

"Thank God," I whisper to myself. Close call. What I don't need is someone else to worry about. 'Cause I'm no good at that. It's enough, taking care of myself.

I try to get up, but my legs are too wobbly. I sit back down, put my head between my knees, try to take a few good breaths.

Here's one thing about being on testosterone. Before the hormones, I was a lot more verbal. I had words for all the feelings. Like, I could describe my emotions in detail, tell you what was going on inside, if I wanted to. Now, I've still got all the feelings, but they're rolling around together in that big red fireball, all knotted up, I have no idea how to pick them apart anymore. So, what I think of as relief turns out to be anger, or maybe it's fear, but if it's fear, why am I laughing, and if I'm laughing, why the fuck are my eyes stinging so hard?

15. Jules

Swish

There's the basket, and the ball, the ground the ball bounces on, and your hands. That's it. The ball bounces. The ball's in your hands. The ball leaves your hands. The ball goes in the net, or doesn't. And you do it again. And again. And again.

Swish

You don't have to worry that the basket is going to crumble. Or that the ball will suddenly grow wings and fly off. The ground is not going to give way.

Swish

Bounce, shoot. Bounce, shoot. You could do it all day. You don't have to think about anything—in fact, it's better if you don't. The sounds of the ball and the rim and the net are the only sounds in your head. And if your palms sting every time you make contact with the ball, well, at least you know it's real. And soon you can zone that feeling out, too. Like you can zone out thinking about Jack, and his angry hard eyes, and how none of the feelings you thought were true were true.

Swish

I manage to avoid my mother for most of the day. I see her in the kitchen getting dinner ready, talking with someone on the phone, probably Bubbe, 'cause it's Sunday, or maybe with someone from SORE calling to tell her the latest reservoir news. She opens the French doors off the dining room, her shoulder locking the phone against her ear. "Dinner in twenty," she calls out.

We eat in the kitchen at the white marble island, pushing aside the stacks of diet cookbooks to make room for our plates. Tonight's dinner is kind of macrobiotic, plus a portion of paleo (for me), and white wine (for her). We do our usual game where she pretends to eat the food and I pretend to like it. Turns out she *was* on the phone with SORE, and the outrage stoked up by that call just might save me from talking at all.

"Can you imagine?" she asks as she spears a soggy Brussels sprout with her fork and drags it around her plate. "Draining the entire reservoir without input from the residents?" *I can't imagine,* I tell her with my eyebrows. "How can they think that would be a good idea?" In between sips of chardonnay she lays out questions to me and then answers each of them herself. Isn't it an eyesore? It certainly is. Do I know what they're planning for it now? Neither do they. Who are these developers, are they more important than the people who actually live there . . . do you, Jules, think a nature refuge . . . so much better than a soccer field . . . the ecosystem of the . . . attracting bad elements . . . crime rate . . . zoning . . . homeless magnet . . . impact studies . . . coyotes—

"Jules?"

"Hey. What?" Truth is, I've been on automatic, nodding and grunting while my mind was playing a slideshow of Jack at the river, still trying to figure out exactly what happened.

Mom sets down her fork. "You're quiet."

I grab at the last thing I remember her talking about. "So, a soccer field, huh?" I say, trying to look interested. "Sounds like a good idea."

"It's not." Her fingers curl around her wineglass. "Okay. What's up?"

"I'm just tired."

"Jules. You've been this way all weekend, ever since the game."

"Yeah, well—"

"You were upset that Jack didn't show up, right?"

"Uh . . ."

"Was he the one you were meeting on your bike ride this morning?"

I can't keep the surprise off my face. How does she do it? Hidden cameras? Drones? She must be a witch.

My mother nods sadly. "Did . . . something happen? Something happened. What happened—don't get up, sweetie, put down your plate. Just talk to me a little. It helps to talk about it."

"It's not going to help, Mom."

"Just give it some time. Things can change."

"They'd have to change a lot," I blurt out, and instantly hate myself for saying it.

"Is it a cultural thing?"

"Uh . . . you could say that."

"Is it because you're Jewish and he's . . . whatever he is?"

"No, nothing like that." I shake my head, wishing she would

stop, but also wishing she would just reach into my mind and grab the answers.

She squeezes my hand. "Sweetie, if you're right for each other, things will work themselves out. It'll happen. Let it evolve naturally."

She sounds so sure. I get this tiny leap in my chest. Could it have worked? Was I missing something? How could it have worked?

"What's the problem?" she asks.

I feel like a twelve-year-old, coming to Mommy with a skinned knee. But I don't know what else to do, who else to turn to.

"Tell me."

There's this horrible feeling, like when you're about to throw up—both panic and relief—that I get when I realize what's about to happen—

"You'll feel better."

—I'm about to ask my mother for dating advice.

"All right." I set down my fork. "So . . . Jack's trans, okay, and he just told me, and I'm not sure how to—"

"He's what?"

"Trans."

She sits with her mouth open, at a full stop. She takes a quick breath in to restart her brain, and then her eyes widen with understanding. "Oh, Jules. So, Jack wants to be a girl?"

"What? No. The other way."

Her eyes almost cross, she's thinking so hard. "Wait. He wants to be a—" And she puts her hand to her lips, like she's stopping the word *boy* from escaping. When she starts talking again, the words come out very slowly. "Jack *is* a girl?"

"No, he's not, I mean, he was, or whatever."

"What do you mean, whatever? Is Jack a girl or a boy? It's not a hard question, Jules."

It is when you don't know the right words. "He's a boy, but he was . . . before, a girl. I don't know how to put it."

"Oh," she says, and I can tell she's still not getting it, but then she repeats it, and that *Oh* stretches out and trails off into a sad little laugh that only stops when she looks at my face.

"Oh. Poor Jules."

There it is. *Poor Jules.* I've heard that coming out of my parents' mouths for as long as I can remember—after every mis-understanding, every boneheaded move I've ever made in my life—that head-shaking, frown-smiling blend of disappointment and amusement.

"Oh, sweetie, I'm sorry." And again, I catch a flash of something in her eyes that she's almost able to hide behind the sad smile. And that almost stops me, but the tiny leap in my chest keeps me going.

"But, maybe . . . I don't know. Could it still work, if I, like, give it time, like you said?"

"What?" My mother sits straight up. "Oh, no. *No.*" She pours herself another glass of wine. "There's not enough time in the world to fix *that.*" She takes a sip, then lets out a long breath, like she's exhaling cigarette smoke. "Jules, being gay is hard all on its own. Trust me. This whole transgender thing? Oosh. Very complicated. You don't want to have to deal with any of . . . *that.*"

That. Like Jack is a *that.*

"But you said—"

"Honey, listen to me. It makes no sense. If you're gay—and that's a *good* thing—then obviously, you don't want to be dating a girl, right?"

"But he's not a—"

She waves her hand, like she's clearing away a bad smell. "Whatever. It's best not to get involved. Okay? It's just . . . too much. And don't lead Jack on. Probably, that poor kid's just confused, trying to find herself—"

"Him," I say quietly, "himself."

"Fine. *Him*self." She shakes her head. "Just let it go. Don't worry. You'll find someone else, sweetie. Someone more . . . appropriate. A nice *boy*. It'll happen."

And she pats my cheek, and grabs my chin, and shakes it. She stares at me, making sure I'm with the program, and smiles. Nothing but motherly love in her eyes.

"Poor Jules."

Tiny leap, stomped.

I let my phone go black and crawl into bed by ten, hoping I can shut down, too. I try not to think of what school'll be like tomorrow. But my mind keeps spinning.

Jack isn't confused. That's not the problem. He knows what he wants. Which, he's made pretty clear, is not me. So why do I keep thinking about it?

"I'm attracted to guys," I say to the night. As in, guy bodies, guy parts. It took me long enough to figure that out. And Jack,

he's a guy, but . . . not . . . like . . . it was complicated. *Complicated.*
Both Jack and my mother used the same word, and as different as
the two of them are, they seem to agree that it's too complicated
for me. So, it doesn't matter if it could work, or how it could work.
I should just drop it. Move on. Find someone more appropriate,
as my mother says. And it's only been, what? A few weeks of
knowing Jack? That's nothing. No harm, no foul. I try picturing
those guy bodies in the dark above me, all the teen werewolves
and basketball stars and superheroes . . .

Only, it's still Jack's face I keep assembling in the air above,
those melting chocolate eyes, the grin, the sudden dimples . . .
Even though Jack says there's nowhere for this to go, that little
strum starts up in my chest again. That pain. My stupid heart
will just not get a clue.

16. Jack

Monday. No.

I'm being forced into life, poked by a . . . foot? I squint my eyes open, there's Dad looming above my mattress in his boxers and T-shirt, his hair doing a complete Einstein. I fumble at my ears, twist out the anti-snore earplugs.

"What are you still doing in bed?" he's saying. "It's already eight."

"Not feeling good," I mumble from under the covers.

"I *thought* something was off last night," he says. "Well, *more* off."

I'm ready to spit out a roll call of symptoms for proof, but instead Dad nods and heads for the bathroom. "You need anything?" he says from the hall.

"I'm okay." I turn back on my side, listen to the pipes rattle and clank as he flushes and washes up. I've already been awake for a couple of hours under the covers, watching the room undarken, listening to the muffled waves of Dad's snoring, and deciding, no thank you, I'm not going to school today.

It's not that I'm chickening out. And no, I'm not catastrophizing. I just need the day to think things through. Regroup.

Dad bangs back in, I shut my eyes but he's right in my ear, the bustling around the room, the mouse squeak of hangers in the closet, the wooden whisper of dresser drawers opening. And not even a hand to my forehead. If it were Mom, I'd have to print out a list of ailments, bookmark three WebMD pages, and act out the last hour of *Terms of Endearment* before she'd let me stay home, so it's good she's 2,500 miles away.

"Big day today," my father announces from his corner of the room. "Your dad has a meeting."

"Audition?"

"*Meeting.* Duvall and Blum Management. Remember Dave Duvall?"

I don't, but Dad's happy to recap, every single detail. At the West Hollywood Carnegie Mellon alumni mixer, he gets his chat on with Dave Duvall, who graduated two years after Dad, and what do you know, he's just started a management company, why don't you stop by Monday, Blum's in NY but come in anyway nine o'clock good? It was good. Very good.

"He's new. I don't know who else he reps, but . . . ya gotta start somewhere, right?"

"Yep," I say in a sickly whisper.

I feel my dad sit down on my mattress. I open my eyes. He's got on a checkered shirt with a tie and a navy blazer, and I don't have the heart to tell him he looks like he's applying for his next temp job.

"You going to be okay?" he asks.

"No, Dad," I croak, "I really, really need you to stay."

"Yeah, dream on, buddy," he says, and straightens his tie.

✤ ✤ ✤

The morning sun is brutal, I'm being cooked like a Thanksgiving turkey under the blankets, but I'm not getting out of bed yet. Funny thing is, with Dad gone, I don't have to pretend I'm sick anymore, but the longer I lie in bed, the more I feel myself sliding into the awful. I want to sleep for about a month, never want to get up.

But my bladder is not with the program.

"Shit," I say, and throw off the covers.

Brian, Serial Killer #1, is sitting on the couch in the unlit TV room, watching the Weather Channel. He's completely still except for his spoon dipping into the cereal bowl and finding its way to his mouth. "S'up," I say, passing him to get to the bathroom. He turns his head slowly like one of those possessed ventriloquist dolls, doesn't say a word, just keeps crunching.

I return to my room, where it's so. Damn. Quiet. For once, there are no trucks, no jackhammers, no construction workers shouting outside. I swear I can hear Brian crunching in the other room, swallowing his last spoonful of what sounds like gears in milk.

It's only nine.

I'd kinda like to Skype Mom right now, but that would totally sabotage my day off—she'd stretch her hand all the way through two screens to feel for fever and know it was bogus. I reach for my phone to text Dad about when he's coming home, suggest a movie we could watch together, but that would only make him suspicious, so I delete delete.

Problem is, I've got Dhyllin on autoplay. Every time there's a moment of silence in my head I'm retracing the trail he must have followed to find Pittsburgh Me. My dad tells Mr. Gene Ramsey a funny side story about my transition, he tells his son Dhyllin ("Why didn't you come in and say hi to the nice brown trans kid?"), Dhyllin does a Google search—even without my first name, he's sure to come across the *Post-Gazette* article that has links to the YouTube channel—and presto bingo, he's locked and loaded. I wonder if he's known since the first day and was just waiting for the right moment, or if seeing Jules and me together at the cemetery triggered something. Either way, it was a dick move. The dickiest of moves.

The mattress. Back to my mattress.

I turn my head and look over at the stack of movies against the wall by the dresser, our emergency supply of DVDs. Half of them have blue Blockbuster Video labels on them with big yellow sale stickers. *Raging Bull, Scarface, Lost in America*, hey, there's the Criterion *Harold and Maude* Dad gave me for Christmas, I could watch that again.

No. Definitely not.

Jules. I wonder how he's doing. It's just about snack time. We'd be meeting up outside Building C, ready for another day of smuggling goods, that's what he called it. Is he missing me? Ha. No, safe to say, Jules is done with Jack. *There goes another one out the door.* I've got a gift for driving friends away, it's my special ability.

I scrunch myself small. This time though, I tell myself, this time it isn't on me, it definitely isn't on me. I yank out my phone again, stare at the text I haven't erased:

> **Why are you hiding?**

I sit up, my fingers typing even before I've hit vertical:

> **why r u an asshole fuck off**

I punch send, give it a middle finger salute, and wait for the regret to roll in.

But it doesn't.

I feel good.

No text back.

I'm gonna be all right.

I'm gonna get out of bed, I'm gonna go to school and not give a shit and sell gulab jamun if I want to because I'm Donut Boy, goddamn it. I'm Los Angeles Jack, and I am handling it.

I'm gonna get out of bed.

But not today.

17. Jules

Monday morning arrives, and it's like I had a fever that broke in the middle of the night. I feel okay, surprisingly back to normal. I get dressed, eat breakfast, head out the door, just like every other day. When I get to school there's no sign of Jack, and I walk over to the sophomore benches and there's Gregg, hunched over as usual, smashing away at his phone. He looks up as I slide in next to him, raises an eyebrow. I shake my head. He nods. I nod back. He nods again, lips tight. And that's it. He goes back to his phone.

I've never been so grateful for the Gregg-ness of Gregg.

I look around the courtyard. Kids are doing their own thing, chatting, playing around, texting . . . and no Jack. It's like a reset. Jack was a kid I saw at Dhyllin's house and then never saw again. I scroll backward through the last weeks and delete everything: I didn't sell Indian donut holes, I didn't go to the Hollywood Forever Cemetery, I never dropped a clipboard in front of Mr. Janssen's class. Never fell on the first day of school. And there, he's erased, and it's just me and Gregg on a sophomore bench. And that's okay. The bell rings, I go to first period, and the day continues, just like always.

And then lunch hits.

A group of ninth graders sweeps up to me even before I get through the archway into the courtyard. They're all smiling with bright eyes. "Where's the Donut Boy?" one of them asks. There's no sign of Jack and his backpack in the courtyard, but before I can answer they rush off again, laughing. I don't get what the joke is, but there's no time to think about it because from behind, a hand grabs my arm, fingers small but strong. It's Jack, coming to get me, *Why are you so late? Come on, those Indian donuts aren't going to bag themselves*, but when I turn around, it's Cecilia staring up at me.

"There-you-are-thank-God-I-found-you-are-you-okay?" she says breathlessly. She pulls me in for a tight hug, then leads me across the quad to the lunch area, where Gregg slouches, like he hasn't left since this morning. "I found him," she announces, kicking his legs.

"Oh, hey," he says, pulling off his earphones. He sits up, looking guilty as hell.

"You must be devastated," Cecilia says to me.

Uh-oh.

"I'm okay . . ."

"Gregg told me you had no idea. Oh my God, to find out that way? Heartbreaking." Cecilia's hand is on her chest, trying to keep her own heart from leaping out in sympathy.

"You saw the video?" I ask Cecilia, glaring at Gregg.

He looks up, pleading. "I didn't show it to her!"

"Oh, he didn't have to," Cecilia says. "It's everywhere."

"What?" I say.

Cecilia's talking even faster than usual. "Of course. Once something like this hits, you can't stop it. It just *goes*."

"Goes where?" I'm having trouble keeping up, my mind is too crammed.

"Jack should have told us day one," she says, flicking through her phone. "It's his own fault."

"Why?" I ask. "I thought you said it's not a big deal at this school!"

"It isn't, but . . . this is different. The video, it's like a *thing* now, it's *drama*, everyone will want to have a take on it: 'Did you know?' 'Could you tell?' 'Who sent the video?' 'Did the boyfriend know?'"

"Why is it Jack's fault?" Gregg asks. "Isn't it the fault of whoever sent the video out?"

Cecilia rolls her eyes. "Oh, Grey-g-g, that's not the point."

"Wait—boyfriend?" I say. "Is that me?" I'm in this alternate reality, where I'm being called out for what was just in my head. "I'm not the boyfriend. I was never the boyfriend!"

"Dude," says Gregg, "it's not like you were trying to hide it or anything. It was kinda obvious."

Cecilia sees the look of panic on my face and starts petting my arm, like I'm her favorite pony. "Don't worry! The whole thing will go away, but the trick is to get ahead of the story. Let me take care of it."

"Cecilia's mom's in PR management," Gregg says. "Like when some actor does a sex tape, stuff like that, she fixes it."

Cecilia gives me a tight smile. "You're going to come out of this just fine. I've been talking to people and I told them you knew nothing about Jack's secret. You were being fooled, too."

"But he wasn't fooling me, he was just—" I try to remember what Jack said at the river, when I accused him of the same thing. "He just wasn't ready." I pull out my phone. "I should warn him."

Cecilia pushes down my arm. "Oh, I wouldn't do that."

"Why not?" I ask.

"It's his problem, let him deal with it. And why would you want to help him anyway? I can't believe he played you like that. He played us all! And can I just say?" She puts out a hand to stop any possible interruption. "I have no problem with trans people, believe me. I just have a problem with *fakers*."

"Cecilia," I say, trying to sound like I'm taking control. "He's not a faker. It's not like that—don't make it be like that—it was just a misunderstanding. Could we just let it die, please?"

"Jules—" She's about to launch into another lecture on crisis control. I can't take it.

"Just stop, okay? Stop talking about it!"

Cecilia stares at me, openmouthed, stunned. Then her mouth closes so sharply I swear I can hear it slam shut. "I was just looking out for you. Clearly, you don't understand the situation, but, whatever. I mean, I've got plenty of other things to do, believe me. God. Ungrateful much?" She snatches her backpack, gives me one furious glare, and stalks off.

Gregg and I sit for a moment, dazed. I stare at the phone in my hand, wonder if I should text Jack, wonder if I should text Dhyllin. Gregg looks around, like Cecilia might still be in earshot, then says quietly, "Seriously, I don't think most people will really give a shit?"

I nod. Slide my phone back into my pocket. Maybe it *is* better to let things be. Things might calm down by tomorrow. No use panicking Jack. And since when have I ever been able to make Dhyllin do anything?

The bell rings. We grab our stuff and start walking across the quad. "Look," Gregg says quietly, "I know Cecilia can be kind of a lot. I mean, once she gets all up into something, she kind of takes over."

"Yeah," I say.

"That's just her style, you know? Bossy, in your face, self-righteous . . . Yeah." Gregg sweeps the hair off his eyes and sighs. "I really like her."

The rest of the day is pretty much anguish, trying to look normal in class while catching every whisper and giggle around me. Whenever a head turns, I think it's turning to look at me; wherever kids are gathered, they're gathered to talk about Jack. Which probably isn't true, but Cecilia's got me spooked.

It isn't until sixth period, history, that something actually happens. We're going over the French Revolution: causes, Louis XVI, storming the Bastille, heads on pikes, guillotines, heads in baskets . . . just a whole lot of severed heads. It's almost interesting enough to keep my mind occupied. Mrs. Coleman, who should have been a theater teacher, is all gritted teeth and defiant fists raised in the air, single-handedly keeping the revolution alive.

"Bread! Bread!" she cries, trying to enlist us into the March on Versailles.

We're supposed to split up into micro-groups to discuss similarities and differences between the American and French Revolutions. "Just grab who you're closest to, clusters of three or four, no more!" yells Mrs. Coleman. Before I can even look around, two chairs clank against my desk. Lowell Taylor and Lily Cho stare down at me, eyes bright and shining like they've just won the Powerball.

Lily Cho is never called anything but Lily Cho. One, because there are three Lilys, but also, because two syllables just wouldn't be enough to sum her up. She's big in every way—in size, in voice, in the way she enters a room. There's no way *not* to notice her. She's usually in leggings, sometimes black, sometimes fluorescent, sometimes covered in yellow happy faces, and they match her collection of cat-eye glasses, which always match her lipstick. She's got a variety of laughs, from under-her-breath snickers to flat-out shrieks, that she unleashes at the quietest moments in class, usually because of something Lowell has whispered in her ear.

Lowell is, well, Lowell. Still handsome. Still intimidating. He's worked out how to be skinny in a graceful way that suits him, not awkward (like me). He's always exactly put together instead of just thrown together (like me). No jeans and hoodies, ever. He's got steel-blue glasses that are a little big for his narrow face, so they almost look like a prop, like he's pulling a Clark Kent, trying to disguise the fact that he's got these sky-blue eyes and creamy skin, a dimple of a cleft chin and hair that stays in place and seems to do exactly what he wants it to do without arguing (like mine).

Not that I've noticed or anything.

If Lily is a shout, Lowell's a smirk. They're always watching, always amused by something. And right now, that something appears to be me.

"Hello," Lily Cho says.

"Hello," Lowell says.

"Wanna group?" Lily Cho asks, like it's the most delicious idea ever.

"Uh, sure," I say, and on cue, both of them immediately sit down. They stare at me, waiting.

"So, uh, the French Revolution . . ." I begin.

"We saw the video," Lily Cho says. Her voice has that kind of high pitch to it that can't be quiet even when she whispers.

"Such a violation of privacy," whispers Lowell.

"A violation," echoes Lily Cho. "So how did you feel when you found out?"

"Let's stay on subject," Mrs. Coleman calls out from across the room.

Lily Cho rolls her eyes and mutters, "Fine."

Lowell sits up straight and says, "Okay, French Revolution. Marie Antoinette definitely got the shaft, historically."

"Definitely," Lily Cho says.

Lowell continues. "But her wardrobe was *legendary*. So that kind of balances it out, historically, don't you think?"

He looks at me like he's waiting for some reaction, like there's a secret password I need to give. I don't know what to say, but I can tell by Lily Cho's sparkling eyes that it's a joke, so I smile, pretending I know what's so funny. He smiles back right at me, and then I smile, for real.

After class, Lowell waits for me by the door. Lily Cho's already halfway down the hall, standing by the lockers and pretending not to look our way. Without her, Lowell's quieter, almost . . . shy. "Hey," he says, "if it's okay to talk about it, I just want to let you know, we got that YouTube link, but we didn't share it. Swear. We didn't even know who Adam was until Cecilia told us."

"Oh . . . okay." I swallow. "Jack."

"Jack. Right." Lowell nods thoughtfully. "We told people not to send it around, but you know . . ." He rolls his eyes. "I'm sure Jack'll be fine. The school's cool."

I nod, relieved. Lowell bends his head toward mine. "Did you really not know?"

I shake my head.

He lifts an eyebrow. "So, now that you do, how are you feeling? Is that like, you know, your thing?"

Out of the corner of my eye I see a couple of girls standing just inside the room. Their bodies are angled like they're in conversation, but no one's talking, and all the listening's in my direction.

"My thing?" I say. I have no idea how I should respond, but I get the feeling that there's a correct answer I'm supposed to give. "Oh, I, um, don't have a . . . thing. I mean—" Lowell's leaning in, waiting for something, another password, what? "I mean, I . . . like guys, you know?" I've said it out loud, finally.

"Ah. Well, okay then. Good that you found out." Lowell smirks,

216

and I realize that what looks like a smirk is actually what his lips do naturally when he smiles. He's got perma-smirk. He cocks his head to the side and squeezes my shoulder. "You're funny," he says, and looks at me brightly. "Well, okay. See ya."

A moment later he's down the hall, reunited with his waiting friend, and I stare after them, still a little dazed, as they disappear down the stairs. Lily Cho's scream of delight echoes up and down the hall.

The GSA student leader chatting me up in history is one thing. Basketball practice is another.

Heading to the gym, I think about Bishop Academy and their locker rooms. They had an entirely new sports building, no rusty lockers there, no chipped tiles or funky mildew smell in the shower room like the ones at Earl Warren. It was shiny clean and sparkling, but I remember it like it was a crime scene. There's where the word *fag* first splatted on me. There's the locker Patrick was standing at when he hurled the word, there's the water fountain where they first called me *Julie*. That locker room was the beginning of the end of my time at Bishop Academy. So here I am now, about to push open the rusty gray metal doors of the Earl Warren gym. What new and special name am I going to be given in the locker room to hound me for the rest of the year?

It gets quiet when I enter. Eyes on me as I make my way to the back row of lockers, not unfriendly, exactly, but curious. Gavin Miller's hanging out by the front, phone in hand, and as soon as I pass him, he pushes himself off the sink he's been leaning on and

217

crosses behind me. By the time I open my locker I hear Tommy McBride, two rows over, yell, "That's Donut Boy? No way!" followed by Gavin's "It's true!" and laughter.

Here goes.

Gavin pops his head around the corner, followed by two other freshmen, Hayden Seidel and Gus Sanchez. "Jules, buddy, how could you not know?" Gavin asks, eyes shining. "Do you need anatomy lessons?"

"Shut it, Gavin," Colton Meyers says under his breath, slamming the locker next to mine and walking past Gavin to the exit.

"Hey, I don't give a crap if he's *gay!*" he shouts after Colton. "But that trans shit is just fucking whack. Jules might be *confused!*" He turns to me, friendly as can be, picking at the red zits crusting his neck. "You want me to draw you some diagrams?"

Hayden and Gus snicker. I know I should say something. Here's where Jack would tell me to stand up for myself, but I can't even think of a joke or dis that will make it all just locker room shit-talking between Gavin and me. I can't think of anything.

"Whatever, Gavin" is all I can manage, and keep dressing. A few more stragglers look in. They hear the edge in Gavin's voice.

"How'd you find out? That musta been a shocker." He pumps his fist in front of his face, the universal sign for blow jobs, then opens his fist in mock surprise. "Uh-oh! Something's missing!" Laughter, and suddenly Tommy swooshes in behind them, rocking an air guitar and launching into a chorus of "Dude Looks Like a Lady." I'm frozen, but my face is on fire.

"Bro." Jamal parts the herd of ninth graders with his easy stride.

He throws his duffel onto the bench between Tommy and me. "Whadya singing that for?" Jamal's tone is calm, but Tommy and the laughter stop immediately. Jamal turns to face him, one hand resting on the locker door. "You know it *literally* makes no sense, right?" He waves his hand in front of Tommy's face. "Seems to me you're the one who's confused."

"Jamal, you heard about Donut Boy, right? There's a video, show him, Gavin—"

"What are y'all, ten?" Jamal says, looking around in disbelief. "Who gives a shit? This is 2015."

Silence. Tommy nods in total agreement, shocked at the JV players. "Yeah, what the fuck, guys? This is 2015."

Most of the kids start to slink away, but not Gavin, who keeps his head cocked high. "C'mon, Jamal, you know you're just covering for him because—"

"Because?" Jamal drops the word like a rock.

Kevin, Jamal's brother, rumbles in from behind. "*Because* Jules drained more points than anyone at the scrimmage last week, and Miller here was throwing up bricks all game."

Jamal squinches his eyes, staring at Kevin. "Nah, he wasn't throwing bricks. He was on the *bench*, remember? Couldn't keep his mouth shut. Right?" He looks square at Gavin, cool and mild. "Or am I *confused* on that?"

Gavin tries for a laugh, but it comes out like a lopsided hiss. "It was just a joke, man, chill out," he mumbles, and slinks away. Jamal turns to the others. "Don't you *juvvies* have someplace you're supposed to be? Or are you just waiting to watch me take off my clothes?" That clears everyone out of my row, fast, except Kevin, who pauses to slap hands with Jamal. "Freshmen," he rumbles, shaking his head, and follows them out.

I finish changing in the corner, as Jamal pulls his shirt over his head and gets on his number fifteen, not even looking at me. I've never realized how much space he can fill, just pulling on his jersey, what a totally different sort of being he is than me.

"Thanks," I say quietly.

"It ain't nothing," Jamal says as he stuffs his locker. "Just some foolishness. Ninth graders come in not knowing how this school works. How we don't put up with that kind of bullshit around here. They'll learn."

"What about Tommy? He's a senior."

Jamal shrugs. "Tommy, he's all right. Doesn't mean anything, just gets too excited when you give him some attention. He's like a puppy that pees on the rug when you get home. A big white puppy."

I smile. "Okay, but thanks anyway."

"No problem." He shuts his locker and turns to me, hair bouncing. "We gotta look out for each other, right? Being we're on the same team and all. At least I think we are, but, hey, you do you." And he smiles, shoots me a wink, and leaves.

A wink. Who winks?

Jamal winks.

And that's it. It's over. For the rest of practice, there's no problem. No one on JV cracks any jokes or treats me any differently. If anything, I get a few more balls passed my way. Even Gavin, though he looks a little more sour than usual, shuts up. It's the exact opposite of Bishop Academy. Even if Jamal weren't the team captain, he's a good person to have on your side.

I guess I'm officially out at Earl Warren High School.

Isn't that what I wanted? Wasn't I looking for exactly this, being out and daring and open? Maybe that video of Jack was the best thing that could have happened to me. It launched me into school a hundred times better than I could have done. Maybe it'll do the same for Jack. I think of texting him, but then I remember: *Let things be.* Don't stir things up. Lowell said he'd be fine, and he'd know.

Let things be.

18. Jack

"Okay, what's up?"

Dad clocks me still in bed Wednesday morning and gives me another foot poke. Have I mentioned how gross his feet are?

I tell him I'm still not 100 percent. "What percent are you?" he asks. His concern isn't the warm melty kind, it's the kind with its arms crossed over its chest and one eyebrow raised. "You know, more than two days off school triggers an immediate call to your mother."

The jig is up. Just as well, my dad informs me he's going to stay home all morning, working on audition monologues, and nothing gets a recovery going faster than being trapped in a bedroom listening to your dad recite Jack Nicholson's speech from *A Few Good Men*, over and over again.

"You want answers? You want the truth? You can't handle the truth!" he says, giving me a preview, jabbing his finger down at me.

I can't. I really can't. If I have to go through a day of that I may get sick for real.

Re-entry. In front of the same school I've biked up to for the last eight weeks, the one I'll be biking away from in eight, unless my father makes like Jesus and pulls off an acting miracle. Two weeks ago, the thought of leaving so soon would've majorly bummed me out. Now, I'm ready to jump either way. Around this time back home, everyone would be in layers, breathing in crisp air, the school lawn would be on fire with leaves changing color. Here, the boring trees are holding on to the same dusty green leaves they've had on all year, and the school lawn is dry and crunchy when I arrive back on campus.

Hello, old man Earl Warren, you decapitated bronze head over the main entrance, spitting distance above me. Don't spit on me, though, and by the way, as I stand here killing time looking at you, I see you could use a little work, I'm noticing those scratches on your forehead from the pigeons trying to get comfortable on your glasses, that gash ripping down your metal cheek like a tear—

"Excuse me!" Students push past, the First Bell Stampede. There's no putting it off.

Jack is in the building.

Classes start. In physics, Gregg tries to catch my eye, but I stare straight ahead, no thanks, I'm good. The rest of the morning I'm slipping in and out of classrooms, strictly lo-pro, no one bothering me. I skip nutrition, got nothing to sell today, and I'm avoiding the courtyard, the sophomore benches, trying to give Jules his space, cut down on the awkward. At lunch, I stick to the science lab, plug in some Kendrick, "Alright," and zone out, munching on a cinnamon Pop-Tart and staring out the window.

Well, look who's out there. I'm not the only one avoiding the lunch area.

Jules is sitting on a grassy strip down the slope on the side of the building—funny how easy I can pick him out, even from up here. He's under a tree, eating lunch, talking. I see two other students through the gaps of the branches, no one I know. The guy's thin and tall and white, a match for Jules, but with lighter hair and glasses that flare at me when he turns his head. The girl's Asian, with pigtails that bounce and hands that move a lot, they swoop and wave like she's performing a magic trick for the other two. There's a shade of pink on her that can be seen from space. Jules sits with his legs shooting out to the left and the other kid sits with his shooting to the right, they look like bookends with no books separating them.

The magic trick is done. Looks like everyone really enjoyed it.

That was quick, Jules.

Good. Good for him. *Go with God*, as my father likes to say, usually when someone cuts him off on the freeway.

I sit back down and crank up the music, hard. *Go with God, Jules.*

Sometime after lunch, I get a feeling. Something's up. There are some whispers from a couple girls seated near me, maybe a look my way, I could just be imagining it, but it feels . . . familiar.

Next class, something more, a little suck-in of silence as I get near a few kids in the doorway and their conversation chops off, and after I pass there's a release of under-breath chatter. I get this Pittsburgh vibe, people trying *not* to look at me. Heads magnetize toward each other, sharing a phone screen, that quick look, and then away.

It's not me, I tell myself, it's not about me. *Don't catastrophize.*
But after fifth period, in the hall, it's unmistakable, a fury of
whispers, exclamations of words I can't hear, *ping-ping-ping* bursts.
Eyes. Flickers. Stares from classmates I've never talked to.

It's happening. Something.

What.

You know what.

My hoodie's pulled up by now. I do my own flicker and
stare, glancing without glancing. It's this game where everyone's
motionless until you look away, then there's quick movements,
sounds. Like freeze tag. And you're it.

End of day comes, finally, *finally,* I push out into the open air
and at first everything feels normal. Everybody's on their way
to the next thing, and the next thing's not me. I'm just part of a
crowd. *Okay. Breathe.* I wonder what all the freak-out was about.
Maybe it was seeing Jules, or just my mind playing with me.

And then I hear it, coming out of a phone somewhere to
my right, only a few words but I recognize them immediately,
the way you know an old song you once loved by the first few
notes:

—*might be trans or know someone who's trans or have questions um
we are saying hello Hello*—

Look at me, not losing my shit. I'm not going to let myself.
That's where all the catastrophizing comes in handy—it keeps
you ready.

There's a group of four girls huddled at a round table nearby, all
in blue and white with frizzy black hair. One girl has her phone

out, and they're surrounding it close, like it's a trash can fire in the dead of winter.

—to like see how we're getting through it. And is there something you'd like to say Adam?—

Yes, yes, there is something Adam would like to say.

One of the girls sees me approaching and elbows another and their eyes all widen in my direction.

"Where did you get that?" I ask them.

"What?" the girl with the phone says blankly, pushing it into her chest.

"I can still hear it," I say.

"It's nothing," says another girl.

"It's me," I say, trying to sound all kinds of reasonable. "Can you tell me where you got that from?"

"Look," says Phone Girl, trying to shut it down, "we support you—"

And then they all join in—little birds chirping their support— they're totally with me, they can't believe I changed so much oh my God!, they like my hair, they think I'm so brave yes so brave brave brave!—but all their words just flap around my head, swooping, I can barely breathe there's so much fluttering in my face.

"You look like an actual guy!" one of them chirps. She really said that, yes she did.

"Great, okay, but—here's the thing," I say, cutting through the cawing. "Thank you, but I don't really care if you think I'm brave. I just really want to know who told you about this, because it wasn't up to them to tell you so if you could just tell me please who—"

"You know it's on YouTube, right?" says Phone Girl. "Anybody can see."

—*say hello Hello*—

"I can still hear it!" I shout.

She looks down. "Dang, I must have pressed replay."

Out of the corner of my eye I see an arm raised, and when I look around there are kids toasting me with their phones and oh yeah, I remember this, it's freshman year, the sequel. Kids are the same everywhere, why did I think it'd be any different. I feel that pressure in my chest, my binder pulsing red and tight through all the layers, *here I am!* and that's my signal to go, because I will not be upset in front of the school, no I will not.

As I'm walking away another kid comes up to me, older guy, looks familiar, maybe I sold him some gulab jamun before, he steps in and says, "Hey, you okay?" But I can't answer him, can't even focus on his face, there are just too many eyes everywhere. "You know my sister is—"

Sorry, man, got no time to hear what your sister is, gotta go, gotta get out of here.

I turn around and take off for the bike racks, wondering how the video got spread around so fast—Jules? Gregg?—but it doesn't matter who. None of them matter. I hear someone yell, and it sounds like my name, but even if it isn't, I duck my head, because when you're trans, all shouts are homing missiles, aimed straight at you.

The yells become trucks, rumbling on my tail. Twice I almost get clipped on my bike, like I'm in a thriller and the shadow government is trying to run me out of town. One pickup truck gets so close I almost smash into a parked car trying to get over. "Go back to ISIS, motherfu—" a man's voice screams out the window. Their bumper sticker has an American flag on it, and Calvin peeing on the word *Obama*, a reminder that, oh yeah, there's that, too.

Why is it still so damn hot in this city? I'm tired of it.

I head for home, thinking of Jules and his new friends, and whether he got so popular by trading in stories about me, maybe complete with multimedia proof. *Boy, what a close call I had!* I can imagine him telling them. *Holy Crying Game!*

As if he'd know what *The Crying Game* was.

Chill. Just chill.

I think of a video Evie and I made, about ways to combat an attack of dysphoria. Like we knew anything. I think we just read a whole bunch of Tumblrs and cribbed from them:

Light a candle

Talk to a friend

Write a poem

Go for a walk

Yeah, like I want to write a poem. And Evie has never lit a candle, guaranteed. Why am I still hearing Evie's voice, when I thought I left her behind in Pittsburgh?

Dad's gone. I retreat to the bedroom, throw my backpack on the floor and scrunch myself into a ball on the mattress. I think of my room back in Pittsburgh, my very own room, and this wave of homesickness hits me so hard I almost push through the wall I want to get back there so bad. I haven't felt this since I got here, missing my lizards, my dark curtains, my bed off the ground, the funk of me, just me. Hell, I even miss Sudhi-Sue.

But mostly, Mom.

Mom doesn't take shit from anyone. She keeps a lot of it away from me, too, as much as she can. I remember two summers ago, when I started my transition, there was a block party on our street, and she dragged Susie and me from family to family. To the people we didn't know she'd introduce us as her son and daughter, and to all the people we knew already she made a point of saying, "And I don't know if you heard, but my *son* has a new name now. It's Adam." And while she was saying this, she looked at them with grappling hooks in her eyes, daring them to look away before she got a nod or a smile. At the time it made me die a thousand deaths, but now I get what she was doing—securing the perimeter. She was making sure that on our block, at least, I was going to be known how I wanted to be known. There were some awkward silences, some forced smiles, but if she ever got more flak than that, it never got back to me.

Bloop bloop bloop bloop. Ring. Ring.

She might not answer. She might be getting my sister ready for bed, or helping with her homework, or—

Mom.

"Jack," she says. She's at her desk in the tiny nook between the living room and the kitchen. Behind her I can see into the room, an arm of the recliner with the purple-and-white blanket thrown on top, best seat in the house, a corner of the coffee table stacked with DVDs we never get around to shelving. Home.

There's got to be an upgrade to Skype, where you can virtually feel the other person's touch, some VR where their long fingers can come through the screen and cup your face, sensors that allow you to feel their arms around your shoulders or get a whiff of the Aveeno Baby lavender lotion that they're always spreading on their hands. Because that's all I want, right now.

Mom looks at me from above her reading glasses—she was doing bills. She stares, sussing me out. "How are you, my darling?" Her mouth tightens and her eyebrows hunker down, she's bracing herself for the worst, waiting for the other shoe to drop. In my mom's world it's always raining shoes.

"I'm good," I say. "How's Susie doing—is she still calling herself that?" Which is a question I absolutely hate, because I used to get that all the time, and yet here it is coming out of my own mouth.

"Susie is fine," she says. "She's going through . . . her Susie things, but she'll be fine. Now, what's wrong?"

"Nothing. Why?"

"You never ask about your sister."

"Okay, how's Nova and Spike?"

"Your lizards are also fine." She takes off her glasses and waits for the bad news that she's sure is coming. When she leans forward, filling the screen, you can really see the pouches under her soft brown eyes, those eyes with the worry spiking through them.

"I'm okay, really. Stop it."

She gives a little sigh and sits back. "Where's your dad?"

"Not home yet."

"Mmm. How's school?"

I tell her school's just . . . fine, but that tiny hesitation gives me away. "What happened?" she asks immediately.

"Nothing."

She raises an eyebrow.

"It just gets a little old sometimes, you know, being The Trans Kid in school."

She nods. "Hmm . . . Well, you know, my darling," she says slowly, "you *are* a trans kid in school. There's no getting around that."

Well, there *was*. But I don't tell her that.

"Are they giving you trouble?"

"No . . . not really. It's just, a lot of eyes on me."

"Hmm." Mom puts a finger to her lower lip, strokes it. She relaxes a little. We've been through this before. "Just be yourself. People will settle down once they get used to you. Most people. The ones that matter."

Not always.

"Is there anyone else there who's . . . like you? That you could talk to?"

I think of Magenta Streaks. My mom doesn't know about me going stealth, don't think she'd understand it. "Not really," I tell her.

"What does your father say?"

I shrug. "I hardly see him."

"Mmm." The lines between her eyebrows furrow a little deeper. "Well, Jack, you're in Los Angeles. I'm sure there are a lot of resources. I know there's an LGBT Center in Hollywood,

I looked it up, and they have a youth—"

I shake my head, because that's not what I want, out here.

"But if you need support, I'm sure you could call—"

"I'm good. Really. I am. I'm just . . . letting off some steam, that's all."

"You can always come home."

She said it. My face freezes, trying not to show how good that idea sounds right now.

"Oh, yeah, it's *so* much better there. I've got *tons* of friends."

"It might not be perfect here, but it's *home*. And I miss you."

"Right."

"I do. I'm counting down the days, believe me."

I think about spilling everything then, about Jules and the video and the water stain over the bed and the serial killers down the hall. But I don't tell her. Mom deserves a break. I can handle this on my own.

"I'm fine."

"Oh, Jack." She sighs. "There's always a period of adjustment, my darling. For them as well as you. I remember when your father and I first moved into our house, I was the only brown person on the block for the longest time, and . . . Remember Mr. Karlin down the street? Older man? He had that little dirty white dog that kept yapping all the time?"

The dirty white dog sounds familiar, but I have no memory of the man.

"You might have been too young to remember him. Anyway, the first time I met Mr. Karlin was when we had just moved in.

I was unpacking and getting the house cleaned up that day, I think I was in sweats and some old T-shirt, taking the garbage cans to the curb, and this man walks by with his dog, it wasn't on a leash and it jumped up at me, barking, oh, I hated that dog, Betty, that was its name, Betty, and he stopped and asked me, I remember this so well, he asked me if I had any extra time available, because he needed someone to clean every other Saturday and did I do light yard work? He also complimented me on my very excellent English."

I can't even imagine. "Did you obliterate him?"

Mom shakes her head. "No, of course not. I was going to be *living* among these people. I had to get along with them." She laughs. "But believe me, for the longest time I never left the house without putting on makeup and a full wardrobe. Heels, even *heels*."

It's like me with my binder and hoodie. Armor. "So, what happened?"

"Eventually, it got better. People recognized me. And then you came along, and there were *two* brown people on the block."

"Did Mr. Karlin apologize?"

"No, but he turned out to be a very nice man. I could never stand the dog, though. Oh, such a . . . *kutta*, Betty was, always knocking down the garbage cans."

"Wait, what is that?" I think of Nani, sipping tea on the couch. "What does *kutta* mean?"

She blinks. "What?"

"*Kutta.* Nani called me that once. I was running around like a *kutta*."

She stares at me a moment, very still, in her eyes I see a downpour of shoes dropping. I wish I hadn't brought it up. "Oh. That was so . . . why do you remember that?"

"Because she sounded so mad."

"She was always so mad. It was her natural state." Mom takes a deep breath. "*Kutta* is a kind of dog. A street dog."

"Oh. So Nani thought I was a street dog?"

"She thought you were . . ." Another deep breath. "She thought I wasn't raising you correctly. I wasn't bringing up a proper Indian . . . child."

I bet that wasn't the word Nani used. A proper Indian *girl* is what she probably said. Why does that make me feel worse than being called a street dog? "Yeah, damn right."

"Jack—"

"So, I disgusted her so much she ran back to—"

"No. No. Don't do that." Mom's eyes can be soft, then hard, in a single blink. "Nani was dissatisfied with *so many* parts of my life. With me. She was very traditional, very rigid, and I wasn't going to buy into any of that nonsense, so . . ." Her hand drifts up and away, disappearing from the screen, off to another continent. "It has nothing to do with you." Mom looks about ten times more tired than she did a minute ago. "Let's not talk about Nani, all right?"

"Yeah. Sure." I need to stop this conversation anyway, I need to get off the screen, because a wave just broke, I feel so goddamn sad right now, but I don't wanna drown my mom in it. "I gotta go anyway, I've got a ton of work to do. Don't worry, it's all good

234

here. Really. Talk later. Miss you, too."

The moment my laptop closes I feel the panic birds arrive, restless and hungry, all snapping beaks and claws. The room's getting darker, the water stain on the wall is the shadow of Nani, staring at me, at her failed *granddaughter*, it's like, she knew about me, even before I knew, and in her eyes that made me a wild dog.

My ribs cinch tighter, squeezing my breaths into tiny gasps.

I don't want to go back home.

But I don't want to stay here, either.

I don't know where I want to go.

"Damn it!" I yell to the water stain. I had a plan, it was a good plan, and now it's all blown up. I want to be Jack again, Jack who's just arrived in Los Angeles. Jack before he met Jules. Strong and sure. Jack when he was Jack and nothing else.

I still can be. Just in a different way. Breathe. Breathe. Buck the hell up.

"It's all good," I repeat out loud. "It's all good." *Breathe.* The afternoon light is almost gone. I try not to disappear with it.

Boom goes the bedroom door, scaring the shit out of me. Dad makes a surprise entrance, I didn't hear him pound up the stairs, he must have popped out of some trapdoor. He's practically glowing, bringing the hall light in with him. "Guess who's the newest client of Duvall and Blum?" he announces, flicking on the light, giving me his best Captain America. "*And* guess who already has an audition tomorrow? *And*—why are you sitting in the dark?"

19. Jules

I yell to Jack, but I'm not surprised he didn't hear me. He doesn't even look back, walking across the courtyard away from the table of girls he was talking to, heading to the bike racks. It's the first I've seen him at school. Not that I'm avoiding him or anything, it's just . . . everything's calming down, and if people see us together, it might start the chatter up again. So even as I'm calling out his name I'm swallowing it, so what comes out is more like a random shout, one strangled syllable that barely leaves my lips. And before I know it, Jack's already on his bike, pushing off on the pedals. And for a moment, it feels like that's how it's always going to be, Jack getting farther away, getting smaller, disappearing from sight.

Over the next few days it's like we've made an unspoken agreement to keep away from each other, which I guess is for the best. Jack's nowhere to be seen during nutrition, and I'm off on the other side of campus at lunch with my newfound friends. I've left the awkwardness of a frosty Cecilia behind (with Gregg parked at her elbow) at the sophomore benches, and somehow gained admittance to the exclusive, gay-friendly club of Lowell and Lily Cho (or Lo-Cho, as they like to call themselves). It just seemed to happen. It's like they adopted me. The three of us sweep out of class as one unit and settle onto our patch of grass for lunch without ever even deciding to, all our movements powered by the sheer wind velocity of Lo-Cho's conversation.

In class, they're low-key chatty, but out on their own, they create this hurricane of conversation, back and forth, back and forth, with me forever trying to just stay on my feet. They speak in shorthand—quick overlapping word bursts, like they're trying to beat each other to the end of the sentence, or like they're building this ladder of conversation with only half the rungs, and when they've reached the top I'm still stuck below, trying to figure out how they got up there. Even when I do keep up, I barely have any idea what they're talking about. So much reality TV . . . who knew there were so many Housewives to keep track of?

Today they're making a life-and-death decision about who would be crowned the best contestant *of all time* from the seven seasons of *RuPaul's Drag Race*. I guess Lo is a superfan of one of the queens, and Cho will straight-out murder him if he doesn't agree with her choice. They go at it for a while, throwing words like *fierceness* and *realness* into the air, and shoving Instagram photos on their phone at each other.

Lowell turns to me for support. "All right, who's *your* favorite?"

I look at both photos and say, "They both look pretty . . . fierce. And . . . real."

Lily Cho is *shocked* that I would dare call her queen real, when she is *so* not about being real, and I realize I'm in over my head and have to admit that I've never seen the show. They both gasp.

"I'll start watching right away, promise."

Lily Cho purses her lips and coos. "You are *such* a baby gay."

Lowell shakes his head. "I don't know. He might not like the show. He's too nice."

"I'm not too nice, believe me."

"Right." Smirks all around. "You are super nice," says Lily Cho, and I know that's not exactly a good thing.

"When are you coming to a GSA meeting?" Lowell asks. "I'm feeling outnumbered."

"Why? Who else is there?"

Lowell scoffs. "Mostly straight girls and a few curious boys. And *Kacey*." He turns to me. "The nonbinary kid with the dyed hair. Never says a word. Extremely dull."

"Lo!" says Lily Cho.

"We need some full-on, conforming, cisgender, m4m gays to attend." Lowell points at me.

"You are a cisgender sexist *pig!*" says Lily Cho, swatting him. I'm guessing I should be shocked, too, but I'm too busy trying to decipher what all those words they're throwing around mean.

Lily pulls herself up from the grass. "Forgot to get my Diet Coke. Anyone want anything?" And without stopping for an answer she looks at Lowell. He nods. She turns to me.

"I'm good, thanks," I say.

Lily Cho keeps staring. "C'mon, what do you want?"

"Okay, um, whatever is fine."

"Diet Coke?"

"Sure, whatever's easier."

She exhales. "It's not like one soda weighs more than the other."

"I want the more *difficult* soda!" pouts Lowell as she jogs off toward the lunch area.

We laugh. The laughter trickles away. Silence.

More silence.

There's always this constant chatter between Lo and Cho, but now that she's gone, Lowell and I seem to be in low battery mode. Mute. He checks his phone. I chew on my cold vegan burrito. I can hear, really clearly, the cars driving by the building.

Lowell's seated so perfectly, legs drawn up, posture straight, that he could be posing for a catalog. His long fingers swipe along his phone so delicately it's like he's petting a very small cat. I imagine him as a homecoming king, waving at the crowd, his crown pushed back at a precise angle for maximum jauntiness. He would, as Lily Cho says, "Work that sash." And who'd be standing next to him? I picture myself, in my sweaty team uniform and scabby knees. Doesn't quite work.

Lowell looks up from his phone, catching me in my stare, and I look away, continue with my chewing. Lowell gives me a friendly smirk. I smile back. There's a pause, each of us ready to jump in.

He goes back to his phone. I swallow. Cars rumble.

"So," says Lowell, head popping back up. "You do basketball, right?"

"Yeah," I say, nodding. "You like basketball?"

He grimaces, shakes his head. I laugh. He smirks.

And that's really all we have to say on the subject.

Swipe. Chew. Rumble.

Lily Cho trudges up the hill, arms full. "I come bearing booty!"

239

Lowell's head snaps up. "Hooray for Cho's booty!" he calls. We both wave and she gives an appreciative wiggle. "What took you so long? We thought you were kidnapped."

And . . . we're back on, full power.

"Look at what I've got!" Lily Cho says in her high singsong voice, all excited. She passes a Diet Coke to Lowell and sets the others on the ground. Then she extends her hand, displaying a little paper to-go bowl, like the kind you get for an order of fries.

"Ta-da," she says.

Inside are two little balls of Indian fried donut holes.

"He's selling them again!" Lily Cho says.

I want to jump up and knock the bowl to the ground. I have to squeeze my hands to keep them still. Of course he's selling them again. Why wouldn't he be? Even without me . . . Of course he would.

"You look nauseated," Lowell says. "Should we not eat them?"

"No," I say. "They're really good. People love them."

"They were going fast," says Lily Cho, settling on the grass.

Lowell rubs a finger over the cleft in his chin, almost like he's still swiping his phone. "I bet he's selling more than ever. I mean, now that he's *known*."

"A YouTube personality!" Lily Cho giggles. "And he's cute—*so* cute! I just want to put Adam in my pocket and *shake* him he's so cute."

"Jack," I say. I can't imagine Jack would be very happy being in anyone's pocket.

"Oh right, Jack. I'm just used to him being Adam in the videos."

"Videos?" I get this sickening feeling, of more videos being passed around the school. "More than one?"

"They have a channel, him and Evie," Lowell says. "They made—"

"—Tons of them," Lily Cho echoes. "We binge-watched."

"*You* binge-watched," Lowell says. "I got bored."

"Didn't you watch?" Lily asks me.

"Uh . . . I didn't." It doesn't seem right, watching Jack's videos like they were just another reality show.

"I was going to introduce myself, but he's *so serious*," says Lily Cho. She demonstrates with a scowl. "Wouldn't even look me in the eye. All business."

Lowell waves a hand. "I'm sure he's fine, if he's back to selling. Are we eating these things?"

I get a sudden twist in my stomach. Just last week we were traveling table to table, every day, so excited, selling these dough balls, and now we're on opposite ends of the school, he's *so serious*, and I have no idea how he's doing.

I jump up. "You know what? I actually don't want the Diet Coke, sorry. Um, I'm just gonna see if they have a Sprite. Anyone want anything?"

I don't know what I'm looking for, or expecting, peeking around the corner at the lunch area like a cartoon spy, but I see Jack right away, circulating, his backpack over one shoulder, just like always. He doesn't seem any more serious than before. Good, I guess. Part of me's glad he's doing fine on his own. The other part of me, the unfair part, wishes he looked just a little more, well, like he missed the company.

"Hey, Donut Boy, can we ask you a question?" I know that voice. I look over and it's Gavin, seated with Hayden and another guy. They're hunkered down, elbows pressed on the round stone table, watching Jack.

They look hungry.

Jack nods, moves closer, his back to me. Gavin runs a hand over his buzzed red hair. "We're a little confused. What exactly is it you're selling?"

I see Jack's backpack slipping off his shoulders. He starts to open it up when Gavin interrupts him: "What do you call them?" Gavin rubs the palm of his open hand with the thumb of his other.

"Indian donut holes," I hear Jack say.

"Are they holes? Or balls?" The two other boys hang their heads down to keep from cracking up, but Gavin keeps his eyes on Jack.

Jack stands with his backpack half-open, really, really still.

Gavin has both palms moving slowly up and down like a scale. "Holes? Balls? Which?"

Hayden whispers loudly, "Maybe both."

The third kid snickers. "Or neither."

Gavin's eyes haven't left Jack's face, Jack's face that I can't see. But I can see his right hand, which is gripping his backpack handle so tightly he's going to tear it right off.

Jack. My heart starts pumping fast. Before I can move, Jack yanks his backpack off the table, knocking a tray to the ground, and turns, while behind him the guys have finally broken into hoots, *Hey, pick that up!* palm slapping palm slapping palm. And Jack walks off, giving them a middle finger over his shoulder, head up and staring hard, without seeing anyone. He enters Building C, and then he's gone.

The lunch bell rings. I look back at Gavin. He stands, his lips curling into a slow, satisfied smile, and then he's gone, too. People surge all around me, making their way back to class, but I can't move. I'm trying to understand how I could ever think Jack was having a smooth time of it, with someone like Gavin around.

I guess I thought, he's Jack, he can take care of himself. No. That wasn't it. The truth is, I wasn't thinking at all. I was so relieved that I wasn't getting the Bishop Academy experience all over again, I wanted to believe it was going to be the same for him. But it wasn't. For all I know, it's a completely different experience being outed as trans than being outed as gay. I have no idea.

Transgender. I hadn't even heard the word until until my last year of middle school. Men who wanted to be women. And then Caitlyn Jenner came out at the end of my freshman year, but I didn't really pay much attention to it. Why would I? I didn't know anyone who was trans. I figured it didn't have anything to do with me.

But now, I know Jack, and I'm still as clueless. I mean, forget about whether or not it would have worked, us together, or whatever. Just on a friendship level, I could have been there for him, like Jamal was for me, when all this came out. Though, if I'm being completely honest here, I don't know if I have it in me to be like Jamal, to be able to stand up to people the way he does.

Maybe I'm not strong enough to be Jack's Jamal.

But, Jesus, I could at least try.

How do I know what I should know if I don't know it?

I wait until Mom has gone to bed before I open up my laptop and start watching. I've got my headphones on and the bedroom door closed, but I still turn the volume down. I feel like I'm reading someone's diary.

I start with the oldest YouTube video, the one sent to me on my phone, but on the bigger screen I see them much more clearly. It was less than two years ago, but Jack-as-Adam looks so, so young. Shy, and sillier than I ever thought he could be. He can barely look into the camera. Evie bounces on the bed they sit on, flips her hair, talks a mile a minute.

I watch the other videos, in order. They must have made at least one a week. Evie has a lot of different looks, mostly by changing her hair, but her face and body stay the same. Adam, though, I watch Adam transform video by video, from the new Adam that he was into the Jack I know. It's incredible, like watching a time-lapse of puberty right before my eyes. And it's not just physical. By the last video, he's got the energy and the confidence that makes Jack, Jack. You can watch Evie fall in love with him in these videos, it's obvious, at least to me, because I can see myself staring through her eyes.

It's past one when I finish watching. The videos answer a lot of questions, but there's still so much I have to learn. I snap the laptop shut and click off the light, but my brain is still on, on, on. Jack's transformation. I can't imagine. Against everything the world was telling him, against what his own body was telling him, how could he have been so sure of who he was? How did he figure it out?

Will I ever be so sure about anything?

hey jack

its jules

duh

hows it going

hows the selling

heard you ran into some assholes yesterday

real jagoffs right

u heard?

i mean i saw

gavin can be a superdick

u should tell someone

dont worry about it

if u need anything lmk

nah im good

ok

Adam: *Hey all it's Adam here*

All alone

And where could Evie be?

Wait what's that sound?

[moaning]

Oh no it's a ghost help

[screaming]

Evie: *Ow why is it so hard to get this sheet off of me ow*

[Title: A Very Special Adam and Evie Halloween]

Evie: *Hi guys it was me could you tell?*

Adam: *Shocker*

Evie: *It's Halloween time*

So we want to talk about our own Halloween experiences growing up

Adam you go first

Adam: *Okay well so when I was young Halloween was like the exact opposite of what everyone around me was experiencing?*

Like for them it was all about dressing up in costumes and being this other thing

you know a superhero or a witch or whatever

But for me it was the rest of the year where I was in costume

The skirts and the hair clips and the wrong shoes

Evie: *Yes*

247

Adam: *And Halloween was the one day where I could be who I really was a boy*

I mean I was a boy who looked like a hobo or a pirate or a baseball player but I was still a boy

I remember this one time I begged my parents to buy me this Spider-Man costume it was like the first store-bought costume they ever got me

And it had all of this muscle padding built into the chest and the shoulders and the arms and I remember putting it on and it was like oh

Yes I never want to take this off ever again

I wore it like every day after school for a week until it mysteriously disappeared

I wish I had it now I could use it

Evie: *Ha you've got your own muscles look at you*

Adam: *No no don't look don't look*

Evie: *Muscles here and*

Adam: *Okay*

Evie: *Here and*

Adam: *Stop no really stop*

Evie: *Okay*

Adam: *What about your Halloween?*

Did you do the Disney princess thing?

Evie: *Are you kidding me no way*

If I tried to dress up as a girl

I would be dead

My father?

248

No.

But seeing all those tutus and gowns come out

All the tiaras and wands

And none of it on me?

I hated it

Oh my God I cried so much

Whenever I had to put on the superhero stuff ugh

Buzz Lightyear no way

Adam: *Too bad we couldn't have switched places*

Evie: *Okay?*

There was one year oh my God okay I was going as a ghost

You know an old sheet like this one?

Eye holes cut out the whole thing that was my entire costume

Big sheet queen size

Adam: *Appropriate*

Evie: *Okay?*

But but underneath that sheet I stole my little sister's Cinderella costume from a year before and I put that on in the bathroom

It had these cap sleeves and the little ruffles all up here

And I wore my jeans under the gown and the gown was a little short so it was perfect

I was like a ghost on the outside

But underneath I knew I was a princess

Adam: *Aw you should have been a ghost every year*

Evie: *Yeah but at the end of the night something slipped*

I forgot what oh I was reaching up or something

and the sheet kind of moved and my mom saw a little bit of

the blue sparkles from the dress
She yanked me home so fast
But thank God it was her and not my father
Never again
Adam: *That sucks*
Evie: *That's Halloween*
But at least now I don't have to wait for a holiday
To dress how I want to dress right?
At least here
Adam: *You can be free on YouTube woo-hoo*
Evie: *Oh Adam I bet you were a really cute Indian pirate*
Adam: *I was*
Evie: *Will you dress up as a pirate this year?*
For me?
Pretty please?
Adam: *Okay moving on happy Halloween everyone*
Evie: *Hee hee happy Halloween*
Adam: *Eat a lot of candy*
Evie: *Be who you want to be love yourself*
Adam & Evie: *You are perfect bye*

20. Jack

It shows how much I've been camped out in my own ass these days that I forget school is celebrating Halloween a day early, even though that giant billboard outside on the lawn has been announcing it for two weeks:

HALLOWEEN AT EARL WARREN

FRIDAY OCT 30

NO MASKS NO WEAPONS

Not that I would have dressed up even if I had remembered—I mean, it's not like I need to draw *more* attention to myself.

The campus is pretty evenly divided on the whole dress-up/no dress-up issue: a third of the kids going full-on with costumes, a third just putting on a wig or a hat and calling it a day, a third not giving a shit. Guess what third I'm in.

Nutrition break. I scan the quad. Your typical outfits: Avengers, wizards, hobbits, witches. Social media is big—I see a couple of Twitter feeds, a few Snapchat animal filters come to life, one junior is an entire iPhone, which I have to admit is pretty impressive, except for where the home button falls on his body. "Wanna wake up my screen?" he wanders around asking. Gross.

And, of course, here they come, the boys dressed up as women, as cheerleaders and lacrosse players or just lazy drag—a towel stuffed under a T-shirt with a wig. I guess there could be some guys secretly expressing their inner selves, but I'm feeling judgy and not buying it. They're doing it for laughs. Take exhibit A, the two across the quad, both dressed up in flaming-red pigtailed wigs with big blue bows that stick out from the side of their heads—they're either going for Pippi Longstocking or that girl from Wendy's. Wait, I recognize these guys, it's Gavin and one of his sidekicks, Gavin the redheaded douche from the holes and balls incident, wasn't that fun—*Holes? Balls?*—I still flinch when I think of it, my chest still tightens, I should have known, *I should have known*, when he called me over that day, just from the look in his eye, that shard of meanness poking out, that he was gonna be trouble.

Fuck him. I'm not gonna be scared off from selling these gulab jamun while I'm here, no way I'm going to eat the cost of these things just because a few slack-jawed freshmen like jerking off to the sound of their own voices. Please. I've been through worse. When I came out as trans in middle school, about three-quarters of the kids I grew up with since first grade just cut me out, I was like Carrie at the prom, everyone running for the doors to get away. So, a couple of jagoffs here in Los Angeles? Nothing compared to that. Some curious eyes, some whispers? Whatever. I can live with that for seven more weeks. Go right ahead, Gavin, keep squeaking in that girl voice, prancing around the lunch table, *Isn't it weird looking like this?* At least I know where to avoid.

I look out for Hernandez, and when I don't see him I kind of walk slowly around the tables nearby, my backpack in my arms. Not much selling's going on today, not with all the candy being slung around. Doesn't matter—selling these things don't have the same Kennywood roller coaster thrill that it used to have with Jules—now I'm just a human vending machine. Oh well, price of doing business.

Gregg's sitting alone at the sophomore benches, no costume. He looks sleepier than ever, slumped over his backpack, not even playing on his phone. I look around for Cecilia but she's nowhere to be seen. That's why he looks so lost. Without her to pull him around, he's like a dog off-leash who doesn't know what to do with himself.

His head jerks up. "Oh hey, Jack," he says, brightening like he hasn't seen me in a while, though we just had physics together three periods ago. "Um, I think Jules is looking for you or something?"

"Well, he knows where I am." My answer drops a little harder than I mean it to. I offer him a donut hole to make up for it. "On the house."

Gregg puts out his hand, I scoop a ball into it, and, *pop*, the whole thing disappears into his mouth. He licks his palm. "Thanks, dude," he says, flecks of gulab jamun glued to his chin. He swipes his face with his hand, and then licks it again. I guess it's a compliment.

"Where's Cecilia?" I ask.

Gregg's head drops. "I dunno. She's hanging somewhere else. I think she's mad at me." When I ask why, he shrugs and flips the hair from his eyes. "Mmmm. I think she thinks I didn't stand up for her or something?"

"Oh." We're silent for a moment. "Is it true?"

Gregg shrugs. "Doesn't matter." He looks up at me. "How are things going with you?"

He's throwing out a line, but I'm not biting. "Everything's good," I say, squinting at the courtyard. "Everything is *great*."

Gregg nods. "Cool . . . Cool." We both stare out, contemplating how great everything is. "Wait," he says, "did I tell you Jules was looking for you?"

"Yeah. I'll keep it in mind."

There's a shout thrown across the blacktop, the kind with an edge to it that cuts through the schoolyard chatter. Gavin's twirling his skirt and hooting, throwing his arms up in the air as he struts. He's on the move, my eyes follow the path he's taking, and I know, I *know*, he's heading to that person sitting alone at the corner of a long table.

Magenta Streaks looks down and away. Their long hair drapes over most of their face, glasses hiding the rest. They're doing their best not to be seen, to ignore the whole situation, but it's not going to go away. Gavin gets right up close to them, shaking his false boobs like he's a pole dancer and Magenta Streak's his only customer.

"Is it like Halloween every day for you, Kacey?"

Kacey. That's their name.

I don't care if this is Los Angeles and the school has all the right rules and rainbow stickers and everyone signs an anti-bullying statement, there's always a bad kid with a sideways smile, or a red Supreme jacket, or a silver nose ring and soccer player legs, to make life a living hell for someone else, as long as no one's around to stop them.

I'm drifting closer without thinking about it, my legs moving on their own.

"—Whadya think, Kacey? D'ya think I *pass?*" I hear Gavin say.

A few stares, some snickers, but no one is getting up. I'm holding the plastic tub close to my body with both hands, like it's a child and I've got to cover its ears, *You shouldn't hear this, little plastic tub.*

"I'm really a woman, too! Look at me!" He grabs his fake boobs and gyrates.

Kacey's quiet, just hunching down, small. That cringe, Evie's body bent that way, too, the day they dragged her off to the bathroom—

(*What are you looking at faggot*)

—the day Adam did nothing.

Jack, though, Jack's a different boy.

"Hey, Gavin," I yell, with a voice that's been waiting so long to come out. I'm so calm I don't even feel the black wings rustling in my chest, though I know they're there. "Hey, Gavin."

I'm so calm.

21. Jules

Quiff is a real word. It sounds like something you do when you're getting high, but actually, it's a hairstyle. All the fashionable teen pop stars wear their hair this way, though on me, it looks more like a guinea pig has set up camp on my head.

I haven't kept up with One Direction for years. I'm really not into that kind of music. And yet here I am, watching YouTube on how to get my hair to look just like Harry Styles's. You wouldn't believe how many videos you can find on just that one subject.

I don't have the length for Harry's man bun, but I'm hoping there's enough for a quiff. It takes a lot longer to get my hair going in the right direction (the One Direction?) but luckily, once it's been blow-dried and brushed back into a small tsunami wave, I have a whole shelf of unused hair care products my mom has bought for me over the years to cement that sucker in place.

I stare into the mirror at my ridiculous self. Too late to turn back now, not without a chisel and a fire hose. I barely have enough time to apply the essential Harry Styles tattoos. Here's the plan: I show up at school with my quiff and tattoos and leather arm bracelet. A guitar if I can find it in my closet. I walk right up to Jack and say, "Hey, Zayn, don't you think we should get the band back together?" And he's going to smile. I'll extend my hand: "Friends?" and he'll laugh and shake it: "Friends."

That's how I imagine the reconciliation is going to go. English accent optional.

Man, Harry Styles has got a lot of tattoos. The anchor, the rose, the heart, and two badly drawn swallows on my chest are all I've got time to marker on before I'm seriously late for school. I'm already in black jeans, boots, and a loose white tank top that I've always been too self-conscious to wear. I finish the look with the leather strap bracelet and sunglasses. I'm complete.

Harry Styles, though, is sexy and cool. What I see in the mirror is Jughead from the Archie comics, trying to look like a rocker. But I can't back out now. I've got to get to school.

My mother stands in amazement, won't even let me out of the bathroom. She doesn't know who I'm supposed to be, but she's still impressed. "Wow," she says, hugging me. "I barely recognize you."

"Don't touch my hair," I warn, "or it's gonna crash."

I kiss her and run out before she starts asking questions. I jog the few blocks to school, where everyone's already filing into first period. No sign of Jack. It's then I realize I've forgotten the guitar. *Damn, this plan's already falling to pieces.*

Entering Ms. Partington's English class, I brace myself for what people are going to say, but it turns out I don't have to worry about that. No one's going to notice me at all. Not with Lily Cho in the room.

Lily Cho blocks out most of the class with her giant sky-blue ball gown, which balloons out at the waist and billows down to the floor like a parachute. She's got on ruby fishnet stockings under the dress and silver heels to finish the look, but what's most impressive is what's towering above her. If I thought my hair was high, her white wig is stratospheric, all swoops and curls with pearls and bows and feathers; it's like a peacock balancing on her head. She looks seven feet tall.

Circling around her is Lowell, who's in a white ruffled tuxedo shirt and a bow tie the same color as Lily Cho's dress, outlined with what looks like pink frosting. On his head is a hat like the Mad Hatter's, only made to look like a wedding cake, with candles stuck in the brim and the pink words "Eat Me" scrawled across the top.

Lily Cho shoos Lowell away with an open fan clutched in her hand, her hair wobbling. "Fly away, *mon petit gâteau*! Feed the masses!" she commands, and Lowell charges cake-first into the giggling classroom. Poor Ms. Partington stares up at a corner of the ceiling, waiting for the frenzy to die down.

Lowell almost runs into me at the door and stops dead. "Whoa. *Jules*." He nods in approval.

Lily Cho sashays up, fanning herself. "Well, look at you!"

"He really Sandied out," Lowell says.

"Yes!" agrees Lily Cho. "He *totally* Sandied."

"I totally what?" I ask, confused.

Lily Cho explains. "Remember in *Grease* when Olivia Newton-John gets all hot and slutty and perms her hair at the end of the movie and struts her stuff at the school carnival?"

"That's you, Sandy," finishes Lowell.

I haven't seen the movie, but I'm pretty sure that's not what I was going for. "Do you know who I am?"

Lily Cho frowns. "Give us a hint."

I make a half-hearted attempt at air guitar. Point to my tattoos. Try to bop to no music. They look blankly. "Come on, *mates*," I say, in the world's worst English accent.

"Some kind of pirate?" Lowell asks.

I give up. "Harry Styles," I say, and they both give a cry of recognition.

"Wrong shirt," says Lily Cho.

"Different sunglasses," says Lowell. "But," he adds, seeing the disappointment on my face, "good arms."

"*Very* good arms," says Lily Cho.

"Well, it's nothing compared to you guys," I tell them.

"That's what happens when your mom does wardrobe for a living," says Lily Cho. She bends forward, or as much as she can without toppling over. "But do you get it?" Her wig quivers with anticipation. She points to herself, then to Lowell.

"Let them eat cake?" I say.

"*Exactement!*" she shouts as she twirls and nearly takes out an entire row of desks.

After class, I shoot a text to Gregg, who I'm guessing will be on his phone for a quick zombie apocalypse in between classes:

if u see jack tell him i want to see him

I immediately wish I could take it back—it sounds like something strict and parent-y, not the light and friendly tone I was going for. But it doesn't matter. Jack will see me in this getup and there's no way he's not going to bust out laughing. It'll be fine.

I tell Lo-Cho that I'll meet up with them in history (Mrs. Coleman will love their historically appropriate costumes) because I'm heading to the lunch area for the nutrition break, but they insist on coming with me.

"I'm not going to miss this," Lily Cho says. "You really think we don't know why you dressed as Harry Styles?"

"What?" I squeak, and it doesn't sound convincing, even to me.

"Harry, Harry, Harry," sighs Lily Cho, "we always knew you had a thing for *Zayn*."

Busted.

"Do you deny it?" asks Lowell, folding his arms.

"We're just friends," I say.

"That is *exactly* what Harry Styles always says," Lily Cho fake-whispers.

Lowell sighs. "I think it's a bad idea."

I feel my face getting red. "Why?"

"Because"—smirk—"band members should never mix." He gestures toward the door. "Shall we?"

The three of us head to the lunch area, Lily Cho using Lowell for support, and I wish it were just me meeting up with Jack, but then the two of them start singing that One Direction hit "Best Song Ever," and it's so cheesy it makes me laugh. This could work. I'd have backup. I imagine a flash mob, all singing and dancing while I extend my hand. Why not? Even Jack wouldn't be able to resist.

"Jesus," Lowell says sharply. He's looking across the yard at a dude prancing around in a dress and red pigtails, hooting loudly. "What is that idiot doing?"

The idiot looks familiar—the way he's walking, the cocky way he angles his head. Gavin. Why is it always Gavin? He's calling out to someone alone at a table, that kid with the dyed red hair and blue fingernails. I can't exactly hear what he's saying, but you don't have to hear the words to know it's not good.

"Kacey," Lowell says.

"Shit. Someone should get Mr. Hernandez," Lily Cho says, but they're both frozen in place, watching. There's only one person moving toward Gavin, and he's moving fast.

"Hey, Gavin!"

It's Jack. His voice has no emotion in it, it's like he picked up something that Gavin had dropped and wants to return it, but the only thing in his hands is the plastic tub filled with the Indian donut holes, and the way he's striding across the schoolyard is almost robotic, tight and tense. He's close enough that I can get Gavin in my view, too. Once he sees who's calling, Gavin stops dancing and smiles like they're old buddies, and Jack stares right back, not breaking his stride, while his left hand dips into the tub and pulls out a dough ball, raises it, and I rush forward, yelling, "Jack! Jack!" but already I know I'm too late.

22. Jack

it's heavy with syrup but oh so light in my hand, the size of a tiny snowball, ready to melt with the smallest crush of my fingers but I hold it like it's a baby bird, ready to fly

and it flies

I can't throw worth shit and it splats on the bench next to Gavin, spraying little particles of sweet soggy shrapnel into the air, misses him entirely but that doesn't matter

hey, it's balls and holes! You got any balls or holes for me?

yes yes I do, here comes one winging your way and this one almost makes the grade maybe 'cause I'm closer but he's got to shimmy his bluebonnet ass to the side to avoid a direct hit and it lands on his sneakers

now he's sideways smiling he's got a batshit grin on his face and his eyes open wide like I just asked him to the dance *oh yes I will, I will dance with you*

and off come the pigtails

fast he's floating toward me fast

my throw misses again but that doesn't matter

I've got lots one for Gavin one for Dhyllin one for Roman with the soccer player legs, these things can't hurt anyone they're too soft but that doesn't matter

I'm not even aiming anymore he's so close, I just dip my hand in and throw, dip and throw and dip and throw, faster faster fly fly my pretties, and one hits him square in his Dorothy Gale checkered chest and his smile curdles into something like a snarl like an animal but that doesn't matter

dipandthrowdipandthrowdipandthrowdipandthrow

and somewhere along the way I dip into nothing, there's no more throw to throw, but that doesn't matter, there goes the tub but he swats it away and I just keep my arms moving whipping air into the air

and he says something but I can't hear it I can't hear anything but the flapping of wings inside me so loud and fast keeping me moving toward him, close enough to dance now and both my arms are throwing

I can't stop me and his fists can't stop me and I'm finally FLY-ING it feels so fucking good to FLY arms FLYING body FLYING it's like the panic birds were pecking at my chest wanting to get out and now I've released them all and they pour out of me into the air into him there's no space between him and me that's not filled with black wings beating

beating

SO FREE—

From behind, arms wrap around my chest (*God not my chest no*), pull me back and away and to myself. The arms fall with me to the ground. In the space opening between me and Gavin sound rushes back in. Mr. Hernandez shouting. Gavin yelling.

Laughter. My own breathing. My name being called, over and over again. *Jack. Jack. Jack.*

Quiet. The taste of blood. Blue sky. Chemtrails, a white spine across the blue. Green ferny leaves, like feathers, on the branch of a tree, quietly nodding. My breath. My breath.

"Jack."

I'm on my back. The pressure of the hands on my shoulders feel like they're keeping me in place, keeping me intact. Holding my body so I can step back into it.

An anchor. A rose. A heart. A bird. A face hovering over mine.

Harry Styles.

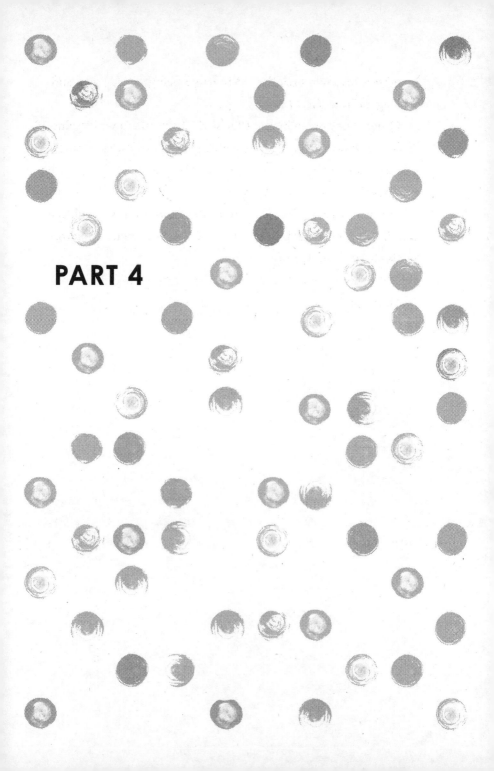

PART 4

23. Jack

Focus on the sounds.

Kids are in the hallway outside the door. Don't understand what they're saying but you can tell from the speed of conversation they're ramped up on sugar, or gossip, or both. Volume spike, a quick babble of words, another spike, a laugh, and they're gone.

Locker slam. Another.

Another.

Keep it together.

A river of conversation, a big group flowing by.

Slam.

Keep your eyes pinned to the nameplate on the desk in front of you. Wooden nameplate. What shape is it? *You know this.* Triangular prism, that's it. Gold letters on a metal rectangle. Keep staring at it. Memorize each letter. M. R. S. C. H. A. N.

There's a little plant next to it, wilted and forgotten, drooping in a pot covered with red foil. Behind the nameplate's a small metal picture frame, but there's no telling who's in it, it's not for you to see.

M. R. S. C. H. A. N. M. R. S. C. H. A. N. M. R. S. C. H. A. N.

Don't forget to blink. Try not to disappear.

Clack-clack-clack down the hall. This must be her, you can tell by how sharp and sure those heels are, echoing and then stopping, no hesitation. Important footsteps. Doorknob rattling, squeaky hinge.

She doesn't speak until she lowers herself into her chair. It complains a little, then shuts up. The nameplate's centered below her chest, a subtitle:

Mrs. Chan

Student Counselor

"Shall we begin?" Mrs. Chan asks, but she doesn't wait for an answer, she swivels back to get at her right drawer, pulls out a sheet of paper. Sets it down in front of her, next to a folder that she's brought in, then *tap-tap-tap* on her keyboard.

"Jack Davies," she announces, like she guessed the right answer in a game show. In the form of a question, please. *What is Jack Davies?*

I am Jack Davies. Jack Davies Jack Davies Jack Davies Jack Davies Jack

She bends herself over the piece of paper, begins filling it out. "Date. It's ten . . . thirty. Isn't it?" I think she wants an answer, but then she saves me the trouble. "Of course. Day before Halloween," she murmurs, continuing to fill out the sheet. "Oh, Halloween. You keep me busy, don't you. Every year. Time?" I look up at the clock behind her, but she's already checked her computer screen. "Ten thirty. Oh. Look at that. Ten thirty on 10/30. Huh."

I may as well not be here. Maybe I'm not. Maybe I've died, a casualty of the Great Gulab Jamun Massacre of 2015. Someone needs to *Sixth Sense* me. What happened to Gavin? Is he a ghost, too? How much of this blood on my hoodie is his?

Mrs. Chan lifts her head. "How's your nose doing?"

So she does see me. "It's fine," I mumble, lowering my hand, looking at the wad of bloody tissues I've been jamming into my left nostril. "I think it stopped."

"Jack."

I know she's waiting for me to look at her. She's the patient type, we might never leave this office. I flick my eyes up.

Mrs. Chan's entire face is built for delivering bad news, eyes that crinkle down like frowns behind her glasses, a mouth that's already disappointed in me. Only her eyebrows are happy to be there—penciled on high, constant surprise, striking out in the opposite direction from the rest of her drooping face.

Focus on those.

"You'll want to get some ice from the nurse after this," she tells me, staring at my face for way too long. "Under your eye. It's starting to swell." Now that she's got that out of the way, she straightens up for official duty. "How it works is this. We are going to fill out an incident report detailing what happened this morning. Then you are going to go have a talk with Mr. Shanley, who makes the decisions about . . . what happens next." Her voice is low and soothing, a hostage negotiator, or a nurse at a psych ward. "At the very least, you will be going home today, in the company of a parent or guardian."

Fine. Good. Get me home.

"There may also be a restorative justice circle. Do you know what that is?" I shake my head, so she explains. It's something about collective agreement and all parties coming together and conflict resolution and something something South Africa, but all I hear is this: me sitting in a room with Gavin and talking things out, about the last thing in the world I want to do.

"I'm good," I say.

Mrs. Chan's eyebrows nudge up another inch. "It's not a choice. Not if you want to stay at this school. But let's not worry about that right now. Let's talk about what happened." She picks up her pen. Clicks it. "You're on, Jack. Jack?"

Jack Jack Jack's my name don't wear it out

"To be honest," I begin slowly, "I don't . . . remember a lot." Which is true, it's not a stall, I'd like a high-def replay of every time my fist connected, every blow to that smug bastard's face, but it's all a blur of colors and movements I can't put in any kind of order.

"According to Mr. Hernandez, you had a physical confrontation with Gavin Miller, is that correct? And that you provoked the incident. True?"

I shrug. She waits a moment, then tries another angle. "Can you tell me how it started? Did you have words with Gavin? Some kind of argument?"

"No."

"You know him though."

"No."

Mrs. Chan's eyebrows are so fed up they've disappeared into her hairline. "So, you went up to a total stranger and picked a fight? Is that what you did?"

I swallow and say to her nameplate, "When I see someone being a total asshole to someone else—"

"Hey, let's be a little more respectful, okay?"

"Okay. When I see someone being a total *jagoff* to someone

270

else—I can say jagoff, right?"

Mrs. Chan's eyes look away while her hand tells me to keep going.

"Then I feel like I need to do something, or something." A surge of electricity zaps the haze—I did do something. I got him back. For Kacey. And Evie. And me. *Fuck you, Gavin, fuck you*—

"All right." Mrs. Chan is finished scratching on her form. "And you think that Gavin was being . . . . *disrespectful*, to someone else. Yes? Would that be fair? Good. And was that someone else Kacey Sherman?"

"I guess."

"Do you know Kacey?" I shake my head. "No? All right. What did Gavin say to . . . Kacey?"

But I'm not getting any more involved. Sorry, Mrs. Chan, this is my stop, let me off here. I shrug. There's nothing else I want to say, no matter how many times Mrs. Chan sighs. She scribbles a little more, moves on to the next box.

"So, your idea of doing something about it is to throw food at Gavin? No, shrugging is not an answer, let's forget about shrugging. A *shrug* does not give us the kind of detail we need for this report."

"I guess I did, yeah."

"Mm. You threw these . . . pastries, am I correct? You had a large quantity of them. Mr. Hernandez also seems to think that you were selling them on school property, which"—she goes back to whispering to her sheet of paper—"is another thing." She's got her pen about to touch down when she looks up at me. "Is it true? Were you selling them? And *try* to answer that without any movement from your shoulders, please."

"Yes," I say loudly, "I was."

Mrs. Chan is so pleased to have something definite to write she almost hums filling in her box. "You are lucky," she says, still scribbling, "that these pastries are not being considered a weapon, which would have gotten you in a *lot* more trouble."

The thought of gulab jamun being like the nunchuck of Indian desserts is so funny I can't help but snort. Mrs. Chan stops skritching, stares at me above her glasses. Her eyebrows dare me to continue.

"This is serious, Jack." Her tone. Did something happen to Gavin? He was surrounded by kids when I came back to earth, and then I was hauled away before I could see him. Maybe I really hurt him. Scarred him. That would be horrible. And excellent. Horribly excellent.

"So, after this . . . throwing of *pastry*, you two got in a physical confrontation, is that correct?" I nod. "What happened?"

My shoulders start to twitch up, but Mrs. Chan's eyebrows keep them pinned. "I don't know. I guess he punched me. Or I might have punched him. I really don't remember. Is he okay?"

She sighs, figuring out how much she'll tell me. "He'll survive. His right hand may have a fracture."

A fracture. That sounds serious. "How did he get it?"

Mrs. Chan looks at me sadly and points a finger at my face. "The same way you got that."

"You mean, by smashing into my face?" No. No. That is unacceptable. "Anything else?"

"No, he seems to be fine otherwise. Don't look so disappointed! It's better for you that you didn't hurt him!"

It's not better. It's definitely worse. All that rage, that righteous fury, for nothing? How pathetic did I look? *He punched like a girl*, the comments will read. I close my eyes, breathe in through clenched teeth, try to swallow down the fluttering.

Mrs. Chan continues with her soothing voice. "However. You did provoke the confrontation. Unless . . . was there some previous incident?"

What is the use of saying anything?

Mrs. Chan sighs again and places her pen down. She glances at the shut door behind me, then clasps her hands in front of her on the desk. Her voice goes even lower. "This is not the first . . . incident, involving Gavin. There have been several." She looks at the mayor on the "D.A.R.E. to Resist Drugs and Violence" poster on the wall, like he interrupted. "Several, yes, already, and it's only October." Back to me: "So it would be . . . helpful . . . if I can get all the facts behind this situation. Helpful to me, and . . . to you, and to . . . others." She lowers her head and looks at me over the top of her glasses.

But there's nothing else I want to say to her, except, get me home. And stop staring at me. It only makes things worse.

Mrs. Chan taps her nails against the folder on her desk, quickly opens it, reads. She opens her mouth to say something, doesn't, shuts it. Closes the file. Clasps her hands again. Her interlaced fingers pulse with all the words she's not saying.

"Jack." She tries again. "Was there something he said to you . . . anything, that might have made you feel . . . un . . . safe?" She says that word slowly and deliberately. "Anything he said to Kacey that you felt made Kacey, *or* you, feel . . . unsafe? Singled out?"

There's what feels like a full minute of silence, where I swear, I can hear the entire building: the ticking of the clock, footsteps, the rattle of combination locks being solved, doors echoing closed. I know what she has in that folder. What she knows. It's all games, but I don't want to play. I just want to dissolve into little pieces of sound, I want to echo down the hallway, blow out through the doors and into the wide-open sky, where the wind can carry me away, *whoooosh*, lost forever.

I shrug.

Mrs. Chan sighs so long I look up, expecting her to be a deflated puddle of disappointment pooling on her desk. Instead, she's staring at me with a sadness in her eyes that makes me think of Mom.

"You know, Jack, if you don't speak up, how do you expect anything to change?" she says softly. "By fighting? You think that's going to solve anything? It won't." She sets her pen down for one last sigh. "We can't help you if you don't tell us what's going on." She pauses, waiting for me to pick up my cue.

M. R. S. C. H. A. N. M. R. S. C. H. A. N. M. R. S. C. H. A. N.

Mrs. Chan keeps looking at me while she punches a button on her desk phone. "Lucy," she says, "please call Jack Davies's father. Tell him Jack is going home now and will need to be picked up."

24. Jason Jules

jack u still around?

My phone buzzes back within a minute, but not from Jack. It's Lowell:

Where are you? You need to come!!

you promised! it is PACKED

I forgot, it's the last Friday of the month—GSA lunch meeting. I run from our lunch spot up to the fourth floor. The door to Mr. Janssen's class is closed, but through the glass pane I can see that, sure enough, it's a packed room. Word must have spread.

Lowell's at the front of the class, his cake hat tucked under his arm. I watch him pace back and forth, his one free hand gliding and stopping and gliding again, like a hawk catching air currents. I hear the students clap at something he says. It's obvious he has no problem talking in front of a whole group of people—only Lowell can be dressed in frosting and cake and still be taken seriously. It all comes so naturally to him.

The seats are taken, kids are lined up against the wall, listening. Mr. Janssen's sitting in the back of the class, looking grim. A lot of tense faces, but none more than Lily Cho, who stands by the windows, tall and terrible in her giant wig and dress, looking like an avenging spirit. In front of her, like they'd just come through the curtain of Lily Cho's gown, sits Kacey, the only person not looking at Lowell. Their hands are on their lap, smoothing the pleats of their kilt, shoulders hunched forward, head lowered and turned away.

Lowell catches my eye and waves me in. I reach for the handle, but . . . I just can't do it. I know I should be in there, to support Lowell, to support Jack, but I can't make myself enter. The idea of being bottled in there for the rest of lunch . . . I feel this restlessness in my legs, just standing at the door. I shake my head and smile. Lowell frowns but keeps talking, and I straighten up from the little window and step away.

In the hallway, pressed against the wall, my legs don't stop shaking. Why am I still so jittery? Moments from the fight keep flashing in my mind: me pulling Jack away from Gavin. Jack striking his arms out at nothing, like he was having a fit, so stiff and sharp and then complete deadweight in my arms. How he never said a word, the whole time. Even when Mr. Hernandez yanked him to his feet and pushed him toward the administration building, he might as well have been sleepwalking. I didn't know where he went, but he was *gone*.

I can still feel his weight against my chest.

Lowell slips out into the hall, closing the door behind him.

"Why didn't you come in?" he asks, a puzzled look on his face.

"I don't know, I just didn't want to interrupt. How's it going?"

Lowell looks skyward, puffs out his cheeks. "Oh, a shit show. We aren't allowed to *say* anything, no *naming names*"—he rolls his eyes—"but everyone wants to know what's going on." He tilts his head closer to mine. "I guess Gavin's been harassing Kacey for months. No one told me! I mean, hello! That's what the GSA's for!"

He stops and stares at the dirt and bloodstains on my white muscle shirt, my wrecked hair and smeared tattoos. "How are *you* doing? You look like *zombie* Harry Styles."

"I'm okay. Had to go to the nurse just to, you know, get the blood off me."

"Yuck." Lowell lifts his chin, narrows his eyes. "You really jumped in there, didn't you? Well, come on in."

But before he can reach for the door, it swings open, and a blue satin tidal wave spills out into the hallway—Lily Cho's dress, carrying along with it Lily Cho, a chair, a trash bin, and Kacey.

"You know I'm not totally mobile in this outfit!" Lily Cho says furiously to Lowell, untangling herself from the chair and pushing it back inside. "You left me stranded!" I've never heard her voice sound so deep and so urgent. "Mr. Janssen's passing out handouts, and—" She manages to get the door shut, takes a few heavy breaths, then swings Kacey in front of her. "Kacey. This is Jules. Jules, Kacey wants to talk to you."

Kacey looks at me with anxious gray eyes that look huge and watery beneath their glasses. They don't even wait for Lily Cho to finish. "How is Jack? Is he okay?" Their voice is soft and low and fast. "I hope he's okay."

"I'm not sure," I say, starting to feel jittery again. "I hope so, too."

Kacey bites their bottom lip, begins twining their hair with nervous fingers. Their fingernails are dark violet, with a yellow lightning bolt painted in the middle. "You saw, you saw what he did, right? For me?" I nod. "He, he didn't have to do that. Why would he . . . He doesn't even know me." It's almost like they're talking to themself.

Lily Cho, towering above, pats Kacey's shoulder and says nobly, "It's what allies do."

"Did Jack also have problems with Gavin?" Lowell asks.

I feel this instant stab of guilt. "They had a run-in last week. Jack told me he was okay, but—"

"Gavin is a pig," says Lily Cho fiercely. "He should be kicked out of school."

"He's mostly just ignorant," Kacey says. "I've known him since—"

"We really need to go back in," Lowell tells me, interrupting Kasey. "If Jack needs support, he should come to GSA meetings. He's always welcome—"

"How would he know that?" Kacey's voice is so soft it's almost a whisper.

Lowell cocks his head toward Kacey. "Uh, what? Anyone's welcome."

"Well, I don't feel welcome," Kacey says to a spot on the floor. Silence.

Lowell adjusts his glasses, like he's trying to see Kacey better. "How can that be? You're here every meeting."

Kacey looks to the wall, tucks their hair behind an ear. "That, that doesn't mean I feel welcome. I mean, even the name: 'Gay–Straight Alliance.' What if you're neither? It's like you're trying to make us choose."

"Oh, come on, that's—"

"That's what?" There's a sudden spark in Kacey's pale eyes. "Words matter. And . . . You should hear what you sound like sometimes. It's not welcoming. You never ask about *my* issues, you don't ever even talk to me."

"I ask for pronouns every week!" Lowell says, looking to Lily Cho for support, but all she can offer is a small wince. Lowell takes a breath, starts again. "If you want to talk, you should talk. I just didn't want to single you out, make you uncomfortable. You don't say much, so—"

Kacey finally looks up into Lowell's eyes. "I don't *say* much because I *don't* feel comfortable."

I wait for the smirk, the putdown, but for once, Lowell doesn't have a comeback. He stares at the wall, takes a breath, and turns back to Kacey. "I'm sorry you feel uncomfortable. No. Wait." He starts again. "I'm sorry I *made* you feel uncomfortable. I didn't mean to. If you want, you can talk now. You should." He sighs. "But we really have to go in, before lunch is over." He looks at the rest of us. "Okay?"

"Actually," I say, "I was going to go to the office and see if Jack's still here, just to check on him, so—"

Lowell throws his hands up and chokes back a laugh, all his frustration funneling my way. "So why did you even come?" He presses his lips together, squints at me.

It's a good question, and I fumble for an answer. "Because you asked . . . and . . ."

"Let's all go!" says Lily Cho. "He shouldn't be alone, poor baby!"

"Oh, let Jules go," says Lowell quietly. "They've got a *history*." And the way he says *history* makes me blush.

"I just want to make sure he's okay," I tell him.

"Of course," he says, and a smirk finally appears on his face, but this one is a small, sad one. "Tell Jack we're behind him." He pushes my shoulder. "Go."

Before I take off, Kacey stops me. "Could you, could you tell him, um, thank you from me?" They've suddenly turned shy again, quiet, twirling and untwirling their hair. "And, and that I'm sorry for all the trouble, for everything?"

"Sure," I say. "But I think that Jack would feel like standing up for someone is definitely worth the trouble."

Kacey smiles for the first time, a sweet, hopeful smile that lights up their entire face. "That's what I thought!" they say. "Definitely he would. Definitely."

Down the hall of the administration building I see Jack, sitting in one of the chairs outside the vice principal's office, head bent down, hoodie up. His arms are locked across his chest, like he's afraid to release them or they'll fly off again. His whole body's so tight and still, I don't know how to approach. *If* I should approach.

Do I sit next to him? Do I stand? The way he's staring hard at the floor, pressing himself into the chair, it's like there's a force field all around him: *do not enter, do not come near.*

"Hey," I call out.

Jack's head jerks up, like I'm someone else he needs to fight, and then he squints at me, confused. I realize I'm not very *me* in this postapocalyptic rocker outfit. I mess up my hair, trying to break up what's left of the lift, smile and wave.

He doesn't return the smile, but I can see his body loosen enough to take a deep breath, and he gives me a small nod. His left hand reaches up and rubs beneath his right collarbone, as if he were remembering my hand pressed there. He's back. I've never seen anyone disappear like Jack did, his body like a cave he could hide in. It scared me. But now he's back. I take a deep breath, too, the deepest I've taken all morning. He's back.

Before I can get any closer, a man comes barreling down the hall past me, the fastest you can walk without running, and heads straight for Jack.

"What the hell, Jack? Are you okay?"

It's his father, out of breath and angry. He grabs Jack's chin and examines the bruises. "God*damn*," he swears. They stare at each other while Rick's breath goes back to neutral. Then Rick grabs the top of Jack's head and shakes it, whether to loosen him up or knock some sense in, I'm not sure. He lets go, pulls open the office door, and walks in.

Jack stands slowly. He shoots one more look at me, adjusts his hoodie, and shadows his dad into the office.

At least I know he's all right. The class bell right above my head shrieks so loudly I almost shout along with it. I trudge toward the archway leading to the courtyard as the hall fills up with students, falling in with everyone else, just one more backpack, one more pair of sneakers, but I feel like I'm in a bubble, isolated from all the chatter by this swelling of relief, and then dread, and then both at the same time. I can't shake it, until turning to go out into the courtyard I almost collide with Gregg coming in.

"Oh good," he says. "I was looking for you."

"Hey." I haven't really seen Gregg much these last few weeks, but there's no time to feel awkward because he's so agitated. His hands are jammed into the pockets of his army jacket and his head's up and darting around so you can actually see his face. It's the most awake Gregg's been since school started.

"Have you seen Jack? Is he okay?" He grimaces, expecting the worst.

"I think he's fine," I say. "He's in Shanley's office now."

Gregg exhales, relieved, and pushes his hair out of his eyes. "Man, that was some crazy shit. I was talking to him, and then all of a sudden, he, like, went into berserker mode."

"Yeah."

"Did you see all the phones in the air?" Gregg shakes his head. "There's gonna be a *lot* of Snapchat videos."

I hadn't even thought about that before now, though of course people would be recording. But it seems like the least important thing to worry about today. "I don't care," I say, and I don't.

"Well, it was good you pulled him away when you did. I

thought he was gonna get slaughtered."

"Me too." The what-if of it makes my skin prickle all over again. "I'm just trying to, you know, be there. For him."

"Yeah. Sure." Gregg pauses. "So does that mean you guys are, like, back together now?"

"No! I mean, as friends, yeah, but more than that, no. It's not—you know . . . we were never gonna—that wasn't going to happen." It's frustrating, having to explain this to Gregg. "Remember? You were there."

"Oh, right." He crinkles his head, like he's working out a math problem. "But I forget. Why?"

"Because, Gregg . . . stuff." It's such a Gregg thing to ask. There are so many reasons and complications, so many unknowns, I don't even know where to start. "Lots of . . . stuff."

"Huh." He nods slowly. "Like what?"

"C'mon, Gregg. *Stuff.*" I swat his shoulder and shake my head at him like the reasons are so completely, utterly obvious, they're not even worth mentioning, but that's only because, at that moment, I can't come up with a single one.

25. Jack

The quietest car ride home, ever.

Usually, there's no shutting Dad off, he's like DVD commentary running under a movie, just constant, constant talk, it doesn't even matter if I've got headphones in or not, he'll keep going. But on this ride, nothing. Dad stares straight ahead, watching the road, biting his lower lip. He hasn't said anything since we left Mr. Shanley's office, nothing about his latest audition, who he met last night at the blah blah blah showcase, the student film he's working on today, or was working on, until he got the call from school.

Nothing. Just silence, crowding the car like a balloon filling up and up and up and up.

It's not until we're halfway home that I remember. "Shit. Just drop me back at school, okay," I say. "I gotta pick up my bike."

The car doesn't slow down. No blinker.

"Dad. Dad."

He answers, low and careful. "You can leave your bike. You're not going anywhere the next four days."

"What, you gonna keep me locked up or—"

He cuts me off with a full-on wrath-of-God look.

"Watch the road!" I shout. "Pedestrians! Jesus."

He jerks the car to a stop. The yoga mom crossing the street with her labradoodle, stroller, and Starbucks looks up from her iPhone long enough to glare at us.

"Way to almost get us killed," I mutter.

He keeps staring at me, even when the cars behind us start honking. "You know what, buddy? You don't get to have that tone with me right now. You really don't. Especially when I had to call the director *on the way to set* to tell him I couldn't be there because my son was being *suspended*. Yeah? Understand?"

I was wrong, silence is better.

He parks on a side street near our house, takes the key out of the ignition, and sits back, rubbing his head. "Jesus." All I really wanna do is get into our room, turn off the lights, plug in the music, and curl into a ball for a few hours. But we both know we're gonna have The Conversation, whether I like it or not. Now. In the car.

"Fighting, Jack? Really?" my dad says. "What's going on, huh? This isn't you. You don't pick fights."

Well, apparently, I do.

"Is it the testosterone? Do we need to get your levels checked?"

I shut that down double fast. "No. Don't blame the testosterone."

"Then what? You didn't even try to explain yourself to Mr. Shanley. You said you didn't know this kid. So, what?"

The problem with parents is they ask all these questions you don't have the answers to, and you might have them if they just left you alone for two minutes, but they never do. They want it all explained right away. So, you have to ladle out some half-truth bullshit just to get them to back off.

"I saw him being an asshole, so."

"Jack. Lots of people are assholes. You don't go around beating them up."

"I didn't beat him up! He's not even hurt! I suck at beating people up!"

"That's not the point!" Dad looks at me with microscope eyes, worried. "Buddy. Look at me. Did he do something to you? I need to know."

I shake my head. "It's just your usual schoolyard thing. Not a big deal."

"Hah." He sighs and sits back. "You know what's gonna happen when I tell your mother, don't you? You'll be hi-ho hi-ho-ing off to Pittsburgh on the next flight."

"Then don't tell her."

He slides his eyes my way. "Jack. When your mother agreed to let you come along with me on this little adventure, we promised, we *promised*, swear-to-God-hope-to die, that you were going to be able to handle being on your own. Being more independent."

"Yeah?" I say, like we'd already ticked off that box.

"Well, obviously it's not working out. You're suspended from school! Two days next week. Does that sound like things are hunky-dory in Jack Land?"

"I'm handling it, Dad."

He grimaces, showing all his teeth, like an ogre. "Doesn't look like it, buddy."

"Come on! You said so yourself, I'm more confident and socializing and—"

"Yeah, but that was before all this."

"It was a one-time thing! I mean, Jesus, you should be happy I was defending myself!"

Dad's eyes bug out, and he points a finger at me, Sherlock Holmes style. "You *were* defending yourself! He *did* do something!"

I pause, then tell him, yes, words were said the day before. And he makes me repeat them. And then his eyes narrow. "That fucker," he says. I don't say anything, because him swearing is a sign, he's stepping away from Parent on High and onto the schoolyard with me, fists up. "Why didn't you tell this to Mr. Shanley?"

"Dad, I'm not going to narc."

He wavers. "Yeah, but . . ."

"I took care of it. It's not going to happen again," I say, steady as a hitman. If this were my mom, that answer would never fly, not in a million years. My dad stares at the windshield, like it's gonna give him answers. I stay still.

"I told you, you should be taking self-defense classes," he says finally. I agree, totally, whatever, yes.

"So, don't tell Mom," I say. "You know she'll only worry."

He breathes out slowly and runs a hand through his hair. "She will." He puts on the stern face again. "You promise me you're okay? You're safe? This isn't a cry for help?"

I need to get out of the car, the air's too thick, the roof's closing in. "Promise."

"And if that jagoff does anything else—"

I nod, absolutely.

"Okay," he says, after a long sigh, "let's see how it goes."

My legs are begging for movement, but I don't open the door, 'cause he hasn't given the sign yet, the release.

"I should call the director, let him know what's going on."

"Is it too late to go?" I ask.

He waves a hand. "Eh, they said they were running late anyway. They might not even get to my scene today. Told me to come in at three, but . . . I'm gonna cancel—"

"No, you should go."

"It's just a stupid student film, anyway."

"It'll be your first LA credit, come on."

"True . . . And it's a whole scene, I could use it on my reel—" He drums his fingers on the steering wheel.

"Absolutely."

"But I should stay home . . . yeah?" He looks at me, like he's asking for permission to go. I'm this close to saying, *Why don't you stay home, we'll make some microwave popcorn, put in a movie, I'll even let you pick, yeah, stay home.*

"Go. I'm good."

He pretends to think for a moment more, but I know he's already made up his mind. "Wait a second," he says as he sees me reaching for the door.

I keep my grip on the handle. "What?"

"Give me a hug." Dad holds out his hands, waves me over.

God no Dad—

"Remember when you first told us you were trans? Remember what I said?"

I shake my head, because all I can think of right now is the house, the room, the mattress.

"I told you that I didn't care if you were a girl or a boy or even a Ravens fan, just as long as I could still give you hugs. Remember that?"

I do. I drop my hand from the door and let him wrap his arms around me even though being touched is pure hell right now. I close my eyes and think that I'm gonna relax into it but I don't and I hope he doesn't feel every muscle in my body just shrinking away, the rustling of wings under my binder. Finally, a tight squeeze, and I'm released. He can't get at my hair so he scrunches my hoodie instead.

"You're my boy," he says, grinning, and I do my best to grin back honest.

I thought I was gonna feel okay once I got to the house. It's all fine while Dad's here, me on the bed, plugged in to my headphones, him bustling in and out of the room, muttering his lines, getting into his part as a cop, but as soon as he takes off, I don't know, the thoughts just start creeping back in. The quiet in the room keeps poking, poking at my chest, at my hips, my hands . . .

I imagine how I'll look on the videos all those kids must have taken on their phones, today, me and Gavin, what comments they'll make, *look at the boy dressed as a girl fighting the girl dressed like a boy!* and for what? It didn't change a damn thing.

He won. I couldn't even land a punch.

I shouldn't have chased Dad away, we could have watched *Aliens* or *The Terminator*, something where the big baddie gets blown away at the end.

(*Holes and balls balls and holes*)

The Terminator. It can't be reasoned with, it can't be bargained with—

(*Holes and balls*)

—it will absolutely not stop. Ever.

(*how much are you—you know, like, your body is it—*)

Flutter flutter flutter flutter.

Deep breath.

Come on. Your mother was badass enough to freeze out her own mother, you can get over a jagoff in the schoolyard.

"Take a walk! Exercise can be really helpful to clear your head," I remember Evie saying on YouTube. "It can also make you feel stronger, more in control of your body when there are so many things that are out of your control . . ." That was YouTube Evie. Real-life Evie would say, "Bodies just fucking suck sometimes, don't they?" Evie got it.

I wiggle my finger like the kid from *The Shining*. *Evie's not here anymore, Mrs. Torrance.*

I know I'm technically grounded, but I figure going out for my mental health gives me a pass. The LA River is close enough that I can get there without a bike. I walk past warehouses and abandoned factories and car shops in my neighborhood, watch them turn into squat single-family houses with dying grass in the yard or no grass at all, just a few cacti heaving out of the weedy dirt lawns behind chain-link fences. An underpass, a few more blocks, then the *click-click, click-click* of skateboards.

Marsh Street Skate Park. Concrete, two ramps surrounded by dirt, but clean. The skaters dress like me, hoodies and baggy pants, hiding everything but their grace and swagger. They roll up the single ramp and down again, and when they fall off their boards they get right back on, no big thing, part of the drill, super chill. I ghost into their bodies when I get near, try them on, the careless shuffle, the loose way they hang their limbs, I imagine myself part of their gang, flying up the ramp, the sudden switch in direction, easy as gravity, the fall to earth, the high five as I roll back to the others.

"Hey." A skater boy, waiting his turn, calls to me. Pointy face, buzz cut, sharp eyes and thin lips like Gavin's. "S'up." A question, or a challenge? The rest of the pack swing their eyes in my direction.

I nod, lift a hand, but whoops my legs have lost their swagger, rhythm's off, moving too fast, these legs wanna leave before the boys suss me out and their chill heats into something else, sorry gotta go. I escape through the archway, into another park, a giant rattlesnake statue on guard, stone coils rising out of the grass, metal tongue flicking. There's a dirt path, a small play area on one side, exercise equipment no one ever uses on the other, and, through another gate, the LA River.

Miles of concrete to get you far away from what you're running from. No one's around, the bike path's all mine. Wilderness down by the river, hard city above. There are hipster fingerprints all over; some of the warehouses along the path have been gutted and turned into art studios, you can see bright slashes of color inside, and murals competing with the rust for space on the outside walls.

Across the water there's a giant homeless camp, more than a camp, a village, jutting out from the muddy bank, in among the bushes, protected by leaning trees looking at their reflection in the water. Blue painter tarps, sheets, milk crates and grocery carts, a few burnt-out TV sets, giant cardboard boxes and even some artwork in frames, propped up on the tree trunks, a scavenger's studio.

Decay, and change.

Evie would love this place. She'd love the color. There's a mural near where she lives, giant letters spray-painted on the underpass, *Polish Hill* in blue and red, outlined in black, the only thing she likes about her neighborhood. That mural would fit perfectly along this river.

Don't think about Evie. She's not thinking about you.

My phone buzzes, and for a hot second I think it's her, damn she *was* thinking about me, that used to happen all the time, this psychic thing, *I was just about to call you when you called!* Evie's texting to tell me to stop being such a drama queen, that I've got it good, and can we meet at Skinny Pete's for coffee, but I have to treat 'cause she's low on cash.

But of course it's not her.

hi

I answer Jules's text so quickly it's like I've been waiting for it all day.

> hey

just got out of practice how ru

> everythings good

really

> yeah

u at home

> down by the river my usual

cool

your dad lookd pissed

I step back from the edge of the river, concentrate on my phone.

> nah hes ok

no way my mom wld be hysterical

ur dads pretty chill damn

> i guess ha

gavins off the team 2 weeks plus 2 day suspension

what abt u?

same mon tues

not too bad

ur staying out of school more days than in

ha yes part of my diabolical plan

MWHAHAHAHAHAHAHA

mastermind

thats me

And it's like we're back at the old Jack and Jules, before the video came out, and the more my fingers type, the more normal I feel. If I could just text with everyone instead of having to actually see them, my life would be So Much Better.

hey do u know the movie grease

duh yeah

am i a sandy

or sandied

WHO IS SANDY

olivia newton-john did someone call you sandy?

lowell did tday in my costume

Jules in his skinny black jeans and muscle shirt with muscles included, the Harry Styles behind me on the schoolyard, pulling me away. It comes back in flashes—him so close to my body, him holding me in place—and it doesn't freak me out like I thought it would. And then I remember the two birds peeking out the scoop of his shirt when I saw him in the hallway, his very own panic birds, painted on, flapping out of his chest just like mine.

> **yes ur a sandy**

> **is that a good thing**

> **fuckyeah**

I search around for a minute and find a GIF of Olivia shimmying in her tight pants and halter top, send that to Jules. It's a long moment before he answers.

> **what**

> **WHAT**

> **man**

And I laugh out loud, first laugh of the day. First laugh of the week.

We text until he's at his front door.

ok gotta go

bye harry

HAHAHAHA

bye zayn

When he signs off, I look up—the streetlamps have switched on, how is it so late? The buildings behind me are dark, the sky beyond the river is a fire dying down. There's a little wind whipping down the path, it's actually getting cold, I get whiffs of rotting green from the water, swampy and metallic.

I stare down at my phone, trying to coax one last text out of it, it's a tiny ember of light I'm holding in my hands, but it's gone quiet. With one click I snuff it out. Time to go, before the river shows its night side and Dad gets home. I hurry down the path. By the time I reach Marsh Park the rattlesnake has almost disappeared against the bushes. I slip through the gate, watched by the ranger who's getting ready to lock up. The skateboarders have disappeared. The shadows are coming out.

26. Jules

"And I'm telling you, Jules, you're going."

My mother sets her shopping bag by the front door and shifts a bunch of poster board signs from under her arm. She was up all Friday night making them, glass of red zinfandel in one hand and a thick Sharpie in the other. "Come on, I'll let you pick," she singsongs, waving the cards in front of her like she's doing a fan dance, trying to entice me.

BOO! on Reservoir Developers!

and

Land Grabs are SCCARRRRY

and her personal favorite,

Don't TRICK Silver Lake!
TREAT our residents RIGHT!

She's on her way to an emergency Save Our Reservoir Endeavor meeting, followed by a *spooooky!* afternoon rally at the small park next to the reservoir. They're hoping for a Halloween media blitz, getting families to join in by bribing them with big bowls of candy and the promise of face painting.

I've told her three times that I'm not going to be there. I've had more than enough of Halloween.

"But it'll be fun! Don't give me that look. It's important to stand up for what's right."

"This isn't my fight, Mom."

"Then support *me* and *my* fight." She hits me again with that singsong voice. "You could dress up. . . ."

"No way I'm dressing up."

"Jules, you looked *great* yesterday. And you really should be in costume for the rally. It plays well on TV, and, you know, *social media*." Mom always whispers *social media* like it's the new hot restaurant she doesn't want anyone else to know about. "I'm going to be Elsa from *Frozen*!"

That seals it. "I'm not dressing up."

"Jules."

"No."

She gives me a stern look, then sighs. "Oh, all right. You don't have to dress up if you don't want to. Though, you know, that *will* reflect on me." She grabs the shopping bag with her costume in it and quickly opens the door. "Okay! I'll-see-you-at-the-rec-center-at-two-o'clock-don't-be-late—goodbye, sweetie!"

She's gone, and somehow I'm going to the rally. How did that happen?

trick or treat

ha i forgot

no tricks thanx

how r u

> grounded

> sounds like you need Halloween candy

> snickers pls

> no candy corn GAG

> do my best anything else

> my bike at school haha

Back online with Jack, when it's just us texting back and forth, it's easy to forget all the *stuff*, the complications. Maybe this is enough. Maybe. Still, I get the idea of swinging by school, grabbing his bike, and wheeling it over to his place. Happy Halloween, courtesy me.

> whats ur address

> ?

> 4 ur bike?

> u know its locked right

> ah shit duh

I'm an idiot. Of course it's locked. There's a pause, and then Jack types in his address anyway.

> just in case

Just in case. Heh. Good one, Jack. We back-and-forth a little longer, and then Jack cuts out with a sudden:

> **shit gotta go dad freaking out**

> **what about**

—but he's gone. I'm not ready for him to be gone, not yet. There's a bag of Snickers on the counter for the trick-or-treaters tonight. I could bike over and drop off some candy bars before heading to the rally, just to surprise him. It wouldn't get him his bike back, but it'd be something sweet.

I throw a bunch of Snickers in my jacket pocket and punch the garage door open. Strap my helmet on and wheel my bike out. I figure, when I see Jack, I'll grab his lock key, bring the bike back to him on Sunday.

A black car roars into the driveway. A nice car. A *super* nice car. Damn, it's a Mercedes Benz C63 AMG, unmistakable, completely tricked out—growling V-8 engine, carbon fiber mirrors, LED running lights—

And Dhyllin sitting behind the wheel.

Someone's just got their driver's license.

Dhyllin lowers the driver-side window and sticks his head out. He's wearing Ray-Bans, and he's so relaxed, one arm slung over the top of the steering wheel, it's like he's been driving for years. "What do you think?" he calls out.

Of course he got his license first. Of course he got a Benz, and it's black and sleek and new. A few years ago, we'd sit on the curb and name all the sports cars that passed by, and now he actually has one, while I'm standing next to my father's bike, a dorky helmet strapped to my head. There's that old feeling, Dhyllin running ahead, always ahead, but that feeling disappears when I remember all the shit he's been pulling on Jack.

I ditch the helmet and lean the bike against the house. Summon my inner Jamal. "I want to talk to you," I say, walking over.

Dhyllin raises his sunglasses. "Pretty sweet, huh? My dad came through. Said if I got my license by Christmas . . . Get in. You gotta feel how it handles."

I shake my head. "I'm not going anywhere with you. I just want to talk."

He shrugs. His eyes disappear behind his sunglasses. "Whatever. At least get in and see what it's like inside."

Okay, I'm not proud of it, but I'll admit, I'm curious.

Inside, the Benz is warm, sending up all that new car smell from the dark gray leather seats, from the wood paneling on the dash. All the outside noises disappear as soon as you shut the door; you can barely hear the engine growl. Dhyllin smacks on the music, and Kanye thumps out beats like he's playing on the dashboard. Before I can stop myself, a "Whoa" escapes from my lips.

He nods. It was the reaction he knew I'd have. Suddenly his hand reaches for the gearshift, and he throws the car into reverse. "Fuck it," he says. "Let's take a spin." The Benz squeals out of the driveway.

"Jesus, Dhyllin!" I yell, strapping myself in, but he doesn't stop, racing down two small roads until we reach Silver Lake Boulevard, a wide street running alongside the reservoir that he turns onto without even stopping.

"You're such an asshole!" I shout at him over the music, but Dhyllin just smiles and steps on the gas. And as we race down the street, zooming by the houses and the baby strollers and the joggers on the dirt path next to the road, my heart is pounding with adrenaline and anger, waiting for the fiery crash that's sure to come. This ride is pure Dhyllin—fast and reckless, not caring what he does or who he hurts as long as it hypes him up.

He's not as good with stopping as he is with speeding, and we jerk to a halt at a turnout at the end of the reservoir. Dhyllin settles back, panting and satisfied. "Ya gotta give it to me, that was fucking awesome."

I'm not giving him anything. "I told you I didn't want to go on a ride."

"Oh, calm down, I'll drive you home," he says. He settles back in his seat. "So. What did you want to talk to me about? Hmm? The fact that you're *gay*?" He smiles, like he scored a point.

"That's not what I was going to talk about."

"When were you going to tell me, huh?" His eyes are hidden behind his shades. His mouth is a straight line that reveals nothing. "You even told Gregg, for fuck's sake. I've known you longer."

"What does it matter when I tell you?"

"It doesn't. I could give a shit." He sits up, puts the car into gear, looks for traffic. "I mean, it's not like it was a big secret anyway."

"What does that mean?"

He scoffs. "C'mon. It was obvious."

"It was not." I don't care if it was obvious—why am I even arguing? I stare out the window, trying to stop myself from playing the same game I'm always playing with Dhyllin.

Dhyllin takes one more look down the street and we pull away from the reservoir and up into the hills. We're quiet as he navigates the side roads that lead back to my house. There's a sourness in the air no new car smell can cover.

"I wanted to talk to you about that video you sent around my school."

He doesn't even act surprised. A little smile curls around his mouth. "Oh, you mean the one starring our tiny terrorist? Our tiny *tranny* terrorist?"

I feel my face burn. "Don't call him that. His name is Jack. And you really screwed him over."

"Did I? Did I really?" Dhyllin says, all innocent.

"Yeah, you did. You outed him without his permission, and now he's getting it from people at school—why is that so funny?"

He's openly grinning now. "Sorry to disappoint you, Jules, but *I* didn't send it out. I heard about it from Gregg. Sorry!" He steps on the gas, and we squeeze between a moving van and a car pulling out of a driveway. "But you should be happy *someone* had your back."

I stare into Dhyllin's sunglasses, wishing I could see behind them, to tell if he's messing with me or not. "What do you mean by that?"

"C'mon. Your first boyfriend turned out to be a girl!" He can't stop laughing. "Classic Jules."

I feel my face flare red. "You don't know what you're talking about, okay? Jack's not a girl, and he's not my boyfriend, but really, it's none of your fucking business."

That stops his smile. Dhyllin's jaw juts out and his face turns sharply to me, then back to the road. The streets are twisty and narrow, and the curves are sudden, you can't see what's coming up ahead. I grab on to the seat, but I'm not going to say anything, because that's what he wants me to do.

"Just trying to give you a hand, Jules. You do know what it means to be gay, right?" Dhyllin's voice is light but he's gripping the steering wheel. "It means you're horny for *men*. You get all hot and bothered by *men's* bodies. Isn't that the *point* of being gay? Wanting some D?" He presses on the gas as he lays out the moral of the story. "It's all about the D, Jules. And the sooner you understand that, the happier you'll be."

He slows to pass a UPS van, and suddenly I notice—he's sweating. He's white-knuckling the steering wheel even as he shifts into higher gear. He looks like someone playing at driving a car.

"Why do you always need to score points, Dhyllin?"

"Hey, I'm just telling it like it is."

"You have no idea how it is." There's a sudden lift inside me when I realize—I'm right. "What do you know about what it means to be gay? Are you gay?"

He glares at me. "I'm not, asshole. So?"

"So, shut up." I get this sharp focus I sometimes feel on the court but never in real life. "You don't get to have an opinion on this. And you're wrong, by the way. It's not all about the D. That's a really sad way to look at things."

He jams on the gas, just as a mail truck suddenly appears around a curve. Dhyllin swerves, barely missing a row of garbage bins set out on the street, but he doesn't slow down. "I just think it's funny—"

"I don't care what you think."

"Oh, since when?"

"Since I realized you were such a dick." *Swish.*

Dhyllin glares at me, jerking the steering wheel sharply to swing the car into my driveway. "Yeah, well, at least I *have* a—"

The sentence cuts short, and so does Dhyllin's car, because my mother's Subaru is in the exact space he thought he was going to be swerving into. Instant warning buzzes, flashing lights on the control panel, and Dhyllin yanks the steering wheel hard, away from the Subaru but right toward the basketball hoop. For a moment, as the car is bucking to a stop, I think we're going to clear it, but then there's a slo-mo battle of car versus pole, screech, scrape, thump, and it ends up a draw, the only casualty being the dangling carbon fiber driver's side mirror and a whole lot of paint.

Dhyllin's mouth gapes. His glasses have flown off his face, his eyes are ready to explode. "Oh my God," he repeats over and over again. He turns to me. "Fucking get out," he says, in a trembling, hollow voice.

I shut the passenger door and stand in the driveway, heart still pounding, watching him reverse and peel off. I know I should be horrified, and I am, but I also feel this tingle of adrenaline racing through my body that feels a lot like victory.

I turn to check out the basketball hoop for any damage, but my eyes never make it there. They get stopped by what looks like an angel of mercy, or death, frozen on our front doorstep. She's dressed in sparkling Disney white and blue, a halo of braided blond hair, a shocked stare, and a bowl of candy slipping from her hands.

The only reason I don't get the electric chair right away is because Elsa-Mom is late for her rally. I try sputtering out an explanation, but she's only got time for some general outrage and a stern warning to park my butt in my room and not leave the house under any circumstance. "We are going to have a *talk*," she says out of her car window before she leaves, spitting out the word *talk* like it's a bitter seed caught between her teeth.

At least I don't have to go to the rally.

> i am so in the SHIT rt now

I text Jack, but don't wait for a response. Maybe it's the adrenaline leaving my body, or the dread of the upcoming *talk*, but I'm suddenly so exhausted, I can hardly make it to my room. I don't even remember hitting the bed, but I crash, big-time.

It's dark when I wake up. What time is it? What *day* is it? I reach for my phone, but it's not on the bedstand or hidden in the sheets.

I try to remember where I left it, but my brain is too fuzzy to map it out. I stumble into the hallway, which is also dark. Maybe I've slept straight through the night, I think, but then I hear the grandfather clock striking seven.

The hall and porch lights are turned off, which explains why trick-or-treaters haven't been ringing the bell. The only light on is in the living room, where my mother is curled up on the couch, reading her phone. She's in her robe, her hair both wild and plastered down, and there's the Elsa wig smashed on the coffee table next to a bottle of open red wine. Cabernet, about two glasses gone. Then I remember that there was already a half-full bottle of zinfandel, the one with the donkey label she likes, on the kitchen counter, which means she's already gone through that one, which means, oh shit. Then: candy bar wrappers littered around her on the couch. *Candy bars.* Double oh shit.

Her phone looks different; it's not shining pink and gold. Why would she take it out of the case? Unless . . . it isn't her phone. Unless—it's mine.

"Mom! What are you doing!"

She looks up at me, glares. Jabs a finger. "Don't." And then a heavier *"Don't."* She leaves me standing there, horrified, as she goes back to scrolling through whatever of mine she's reading. *Tap tap* on the screen, *my* screen.

"Why do you have my phone?" She ignores me. *Tap. Tap.* I guess passwords don't work when the person who set them up is doing the hacking. *Tap. Tap.* Finally, she places it down on the couch next to her, reaches for her wineglass. The cords of her neck muscles jut out, tighten as she swallows.

I take a breath and say, as calmly as possible, "Can I have my phone back, please?"

She points the wineglass at me like it's a microphone. "Do you know who I was just talking to? For forty-five minutes? *Dhyllin's mother.*"

I need to get through this as quickly as possible. "Okay, so, what happened was—"

"*Dhyllin* came home in tears. *In tears.* Janelle said he came over to show you his new car, and *you* pressured him into taking a drive."

"That's bullshit."

"Hey, *enough* with that mouth. We'll get to that." She takes another sip, rolls it in her mouth as she shakes her head. "A brand-new car, Jules. *Brand-new.*"

She makes it sound like I was the one who had personally smashed that brand-new car into the basketball pole. She's talking slower, more carefully, dropping words like sledgehammers. "What were you *thinking*?" she demands. "You could have been *killed.*"

"Can I just, can I tell you what really happened?" I ask. She purses her mouth and looks up, daring me to continue. There's a stain of something dark on her chin, wine or chocolate, that I try not to focus on. "I didn't want to go for a ride. I told him no, okay? He forced me."

"*Forced* you? How did he force you? Did he hold a *gun* to your head? Tie a, tie a *rope* around you and drag you—*lasso* you in? What?"

Her voice is mushy, so I know we're way past happy tipsy mom and square into sloppy slurry mom. I haven't seen that mom since right after my father moved out. When she's at this stage, it's all about getting her to bed. She probably hasn't eaten anything, either, except those candy bars, and God knows what they're doing to her system. The smart thing to do? Just back down and apologize, leave it for tomorrow.

But I don't do the smart thing.

"Why do you believe him and not me?"

"*Dhyllin* is one of your oldest friends, Jules. Why would he lie?"

The words can't come out fast enough. "Because he crashed his new car and doesn't want to get in trouble!"

She waves a hand at me: *Oh, please.*

"Mom, does that sound like me? Does it sound like something I would do?"

Her head snaps up, eyes shining. "I don't know, Jules. I don't know *what* you'd do. You are, you are, *full* of surprises."

She swipes her hand down hard on my phone like she caught it escaping.

It's chocolate, definitely chocolate on her chin.

"Dhyllin's mom told me he lost control of the car because you were *distracting* him. He said you got all upset because he was trying to *warn* you—"

My whole body braces.

"Because, *because*—" My mother presses her lips together tight, then lets it all spew out. "—you are dating that *transgender person*." The words fit awkwardly in her mouth, a foreign sound, an accusation.

I deal out my words slowly and carefully, because if I don't, I might shout them. "I am not. Dating. Anyone."

"Oh please. Look at all these messages—" She scrolls frantically.

"Stop going through my texts!"

I reach for the phone, but she pulls it away. "You think I can't read between the lines?" I feel sick. In my head, I'm snatching the phone back and running upstairs, I'm getting into my bedroom and slamming the door and never coming out. If she starts reading them out loud I think I will die.

But what she's reading is too exhausting, she can't bear to look anymore. "You were keeping this from me. I thought we put a stop to it," she says, clutching the phone to her chest. "We *talked* about this, Jules."

You talked about this, I think, staring at the chocolate smudge, watching it stretch and shrink as she moves her jaw. I close my eyes. "We're just friends, Mom, okay? Will that make you stop?"

"No. No no." She taps the phone. "Don't try to fool me. There's something more going on." She lays her palm on top of her wineglass. "Isn't there, Jules. Hmm? Yes or no."

I don't say anything because, if she won't believe me even when I tell her the truth, what else can I say? But there's also something else that keeps me quiet. I'm afraid that I *can't* fool her, that even drunk and spouting crap she's circling something hidden and private that I'm not ready to deal with yet, especially not with her.

"Don't worry about it, Mom."

This only sets her off. "How can I *not* worry about it? You have no idea what you want, Jules! You don't know what you're getting yourself into!" She waves the phone at me like Jack's somewhere inside it. "This person is heading for a lot of trouble. Sending out videos, getting in fights—you want to be associated with that? That's their life, not yours! You want it to be like Bishop Academy again? Do you?" Her voice thunders, then crumples. "Isn't being gay *enough*? Do you have to add on to that? I'm so scared . . . I'm so scared for you!"

The weeping is worse than the yelling. I stare at my mother, and, yeah, there's so much wrong in what she's saying, so much awfulness, and inside me, muffled, there are these flares of anger, and shock, and disgust, but in the end, it's my mother, crying in front of me, and all I can think about is trying to make it stop. I know that underneath the wailing she wants this confrontation to end, too; all I have to do is nod and agree, and that will flip the switch in her head, and we can put this situation to bed, tuck it in and let it pass out until tomorrow.

"Mom—"

But then I notice what's been lying on the couch next to her, smiling up at me, and all that gets swept away.

"What are you doing with that?"

Her head jerks like she just woke up. "What? What?" Her eyes go to where I'm staring. and she smashes her hand down quickly on the photograph of Rick Davies's face. "I needed to know who these people are!"

His headshot. She must have snuck into my room like a ninja when I was sleeping and dug it out of my desk drawer after she grabbed my phone. I'd say it was a new low for her, but for all I know, she's been doing this my entire life.

She waves the headshot in front of me. "I mean, they're from . . . *Pittsburgh*. Why are they even here?"

"Mom, Mom! It's none of your . . . goddamn business! Really."

Her back stiffens. All her tears have disappeared. "It. Most. Certainly *is* my business. And don't use that language with me!"

"You can't go looking through my stuff, and you can't look through my phone."

"Oh, I can't? Who says? Who pays for that stuff and your phone, hmm?"

"Uh, Dad?"

We're both in shock that that came out of my mouth.

"I think I'm keeping this, thank you," she says, icy, slipping my phone into her robe pocket.

"For how long?"

She raises her chocolate-dipped chin high. "As long as it takes for you to start acting normal again. Stop being so ungrateful. Apologize."

But I won't apologize. And I won't start acting normal, either. I nod and say, as cool as I can, "Okay," then turn and leave. It's not until I reach the second floor that I yell, "I wish his whole windshield had gotten smashed in!"

No answer.

In my bedroom, I need about five deep breaths to get steady before I open my laptop.

His texts are hours old:

> **why u in the shit?**
>
> **u throwing pastries?**
>
> **DONT DO IT MAN!!!**

I want to type something back, but I worry about my phone pinging in my mother's hand, and anyway, there's just too much to go through. Dhyllin seems like years ago. I close my laptop and pull out the mini Snickers from my pocket, cram two in my mouth, but before I can finish unwrapping a third, my eyes begin to close. It's impossible that I should be so tired after I've just woken up, but I think she's drained all the energy out of me. I crash again, and this time, I sleep clear through to morning.

27. Jack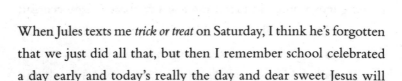

When Jules texts me *trick or treat* on Saturday, I think he's forgotten that we just did all that, but then I remember school celebrated a day early and today's really the day and dear sweet Jesus will Halloween never end? Guess not.

I'm giving myself a pass for being confused—Dad's distracting me with his caged animal act. You'd think shooting his first Los Angeles movie would let him kick back and enjoy, but he's full-on manic monkey this morning, pacing the room, kicking my mattress with that poke-y foot of his while I'm trying to text.

"What am I even doing here? Your mother should have stopped me. This is insanity. Why are you still in bed? It's almost noon." He doesn't understand I'm actually doing something here on this bed, I'm carrying on a conversation he keeps rudely interrupting.

> **no tricks thanx**

> **how r u**

> **grounded**

"I could have shot that movie better. *You* could have. Absolutely. What a Mickey Mouse operation."

I can tell this dumpster fire isn't going to burn itself out any time soon, so I roll myself out of bed and head for the bathroom, grabbing up my binder and clothes on the way. "Dad, they're students, remember? That's why they call them student films."

He keeps ranting through the bathroom door while I pee and change. "Three hours, three hours before they get to my scene, all my energy just leaking into my frigging shoes, and when they're finally ready, we're losing the light!" He follows me into the kitchen. We eat a late breakfast, cereal with just-expired milk, and Dad can barely get in a spoonful of his off-brand Mini-Wheats, he's so teed off. "What are they teaching these students anyway? How to screw over the actor?"

Jules texts that he wants my address. For what? Oh, right, but my bike's locked up, Jules. I give it to him anyway, *just in case*. I hope he realizes that's a joke.

Dad keeps talking, projectile spitting his milk back into the bowl, he's so outraged. "I was completely in shadow! Just the back of my head in the shot! How's that gonna help me at all? Believe me, I could have been a hand puppet and no one would know."

hey lowell from gsa said

theyre behind u

ok

he wants to know if u want to come

315

to a meeting

idk not really my thing

—which is my way of saying, hell no, sitting around jawing with a group of cis people about the one thing you don't want to be reminded of? Yeah, I know, solidarity and visibility and pride, but . . . can I just do those things later?

"And where's my manager? What's Dave Duvall doing for me? Nothing. Three times I called yesterday, and not one word. I hear nothing from him. What's he so busy with? Not me."

Also, going to a GSA meeting would mean sharing space with Lowell, and I'm pretty sure that name's attached to the guy with the glasses under the tree with Jules at school. *Jules and Lowell sitting in a tree, K-I-S-S—*

Dad follows me into the room, sits on the end of his bed, sad and unshaven. He's worn himself out. "And where is this partner of his? I think Blum's completely fabricated." Dad points an accusing finger at me. "There is no East Coast Blum! What kind of scam is being perpetuated here?"

I put down my phone and sigh. "Forget it, Dad, it's Chinatown."

"You bet your ass it's Chinatown, Jack."

Dad finally decides to shake things off and go running, and while he's gone, I know I shouldn't do it, but, can't help it, I go online. Not to find videos of yesterday's cringe-fest, no, God no, I'm searching for something else, scrolling through Tumblr, YouTube,

Reddit, Google, like they're thrift stores and I'm pawing through the bargain bins, looking for that one special item:

gay FTM boy dating cis boy

But there's nothing that fits, or at least not for me, no bouncy stories of gay high school trans-cis romances, just like I thought, there's no movie for this and IT DOESN'T MATTER ANYWAY, why am I even looking? I'm just picking at that scab a little more. Yeah, Jules and I are texting again, and sure, he did swoop in and pull me away from Gavin, but none of that matters because the ship has sailed, Jules is all squared away. Why would he want a trans Jack when he can have a cis Lowell, fully equipped, right out of the box?

Forget it. Wait until after high school to make any sense of this dating shit. Wait until later.

Later, except, what do you do with these endless minutes of Now?

Laptop snicks shut. The quiet pushes down my eyelids, is it already time for a nap? But no, I can't, my brain won't let me, 'cause when I think of nothing, everything buzzes in.

Bzz bzz

It's my phone, Jules again, c'mon, why does this sailed ship keep texting me? Don't interrupt my wallowing, man. He's in the shit about something, but before I can find out more I hear my name being called from outside. "Jack!" Dad yells, kind of pained and out of breath. "Help me!" I throw on my sneakers and head for the door, sure he's had a heart attack.

He meets me halfway up the stairs. "There's more in the car," he says, panting.

"Are you insane?" He's got two huge dumbbells in his hands, he can barely keep them from scraping the steps. "What are those?"

"House sale," he gasps. "Three blocks away. Dirt cheap. Guy died. Don't look at me like that." He jerks his head toward the car, still huffing and puffing. "Go down and get the rack."

In the bedroom, my dad moves the case of instant ramen to the top of the dresser, shoves aside the open suitcase holding dirty clothes, and plants the dumbbell rack in its place.

"They gave me the rack for free if I bought the whole set!" he says, all sunshine.

I ask about his sanity again, because, come on, this is the guy who won't buy name-brand cereal. "We're going to be leaving soon. What are you going to do, stow them in your carry-on?"

He's got this all figured out. "Business expense! It's an investment. Come on, you see what guys look like out here! They're all *GQ* models. I gotta compete, right?"

"I don't think you're competing with *GQ* models, Dad."

He ignores me and starts loading the dumbbells onto the rack. "It's about being camera-ready. Pittsburgh fit is different from LA fit. I need to get more . . . pumped."

"In six weeks?"

"Almost seven weeks, Jack!" he roars, shaking a ten-pounder like it's warding off evil. "Seven weeks! It can't hurt!" He hands it over to me. "You said yourself you wanted to bulk up. Well, here's your opportunity. *Our* opportunity."

He has a point. When you start on T, you think muscle'll start

318

sprouting up all over, Popeye on spinach, but it doesn't work that way. And going to a gym? No way. Not now. But with these . . . I do a few curls with the weight, imagine a jacked-up Jack.

Yeah. Too little, too late.

By evening, all that enthusiasm Dad picked up along with the weights has drained away. Somewhere between ordering our Yoshinoya beef bowls and setting them down on the sticky kitchen table, he's back into his funk. Every grain of rice he lifts has the weight of boulders, each swallow of chewy beef comes with a sigh.

"It's been quite a trip, hasn't it?" he asks, out of nowhere. "You happy you made it?"

I nod.

"It was quite a ride." He takes another bite, sighs, stabs his chopsticks down, stares into the air. It's almost over, for both of us, the Great Experiment roller coaster is pulling into the platform, exit on your right, check your possessions. Game over, man, game over.

"It's a different life out west, isn't it," he says. "Can you imagine living here?"

"Sure," I say. "Why?"

He sighs and shakes his head. "No reason. Doesn't matter. You miss your mom?"

"Yeah, I guess."

He runs his hand slowly over his stubble. "Well, you'll see her soon enough. Home again, home again."

319

Home, yeah, but what does that mean, exactly? I mean, after Evie, it felt like I didn't belong in Pittsburgh anymore, and here— here there's Jules, but in a way, that's even worse. I really don't belong *here*, either. I wonder if my dad's mood has darkened mine, or if mine has darkened his. I guess it doesn't matter.

We decide on a night of *One Flew Over the Cuckoo's Nest*, 'cause that's what you need to lift your spirits. While he gets that set up, I clear all the takeout from the table and dump it in the garbage. As I'm getting the last of the gulab jamun out of the fridge, my phone buzzes, not a text, a call. It's Jules. Weird. I answer. "Hey."

No *hey* back. Nothing. Just silence.

"Hello?" I say. "Is this the trick part of trick-or-treat?"

And he's gone. Call ended. Twelve seconds. I stare at the phone, waiting for him to call back, unless it was a butt dial—

"What the fuck!" I yelp. There's a giant demonic bunny leering at me from the doorway—ragged gray fur, twisted ears, a mouthful of sharp teeth and empty eyes. It leans forward like it wants to eat me.

"Pretty good, huh?" It takes me eight fast heartbeats to recognize the muffled voice.

"Jesus, Randy," I say.

The nightmare bunny peels back its head and there's Randy inside, smiling with all his (real) teeth. "I'm Frank the bunny. Get it?"

"I get it, *Donnie Darko*. You're gonna give me nightmares."

"Sorry, little man," Randy says, grinning. His glasses are all fogged up underneath the costume, his hair is extra greasy, he's almost as scary out of the bunny as he is in it. "Halloween party."

Maybe that's where Jules is, he's at some loud costume party with his new friends, couldn't hear me . . .

"All right, time to go," Randy says, throwing his rabbit head back on. Not surprisingly, his fur already smells like weed. He nods creepily. "I think I'm gonna score tonight."

"Yeah, good luck with that," I call out as he hippity-hops out the door. Great, even the greasy evil bunny is gonna score, and I'll be home with my father watching a bunch of men dancing around a psych ward. "Hey, Dad!" I call out, looking into the TV room, hoping he could catch Randy before the bunny hops into his car. But Dad's not in there, he's standing in the middle of the bedroom, completely still, phone pressed against his chest.

"Jack." He's giving me that look like I'm the son he thought had died in a shipwreck. He turns his hands up to the sky. "It's a Hail Mary pass. A deus ex machina. The gods are *smiling down*."

"What are you talking about?"

"Tomorrow night, Jack. Guess who's going to a big producer's house?"

"You are?"

"No. *We are*." There's no way he could smile any larger without breaking his face in two. "I just got off the phone with Jules's mother. She's inviting us to dinner!"

"*What?*"

Dad pumps his fists like the Bucs just completed a triple play. "Jules came through! They wanna meet us, they have my headshot! Jules's dad, Alan Westman, is gonna be there. *Alan Westman*." He slaps his hands together. "This could be it, Jack. A game changer. Something's *gotta* come out of this. Isn't it great?"

28. Jules

Early Sunday morning, I wake with a stiff neck, a pillow stained with chocolate drool, and a string of unanswered messages from Jack on my laptop:

> dinner w the westmans!
>
> why ddnt you tell me?
>
> where r u?
>
> i get to see ur mansion
>
> hello
>
> hello

I have no idea what he's talking about, and I can't text back. I don't think my mom gets that I can message on my laptop, but if she found out, she'd take that away, too. So I try Skyping. I enter his number, already sure he won't be awake yet, but after four rings Jack's face appears in the box on my screen, yawning.

"Dude," he whispers, rubbing his eyes. He looks like he's in heaven, white everywhere. His voice has a strange echo to it. "You're Skyping me?"

"Where are you?"

"In the bathroom. My dad's still sleeping."

"So's my mother," I say, but I'm whispering just in case. "What do you mean about dinner?"

"My dad's calling you the game changer. He's says he'll thank you when he wins his first Emmy." Apparently, my mother's had this whole conversation with Rick after I went to bed. When I hear she's invited the two of them to dinner, I get this knot in my stomach, and when he mentions that my father's going to be there, too, the knot just tightens. My father hasn't done anything socially with my mother since he left. The last time I saw him was at the beginning of summer. The fact that he's making time to visit means . . . it's a Thing. But what kind of thing?

"Jules? Jules," Jack says. "I thought you were frozen for a second. What's wrong?"

I shake my head. "I'm just . . . confused. I didn't know anything about this."

Jack pulls back to give me a sideways look. "C'mon. You arranged the whole thing."

I shake my head. "It wasn't me. It's all my mother."

"Why would she do that?"

"I have no idea. It makes no sense. We got into this huge fight last night." And I tell him about Dhyllin and the car, about him talking smack and me smacking back, and the accident, and getting my phone taken away . . . but I don't mention that

Jack's part of what my mother and I were fighting about. I mean, what can I say? That my mother thinks we're dating? No way I could tell him that. It's not true, and at the same time, it's too close to true.

"I told you Dhyllin was a jagoff," says Jack, satisfied.

"Yeah. But, you should know, he said he didn't send out the video."

"Liar. *Anyway* . . . ," he says, dismissing Dhyllin with a wave of his hand, "your mom, she knows about me?"

I nod.

"Okay." Jack scrunches his (beautiful) eyebrows down, which I can't help obsessing about even in freak-out mode. "Maybe . . . it's like a peace offering. Like, she's seen the error of her ways, and she wants to do something nice for you."

"Maybe. I guess. But—" I'm so close to telling him everything. "She's been really weird lately, so, I'm just saying, if you didn't want to come, that would totally be cool."

"Are you kidding? It's the most excited my dad's been since we got here."

"Well, tell him . . . not to get his hopes up."

"Too late for that." Jack's face looms closer, searching. "Do you . . . not want us to come?"

I look at Jack's eyes, suddenly wary, so ready to close off, waiting for me to answer.

"No, no . . . I do. Really. I do."

How can something be so true and so false at the same time?

❖ ❖ ❖

The hardest part of the rest of the day is pretending I haven't heard anything, waiting for my mother to drop the news. She doesn't get out of her room until ten, moving slowly and carefully into the kitchen, obviously hung over. She starts the coffee. I finish my bowl of cereal. Minimal conversation. Neither of us mentions last night. Neither of us wants a second round.

It's not until she starts pulling open cabinets, looking for ingredients, that she drops the news. "Oh!" she says, like she just remembered something delightful. "We're having dinner guests tonight. Your friend Jack, and Jack's dad." She looks at me over the cabinet door, her eyes wide and watchful.

"Oh," I say, just as casual. "Uh, why?"

"Well," she says, like she's thinking it through herself, "Jack seems . . . important to you, so I thought it would be good to get to know them. Jack's father was very appreciative. He said he's missed having a nice home-cooked meal." She smiles gently. "Won't that be nice?"

Her words sound reasonable, even kind. I can almost believe Jack was right, that this is my mother's idea of a peace offering.

"Okay," I say slowly. "Can I have my phone back?"

The smile never leaves her face. "Is that an apology?"

It would be so easy. But I can't. I just can't.

The smile tightens. "Then . . . no."

At six forty-five, the doorbell rings. I open the door, not knowing who I'm most nervous to see on the other side of it. It's my father. "Hey, champ," he says, and ambles in.

"Why did you ring the doorbell?" I ask. "You've still got a key, don't you?"

"Yeah, but, it's the right thing to do," he says. We stand in the hall. He's got his usual red windbreaker on, his usual Dodgers cap, his usual pained, awkward smile. "You look so tall. And thin," he says, like he always says. "You gotta get some meat on those bones. How's school going?" I shrug. "You, uh, doing the, you're playing basketball, right?" I nod. He takes off his cap, scratches his head. "Yeah, I gotta catch a game." The cap goes back on.

"Starts in a week," I tell him. My father asks me to send Denise, his assistant, a schedule so he can set up a time. I nod. He nods. I wait the three seconds before his usual, "Well, you've certainly got the height for it."

My mother calls from the kitchen, her voice super frothy and company-ready: "Who is it, Jules?"

"It's me," my father yells.

"Oh," she says, froth gone. "The garbage disposal is not working again."

"You gotta jiggle the thingy. Remember? Did you jiggle the thingy?"

"You come and jiggle the thingy!" she yells back, but my father doesn't move.

He sniffs the air. "What culinary delight awaits us, I wonder?"

"Brown rice lasagna with cashew cheese and spinach."

He winces. "Right. Soggy paper towels covered with tomato sauce and plastic, yeah?"

But I'm too tense to smile, even if I wanted to. "What's going on here?" I ask, hoping my dad will, for once, give me a straight answer.

He shoves his hands into his pockets. "So, a lot of, uh . . . changes happening, with you." He takes my silence for a yes and nods. "Yep." It takes me a second to realize this is my father's way of acknowledging I'm gay. This is my big coming-out-to-Dad bonding moment. Wow. "And we're, uh, meeting your . . . friend, right?"

"Jack," I say, and I can tell by how his lips press together that he's already been filled in on Jack. My mother's summoned him. "You haven't met a lot of my friends."

My father holds up his hands and shrugs, like events are totally out of his control. Which is, kind of, bullshit. He didn't lose control, he just gave it up, because he didn't want the responsibility. My father can run an entire film production but can't manage a family of three.

But maybe that's just my mother, whispering in my ear.

It's all bullshit.

"You okay?" my father says.

My mother hurries out, wiping her hands on a kitchen towel and smoothing her skirt. She is *dressed*. "You're not on set, take off that hat," she says to my father. The baseball cap comes off. She looks at me and my hoodie, clearly disappointed. "I thought I told you to change." She bites at her fingernail and looks around the room, like something's missing.

"What?" my father says.

She's nervous. She's doubting. Whatever brilliant plan she hatched during her binge last night is not looking so peachy today. My parents exchange a look, and she actually grabs on to his arm. "We can't cancel, can we?"

My father sighs, gives her the smallest shake of his head. "Let's just get it over with."

And the three of us stand in the hall, waiting for a dinner party none of us wants.

When the doorbell rings, we all jump.

Jack

It's almost a relief, standing on the porch, staring at smiley Mr. Scarecrow stuck on the front door, under the glow of the outside light. No more time to strategize or catastrophize, no more Dad annoying the shit out of me by rooting through my clothes, giving me last-minute, too-late-now etiquette lessons. Showtime.

This isn't going to be bad. Two hours for dinner, maybe two and a half, tops, being it's a school night. Two hours, that's barely enough time for just one of Dad's stories. In two hours, I'll be back at the house and back in my hoodie and all will be well with the world.

And—I get to see Jules. So that's something.

"You look like you're posing for a mug shot," my father says to me out of the side of his mouth.

"I look how I look."

"Try to smile a little, okay? Act pleasant."

Why do parents think that telling their kids to smile will

actually work? That hearts will automatically burst from our eyes and rainbows will shoot out of our asses upon command? Can they really expect anything from that request but a death-ray stare?

My dad's already sweating hard. The deodorant he slathered on is working overtime, sending out puffs of Old Spice mixed with the fumes of his aftershave that I can smell even in the open air. He reaches out and rubs my shoulder, like I'm the one who needs calming down. "Okay, ready, buddy?"

I look up at him. "Just don't—"

"What? Don't what?" he says, all alarmed.

"Nothing. You look good." I give him my best skeleton grin. He takes a breath, rings the doorbell.

Right away, they pop up together from behind the door to greet us, whoa, instant Mom and Dad, like we're trick-or-treaters and they want to see the cute costumes. Introductions all around. Jules's dad, Alan, has the same tall stoop as his son, same shade of sandy hair, same jaw, and mom, Linda, passed along her pale skin and those wide, nervous eyes. At first, it's all cooing and huzzahs, hellos, so pleased to meet yous!, you shouldn't haves!, arms reaching out to do-si-do and Linda is one huge smile grabbing the Two-Buck Chuck wine Dad brought. Alan gives me a firm handshake, and when I'm released from that, at the edge of all the parental clustering, I'm finally standing in front of Jules.

Jules looks totally miserable.

And then, suddenly, he doesn't.

Jules

Jack's standing in front of me, hoodie gone, he's wearing a red, untucked flannel button-down, large enough to look like he borrowed it from his dad, over a black T-shirt, and the swoops of his hair have been smashed and flattened into submission. He looks so different, so *tamed*, and for a second, it's like I'm the one meeting him for the first time. But then he catches my eye and grins, and it's the same Jack, of course it is, there in the sweet smile, the dark and glowing eyes, not tamed at all, it's Jack just as he ever is, as he always is, *here*, in my house, and all the worries about my parents and this evening and any other *stuff* disappear. All I see is Jack, and suddenly everything gets super, super clear:

I do know what I want.

I'm sure. Absolutely sure.

And it's not complicated.

It's Jack.

Of course, it's Jack.

But before I can say anything, I'm being pulled away into a bear hug by Rick. Over his shoulder I see my parents cornering Jack, hovering over him, and I can't shake the feeling that they're sizing him up. I see my mother pointing out the bruise under his eye, and I start to worry, but then the grown-ups, like large planetary masses, start gravitating toward each other, chattering, and Jack manages to slip in between them. Suddenly he's by my side, safe.

Jack's by my side. Jack's in my house. Everything's fine.

"I brought something, just for you," he whispers secretively, and lifts his left hand, which has been palmed over a small paper cup. He grabs it with his right hand, and we both lean in as he reveals the contents.

My eyes widen. "You," I say, "are a badass."

"Last two," he says, handing me the cup with the glistening gulab jamun nestled inside. "Be careful. They're weapons-grade."

"What's that?" my mother calls out, all chirpy.

I quickly whisk the cup out of sight. "Nothing."

Her eyes darken for a moment, and her mouth closes on the way to a frown but doesn't quite make it there. She swirls around to the other adults. "Shall we sit?" she asks brightly, and sweeps her arm toward the living room.

I match my mom's gesture with an arm sweep of my own, just for Jack. He answers back with a little bow. Our laughter carries us into the room, while my mother follows behind, calling for drinks.

Jack

We get herded into this massive room, and, okay, Jules's house isn't a mansion, but it's close. The living room is twice the size of our TV room back home, easy, maybe even three times, it's hard to tell when the ceiling's so far out of reach, like in ski lodges you see in movies, with the wooden beams and the big French doors and an honest-to-God roaring fireplace that runs on its own. Photos of Jules everywhere, birth to basketball. It's picture-perfect.

There's definitely a vibe in the room, but I can't figure out what it is because everyone seems to have their own vibe. Linda swoops around, getting drink orders, but her eyes keep sliding over to me. Her smile is so tight you could jump rope with it. Alan looks lost in his own house, wandering around until he finally finds a seat. And Jules . . . maybe I've forgotten what it's like around him, but he's turned up his goofball frequency so high, he can barely stay still, giving me these looks I don't know what to do with, welcomes and warnings.

"No, just sit, Alan, let *me* get the drinks," Linda says with a high, pinched laugh. Alan doesn't laugh back, and he doesn't get up, either. She echoes her own laugh so it doesn't get lonely, and my dad throws in a pity chuckle before she exits.

My dad, he's the only one in full party mode—he's a one-man band, sitting forward, hands in motion, working the room, spinning stories about this crazy old town of LA, let me tell you, boy howdy we're not in Pittsburgh anymore. We're each on our own little furniture island, Dad and me camped out on a couch with these throw pillows on it that are so nubbly and soft I can't stop touching them, I want my *life* to be made out of these pillows. Alan's sunk into his leather armchair, drumming his fingers against it like he's waiting to be called into the dentist's office. Jules is stranded on a piano bench, his leg bouncing up and down like a jackhammer.

I'm being tilted. Dad has grabbed my shoulder and is rocking me back and forth. "Right, Jack? Right?"

"What?" I say.

"You love old movies, right?" he says, then turns to Alan. "He loves 'em. It's something we share. Right, Jack?"

"*Classic* movies," I say. "Yeah, they're good."

"Of course, what he considers classic movies is different than what *we* consider classic movies. I mean, *Jaws*, come on." Alan doesn't come on, so Dad turns back to me. "Give him a line, something from one of our favorite movies." He's smiling at me, but there's something in his eyes that's saying, *Help me out, don't get snarky. Get up on your hind legs and dance a little.*

I don't mind, it's for a good cause, but before I can even come up with a quote, Jules calls out, "The earth is my body, my head is in the stars."

Damn. Way to go for the deep cut, Jules.

Alan turns his head, puzzled. "What is that?"

"*Harold and Maude,*" I say. I look at Jules, and we both smile. It's like a secret handshake.

"Hey, how did you know that?" Alan asks Jules, and when Jules doesn't answer, Alan turns to my dad. "I try to get him to go to movies with me, but it's not his thing."

Jules's smile slams to the ground. "When?" he says in disbelief. "When did you *try*?"

Alan shrugs. "I did." Jules turns away, glares at the floor.

"He came to *Harold and Maude* with us at Hollywood Forever," my father says. "Very fun."

"Oh. Well, okay then," Alan says, but Jules still won't meet his eye. "I guess things change."

My dad leans forward. "But you know what else I love

watching? Those Trouble in Paradise movies you make for Lifetime. So good."

Alan clears his throat. "Really?" He rolls the compliment around in his mouth like the taste is off. "Huh."

"No, really!" Dad protests. "Those movies are exactly what you want after a long day at work. Beautiful beaches, girls in bikinis, a little romance, a little mystery, what's not to like? My wife and I eat them up."

I happen to know my mother hates those kinds of movies, she'd throw a shoe at the TV if she were forced to watch one.

Alan looks at my dad, sudden understanding puckering his lips. "So, what is it exactly that you do?"

My dad practically leaps off the couch, he's so excited to get that question handed to him with a shiny bow attached. "Oh, you know, just another actor in Hollywood, looking for his big break. I'm in the middle of this Great Experiment—" And it's time for another showing of Rick and Jack's Excellent Adventure. I thought it would be excruciating to hear him go through it again, but he's telling someone who might actually be able to get him work, so I listen, half hoping something good will come out of it.

But Jules has other ideas. He flicks his eyes over to our two dads, makes sure mine has his occupied, and tilts his head in the direction of the stairs. Raises his eyebrows. I nod quickly. "C'mon," he mouths, and we both stand up to make our escape.

Jules

"Where do you think you're off to?" My mother stops us just as we reach the stairs. I was thinking of going to my room, or the den, or the backyard, or any space that didn't contain parents, but she steers us right back to the living room. "Don't go anywhere." She's carrying a tray of drinks. "Time for a toast," she whispers to us, smiling.

"Don't toast, Mom," I say, but she's already passing out the drinks. A bottle of beer for Rick, a soda water with a lime for my father, two lemon San Pellegrinos for Jack and me. Last, she pours herself a glass of chardonnay, and I can't help wondering how many of those are already in her by this point.

"I just wanted to say," she announces, raising her glass. Rick quietly dribbles the beer from his mouth back into the bottle. She pauses and looks around, like she's waiting for someone else to join in, but no one does. "Well, first of all, *welcome* to our guests. I'm so glad to finally meet Jack. I've heard so much." She gives him a smile, a little too sunny, a little too long. "You know . . . Jules is new to Earl Warren, and I had my reservations, you know, I can't help but worry about my baby at school, we *all* worry about our babies, that's what parents do, we want to keep them safe, help them make good choices, it's such a confusing time, you know, even when they're in high school they're still so young . . ." She gestures at Jack. "So young!" She stares at him, shaking her head, like she can't get over how young he is. My father clears his throat, and my mom gives a quick little laugh. "Where was

I going with this?"

"Linda," my father says.

"What?" she snaps, under her breath.

"You missed the news—Jack isn't going to be at Earl Warren too much longer."

"What?"

"Yes." My father leans toward her. "They go back to Pittsburgh, *in six weeks*."

"Oh!" That short-circuits her brain. "But that's . . . that's no time at all! Oh!" She exhales twice, quickly, somewhere between a breath and a laugh. "Well," she says, raising her glass, "forget what I was going to say. Here's to your time in Los Angeles!"

I've never been more relieved for a toast to be over.

My mother pours herself another glass. "Jules, you never told me!" She's almost giddy.

Rick holds up his hands. "Well, wait, we'll see. It depends on what comes up in the next six weeks, right?" He leans in toward my father, man-to-man. "It's flexible. I could be here longer. Depends."

"Depends?" Jack turns to his dad, eyes questioning, but my mother gets in first.

"And your wife, doesn't she mind? Why doesn't she come out, too?"

Rick bobs his head from side to side. "Well, right now, she's the breadwinner, she's gotta keep that job, right?"

"She *works*," my father says. My mother smiles her scariest

336

smile and toasts him with her glass.

"Plus, she's holding down the fort at home. Taking care of Jack's little sister, Sudhi."

Jack quietly corrects his dad. "Susie."

"Right. Susie. Hard to keep track sometimes."

My mom says, "Oh, so you have two . . . children." And there's that pause between *two* and *children*, and the way her mouth was scrunching up to form a different word, that makes me think, *No, Mom, no.*

Jack

The conversation has somehow slid into my family life. There's a sudden change in the air, electricity building up like right before a thunderstorm. I can tell Jules feels it, he's staying still, tight, watching his mom. Alan feels it, too; his hand curls into a fist on the arm of the chair. Only Linda and my dad are oblivious, my dad dancing and jabbering away like a trained monkey she's got on a leash.

Fuck.

"Does everyone in your family change names?" Linda says, and she and my dad laugh like that's the funniest thing ever.

"It comes from my side of the family. The actor side, you know, stage names," he says, and winks at me, just a little wink, isn't this fun? *Yeah, Dad, I'm about to be hit by lightning, and you're giving me a little wink.*

"Sudhi, did you say? That's an interesting name. So *pretty*," Linda says, and then she thinks about just how pretty that name is.

337

No. No no no.

"Is that . . . what's the origin of Sudhi?"

"It's an Indian name," Dad says, happy to show off. "Means excellent wisdom."

"How interesting." Linda shifts over to me and my heart beats like flapping wings. "And I know—"

Don't. Don't don't don't.

"You must have another name, too, right? Is it just as pretty?"

I look at my dad. I think he's gonna come barreling in any second now, he'll take over, lay it all out, tell her—well, actually, grown-up-to-grown-up, that's kind of a shitty thing to ask—but all he does is look back at me with a clamped-on smile, like he's waiting for the answer, too. And I can't look at Jules and I can't look at Alan and I can't look at Linda so full of curiosity it's just spilling out of her eyes, and so I look down and I laugh a little to myself, well well, here we are.

"I, uh . . . don't, go by that anymore."

"What?" Linda says.

"Mom," Jules says from far away.

"I hope it's okay to ask," Linda says, but she's talking to Dad, like he's the one who would mind. I don't see her face, but I watch her hands cycle in the air. "It's just all so new to me—"

"Maybe Jack doesn't want to talk about this right now," Alan says. It's a save, but unbelievably, *unbelievably*, my dad raises a hand to stop him.

"No, no, it's okay. We're pretty open about all this, right, Jack?" He puts his hand on my shoulder, but it might as well be across the room for all I can feel it.

Linda hisses a tight "I'm just trying to understand, Alan," behind her, then floats back our way, a cloud of sweetness. "I have to say, this is something *I* never had to deal with in high school." And she gives a tinkling little laugh. "Times have changed!"

"Yes, they have!" Even though he's sitting next to me, Dad's voice sounds way way far off. "Changed for the good!" Somewhere he's grabbing my shoulder again.

"Absolutely!" agrees Linda.

"I think the lasagna's probably ready," says Alan across space.

"Is something burning, Mom?" I hear Jules ask.

All the voices are floating up like bubbles, but not Linda's, hers gets sharper and sharper, a direct line straight to my ears. "To be totally honest, I've heard of, you know, the men being women thing, like Caitlyn Jenner—I read that *Vanity Fair* article—but I forget it can go the other way. You never hear about that! Isn't that interesting?"

I'm diving down deep, trying to get away from that voice, or at least muffle it. Jules is somewhere on the surface, protesting, but he can't stop it, no one can. She just keeps talking. "It's everywhere now, this transgender thing. It just popped up out of nowhere, and now, well, it's the latest style!"

I can't breathe. I'm drowning, in bursts of black and red, my mouth clamped shut. Underwater silence, and Dad . . . *Dad* . . . "Well, uh . . ." I hear him swallowing, I hear his lips smacking together, trying to pull up words, I hear a sweaty little laugh, and

I know he's not gonna be pulling me out.

"Jack's . . . always been very fashionable. Right, Jack?"

Whooooosh back up I come.

His hand's on my shoulder and I mean to brush it off but instead, *smack*, I swat it away. Hard. "*What the hell, Dad?*" I yell. "Why are you letting this happen?"

Somehow I'm standing up, everyone's staring at me, I'm looking at Linda, right into her eyes, zeroed in, I want to rain down on her with flames and thunderbolts and all the righteous words.

"You can't— You can't ask those kinds of—why would you think it would be okay to say—"

But I've got no flames, no thunderbolts, and the words, I don't know the words, don't know my lines, it's just me, only me, why is it always only me.

I look at Jules, he's standing, his body a wince, head hung so low he might as well rest it on the ground. Yeah, I don't want to see this, either. His eyes slide up until they meet mine, and in them I see, what, pain, regret, I don't know, hey aren't you glad we came.

I tell him what we both know. "This is so fucked."

And then the room's up for grabs, but I don't care, because I am getting out.

Jules

Jack's standing. Everyone's standing.

My mother's flapping her hands, asking what she said that was so wrong, and my father tries to shut her down, and Rick's got his arms in the air like he's being arrested, saying, "Whoa, whoa now," and in the center of it all is Jack, silent and trembling, looking like he might faint, or explode.

And where am I?

My mother's voice slices through everyone else's. Her body is backing up from Jack, but that voice keeps pushing into him. "I can't what? I can't what? Just tell me, tell me what I said! I really want to know!"

"Let's everyone just calm down—"

"Did I say something wrong? What did I say?"

"Mom, STOP!"

All the adults turn to me, as if they'd forgotten I was still there.

"Just stop." I don't know what else to say, but it doesn't matter, because at that moment Jack, badass Jack, turns away from the group and quietly walks out the door.

Everyone freezes until the door clicks shut. Rick breaks the silence. "I should—let me—he's just—he's been having a hard time at school lately. I . . . Let me just go . . . check on him."

"Of course," says my mother, quickly.

"I'll go, too," I say.

"No," my mother and father say together, the first time they've agreed on anything in ten years.

"It's okay, I'll be back in a minute," says Rick, and then he's gone.

My family splits and retreats to separate corners without saying a word, like we're all in a time-out, in suspended animation until we see if they're coming back. My mother goes into the kitchen to poke at dinner, my father sits back in the armchair shaking his head and pulling out his phone, and I stare out the window at nothing, wondering why I didn't follow Jack out the door.

29. Jack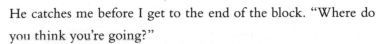

He catches me before I get to the end of the block. "Where do you think you're going?"

"I'm walking home."

"The hell you are." Dad plants himself on the sidewalk right in front of me. "Get back in."

"Are you joking?"

"Jack. Now."

"No way."

We stand on the sidewalk, neither of us going anywhere.

Dad breaks first, his hands shaking in front of him, choke position. "Why are you doing this to me?"

I feel so, so ready for him. "I'm not doing anything. You can go back in. Go ahead." I gesture toward the house. "Go finish up all your ass kissing."

"Hey!" My dad grabs my arm as I try to pass him. He lowers his voice. "It's called being a grown-up. Being polite."

I shake my head, not buying it. "It's called being pathetic."

"What is your friend Jules gonna think, huh? Acting like this."

"It doesn't matter. Nothing matters."

"Oh, stop being so dramatic," he says.

"I must get it from your side of the family," I shoot back. "The *actor* side."

That hits. He takes a breath. "What did you want me to do, yell at your friend's mother? What could I do?"

"You could have supported me!" And it feels really good to spit that out, until the pain kicks in. I wanted it to come out snarky but it ended up true.

"Come on. Haven't I always been there for you? Been on your side for everything? Jesus, give me some credit. I thought we were open about you, that you were fine with talking about it."

"Not like that! Really, Dad?"

"Okay. Okay." He reaches out his arm slowly. "We'll go back in. Have dinner. No more joking."

I'm shaking. He's so fucking dense. "It wasn't joking, Dad. It was *mocking*. Oh yes, being trans is *the latest style*. That's why I'm this way, because *I'm just so fashionable*! And hey, what's my dead-name? Is it a pretty name? Let's just throw that around! For fun!"

Dad looks scared, afraid I'm going to lose it in the middle of the street. "Jack. She was just ignorant. She didn't know what she was saying—"

"But you did! And you laughed!"

"It was just— I—" but he doesn't know how to continue. "Jack."

I'm in control. I'm not going to dissolve. I'm not going to disappear. I'm not.

"And for what? He's not going to give you a job, okay? It's not going to happen, Dad. This experiment was just a stupid idea."

That stops him cold, he's not even trying to form words, but I

344

can't stop mine from pouring out. "You're not going to make it here, Dad. You're too old."

"Jack—"

"We're going back to Pittsburgh. So, get used to it—" There's something about my dad's expression, it cuts me off. "What?"

He talks really slowly. "I don't know that, Jack."

"I do. Everyone does."

"No, I mean . . . I don't know that I'm going back."

I just stare at him.

"I think I'm going to stay awhile more."

"What are you talking about?"

"I want to live out here, Jack. I don't want to go back to Pittsburgh. Four months isn't enough time. I'm just starting to figure things out."

I almost laugh, the idea's so ridiculous. "Mom would never agree to that."

"Let's go back to the car and—"

"No way she's going to move out here."

"I know. She's not."

"So what are you—" and then every part of me wishes I hadn't started the question.

"We're gonna try . . . living separately, for a bit."

A dog barks. I hear the buzz of the streetlamp above our heads. Traffic.

"Mom . . . knows about this?"

Dad nods slowly.

"So, this whole *only a few months* thing was just a lie?"

"Can we walk?"

We start back the way we came, and each step is slow and careful, walking through a minefield. "It wasn't a lie. We thought that if something big did happen, that would change everything. We would all move and it would give us a new start. And if it didn't . . ." Three steps in silence. "Jack, things haven't been good for a long time. You must have noticed."

I didn't. I thought the tension in the house was mine, all mine, reflected out.

"I was unhappy, for a lot of reasons, and I made your mother unhappy, and something has to change. You understand, right? I need to reinvent myself, too."

"I'm not reinventing myself. This isn't an *invention*, it's who I am."

"You know what I mean. And when I saw how brave you were to do what you're doing, discovering who you really are, it really inspired me."

"Wait." I'm dizzy. I want to hurl. "You're putting this on me?"

His face goes pale. "No. God no. No. That's not what I meant—"

"It's my fault?"

"Jack, I didn't mean it to sound like that."

A million pieces of me are about to explode into the air. In space, where no one can hear you scream.

"Jack?" We're at the car. "Let's not talk about this here, okay?" my father says. "You just wait by the car. You don't have to go back in. I'll say our goodbyes and I'll be right out. Okay? Just stay here. It's gonna be fine, buddy. Trust me."

I don't trust him. Not anymore, or ever again. Never.

I watch him jog up to Jules's house. He doesn't even knock, just opens the door and slips inside.

A dog barks.

The good news is, I haven't exploded into a million pieces. I haven't disappeared. I'm still here.

The bad news is, it feels so much worse.

30. Jules

The door opens, Rick alone, and the house springs back into action. My parents must have been listening because they come to the hall right away, all understanding nods and sad smiles, but no questions, because that would have just delayed him leaving. He tells us, Jack's not feeling well, so sorry to cut things short, and dinner smells fantastic but he's got to go. Of course, of course, my parents say really fast. Everyone is so ready to accept the lie. My mother wants to know does he want to take some lasagna home, but he thinks he'd better get back to the car, and everyone agrees, absolutely, so nice meeting you, and there are promises to do it again soon, rain check on dinner, good luck and be careful on the twisty roads, so dark already, no more daylight saving time, and then, as they're shutting the door, hope Jack feels better, any time, good night.

Silence.

"That went well," my father says.

"At least it's over," my mother says.

I lean my head against the threshold to the living room and close my eyes, listen to them bustle around the room, the clinking of glasses, the shuffle of furniture.

"They left before dinner. I guess they dodged a bullet."

"Oh, ha ha."

"The father."

"Ugh, the father."

I don't think they even hear what they're saying. It doesn't matter how many years they've been separated, it's like you wind them up and away they go, like this was just another party they were cleaning up after, like they hadn't just destroyed someone's life.

Destroyed mine, too. I wonder if Jack will ever talk to me again.

"Jules, wake up. What are you doing, holding up the wall?" my mother says, passing with the tray of glasses.

"You know, right," I say, "that you made Jack physically ill?"

"*I* didn't make Jack ill." She pushes the tray of glasses into my father's hands, gestures toward the kitchen. "There's obviously anger issues going on there."

"Do you blame him?"

"All right," my father calls out from the kitchen.

"Fine. I'm an awful person for just trying to understand things. I'm a monster."

"You wouldn't stop!" I shout.

My father reappears. "Okay, okay," he says, "it's over. Nothing we can do about it now."

My mother jumps in. "I feel bad for Jack! I do! I blame the father. And also, the mother, though I've never met her. I mean, how can you let someone so young make that kind of choice?"

"He didn't *choose*!" I say. "Did I choose to be gay?"

My mother waves her hands in front of her face. "I didn't say that! I didn't say that! It's totally different—"

"How?"

"It is! It's—all right." She takes a deep breath. "I don't think you can make that kind of huge decision when you're just a child. I don't believe it. I'm sorry, but I don't. What she's doing to her body—"

"He! HE!" I shout. "It's not that hard, Mom!"

"Why are we still talking about this?" my dad says.

My mother stares at the ceiling and takes a long breath. "Your father's right. Let's just drop it. None of our business." She keeps looking at me, her face getting sadder and sadder. She reaches out a hand and almost touches my shoulder. "I know it seems like a big deal to you now, sweetie, but they'll be gone soon, and trust me, you'll move on. Okay? Let's eat." She heads for the kitchen.

They're going to be gone soon. You'll move on. Of all the awful things my mother has said, this is the worst.

"I'm tired. I'm just going to go to my room."

"C'mon, you'll feel better if you eat."

"I'm not hungry."

"Of course you're hungry. And I think your blood sugar's low."

"Let him go," my father says. "He said he's not hungry. Stop trying to micromanage."

My mother wheels around. "Don't tell me what I should or should not do. It's not micromanaging, it's called being a responsible parent. It's called taking an active role in your child's—"

"Okay, here it is, finally," my father says. "You think I'm not responsible? So why am I here? Answer me that—"

But I don't have to hear any more of this, I've already escaped up the stairs, letting the two dinosaurs battle it out. It's the fight that never ends, and I know all the words by heart.

I lie on my bed, my mind racing, racing with all the things I should have said. *You are being horrible, Mom.* My body tenses and buckles with embarrassment, replaying the night. My mother doesn't understand. She doesn't want to understand. And yet, she just keeps talking.

—*the men being women thing*—

I squeeze my eyes tight, trying to blot out the sound of her voice.

—*What she's doing to her body*—

My mother is so wrong. How can she be so wrong? I mean, it's not hard to find out things. It's all there on the internet, one search on Google and you can get all your questions answered. You'd just have to *care* enough to look.

Really, though, who am I to talk? It took me long enough to do just that. Why did it take me so long?

—*They're going to be gone soon. You'll move on*—

Why *does* it take me so long? If I care—

—*Okay, so now you know. Does it matter?*—

I do care. I do.

I—

I sit up.

She's right.

They will be gone soon.

Jack'll be gone by the end of the semester.

What am I waiting for?

I open up my laptop and log in.

are you ok? home yet?

let me know youre ok

that was awful

so so sorry

parents dont know anything they dont get it theyre just making it up

if youre spying mom its true STOP READING

jack remember the question you asked me before?

ive got an answer

sorry so slow

no it doesnt matter

it doesnt

im with you jack

always

♥

I lie back on the bed, waiting. Finally, after ten minutes dis-
guised as a decade, a response:

> **im ok**

And then, a photo: it's so dark, it's hard to make out. There's a
glare of orange streetlight bouncing off a traffic sign with double
curving arrows and the word *Only* under them. A chain-link fence
with a gaping hole, opening onto a dirt trail. Beyond that, some
kind of concrete slab, and in the distance, a bridge, or a tower.

It looks like a place I should know. Maybe it's near his house,
and he's telling me he's almost home?

> **??**

No reply.

There's a metal scraping sound on the street. I look out my
window and see a car pull up in front of our house, directly under
the lamplight. A Chevy Malibu with a cherry hood and a red
battered side door.

My heart leaps. They've driven back. Jack read my texts and
posted the arrows to tell me they're turning around. He wants
to see me. Without thinking, I grab my backpack, my wallet,
and my keys, just in case. I close the bedroom door behind me
as quietly as I can and sneak down the stairs. In the kitchen, my

mother and father are still at it. What more could they have to say to each other? I don't care.

I get out through the sliding door in the study, because the front door is big and loud. I circle around the house as fast as I can, but when I get to the front, it's only Rick, standing on the street, head swinging wildly from side to side, searching for something, while his hand beats down hard on the top of his head.

"Rick?" I say, stepping out from the shadow of the oak tree in our front yard.

He falls back. "Jesus, you scared me!" he yelps. "Where'd you come from?"

"I saw your car out my window." I keep my voice down, hoping he'll do the same.

"Oh. I was trying to make up my mind . . . to, you know, knock . . . I don't want disturb you all . . ."

"Is everything okay?" I ask, though clearly, it's not. Rick's eyes keep darting up and down the street.

He runs his hand over his head, making his curly hair stick up wildly. "Listen, did Jack happen to come back this way?" he asks. I shake my head. "Yeah, I didn't think he would. But I can't think of . . . where else . . . Oh, God."

His face screws up. It looks like he might cry, which freaks me out a little, but I keep it together. "Did something happen?" I ask.

"He was supposed to be in the car waiting for me, but he wasn't. I thought maybe he walked home but he's not there. What *happened* is he has an idiot for a dad. A fucking—excuse my French—idiot." Rick bites his upper lip, over and over again.

"Do you have any idea where he might be?"

I shake my head, because, technically, I don't.

Rick puffs up his cheeks, blows out. "He's pretty pissed at me right now. Of course he is. He should be. I'm sure he's fine, he can take care of himself. I guess I'll . . . go back home. Look, if he calls or something, could you just let me know? Tell him I'm not angry or anything. Tell him . . ." His voice breaks. "I'm sorry."

He lays a heavy hand on my shoulder, gives it a squeeze, and then he's gone, the Chevy rattling off into the night.

I think of the photo, of Jack setting off on foot, of what direction he might have taken, where he would have gone. I try to remember if there's a bridge nearby, or an overpass, or a chain-link fence with a dirt path . . . and then I see it. Of course.

I know where he took that photo.

I hop off my bike and steer it onto the scrubby strip of dirt between the street and the fence. The bike was a lucky break. I would never have been able to get it out of the garage without being heard, but it was outside, leaning against the wall, where I had left it to get into Dhyllin's Benz, a lifetime ago.

I find the spot almost immediately because it's a place we've driven by a thousand times before. Right where the exit ramp from the highway merges onto Glendale Boulevard. I recognize the bridge, the overpass, the exit sign, only I never noticed the fence before, with the busted chain-link, because, why would I? Why would I ever want to break into the LA River at night?

A car roars by close, I feel the wind of it, and the rattle, and

I fall back into a bush covered in dirt and dirty flyers that have blown into it. One of the passengers yells something angry as the car screeches into the turn without stopping and then it's gone. I'm alone.

The break in the fence is perfectly sized for a bike and rider. The torn chain-link parts on either side like a curtain. The asphalt is broken up around the opening, and I imagine a giant Autobot crashing down on this spot before tumbling into the river beyond. There's broken glass near the hole, and a few beer cans crumpled in the dusty weeds. The only light's from the bridge above, and from the buildings past the electrical towers. There's no one in sight, but that doesn't mean they're not there, just beyond, waiting to jump on any fool who thought it was a good idea to walk in.

Here I go.

The bike path stretches far either way I look, and the pools of light along the path only make the shadows in between them that much darker. Rising out of the river are these giant concrete walls that look like stone submarines surfacing. The water looks black and murky, except for where it reflects the streetlights in a glowing oil slick of greasy radiated orange.

I wish I had my phone. I wish I had a flashlight. I wish I knew exactly where Jack was.

I push off in the direction of where I first met Jack, though I hope to God he isn't that far away, and that he's safe. The LA River seemed sketchy in the daytime, but now it's graduated to full-on dangerous. My heart is beating so fast I'm afraid it's going to give me away. I hear highway noises in the distance, but they're too far away to help. The path is so empty. I wish there were people around, but then, on second thought, maybe not.

I let myself coast, because I've got to look for Jack along the path and also down the concrete slope to the water and also, I've got to watch for gangs. And zombies. And gangs of zombies. *Please, Jack, don't get overrun by gangs of zombies.* Scanning the river, I see shapes in the shallow water. They could be fallen branches, or shopping carts, or bodies. Luckily, none of them looks Jack-size.

Something up ahead, against the railing, in the shadows. A person. It could be Jack. What if it's not Jack? Please let it be Jack. It is Jack.

Jack.

He's squatting and holding on to the middle crossrail, looking down at the river. I don't know if he's huddling there because he's cold, or winded, or hurt, but I'm just so relieved to see him I don't care. I lean my bike against the rail and squat beside him. "Hey," I say, putting my hand on his back. "You all right?"

He doesn't move, but I can feel the strain of muscles beneath his shirt tensing. "I'm sorry," he says quietly, not looking at me, "could you not touch me, okay."

"Okay," I say quickly, moving my hand. I grab the midrail instead. We both look out.

"Do you hear them?" he asks.

"What?"

"The frogs. There are actually frogs."

I quiet, and wait, and there they are.

357

We listen to the frogs.

"Why are you here?" Jack says to the river.

There's so much I want to say, to answer him, things I'd thought about on the bike ride over, all my gigantic revelations. I want to pour my heart out, tell him everything . . . but . . . the way he's huddled there, disconnected, gripping the bar like he's afraid to let go—

Instead, I say, "I just wanted to, uh . . . make sure you knew that . . . um . . . the end of daylight saving time works the same in California as it does in Pennsylvania, in that it . . . uh . . . gets darker earlier, which is why it's . . . so dark now."

That gets him to look at me, at least for a moment. "You are so weird."

I nod, and we both stare into the dark. There's another long silence, and then, out of nowhere, "I miss Evie."

"Yeah?"

He nods. "We were really good friends. She would call me out on all my shit, but she knew me, you know?" His voice is flat and quiet. "I kinda fucked it up with her. I do that a lot." He's barely whispering now. "I fuck things up."

"Not tonight. That wasn't on you. It wasn't."

Jack shrugs and turns back to the water, shivering.

"We should get out of here, okay?" I say. He shakes his head. "Your dad's worried about you."

"Excellent," he says, looking up, a little Jack fire in his voice. "I'm not going back to that house. I'm not staying with him anymore. Forget it."

"Yeah, but . . . you gotta go somewhere. What are you going to do, sleep here?"

"Why not? They do." He gestures out to the tarps across the water.

"Come on. Do you want to come back to my house?"

He stares at me. "Were you *there*?"

I shake my head quickly. "Right. I know, I know, it was ugly. I'm sorry."

He turns back to the water.

"So what are we going to do?"

"You should go home. Don't worry about me, I'm good," he says automatically, but there's no weight behind his words, it's just air leaving his lips.

"Jack," I say as gently as I can, "I don't think so. I don't think you're good, right now."

He bites his lip, takes a deep, shaky breath. "Yeah . . . Yeah, you could be right."

There's a pause, and then his hand moves along the crossbar closer to me. I slide my hand over. They touch, barely.

He looks out at the water. "I always think I'm better. I think I'm okay. That I can handle it. And mostly I am. I can. But . . . I don't know . . . sometimes it's so hard, you know? Just to . . . hold it together, sometimes . . . and I'm . . . afraid of what will happen . . . if I don't."

The side of his hand presses into mine. I press back. "You don't have to do it alone."

He slides his hand away and shakes his head: *no no no.*

"Let me help."

Jack pulls himself forward against the railing, away from me, like he just spotted something below, but he's not looking at anything. His eyes are closed, and his head is pushed against the crossrail, hard. "Jules, just go. I don't need to be rescued, okay?" His voice is tight. "You should go. You don't want to be here. It's cool. Go."

My eyes sting with a sudden fire. "You know what? I'm tired of people telling me what I want or don't want. Okay? I *want* to be here. With you. And I'm going to stay here, as long as I *want*, which is . . . as long as you're gonna be here." And before I lose it completely: "I want to be here with you, Jack."

He curls tight against the railing, and I think he's pulling away, but then he pushes off, lets go of the bar, lets go of his breath, and I'm there to catch him. He buries his head in my chest and I circle my arms around. His crying is silent, more like gasps for air, coming quick and hard, the same rhythm as my heartbeat.

I hold him like that for a long time. There's no room in me for fear, or worry, or even thought. There's only the warmth of his body, his slowing breath, my heart.

When we finally pull apart, our legs are stiff and have gone numb, pins and needles. We need to grab the railing to stand up. We look drunk, it's kind of funny, but then Jack ducks his head away, suddenly shy. My hoodie's wet, and when I touch the place where Jack's head has been, I feel the keys around my neck. I remember how my dad always said, *You can stay over anytime*, and I'm hoping he really means it.

***

Later.

I'm lying in the dark, listening to Jack sleep.

I should be asleep, too, but even as my eyes flicker shut I'm running through events, moment by moment. It took us two buses to get to my father's condo in Santa Monica, and I want to remember every minute:

Us trying to figure out how to get to Santa Monica, and Jack asking me if there was public transportation and I have no idea and Jack asking if I'd ever ridden a city bus and giving me that look when I tell him never;

And the bus to Echo Park, and then another to Santa Monica, a long ride but that's okay because we sit next to each other and can't help that our shoulders sometimes press together;

And me texting Rick on Jack's phone, because Jack didn't want to, telling him everything was all right and we're staying at my dad's, don't worry, and there's already a bunch of messages from him but Jack doesn't look at them, just puts his phone away;

And passing through Beverly Hills, where Jack tells me about how his dad wants to separate from his mom and stay in Los Angeles, and I reach for Jack's hand next to mine and give it a squeeze, hoping he can't tell through my fingers that my heart just did a totally inappropriate happy dance;

And Jack passing me his phone that's about to die and on the screen is a Tumblr blog called *missing evie*, and there's a map of Pittsburgh as a cover photo and he tells me, *Start from the bottom*, and looks out the window;

And by the time I finish the last post there's nothing I wouldn't do for him, and I whisper, *She'll come around*, but Jack's sleeping, and when I look up, there's a sign welcoming us to Santa Monica, and when I look down, his phone has just death-spiraled, and I nudge Jack and tell him we're almost there and he asks sleepily, *But where's the ocean*;

And us being checked in the lobby by the doorman guy, who gives us major stink eye, and how I'm afraid that he won't let us up even if I have the key, but it doesn't matter because my father's home;

And my father's face when he opens the door, full of questions, but when he sees Jack he tucks them away and calls my mother to make sure she hasn't called the police and he tells her I'm safe and tries to convince her there wasn't any abduction, and he passes the phone over to me but I shake my head and he takes it back, telling her, *I'll call you in a minute*;

And him saying, *You look dead on your feet* and Jack nods and my father shows him the guest bedroom before he takes me into the living room so we can talk, and he knows most of it because Rick called Mom and Mom called him, and my dad does a lot of sighing and says, *We can get it all straightened out in the morning*;

And seeing Jack already asleep when I come back in the room, curled up on the bed with his clothes on, fists covering his chest;

How Jack's black hair curls on the white pillow;

How Jack's eyelashes are still wet and spiky;

How Jack is handsome, and beautiful, and all those good words;

How Jack sleeping is him saying, *I trust you*, or maybe just,

362

I'm really tired;

How I cover him with a blanket;

How I don't sleep on the couch in the living room but on the floor next to the bed because I don't want him to feel alone;

How I match my breath to his;

How I imagine my chest against his back, feeling those breaths;

How I'm lying in the dark, listening to Jack sleep.

31. Jack

The coyotes wake me up, they sound like they're right outside the window, screaming and yelping, ripping into the quiet like they hate it. They're coming for me. I'm in the serial killer house, how'd I get back here? Where's Jules? There's a high-pitched squeal, I wonder if it's a cat or a raccoon getting torn into, but I'm not sticking around to find out.

I step out into the hall, just in time, there's scraping and snarling on the other side of the door as soon as I've closed it, they've broken in. *Go. Go.* But the hall is longer than I remember, it stretches on and on, the kitchen's nowhere, I'm turning corners, running past locked doors, I know they're locked without even trying. Finally, there's the end, the exit, it's where Serial Killer #3 lives, I've got to go in. When I push the door open, there are steps going down, like to a basement, but it's a kitchen, no, it's the back room of a store, it's Punjab Spices and Sweets and I know this because the smell of rose water is overwhelming.

Only a weak light over the sink, someone eating at a table, at first I think it's the old lady who works there but this person is like three times her size, Brian-size, could that be him in a costume? but the figure speaks and the deep voice with the Indian accent

364

is definitely not Brian's.

"No need to stare in the dark. Turn on the light if you are wanting a look."

A light blinks on, automatically, but she's still half in shadow. She's gigantic, with broad shoulders and a square face, solid bulk wrapped in a sari of saffron and paprika, a river of blue lotuses snaking along the border. She turns her head to me, glaring, her red bindi glowing between two fierce eyebrows on her lined, dark golden face, the giveaway Adam's apple bobbing up and down as she swallows down gulab jamun, *my* gulab jamun, there's the Tupperware by her elbow.

"Come, come, *puttar*," she says, a voice filled with gravel, her massive hand holding a ball delicately between a thick thumb and finger. "I am not going to bite."

I'm not so sure of that. I watch her pop an entire dough ball into her mouth, thin and wide like a frog's but with lots of pointy teeth inside. She's got the same wiry hair as my grandmother's, pulled back in a tight bun, crackles of white running through. Maybe she's swallowed Nani whole and put on her sari. And is going to gulp me down next.

"Why are you eating those?" I ask.

Her sticky mouth spreads into a smile, and she licks her fingers, one by one. "I couldn't help myself, *puttar*! I was so hungry, and there they are, waiting for me! Just like an offering." She places her right hand over the other onto her chest. "Ardha accepts."

And then I realize that the part of her I thought was her in shadow is actually the color of her skin on the right side of her face and body, a soft midnight blue. "Wait, are you a goddess?" I ask.

"Ha!" she scoffs. "Biology major. Only students live here, remember?"

"Where've you been hiding?"

Ardha raises her eyebrows. "Hiding? I don't hide, child. Do you think there is any hiding *this*?" She waves her hand around her whole body and laughs, a rolling boom of sound that's gonna wake up the entire floor.

"Jack." She knows my name. "Do you like my lizard, Jack, hmm?"

She points to her right shoulder. "Holy crap!" I say, stepping back. A small blue-green lizard appears out of nowhere, clinging to the folds of her drape; it was so still I must have missed seeing it.

"You can pet him but be careful. His coat—"

"Is shedding," I say. "Yeah, I see that. I've got two at home."

Ardha throws her hands up in mock surprise. "Oh. *Two.* You are knowing *so* much." She stares at me, unblinking, expecting something. I want to round my shoulders but my binder keeps pulling them back, why am I wearing my binder at night? But no time to wonder, Ardha keeps staring, putting a finger under her chin and drawing it down. "So, little lizard boy, how is it with *your* shedding? Hmm? Enjoying your new skin?"

My mouth clamps shut but somehow the words come out anyway. "I would if everyone would just shut up about it. When do I get to stop all this coming out, all the time?"

Ardha's laughter echoes around the room, her whole body shakes. The bells dangling from her enormous earlobes jingle with her. She stops, stabs a finger at the table like she's stubbing out a cigarette. Her eyes burn bright. The lizard's eyes light up, too. "It will never be over. You will always be coming out, because you will always be new. Every day you are changing, your cells change, your thoughts change, you *are* change. That is what it means to be alive." She runs her hand over her head, and her fingers leave streaks of pomegranate red in her hair. "And every time you change, you must find a way to present this new self to the world. This glorious creature you are becoming."

I glare at her from across the table. "I'm not a creature, okay? And why do I have to present myself?" I do my own pointing. "It's like, if you had a tail, and you could hide it from everyone, why wouldn't you? It'd be insane not to. Who wants to go through life being called Tail Boy? Having to explain your tail every day? What's wrong with hiding it?"

Ardha raises her shoulders to her ears, arms reaching out. "Nothing! What do I care? It is your tail to show if you wish to or not. But . . . have *you* looked at this tail, which is a part of you? Is it a nice tail? Is it prehensile? Does it regenerate?"

"I'm not a lizard!" I yell to her face. And the lizard on her shoulder barks back, it's a dirty white dog, sitting on her lap. "I'm not a *kutta*, either!"

She's still as a statue, eyes flaming right into mine. I'm sitting now and she towers over me. "You are not this, you are not that. But what *are* you?"

It's hard to breathe, like she's pressing on my lungs. "Leave me alone!"

367

"Is that what you want, to be left alone?" Ardha asks softly. She straightens, brings her hands to her head. "So much fire. Good." She releases her hair, molten brown flowing to her shoulders, strands of turquoise joining the red where her hand has touched. "Just be careful not to burn yourself." She shakes her head and the colors shimmer and spark against each other. "Ah, *puttar*, it is so so strange," she says, her voice far away but deep inside me, "why this world cannot embrace the infinite variety of human life."

She strokes my hair, one warm leathery palm cupping my entire head, and I close my eyes, automatic, her hand is a lullaby. "These are the words." Her breathing's slow and steady, the push and pull of the ocean, I can smell brine in every exhale. "Expand! Don't contract."

She comes closer, I can feel her breath tickle my ear as she speaks again, but her voice has changed, it's higher and lighter and so familiar I want to cry.

"There's room in this fucking universe for all kinds of people, Adam. Even you. So, go ahead, take up some space."

Blink awake.

Evie, wait, don't go, I close my eyes again, try to keep her with me, bring her back under my eyelids, but she's gone, already fading, scraps of images that dissolve as soon as I flash on them, and where did this Ardha come from?

When I wake for real, I don't know where I am, there's no scary wood paneling in front of me, I'm not on a blow-up mattress.

What? Oh, right. Last night. Longest night ever. Good morning, Santa Monica.

Jules is snoring, right below me, well, not exactly snoring, not heavy artillery like my father, more like cooing. Like what cartoon babies sound like when they sleep. His mouth's open, he's wrapped up in a white comforter on the ground, a puffy cloud with his big old legs sticking out, jock angel fallen to earth.

A jock angel who let me have the bed.

I roll onto my side for a better look, and that's when the pain hits. My ribs, below my chest on the right, all daggers. I gasp, and sucking in that air makes them stab even more. I flop onto my back.

Shit. Shit shit shit. Grit my teeth, try to catch a breath, work up the courage to move.

"What's wrong?" Jules's head pops up like a gopher coming out of a hole.

"Nothing," I gasp, jabbing my elbows into the mattress to get up. Luckily, the bathroom is only steps away, connected to the bedroom. I swing my legs around, setting off another burst of red sparks, ouch, and set them on the floor.

Jules starts to rise, "Let me help," but I've already used his shoulder as a launchpad to shoot myself across the room, holding on to my side.

Slam the door behind me. *Okay, next step.* The bathroom's got an entire wall of mirrors but I just have to deal with it. I turn my back and rip off my shirts as fast as I can to get down to my binder. You're only supposed to wear it for like eight hours, never overnight, Binder Use 101, you could fracture a rib or fuck up your breathing. Plus, all that heaving and sobbing from last night probably didn't help. *Shit.*

I squeeze out of the squeeze, take a few deep breaths, already it's better, just being released. Under my right arm I'm ready to see a gaping wound, a rib poking out, but all I can find is a tender spot below my armpit. I cough a few times, because I remember you're supposed to, and some crap clears from my lungs. Wait a minute. Feel around again. It's still tender, some aching in my back, but everything else seems to check out. Relief.

"Jack?" Jules calls from behind the door. "You okay?"

Like a reflex, my hand shoots out and slams down the bathroom light switch, sorry, nobody home, go away. I scramble for my T-shirt, pull it over my head, trying not to groan. Throw my flannel shirt on, but having Jules so close on the other side of that door flutters up the panic birds so I'm having trouble doing the buttons up right.

"Jack?"

"What!" I yell, undoing the buttons.

"Is it your binder?"

Everything stops. "What?"

"You're not supposed to wear it at night, right?"

I'm freeze-framed, world-rocked, I've entered into an alternative universe, I— "How did you know that?"

"You did an Adam and Evie YouTube about it, remember?"

I scroll through all my emotions—amazed and freaked and super impressed, but mostly I'm so confused it just chills my shit out. I flick on the light, try buttoning my shirt the right way.

"Yeah," I call out, "it was the binder. I think I'm okay now."

"You sure? 'Cause you know you could get serious damage if you—"

"I know! I know!" I yell, but then add, quieter, "It's just a bruise. Pretty sure."

"Just to be safe, maybe we should go to a—"

"Don't worry! I'll keep an eye on it."

I'm finally buttoned, but still, I know I can't open that door. Even with my shirt untucked and me hunching my shoulders, without the binder all I can see in the mirror is chest chest, roundness and shadows. I tell myself I'm exaggerating, it's fine, but then I think of Jules, where he'll look as soon as I enter the room.

I can't open that door.

"Hey . . . I'm having a problem, um . . . the binder's off, but now . . . uh . . . I don't know if I can—"

"Wait," Jules calls out. "Hold on." There's a pause—he's closer to the door. "I'm not coming in, okay, I'm not coming in, I swear." The handle moves down, the door cracks opens, it's a horror movie come to life . . .

And there's Jules's blue hoodie, bunched up in his hand.

"Would this help?" he asks, from the other side of the door.

I never knew I could feel so grateful.

The hoodie is bulky and ridiculously big on me, which is why it's perfect. It's got Jules's smell all over it. I never thought about Jules having a smell, but there it is, all around me as I pull the hoodie on, and I'd be lying if I said I didn't breathe in a little deeper before it went past my head.

When I open the door, Jules is standing there in his white T-shirt, extra tall and gangly, his hands stuffed into his jeans pockets, and he looks nervous, but not in a bad way, not like he's afraid of what I'll look like, but that he's just worried about how I am. He sees me, and his eyes don't dart around, or try to avoid, he just . . . sees me.

I give him a thumbs-up and he grins, relieved.

I nod. "Dude."

He nods back. "Dude."

Which is pretty much exactly the right thing to say.

There's no one around when we leave the bedroom. We walk into the kitchen with our hands in our pockets, keeping our distance, awkward, but not a bad awkward. Alan's left a note on the marble kitchen counter:

Had to get to work. I know you teens like to sleep late.

Help yourself to anything.

When you talk to your mother, if you could tell her it was not my idea that would be helpful.

Contact Denise if you need an Uber back.

Good luck,

Dad

"Good luck?" Jules says. "Great. Thanks, Dad, see ya next year." He tosses the note back.

I lean up against the counter. "But he left you money." I point out the cash next to the note.

"Yeah, that's what he's good at," Jules says under his breath.

"Okay, the fact that there's a fifty-dollar bill on the counter you're not snatching up right away—means you're a rich kid."

He flips me the finger, and it feels normal again, and then we smile, and it's back to awkward. "I'm starving," Jules says, and opens the refrigerator. "Ergh. Perrier, butter, mustard, lime. This place sucks."

"This place rocks," I say, scoping out the living room, because it's easier than staring at Jules. "Look at it, it's like mint condition, all sunny and shiny, *and look at these posters!*" All my favorite movies are framed white on the wall. "They're in different languages!" I put my hands on an extremely cool *Easy Rider* one-sheet from Japan. "Hey, he said help yourself to anything. . . ."

Jules shrugs. "Go for it."

"And you can see the ocean!" I say, peeking out the sliding doors to the small balcony. "Jules, you picked the wrong parent to live with."

"Well," says Jules, "who knows, that might change, depending on—"

He sighs. I know he's thinking of his mom, steam coming out of her ears, her pitchfork raised, *because he's missing school.* That makes me think of my dad, who's not off the hook, who's still a jagoff, but probably still needs to hear from me, too. We both know it'll only get worse the longer we wait. So, I find a charging cable on the counter and plug my dead phone in, and Jules heads for his father's room to make his call on the portable.

As soon as my phone has a sliver of green, I open my messages. There are just too many from Dad, so I start texting without reading any of them.

> hi im fine in santa monica will get back soon

Dad's reply is instant:

> Okay. Glad you texted. Glad you're safe.

> You don't have to call me but PLEASE call your mom, she's very worried. She knows everything, I had to.

> See you soon. Love you.

I call her work extension, and she picks up right away.

"Hey, Mom."

"Jack." And then there's her silence and my silence having their own conversation. It's not that we don't know what to say, it's just that there are too many things to say. I don't know if I should feel sorry, or angry, or what. But then I hear her raggedy breath and I realize she's crying.

Mom hardly ever cries. And *never* at work.

"I'm fine, Mom, really."

"Are you sure?"

I think a moment. "I'm . . . on my way to fine. I was a little out of control before, but I think I'm okay now."

Mom takes a big breath and her voice gets solid again. "You need to come back home, Jack. I don't like having you so far away. Enough is enough. You need to come home."

"I know. I agree. I do."

"Oh, Jack." She gives another long exhale. "Never do that again, all right?"

"I won't."

"I miss you so much. And whatever it is, you've got support here—" but she cuts herself off, and I hear her say to someone off the phone, "Yes, I know, I'll be right there." Then she's back in my ear. "Jack, we'll get through this. Together. I have to go into a meeting right now—"

"Sure, go, no problem."

"—but I'll call you this afternoon. Make sure you pick up. All right?" She whispers, "I love you, Jack," and I think we're both gonna break.

"Love you, Mom."

I'm about to click off when I hear her voice. "And, Jack—?"

"Yeah?"

She pauses. "Don't blame your father for everything, okay? It's . . . not so simple. These things are never simple. We'll talk."

She hangs up. I'm alone in the kitchen, waiting, checking out my other messages and holy crap, there are about a billion from Jules's phone from last night, I'm guessing his mom got busy, trying to track us down. I'm about to erase them—who wants to wade through that toxic dump?—when I remember the one text I do want to look at. I scroll up and up and up, past all her exclamation points and all-caps, and find the last text the real Jules sent me:

im with you jack

always

♥

I stare at it and stare at it, hoping it's gonna tell me what to do.

Jules trudges in. He falls on the couch, his head hanging over the end. Big exhale.

"How'd it go?" I ask.

"Brutal. But I was expecting that, so . . ."

"Yeah, me too."

"I think the only thing that saved me is that right now she's madder at my dad for some reason. Like she's furious that he left us alone. And that he didn't try to get me to school today."

"If you were suspended like me you wouldn't have to worry. Did you mention that to her?"

He snorts. "Right. That'd go over big." He swings himself up, sits by me. "I told her we'd get back as soon as we can, she wanted to call an Uber, but I told her no, I mean, I was kind of hoping we could take the bus back but she wants me to—" and then he stops himself. "It doesn't matter what she wants. We'll get back when we get back." He looks over at me, like he just invented parental rebellion. "Right?"

"You know . . . ," I say.

"What?"

"My phone still needs to charge. Can't go home without a working phone, yeah? In case someone needs to contact us?" I walk up to the counter, slap my hand down on the fifty. "And we need breakfast. Most important meal of the day. So, we leave my phone here and get something to eat. And since we're already out, I gotta see the ocean, right?"

Santa Monica has a totally different vibe than Silver Lake and Atwater Village. The breeze, the salt in the air, the people actually walking around on the streets. Even more tourists, if that's possible. Breakfast is French toast crepes with bacon on the Third Street Promenade, dessert is beignets, so much powdery goodness, and just like that, a fifty-dollar bill has almost been sucked dry.

We slurp on boba chai lattes on the way to the beach. Our bodies have magnetized, we always seem to be bumping into each other, tangling our steps, the pull closing up space between us, but I know, I *know*, even if Jules doesn't, that it'll only get harder from here on out.

"Hey, check out that guy," I say, nudging Jules. There's a hugely buff gym rat in a tank top, board shorts, and baseball cap, across the street. "Pretty hot, huh?"

"Duh," says Jules. "He's looks like an underwear model." He looks again. "Wait, I think he *is* an underwear model. Isn't he on the Calvin Klein box?"

"Yeah, I think they grow them out here." This is excruciating. "Look at him," I say, pointing out a skinny, curly-haired dude with retro shades and a porkpie hat, lounging at a Starbucks. "He's got that sexy Brooklyn hipster vibe going on, what do you think of him?"

"Umm . . ."

"And what about that guy? He's kind of geeky-cute—"

Jules looks down at me. "And what about you?"

Ignore. "I mean, look at all these men. There are so many possibilities out there."

"Jack, they're all, like, adults."

"Okay, so what about that guy at school, the one you hang out with?"

"Lowell?"

"Yeah, Lowell. He's like a cool guy, head of the GSA, what about him?"

"What about him what?"

"Could you see going out with him?"

"Hmm." Jules sucks down his drink, considering, and part of me is like, fuck, hit the mark, but then he shakes his head. "No . . . ," he says slowly, "I mean, he's nice, but . . ." Shrugs. "Why're you trying to set me up?"

"I don't know, it's just— I think you need to consider all your options."

"I don't need options."

"I mean, your first relationship should be, like, pow, perfect. Easy."

He shrugs again but gives me that *Where is this going?* stare.

"And I'm heading back to Pittsburgh, you know, I'm not going to be here too much longer, so—"

"Yeah, I know." Jules stops walking. "I know. And it sucks, but . . ." He looks really annoyed. "Look, if you don't want to, like, go out with me or whatever, that's cool, okay? Just say it." I don't say it. "I mean, you told me I never choose anything, so here I am, making a choice. Who says I can't choose something that's not so easy? I mean, maybe not so easy is worth it, you know?"

But I can't let it go. "I'm just saying that for your first perfect boyfriend, you should be with someone who's not going to add all these complications—"

"How many first boyfriends have you had?"

"None."

"Then why should I take advice from you?" he says, and when I don't have an answer to that, he drops the invisible mic in front of me. "Boom!"

We sit on the beach, the Santa Monica Pier on our left, volleyball players on our right, the ocean glittering calmly in front of us, no waves. It's not cold, but there's enough breeze for us to push against each other, for warmth.

"I don't want to go back home," Jules says quietly.

"Yeah." We stare at the water. "We could just live out here on the beach."

"Hey, I'll do it if you will."

"Jules."

"Mmm?"

I pull away. "If we want to even try to do this—" My open hands shuttle between us.

"What? Go steady? Hold hands? Make out?"

"Shut up. Listen." Jules loses his sleepiness, sits up. *Here goes.* "There's, like, a lot of me"—and I circle my hands around my upper torso, my lower torso, and just that motion is, *God, how am I even doing this*—"that I'm not so comfortable with anyone seeing. Or touching. I mean, that might change, but, for now . . . I don't know. I'm just telling you."

"Okay," he says, serious now.

"I mean, there are . . . things we *can* do. For sure. But there are other things that . . . I don't know yet."

"Got it," he says. "I mean, I think I do. I probably don't. But . . . we'll figure it out. Let's just see how it goes?"

"You're okay with that?"

He nods. We go back to staring at the water. Our hands become little crabs, sidestepping their way on the sand to find each other.

He's doing his best not to let me see him smile. "What?" I say.

Jules pauses, and he looks, I've never seen this look on him before, it's kind of shy and sly at the same time. "There are things we can do?"

I grin my own kind of shy and sly, and nod.

"Can I ask a question?" He takes a breath, and I brace myself. "So, here"—rubbing his eyebrow—"is this, like, a safe area? To touch?"

That wasn't a question I was expecting. "Uh, yeah?"

His cheeks pop bright red. "I just always wanted to . . . I really love your eyebrows."

It's just so stupid silly, I have to laugh, and he laughs back, and I say, "Okay, knock yourself out," and he leans over, stretches a finger, and strokes my right eyebrow, really slowly. He makes a careful loop around the piercing, and suddenly it stops being silly, when did that happen? It feels so serious my heart could stop.

"Okay?" he asks.

More than okay. I nod, and we look at each other, eyes just overflowing with amazement, with possibilities, with O brave new world.

"Any other questions?" I ask.

He hesitates, then lifts a finger and draws a circle around his lips, eyes questioning.

I nod again, quickly, because it's faster than words. He reaches out, all his fingers now, leaving a trail of sparks where they touch my smile.

"Jack—" he says, but there's no time for speaking, no way, cue the fireworks, the orchestra, the Hallelujah Chorus, I'm going in.

We kiss. And kiss. Two boys kissing on a beach, in Santa Monica, because we want to, because we can.

And five hundred years later, when we finally pull away from each other, grinning like fools, Jules says, "You have to admit. That was pretty perfect."

I have to admit.

32. Jules

Wednesday, we walk into school hand in hand.

Yes, it's a statement, it's a dare, a let's-just-get-it-out-there kind of move. But the main reason we meet each other on the corner and lace our fingers together has nothing to do with being brave or political. It's just this: there's so little time left. Like, nothing. We wasted so much of it, and now we have to make every minute count. Jack's mom agreed to let him finish the semester but winter break is just around the corner, and I can't even think about what happens after.

Just stay in the moment.

Entering the quads, it's scary as hell. It's crazy exciting. People are staring, people are not staring, I don't care. I do my best to walk like it's no big thing, like I do this every day, but inside, I want to pump my fist in the air and do a victory dance as "We Are the Champions" plays in the background. Instead, I squeeze Jack's hand. He squeezes back, harder. For such a small dude, Jack's got *grip*.

"Watch it, man," I say, "that's my shooting hand."

Like it or not, school's gonna be the easiest place to see each other. I'm not pushing my luck at home, which seems to be operating on a don't ask, don't tell basis—she doesn't ask about Jack and I don't tell her anything. I think me going to my dad's condo really scared her. She's stopped drinking, for now. Alcohol disrupts her intestinal microbiota, she says. I watch her watching me, looking for clues. She's trying to be hands-off, but I know what's she's thinking: Jack will be gone at the end of the semester, and if she just waits it out, everything will go back to the way it was. And it's fine if she wants to think that, because she'll be waiting a long time. A long time.

Passing the basketball court, I see a couple of my teammates shooting hoops. I give them the chin raised, *s'up* nod. They nod back, we're all so cool, and then of course my legs tangle, 'cause that's what they do. Jack jerks me back up before I full-on trip. "Thanks," I say.

"Baby Giraffe," Jack says, remembering something.

"What?"

He smiles. "Never mind."

Cecilia and Gregg are back at the sophomore benches, tapping away on their phones. As we pass, Cecilia looks up and kind of freezes, then gets herself going again with a toss of her hair. "Well, good," she says, and gives a sunny smile that stays longer on her face than it has to. Gregg beams and shoots me two giant thumbs-up, and I can't help but grin back.

We walk on.

I jostle Jack. "Hey, you know what would be really good right now? One of those Indian donut holes. That would be really tasty—"

"Shut. Up," Jack says.

We're almost to the main building. If Jack's tense, he's not showing it. He's quiet, but I have to remember that's not always a bad sign. "You okay?" I ask.

"Yeah, just want to get this over with."

There's a sharp cry behind us. Jack ducks his head and whirls around, but I already know what's coming. "What is this, what is *this*?" says Lily Cho, pulling Lowell along with her. Her voice is back to its usual high pitch. She lets go of him and spreads her arm wide—"Soooo cute!"—then mashes Jack and me into one big hug. "I knew it, Mr. Styles," she says, wagging a finger at me.

Lowell's cool as ever, giving me a raised eyebrow and greeting Jack with a finger flutter. "Thanks for meeting up. Jack, can we talk a little?" Jack nods. "So, about the whole restorative justice circle thing this morning. I talked to Mr. Janssen, the GSA sponsor, and he's agreed to be there, but only if you want."

"Oh, um, okay, sure," says Jack, looking at me, and then back to Lowell. "Thanks."

"Of course." Lowell pulls out his phone to text Mr. Janssen. I can tell he's being more serious with Jack, more careful. He's keeping his smirks to a minimum. "And the student you rescued, Kacey—they want to support you, too, and they're already in, giving their side of the story, so there you go."

"Oh. Now I'm kinda more nervous," Jack says. "I thought this was just kind of a stupid—"

"Just *speak your truth*," Lily Cho declares, underlining every word, "and you'll be fine."

"Nothing to worry about," says Lowell. "Gavin's a knuckle

scraper, everyone knows it."

"And, *Jack*," says Lily Cho, "we know you might feel awkward at lunch, you know, at the *scene of the crime*—"

"Hadn't thought of that," mutters Jack, instantly awkward.

"So, we thought you could eat with us, over on the grass by Building C. Very exclusive. Wouldn't that be good, Jules?"

"Maybe . . ."

She shakes her head. "Forget maybe, the correct answer is yes."

"Uhh . . ." I look at Jack, who gives a tiny wince only I can see. "You know what? I think we're good today. But thanks."

"But—" The bell rings, cutting off Lily Cho mid-protest.

"All right," Jack says. "Here goes." Without thinking, we reach for each other's hands. Jack puffs out his cheeks, exhales. "Fasten your seat belts—"

"—it's going to be a bumpy night?" Lowell says, his trademark smirk flipped on. Jack looks at him, surprised, and they share a smile that I'm not entirely happy about. Lowell turns on his heel, gives a wave. "Good luck."

"Good luck!" echoes Lily Cho, and she and Lowell march off to first period.

The stampede begins. "I'd better go in," says Jack. "See you at nutrition." Our hands squeeze together, saying their own goodbye.

"Hey, Jack!" I catch him just before he goes through the doorway. He turns around. I jab an angry finger his way. "No movie quote sharing with anyone else!"

That gets the smile I was hoping for. "Then catch up, bro!" he yells, and disappears into the building.

33. Jack

I'm wearing Jules's hoodie for luck. Haven't even washed it. No way.

Dad wanted to come with me to the big school showdown, but I told him no, didn't see how him being there would be much help to anyone, at all. That's pretty much the most I've said to him since I got back from Santa Monica, also the nicest I've been to him since I got back from Santa Monica. It's pretty frosty in the serial killer house right now, don't know how long the cold front's gonna last, and for now, he's taking it. It's not easy, sharing the space, no bedroom for me to slam myself into, so I curl up on my mattress with my earbuds in and face the wall, and he tries to make himself busy someplace else.

But. Not that I'd tell him this, but Dad gets points for convincing my mom that I didn't have to get on the next plane home. "Nita, he wants to stay. It's only six more weeks and I promise, I *swear* on all that is good and holy, I will watch him . . . no, I will *not* drop the ball, or the boy, this time . . ." He pulled out all the stops with that phone call, lots of promises and begging and general dirt-eating. I have to give him props.

Not that I'd tell him that.

Not one second longer, Mom said. So now, I've got to save up all my seconds here, 'cause they're not gonna last.

I wait outside Mrs. Chan's office door. *Speak my truth.* What kind of California crunchy idea is that? Mr. Janssen arrives, gives me a nod and a little smile that's tight but warm. He pauses before he opens the door and says to me, quietly, "We can do better, Jack. As a school. We will do better." And he goes in. A minute later, Mr. Shanley, the vice principal, strides past and enters the office without even looking at me, bored and bothered. So much for doing better. Two seconds after that, Mrs. Chan's head pops out. "You can come in now, Jack."

I'm the last one to the party—Gavin's already seated.

So, the thing about a restorative justice circle is, it sounds like it's gonna be the UN, or a Jedi Council, something like that, but really, it's like being sent to the principal's office, but with less shouting and more people. Gavin and me, Mrs. Chan behind her desk, Mr. Janssen and Mr. Shanley standing on the sides, referees waiting to drop a flag.

Mrs. Chan lays out the ground rules: mutual respect, active listening, common understanding, violence is never the answer, all that stuff. "Frame what you say in terms of *I*," she warns. "Not what the other person did, but what *I* did, what *I* felt. Understand?"

Gavin goes first. He stares at the floor and says his piece, mumbles all the right words in the right order: *I wasn't aware—*, *I did not mean to—*, *I respect—*, but the words drop out of his mind the minute they leave his mouth—he's a fourth grader reciting a book report on a book he didn't read. When he's done, he crosses his arms and slouches back in his chair, instantly tuned out.

Mrs. Chan gives me the nod.

So, yeah, I speak my truth. Lay it all out. What I did. How I felt. What it's like to be a trans kid in a cis world that doesn't know how to deal with you. There are some awkward silences, lots of hitches and stumbles—it's hard to remember all those *I*'s I'm supposed to be framing with my heart thudding so loudly—but I get out most of what I want to say, and what I say, I mean.

That's it. Mrs. Chan sums everything up in a nice neat box, we make promises, we *sign* promises, and VP Shanley issues some carefully threatening remarks. Then we stand, so Gavin and I can give each other the mandatory handshake.

Did it matter? I don't know. Mr. Janssen was listening, leaning forward and nodding. Mr. Shanley was on the other side, checking his watch. Mrs. Chan was at her desk in the middle, scribbling, scribbling on her paper, getting it all down. And Gavin? When I stick out my hand, he barely touches it, like he's afraid of contagion. His eyes don't meet mine and his lips are already curling with the things he's gonna say to his buddies after he leaves.

That's the way it is. There are always going to be Gavins, and whether this one learns and grows and marches in a Pride parade, or if he stays exactly the same, I have no control over that. But I got to say what I needed to say. And he had to sit and listen to it.

So, I guess that's something, though it doesn't seem like enough. Maybe it never will.

"Back to class, please," Mr. Shanley barks.

Leaving the office, all I want to see is Jules, Jules and his goofy face, but someone else is waiting in the courtyard for me. They can't wait for me to come down the steps as I push through the doors of the building, they rush up to me and stand, shivering, twining their magenta hair around their nervous fingers.

Kacey, at long last.

"Kacey, right? I'm Jack."

"I know," Kacey says quickly. "How did it go?"

"Uh, good, I guess. I heard you spoke up for me, so, thanks."

"Of course!" Kacy is beaming. "And, and did you hear what else? I told them how I felt, about the school and all, and Mr. Janssen said they'd consider changing the name of the GSA so it's not the Gay–Straight Alliance anymore! It could be, like, the Genders and Sexualities Alliance. Isn't that great?"

I smile. Kacey reminds me of Evie and me, the way we were in the beginning, there's so much hope bouncing around in their eyes. "Well, it's going to take more than a name change, but, yeah, it's a start."

"We're making a difference! I've never done anything like this. So, thank you."

"I . . . really didn't have anything to do with it, but, cool."

"No, you did. You absolutely did. I would never have spoken out if it weren't for you."

"Okay . . . well, then, good." I look around, wondering which building Jules is going to be coming out of, but Kacey's voice pulls me back.

"So, it's better, isn't it?" they say.

"Is what better?"

"Being out. At school. Aren't you glad?"

A shiver, a rustling, up and down my neck. "What do you mean?"

"It's just—" Kacey hesitates, fingers grabbing at their hair like they're trying to pull the pink off. They bite their lower lip. "I know you," they whisper, finally.

"What?"

"I know you," Kacey repeats, "from before. When you were Adam."

I freeze, but Kacey flows on, a flood of breathy, halting sentences. "Your videos with Evie, they like literally *saved my life*. I followed everything you did. I mean, you guys helped me understand who I am, you made sense of me not making sense! You were so happy together, and that gave me hope, too, you know, *be who you want to be, you are perfect, love yourself*, all that, it made me feel like everything was going to be okay. I was jellybeanz2002—do you remember you answered an ask of mine?"

I shake my head. At this moment I couldn't remember my own name, any of them.

"But then, then you guys stopped posting and the Tumblr shut down, and I had no idea what happened, it was super frightening, like, I felt totally abandoned, you know?"

I don't know, I'm dizzy, I'm looking at my life from the wrong end of the telescope.

"And then it was so weird, but on my first day at Earl Warren, I was feeling super anxious, and suddenly . . . there you were! It was like this *miracle*, my number one wish come true, like you appeared just to be this *light* for me, to guide me through high school. That's how it felt!"

Kacey's head drops. "But then . . . but then you were like *that*. I just didn't get it, you weren't like the Adam I knew *at all*, you just ignored me, and it felt so hurtful, like you were saying, 'Be who you want to be, but don't bother me.'" Kacey picks up speed now, talking fast, like a timer's about to go off. "And it's been so hard this year, with Gavin picking on me almost every day and no one really caring, and the GSA, they didn't understand, and you weren't at the meeting to help explain things, you weren't interested in helping at all, like I'd see you in the courtyard and you were fitting in like I can never fit in, it was like you were *hiding* . . . it wasn't *right*."

I shake my head, I'm watching a horror movie where they're about to open that door, the door to the basement, don't open it, Kacey, but they keep reaching out their hand. . .

"And so . . . and so . . ."

I can barely swallow. "So . . ."

"So," Kacey whispers, face pulled into a wince, "I sent out the video."

I'm cold. All the blood has left my body. I can only stare.

"I know!" Kacey's voice spills all over me. "And I felt awful about it and I wanted to take it back right away but I couldn't, and then it spread and—"

"That is—" My blood surges back, pounding into my skull. "That is completely *fucked up*."

"—and I'm so, so sorry."

"You don't get to make that decision for me! How could you do that?"

As my voice gets louder, Kacey's gets quieter. "I don't know, I wasn't thinking, I guess I thought, I thought if people knew you were trans . . ."

I hammer into Kacey with every word. "Yeah? Then what? What?"

"Then I wouldn't feel so alone."

I feel the blood pounding in my head, I'm waiting for the beating of those sharp wings, the fireball I know is going to erupt. I stare at Kacey and take a breath—

And another breath.

And another.

No wings, no fury. Just Kacey, standing small in front of me. So familiar. The hurt and the fear in their eyes, I've had burning in my eyes, I've seen flaming in Evie's eyes. All of us, the same, trying to get by, trying to connect, trying to figure it all out, and fucking up, and trying again. I mean, it's a whole new world out here, there are so many battles we have to fight. The last thing we need is to fight each other.

"Okay." It takes me a couple more breaths to get to even. "That was not . . . you should never out someone, ever. It's a personal decision, and outing can be really dangerous for the person. Yeah? But . . . it happened, and . . . we all screw up sometimes, and . . . and I'm sorry for my part in that."

Kacey nods.

The bell rings. Any moment now, the slam of the crash bar,

the doors opening, the crowd pouring out.

I hold out my hand. "You're not alone, okay?"

"Okay." Kacey slowly reaches out and slips their hand into mine. Their fingers are pale and cool and so delicate I'm afraid of crushing them.

So, I don't.

princess bride

hey look whos back on tumblr its me

this is 4 u evie even if u never see this hello hello hello

recap my name is jack now not adam and im in la not pittsburgh but ill be home in a week dont know 4 how long well long enough 2 get my head together

and when i get 2 pittsburgh im going 2 find u evie im going 2 go full on princess bride and track u down like dread pirate roberts hear this now i will always come for u

and when i do im going to say all the words to u the good words i should have said b4 just wait for me itll be worth it promise

ive changed evie maybe its the california air maybe its the schools here that tell u to speak ur truth and frame it in terms of i (yeah they say things like that) but i think ud like this me this who i am

i am a boy

i am trans

i am gay

i am brown

i am part indian

i am part everything

i am short

i am fire

i am fucking fantastic thank you

and i am not going anywhere

well except to pittsburgh where i am going to find u because u know wuv twooo wuv

speaking of true love evie theres a boy here i want u to meet his name is jules (u would like him but u cannot steal him)

jules is my westley my buttercup he is my orlando who doesnt want a rosalind he loves ganymede and ganymede loves him

ganymede is going 2 be out of his fucking mind missing orlando

i will tell u all about it when i see u

evie please be there please

love urself u r perfect

see u soon

#adamandevie #jackandevie? #julesandjack #goodbye-losangeles #hellopittsburgh

 missing evie

princess bride— 1 comment

**princess bride—
1 comment- EV4ever**

Finally, you pick a movie I actually like. Inconceivable.

Sometimes hashtags DO work. Yes, calm down, I'm here. You don't have to shout. It just so happens that I went away too. Long story. I'll be back in the Pitts soon, hey if your dad is famous now he can pick me up on his private jet haha. But back off, Dread Pirate Roberts. I'm not your Buttercup. If I want to see you I will. I'm not saying I'm not still super pissed at you and you know this girl does love her grudges but post when you get back and we'll see.

And you're totally buying the coffee.

EV

**princess bride—
1 comment- missing evie**

as you wish

34. Jack & Jules

Jules

It isn't dark, just the moment before it gets dark, when you can feel the evening coming on before you can see it.

"That wasn't too bad," Jack says, breathing heavily.

I shake my head. "Not bad at all. Can't believe I've never come up here. Thanks for making me do it."

We catch our breaths and pull each other up the final bit.

We're sitting on top of the world. The only way to go is down.

Jack

A bunch of tourists arrive at the same time we do—damn are they loud, waving their selfie sticks in the air—but this little rocky hill we claim as our own. I can't believe it's December and I'm sweating in a tank top. Yeah, that's me, rocking a sleeveless muscle shirt over my binder. Still need to get the muscles, but why the hell wait, right?

Jules ruffles the top of my head; I can feel every hair pull back and forward and back. He says, "I miss your swoosh. I'm still getting used to the flattop."

"I'm still getting used to you touching my hair," I tell him, though secretly, I never ever want to get used to it. I want to feel that prickle, that electric tingle every time his hand skates over my head. Every time.

Jules

I tell Jack I love his new haircut, but he slaps my hand away. "Wait till it starts disappearing," he says. "You won't like it then." He starts messing with his scalp. "Receding hairlines can be a side effect of testosterone. I think it's already starting—feel how thin it is over here?"

I pull his hand down gently. "Then we'll both get buzz cuts," I tell him, still holding his hand. "It'll be fine. It'll be . . . our thing." And then I have to quickly look out over the mountains, because my eyes are stinging, and it's not from the sunset.

"We should get back," I say, when I can speak again. "The park closes soon. We don't want to get trapped in here with all the coyotes."

"Yeah," Jack says. But neither of us moves.

Jack

Neither of us moves. We stare down at the back of the Hollywood Sign, it's so close I could hit it with a rock. Not what I was expecting. I mean, from a distance, it looks monumental, California's Mount Rushmore, but up close, from behind, it's just thin white letters standing on a hill, propped up by white scaffolding you don't see from below. Not much to look at, just . . . letters.

But the view is pretty spectacular, just the same.

"How long?" Jules asks, again, and I know he's not talking about sitting in Griffith Park.

Jules

It hasn't sunk in. I won't let it sink in. That's why I ask so many times, hoping a different answer's gonna pop out.

"I told you," says Jack. "Probably summer, if my dad's still out here. I don't know, it's all up in the air." He sighs. "The Great Experiment ends on Friday. Then it'll just be the Shitty Separation."

"And you have to go—?"

"Yeah. I do. I do." He won't look at me.

"Summer's too far away," I say. "I'll try to come out spring break."

"Your mother's gonna love that."

"Doesn't matter. I've got birthday and Grandma money."

"Rich boy," Jack says, but he smiles.

"Still too long," I say, and squeeze his hand.

He squeezes back. "We'll always have Paris."

"What?"

Jack bumps my shoulder. "Never mind. A movie for next summer."

Next summer.

Jack

I don't want to think about next summer.

Next summer's a lifetime away.

But now is now.

I raise my head up

Jules

I bend my head down

Jack

My hand on his neck

Jules

My arm around his waist

Jack

And we kiss.

Jules

And we kiss.

Jack

And we kiss.

And then we lean against each other;

my head rests against his shoulder

His head is on my shoulder

When I breathe in

I have to remember this

He breathes in

This moment

When I breathe out

This sunset

He breathes out

And the moment when

I hold his hand

I hold his hand

And neither of us lets go.

Acknowledgments

Writing is usually such a solitary experience, but in the case of *All Kinds of Other*, the opposite's been true. I have met and worked with so many wonderful, caring people during the shaping and producing of this novel that it's hard for me to adequately express how grateful I am to all of them.

First and foremost, many thanks to Kevin Theis for accepting an offer of hospitality those many years ago, and his son Milo Theis, who walked through my front door and changed my world. This journey started with you.

I was lucky to have the most helpful resources to guide me in creating my characters and the world they live in. Here in California, I thank the Burbank PFLAG, Ray Chang, and teachers Heather Scott Partington and David Gonzales for their most excellent input. In Pittsburgh, I am so grateful to Adriane Harrison and her daughters Ellie and Darcy, Katherine Bienkowski from Allderdice High, Parker from the Pittsburgh Equality Center and all the amazing kids I met there, for sharing their experiences with me.

I also had my very own Baker Street Irregulars in the form of students Penelope, Ty, Xavier, Bob, and Victor, who gave me insider tips on teenage life and kept me current. My biggest hug to my son, Ben, for sharing (unwittingly or not) his high school life for inspiration and accuracy, and to my husband, Doug, for letting me stay a juvenile during this writing process.

My gratitude to the Writing Workshop of LA, the Yefe Nof Residency, and the Hatchery for giving me the space, both literally and mentally, to complete my book. Diane Wagman, Heather Dundas, and Kelley Coleman, thank you for your formidable support and wisdom; you are the very best Flora, Fauna, and Merryweather a writer could ask for. Thanks also to Meryl Friedman, Doug Wood, and Sheila Donohue, readers extraordinaire.

I'm ever grateful to my agent, Christopher Schelling—sharpshooter, confidante, and therapist—for championing this book and finding it a home at HarperCollins.

What a gift to be given an editor like Andrew Eliopulos, the steadfast ranger who took such care of my forest when I was wandering lost amongst the trees. Thank you for believing so passionately in these two boys and for your careful and focused care. And thanks to Courtney Stevenson, who grabbed the baton with gusto and carried it so ably to the finish line.

Thanks to Anke Gladnick for their soulful cover illustration, and David Curtis for the amazing design—who knew I could fall in love with a book spine? Thanks to everyone at HarperCollins for their support and acumen, especially Laura Harshberger, Lana Barnes, and Jessica White for gently but insistently whispering in my ear during the whole galley process. Mitch Thorpe, Michael D'Angelo, and Megan Beatie—God bless your mighty trumpets.

And to Ezra Furman—your music is deep in the DNA of this book. Thanks for lending me the lyrics.

I'm so blessed to have met so many from the trans community as well as their allies, who have shared their time and stories so freely, among them Milo Theis, Conner Oswell, Ryka Aoki, Shaan Dasani, Ash Nichols, Skylar Kergil, Ryan Cassata, and Juhi Kalra—you all have been such inspirations for me. It's to you, and to all the queer kids—all the *others* out there fighting for their space in the world—that I dedicate this book.

Turn the page to read a bonus chapter to

All Kinds of Other by James Sie,

Homecoming!

But first, a note from the author . . .

One of the most difficult challenges an author faces in writing a novel is figuring out when the book is finished. Not so much what that last page might be (very often we've known the end from the very beginning, using it as a compass to direct the story in the right direction) but whether we've spent enough time in our characters' lives and when it's time to leave them. You want to make sure it's a rich and satisfying narrative for the reader, of course, but you also don't want to overstay your welcome. Leave them wanting more, as they say.

In writing *All Kinds of Other*, there were a lot of adventures I had in mind for my boys before their final parting. After all, they still had almost half a semester's worth of time left together after their trip to Santa Monica—basketball games, homecoming, Thanksgiving—there were a lot of stories that could be told. But in the end, I decided not to include them because I've always felt that their moment of connection was the most important part, and if I could just get them to that first kiss, then I could safely leave them to move forward on their own.

But sometimes, I wonder.

Since the publication of the book, I've heard from some

readers who wanted to spend a little more time with Jules and Jack together in their well-earned joy. To that end, here's a new section that takes place a few weeks after they've returned from Santa Monica but before Jack leaves for Pittsburgh. It was such a pleasure to peek back into their lives. I hope you enjoy this bonus scene as much as I enjoyed writing it.

Be well, and thanks for reading,

James

Jack: Hello hello it's me did you miss me

For some of you out there I'm Adam uh I used to have a channel Adam and Evie here for you but things have changed

A lot

My name is Jack now and it's just me well actually not just me there is this other person sitting right here

This very quiet person sitting right here

Do you want to introduce yourself

Jules: What

Oh you mean oh okay um my name is Jules

Jack: He's new to this

And so yeah

I'm a little surprised that I'm back here

I mean like I haven't had great experiences lately with my online videos

Jules: That would be accurate

Jack: But I don't know I just wanted to

I guess document my time here in Los Angeles and with Jules

Um Jules and I are like I guess you would call dating

And it's pretty new so we thought

Why are you shaking your head

Dude are we not dating

Jules: No we are it's just

Jack: What

Jules: It's just you know

It just feels weird this doing this

Jack: You said you wanted to

Jules: I said I would

Jack: You wanted to

Jules: But it's still weird

Jack: Well you'll get used to it anyway

We thought it might be fun to talk about some of our experiences together

Jules: Oh man

Jack: There aren't a lot of videos with

You know relationships like ours so okay

I'm a trans boy

Jules: And I'm a um cis boy

Jack: And

Here we are

Jules: Yup

Jack: It's Friday night and

You might be wondering why we're all dressed up

Matching suits pretty sick huh

Jules: A friend of mine her mother works in wardrobe for a TV show so she fit us with these

Jack: Can you guess what for

Pretty obvious right

Tonight was

Homecoming

Woohoo homecoming

Jules: What are you doing

Jack: I'm going to talk about our homecoming experience

Jules: Oh you are are you

Jack: Do you want tell the story Jules

Jules: No no you go right ahead

Jack: Okay so

We walk into the gym

And it's all decorated with streamers and a mirror ball and these giant glittery stars

And we enter in our matching suits holding hands and it feels like

Time just stops

Everyone is silent

But then Mr. Janssen the physics teacher starts clapping

Really slowly

And then everyone starts clapping

Faster and faster

And the music starts

And we're all dancing together

Jules: Who's dancing

Jack: All our friends are on the floor and Mr. Janssen is dancing with the guidance counselor and even that basketball guy Jamal he's dancing with Lowell the head of the GSA can you believe it

Jules: I don't believe it

Jack: And then they announce the homecoming king and queen

And

it's us Jules and Jack

Two homecoming kings

Sashes and crowns

And one big kiss

The whole school goes wild

Even Gavin the bully is clapping

Jules: Come on

Jack: And then a car a convertible drives into the gym

Jules: Too much

Jack: And we get in and it shoots up into the sky and we wave goodbye to everyone

Jules: All right now you wrecked it

Jack: And and

(laughter)

Jack: No way I would have gone to homecoming are you kidding me no way

Jules: Nice fake out Jack

Jack: Didn't you like the story isn't that like everything you ever dreamed of

Jules: No that was just something from before I

I don't care about any of that now

Jack: We could have gone but why

Jules: Exactly

Jack: We went to the movies instead

Jules: He made us get all dressed up just to go to

Jack: We went to the Egyptian Theater

So beautiful

Best movie theater ever

Jules: Good popcorn

Jack: We saw The Shining

Jules: Freaked my shit out

Jack: Perfect it was perfect he totally screamed

Jules: I totally did not

Jack: You screamed

Jules: Okay maybe I yelled once

Jack: They were showing a double feature but we cut out

Barry Lyndon is so freaking long

Jules: And also

Jack: Also oh right

Apparently we've got other plans tonight so

Jules: So

Jack: So yeah we're going to have to sign off right now and

Jules: Get to those other plans

Jack: Right

Okay thanks for watching our very first Jules and Jack video

Jules: Jack and Jules

Jack: I don't know how many of these there'll be

I'm not going to be here too long

Jules: Okay okay don't remind me

Jack: But subscribe if you'd like and

Jules: Can I say it

Jack: Say what

Jules: Be who you want to be love yourself you

Jack: No no that's not ours

That's

We're our own thing

Jules: Okay

So what do we say

Jack: We say

Dude

Jules: Dude

Jack: Take up some space

Be bold

And

Jules: And you are perfect

Jack: You are perfect

Jack & Jules: Bye

Jules

"That wasn't so bad, was it?" Jack grabs his phone from where it's been propped up on the marble counter of the kitchen.

"No, that was, uh, fun," I say, though all I'm thinking about is what's next.

"I'll clean it up and post this weekend, if that's okay."

As Jack fiddles with the phone, looking ridiculously fire in his pink—no, salmon—suit (Lily Cho corrected me on that, and the color doesn't look nearly so good on my pasty skin), I'm working out just how much time we have left in the night for my plan. It's like the gods have set me up with a wide-open shot, and I don't want to blow it. So many things have fallen into place—my mother going away for the weekend (sorry you're sick, Bubbe, but thank you); me not having to go with her (it was homecoming, after all); Gregg's dads offering to let me stay with them; an early movie showing at the Egyptian—I had to go for it.

And Mom didn't even ask if I was going to homecoming with anyone. So I didn't have to lie.

When Jack showed up at Gregg's house wearing the same suit I was in, Gregg's dads practically swooned. Steve had tears in his eyes, swear to God.

"I wish Gregg were going, too," he said, pouting.

"BOOM! KILL SHOT!" Gregg yelled from his bedroom.

"Gregg!" Danny shouted up the stairway, "Jules is leaving!"

"One minute!"

"I don't know why you had to take an Uber," Steve said, staring at the car waiting in the driveway, "We were all ready to chauffeur you—"

"Uh, no thanks," I said, so quickly that Danny squinted his eyes at me. "We just wanted to, uh, make it special? So, we, uh—"

Jack stepped in for the save. "It's an Uber Black," he told Danny and Steve.

"Oh!" Steve and Danny said at the same time, nodding.

"Leave them alone, Ba," said Gregg, thundering down the stairs. He stopped short and staggered back as soon as he saw us in our matching suits. "Whoa. You guys—nice! You really look like you're going to go to—I mean . . ." He stopped, catching a hard glare from me. " . . . have a good time! At *homecoming*."

Danny and Steve looked at each other, doing that couple's telepathy. Finally, after one long, excruciating moment, Danny turned back to me. "You know your mother made us swear that you were to be home by twelve, yeah?"

I nod.

"Well, okay then," Steve said, putting an arm on his husband's shoulder. "We'll see you by then. Have a good time. At *homecoming*."

Now, back at my house after the movie, time is racing by. Midnight curfew means we have barely two hours left alone.

Jack slides his phone into his pocket. "Okay, so what are these mysterious plans you've got?"

I extend a hand. "Follow me."

His hand leaps into mine. I love how warm it is, how all his fingers fit snug in my palm. I love everything about his hand.

I lead him into the living room. He hasn't been here since, well, the Incident, and I'm afraid it's gonna retraumatize him, but he immediately jumps onto the couch and grabs a white fluffy cushion. "My favorite pillow! Did you miss me?" he says, hugging it to his body, then looks up at me, grinning. "Okay, bring it on."

And I realize that this is the first time we've been alone together, really alone, not somewhere outdoors or in a stairwell in building C, sneaking kisses.

The room gets real quiet and still, like it's holding its breath.

"Uh . . . Jules?"

"Right. Okay. Right." I walk up to the fireplace mantel, making a big deal of taking off my suit jacket and draping it over one arm.

Jack pulls off his own jacket. Just that action gives me major flutters. *Concentrate, Jules.*

"Here goes." I grab the remote control, press a button.

From the ceiling above the mantel a large screen slowly descends.

Jack's hands cover the lower half of his face. His eyes are approximately the size of Oreos. A muffled "Oh. My. God!" comes out from behind the hands.

"And, look, look!" I say, grabbing DVD's from a shelf and sitting next to him. "*Taxi Driver. American Graffiti. The Godfather*—the ones you told me I had to watch, to catch up! Some of these are a little long, but there's also a bunch that—what?" Jack's head is shaking. His hands haven't left his face. I rush to add, "Yeah I know we just came from the movies, so we don't have to watch anything, I just thought—"

Kisses. Kisses and kisses and kisses.

"I don't care what we watch," Jack says quietly, when he settles back, "as long as I'm watching it with you."

In the end we choose *What's Up Doc*, mostly because it's under two hours and Jack says I have to "learn my history." I load the DVD, then settle back on the couch, remote in hand. "Now, don't give me grief about this." I touch another button. Instantly, the curtains draw themselves closed, the lights overhead dim to little star prickles, and Jack's hands are over his mouth again. I hear a high-pitched squeal.

"Too much?" I ask.

"Exactly enough."

The Warner Bros. logo, in gold, appears on the screen. Jack throws the cushion onto my lap and nestles against me, head on my chest. This is so much better than sitting in a movie theater.

A woman starts singing "You're the Top" while a book gets opened. The opening credits roll.

Suddenly Jack pulls away like he's forgotten something. I look over. He's staring at me in the dark. "What?"

"Hey. Your shirt . . . it's kind of scratchy," he whispers. Even in the dark I can see his eyes gleaming. "Don't you think it's scratchy?"

For once, I click in right away. "Uh. Yeah. Yeah it is . . ." I say slowly, making sure I'm getting what he's saying. He ducks his head, then looks up at me, and, yes, I'm getting what he's saying. I reach for the buttons of my shirt, but I must be going too slowly, because before I even get two buttons undone Jack's fingers are flying over the rest. I lean forward, and he helps me pull off my shirt. I've never felt so exposed, or so happy to be exposed, in my life.

But Jack doesn't settle back down. He's frozen, hesitating, like he hasn't decided if he wants to settle back down. Please want to settle back down, I pray, thinking maybe he's horrified by my scrawny-ass chest. He turns away.

He's unbuttoning his own shirt.

I can't even breathe.

Jack exhales deeply, then pulls his shirt all the way off. There's his binder underneath, barely visible against his skin in this movie light, a tight, sleeveless tank top. It's the first time I've seen it entirely.

And then he dives back onto me—his head's on my chest, his hair tickling my neck, the warmth of his arm around my waist, skin to skin, and—and I'm really grateful that pillow's on my lap.

"Yeah? Okay?" I ask.

"Yeah, okay," he breathes.

This is so much better than being in a theater.

The credits are still going. Jack turns his head up to me. "Your heart is beating so hard," he whispers.

"I can't help it."

Jack traces a heart onto my heart. He runs his fingers along my arm, and I feel lightning all the way down. He takes my hand and places it on his chest, over the binder. "So is mine." And then he turns my hand over and kisses my wrist.

The opening credits end. The movie was directed and produced by Peter Bogdonavich. And that, really and truly, is the last thing I remember seeing on the screen.

But it's my favorite movie now, all the same.